She looked down at herself now more than half-undressed, her clothes strewn across the floor. Other than his missing hair ribbon and coat, Ty was still clad. The light played along the loose folds of his shirtsleeves and at the ruffles at wrist and neck. She reached out to trail her fingers down his still buttoned waistcoat, noting how it fit so smoothly over his torso. "You are not playing fair, Tyrus Fortune," she said.

He merely arched questioningly while his gaze played over her, touching as warmly as the light from the candle's flame.

"You have on far more than I do. I demand the removal of something before this goes any further."

He lowered his head with a wicked grin and reached up to unfasten his Steinkirk from about his neck. He tossed it over his shoulder toward a chair but missed. "Satisfied?"

She returned his grin with one of her own. "Not yet, but I soon hope to be."

Other Books and Stories by Michele Stegman

Fortune's Foe

Mr. Right's Baby

Conquest of the Heart

"The Shrew That Tames"

"A Pirate's Tale"

"The Admirer"

"The Christmas Pony"

"A Book of Life and a Trick" in *How I Met My Husband*

"Samaurai Cat" in *Cats on the Keyboard*

Fortune's Pride

MICHELE STEGMAN

MYTHICAL PRESS ★ DAYTON, OHIO

Fortune's Pride
ISBN 978-0-9967976-5-8
Copyright © 2008 by Michele Stegman
Cover art © 2013 Jennette Marie Powell Heikes
Photos used under license via romancenovelcovers.com and bigstockphoto.com

This story is a work of fiction. Names, characters, places, and incidents are either products of the author's imagination or are used fictitiously. Any resemblance to actual events, locales, business establishments, media titles, or persons living or dead, is entirely coincidental.

Chapter One

As soon as Tyrus Winthrop Fortune saw the Irishwoman, he was sure there was something not quite right. He had spotted that red hair while still on board his brother's little ship, the *Fortune*, coming up the river. He had seen the easy way she laughed with his other brother, Matt, while they waited for Nate to dock his ship. He had seen the way she helped his heavily pregnant sister, Mariette, make her way down the dock of his family's plantation.

As he kissed his mother on the cheek and accepted an enthusiastic but unwieldy hug from his sister, he had seen how easily his family accepted this interloper as if she were one of them. As his brother, Matt, wrung his hand, gave him a hearty backslap, and huge grin, Ty noticed how the Irishwoman pushed an undisciplined strand of curly red hair out of her eyes and looked at him with one cocked eyebrow, as if assessing him and finding something slightly amusing.

There was nothing amusing about him. He was quite properly dressed in the latest London fashion. She, however, looked like a hoyden.

His mother pulled her forward. "And this is Irish."

Oh, he knew who she was. His family had mentioned her in

several glowing accounts in the letters they had written him while he was in London.

Irish presented her hand to him with a challenging tilt to her head, as if she half expected him to dismiss her out of hand. But the gentlemanly manners his mother had tried to inculcate in all her children had taken strong root in him. He would not be so dastardly as to ignore the hand of a woman his mother was presenting to him in good faith. Not even if he had a niggling suspicion that faith was misplaced.

He took her hand and made a very courtly bow over it, even though he could not help noticing that "Irish" had neglected to wear a fichu tucked into her bodice. Yes, it was quite a hot summer day, but it was shameful to display such a heathenish amount of skin. Creamy white skin that looked as soft as satin and the enticing curve of two perfect breasts that should have been decently covered.

Her hand was not soft. It was firm and competent and the palm slightly calloused. But when he touched his lips to the back of that hand he found the skin there as soft as the upper curves of her breasts looked. The feel of it against his mouth took him quite by surprise so that he gasped and jerked erect, then wished he had an excuse to kiss that hand again. He couldn't, of course. That wouldn't be proper. But he couldn't help running his thumb over the back of her hand...before he remembered himself and hastily let it go.

"Irish...?" He left the question hanging, waiting for a proper name. A surname. Something he had asked his family a time or two in his letters over the last two years. Something his family had failed to mention with irritating consistency. Now he waited with his own cocked and questioning brow for the answer.

She gave him a smile that was almost coquettish. But he had been flirted with by the most accomplished women in London. He was not going to accept a mere smile for his answer. Not after waiting for one for two years.

She shrugged, causing those breasts to momentarily lift, and entice. He forced his gaze upward to her face.

"Just Irish," she said, clipping the words off with finality, locking and barring the door.

Her voice was as strong as her hand and he could hear her Irish brogue even in those two words, the lilt, the extra attention to the "r". Just Irish, indeed. But what else?

He started to ask again, to demand more information of her, but his mother was taking his arm to introduce him to his sister's husband. He turned away from the little baggage, but not without a scowl that promised he would not forget to return to the topic later.

Ty approved of Mariette's choice of a husband immediately. He shook hands firmly as they took each other's measure. The man was half-Spanish. England was presently at war with that country but Alejandro's father was English, and Ty had made it a point to meet him while he was in London. Alejandro came from good stock, and it did not matter so much in the colonies if a man were a bastard.

"Welcome home, Tyrus," Alejandro said, one arm lovingly about Mariette.

"I'm glad to be back," Ty answered, noting with approval that Alejandro spoke without a trace of a Spanish accent, and didn't cut his name short the way the rest of his family did.

"Shall we go into the house?" his mother suggested. "Dinner should be ready."

"I'll just pop into the kitchen, then, and see how that stew is coming along." Irish picked up her skirts and turned to skip up the steps to the house, and Ty caught a quick glimpse of trim ankles and outlandish green dancing slippers. Dancing slippers?

He nodded in approval at the retreating backside of the Irishwoman about whom he knew as little now as he had in London. At least she seemed to know that she wasn't part of this family. She knew her place was in the kitchen. It only made him wonder why she had been down on the dock with the family to welcome him home.

"Irish has been such a comfort since she came to stay with us," Ty's mother said as she took his proffered arm to walk at a more sedate pace up the steps.

At the top they paused to wait for Mariette who, with the help of her husband, was taking the steps one at a time, breathing heavily. Matt and Mariette were twins, and looking at the size of his sister, Ty wondered if she could be having twins, as well. It seemed impossible that his impetuous, sometimes wild and irresponsible sister, was now settled down with a husband and about to be a mother.

Ty's gaze swept to the docks where Nate was directing the unloading of his ship, piling Ty's luggage up to be taken into the house. The river looked the same as it always had. He turned back to look at the house he had been born and raised in. There was the addition on the side his mother had written about, a sun room with large windows. Otherwise, it was also just as he remembered it—grand and sprawling, two storied, and now, with the addition of the sunroom, the two wings of the house were nicely balanced.

"It was Irish's idea to add the sunroom," his mother said, making him grind his teeth. "Do you like it?"

"Hmm," he answered noncommittally. "Do you always take the suggestions of servants on such monumental matters?"

His mother shrugged. "If it is a good idea, does it matter where it comes from?"

He hated to admit that whoever had had the idea, it had been a good one. He was spared the necessity of answering, however, because Mariette had finally made it to the top of the steps and his mother urged him on into the house.

Ty took a few minutes to freshen up then joined his family in the dining room. The table was set with his mother's wedding dishes and he was surprised to see that a place had been set at his father's place. He wondered if his mother did that every night while his father was off chasing Spaniards in this horrible war.

Alejandro helped Mariette into a chair and Ty held his mother's chair for her. Nate and Matt sat down and Ty reached for the chair at his traditional place at the table next to his mother, but her hand on his stopped him.

"Sit there, Ty," she said.

He stopped, incredulous. "Father's place?"

"Your father isn't here and you are the oldest. It's proper."

He nodded his acquiescence and took his place at the head of the table, wondering why an extra place had been set. It didn't take long for him to find out.

Irish came in bearing a huge bowl of stew. He tried not to appear condescending as he smiled pleasantly at her, as if giving her permission to serve. She, however, was not cowed into proper humility at all. She gave him a saucy grin and a wink as she set the stew in front of him, and he could not help himself from taking advantage of the view he had of some very deep cleavage. He could feel himself growing warm and tore his gaze away. Insolent wench!

It was then that the Irishwoman managed to totally surprise him. She moved around the table and sat down, cool as you please, right in his traditional place next to his mother. He would have thought she was doing it just to flummox him except no one else seemed to note anything unusual at all. Had she managed to worm her way into the very family circle?

"Tyrus, will you say grace?" his mother asked.

Ty managed to unclench his teeth long enough to say the prayer.

The same two servants, Ruby and Dee-dee, who had been there all his life, began to ladle out the stew and serve the meal. They grinned at him and welcomed him home, placed bread at his side and a bowl of stew in front of him.

"Tell us about London," his brother, Matt, asked.

"Yes," agreed his mother. "Are we terribly out of style here in the colonies?"

"You could never be out of style, Mother," he answered chivalrously but truthfully. "But I've brought fashion dolls for you and Mariette so you will be able to see for yourselves just what the ladies are wearing in London."

"No matter how up to date your dolls are, Ty," said his sister, rubbing her distended abdomen, "I'll still be hopelessly out of style by the time I can fit into a normal gown again."

"Has parliament considered passing a law against impressing our sailors into the navy?" Nate asked.

Ty looked at his youngest brother, now nineteen and already a man with his own two ships plying the coastal trade. "You seem to do all right, Nate. I didn't notice a lack of men to help sail the *Fortune.*"

"That's because I'm willing to pay better than anyone else. I want the best on my ships."

Ty could hear the pride in Nate's voice. His brother was doing well. He listened as his family began talking of trade, and sank into that familiar atmosphere he had missed so much the last two years. He looked around the table. Anyone could tell that they were a family. Nate and Matt looked much alike with their black hair and remarkable blue eyes. Ty's eyes were blue, too, like their father's, but of a grayer shade. Mariette had black eyes like their mother and all of them, including their newest family member, Alejandro, had black hair. They all fit. All of them except that bold splash of red at the end next to his mother.

Irish didn't have blue eyes or black hair. Her hair was red and unruly and her eyes were green. She was obviously not part of this family. She didn't belong at this table. So why was she here?

Yes, he knew the story. Mother and Mariette had both written to him telling him how the woman had helped Matt and Mariette escape from the Spanish. But that didn't explain why she now seemed to be included in the family. It wasn't right. But he would talk to his mother about it tomorrow. Today was a day to catch up and just be glad to be home.

Ty took a taste of his stew, then another. It was delicious. He picked up a roll and pulled it apart to butter it. A yeasty fragrance wafted toward him. Bread was his favorite food, and as he bit into the roll he thought it had to be the best one he had ever eaten.

"Do you like the rolls?" his mother asked.

"Mmm," was all he could answer, his eyes half-closed as he savored the rich flavor.

"Irish made them," Mariette said.

Ty's eyes sprang open and he nearly choked. Irish again! He put the roll down before he crushed it in his fist. "I'm glad you found someone to replace Mary," he managed to grit out, "but I'm surprised that our new cook is eating with the family."

There was dead silence for a moment. Then Mariette burst out laughing. She laid one hand on his arm with the other at her breast, as if trying to catch her breath from laughing so hard. "Oh, Ty, we've missed your dry sense of humor."

The rest of the family took up the laughter.

Had they all gone insane? What spell had this red-haired witch put on them?

But that red-haired witch was not laughing. She was looking down at her stew, pushing the rich chunks of meat and vegetables

around aimlessly, her spoon clutched tightly in her hand. She was
the only one who seemed to know that he had meant every word
he had said, that she was not fooling him in the least. She did not
belong at this table and they were the only two who seemed to
know it.

Then her head came up and she looked right at him with a
challenge in her eyes. She scooped up a spoonful of stew, stuck it
triumphantly into her mouth and began to chew. She might know
that she didn't belong at this table but she was letting him know
that she was staying, whether she belonged or not.

The battle lines were drawn.

For the rest of the meal he tried to ignore Irish's presence at
the other end of the table. He answered his family's questions about
England, heard about Matt's most recent visits with his Indian
friends, Mariette's description of hers and Alejandro's home, and
his mother's concerns for his father's safety.

Near the end of their dinner a gangly dog came padding into
the room as if he belonged. Ty started to get up to shoo him out
but no one else seemed to pay much attention, and the dog lay
down beside Irish. He noticed that she reached down to pet him
and slipped him a piece of meat from her stew. Now was not the
time to say anything, but that would have to stop.

Dessert was his favorite—apple turnovers. He didn't ask who
made them. He just enjoyed them, eating three and savoring every
bite.

Mariette's condition made her tire easily so the women left the
table soon after, and Ty spent the next hours talking to his brothers and getting to know his new brother-in-law. He drank a little
more than he usually did but not enough to keep him from walking fairly steadily up the stairs to his room, loosening his stock and
undoing the buttons of his shirt on the way.

Irish lay back stiffly onto the soft pillows of her bed and stared wide eyed around her room trying to unclench her jaw, her hands. She had thought she was safe. She had thought she had a place with people who cared for her. Now all that seemed threatened. She should have known there would never be any safety for her.

When she had arrived in Charles Town with Mariette, the Fortune family had welcomed her warmly. They had assumed that she was a well-to- do woman beset by tragedy, and that tragedy had made her reluctant to talk about herself. She had not disillusioned them. When they had asked questions, it had been easy to change the subject or pretend a sadness too great to reveal.

As the days and weeks passed, they seemed to forget that they knew very little about their guest...and certainly none of the truth. They offered her the best they had in return for the little part she had played in helping Matt escape from the Spanish. They treated her as if she really were one of the family.

Only she knew what a fraud she was, what a lie she was living. Every day she walked a tightrope of fear. Fear of discovery, fear that the Fortunes would suddenly decide to question her in earnest, fear that they would ask her to leave.

They had been more than generous with her, even letting her have part of the money from the Spanish ship they had brought into Charles Town as a prize. Now that bit of money had grown thanks to Nate allowing her to invest in his shipping business. But she didn't have enough, yet. Certainly not enough to keep her safe. Maybe she would never have enough. As if she even knew how much that would be.

She had made herself as useful as she could to the family, hoping they would come to think of her as indispensable. And she was glad to do what she could for them. They had given her so much. When their old cook Mary died, she'd taken over supervision of the kitchen, teaching some of the servants how to make various dishes.

When Mariette and Alejandro moved into their own home, Irish had taken over supervising the servants in their household chores. Whatever needed doing, she did with a willing hand and a glad heart. She had thought she was safe.

Mariette and her brothers had spoken often of this eldest brother who was away in London. They spoke of his stiff pride and his perfect manners, the way he never seemed to get disheveled or dirty no matter what he was doing, how he insisted that they all behave with propriety, and how they had worked together to thwart him with their antics. They spoke of his priggishness and they spoke of his compassion, but always they spoke of him with love. And they looked up to him almost in awe. Their perfect brother who could do no wrong. When they had learned he was coming home, they had been joyous.

But Irish had been apprehensive. Tyrus Fortune had seemed different from the rest of the family. They had told her how easily he saw through them and usually caught them when they tried some outlandish prank. Would he see through her as well?

Now that she had finally met the great Tyrus Fortune, she was sure he had looked into her very soul and found her sadly wanting. But she had also seen into his soul. He acted stern. He scowled at her. He looked so prim and starched she was afraid he might crack. But underneath it all, he seemed to be the one who most feared that he might crack—that if he unbent just a little, there would be no stopping the unbending.

For some absurd reason she wanted to be the one who taught him to let go. She wanted to see his stock loosened, the ends dangling beside the open throat of his shirt. She wanted to see if his chest was as hard and perfectly molded as it seemed beneath his coat and waistcoat and shirt. She wanted to see him relaxed with one leg thrown over the arm of a chair, to see the bunch and release of those strong thigh muscles as his leg swung casually back and forth. She wanted to see him...smile.

She was sure it could happen. She knew he was capable of melting. When he had kissed her hand, when his lips had touched her, it was as if something hot had run up her arm. Something hot and melting. And he had felt that melting heat, as well. She was sure of it. It was why he had jerked away so quickly, why he had looked so surprised, why he had forced his mouth back into the hard, firm line it had momentarily lost. The heat of that simple kiss had started to melt something inside him and he had been as afraid of her as she was of him. Afraid and attracted.

She knew he was afraid because he had jerked away, and attracted because he had allowed himself that brief caress of her hand with his thumb before he let her go. A caress that had sent another surge of warmth through her.

But if he was afraid and attracted, so was she. It would not be easy walking a tightrope of fear and attraction. She had to be careful. She could not let her attraction for Tyrus Fortune overcome her caution. If she gave away too much, if he found out who she was, how long would it be before he asked her to leave?

Or would it be worse than that? Would he root out her every secret, find out who she was and turn her over to the law?

She squeezed her eyes shut and tried not to cry. Life had been so good. For two years she had lived as she had never hoped to live. She ran her hand over the clean, smooth sheet, rolled her head on the down pillow, felt the light silk nightgown she wore. In a moment it could all be taken away.

She still had her money. Even if they turned her out, she had enough to live on for a while. Or would they take that away, too, if they found her out? Or worse, would she find herself in jail?

She had thought she was safe until Tyrus Fortune came into her life. She had worked hard today to make sure the house was in good order and the dinner a special one for the returning eldest

Fortune son. Her mouth twisted wryly. He had seemed to be enjoying it until Mariette told him who made it. She had seen the way he had looked at her at the table. He wanted her gone. She was as much a threat to him as he was to her. She was a mystery he did not understand and it bothered him not to understand everything around him. And he didn't understand his attraction to her.

Why was he so suspicious? Would she be able to allay his suspicions as she had the rest of the family's? Perhaps she could use his attraction to her to keep him off balance long enough for him to accept her presence in his family. She would flirt and flatter but keep him at a distance. That was the key—to keep him at a distance.

Attraction was a double-edged sword, it could end up unbalancing her, make her lose her caution. She must not let that happen. What she must, must, must do, was keep this place she had made for herself. This place she had been safe in for two years. This place she wanted to remain sealed in forever. It was too good a place to lose. She would hang on in every way she could.

Paddy gave a whine and she reached down to pet him where he lay on the floor beside her bed.

"Don't worry, Paddy. We've come this far. We'll be all right. We'll show Tyrus Fortune he can't get the best of Kathleen Moira O'Conner." She spoke softly, especially those words that she must never say out loud to anyone. Her name.

Tyrus Fortune had laid down a challenge and she would meet it, just as she had met his glare at the table with an impertinent bite of stew. No matter what she had to do, she would keep her place. She would be safe.

With that determination to comfort her, she fell asleep.

Ty made his way down the long upstairs hallway, putting a hand out once or twice to steady himself against the wall. Surely he had hadn't drunk that much. It must be the darkness of a moonless night. He found the door of his room and fumbled with the knob until it finally swung open. A growl greeted him.

"What the hell?" he muttered.

The growling stopped and a soft thumping began. There was the click of nails and the soft pad of paws crossing the wooden floor, then his hand was being licked. Absently he patted the dog, assuming it was the same one that had made itself at home in the dining room earlier. "What are you doing in here, fella?" He felt a wagging tail whip against his legs as he turned to open the door again.

"Go on, get out," he said softly.

The dog just whined and sat down.

"Oh, hell, stay then. Just don't expect me to feed you from the table."

Ty pulled off his shirt and kicked off his shoes. He shook his head wondering where his coat and waistcoat were. It wasn't like him to shuck them off and leave them lying like Matt usually did. Oh, yes, he had given them to a servant to take to his room. He unbuttoned his pantaloons and stepped out of them, folding them neatly over the back of a chair with his shirt. He lined his shoes up neatly under the chair. It was too dark to put them into the wardrobe tonight and he didn't feel like lighting a candle.

Wearing only his drawers he padded to the window to open it, but it was already open, a soft breeze moving the curtains. For a few moments he listened to the sounds of insects filling the night. He had missed those sounds. He took a deep breath. He had missed the smell of the land and the rice paddies. He had missed this house and his family. He was glad to be home at last.

He went to the bed, pulled back the sheet, and sat down on the edge. That's when he realized that the dog wasn't the only invader in his bedroom.

Chapter Two

IRISH WOKE UP WHEN SHE FELT THE SHEET LIFT AND THE BED dip. "Paddy?" she murmured and reached to pat the dog. But it was not Paddy's soft, floppy ears or wet tongue her hand encountered. It was firm, warm flesh. Puzzled, she splayed her hand over that flesh. The skin was smooth, the muscles hard and the body leapt off the bed.

"What the hell?" a deep masculine voice yelped.

She sat up, pushing hair out of her face. Her eyes widened as she recognized her intruder. "Tyrus Fortune! What are you doing here?" she demanded.

"What am...?" He seemed genuinely confused, but that changed quickly to belligerence. "What are you doing here?"

"Sleeping."

She was wide awake now and could see him dimly against the window.

He was certainly one fine figure of a man, with or without clothes. She saw him plant angry fists on his hips and lean forward.

"Did my brothers put you up to this?" He threw up his hands. "I thought they had grown up a little. I'm going to have their hides for this."

"What are you talking about?" she asked.

"You—being here."

"Why should your brothers have anything to do with it?"

His fists went back to his hips and he stalked closer to the bed, blocking out what little light there was with his broad shoulders. "So this is all your idea?"

She rubbed her eyes. Maybe she wasn't quite awake. But this was too bizarre even for a dream. Of course it was her own idea to be asleep in bed in the middle of the night. "Yes," she said.

He reached over and jerked the sheet away, uncovering her, then, taking her by the arm he began pulling her from the bed.

"What are you doing? Let go of me!" She struggled, but her strength was no match for his. Panic began welling inside her. This couldn't happen again. She wouldn't allow it! This wasn't St. Augustine and this family was good and upright. But maybe one of them had learned a few things while he was in London. By this time she was on her feet beside him. She opened her mouth and began to scream. He stopped her with a hand clamped over her mouth.

"Do you want to wake the whole house, you little tart?" he snarled.

Yes, that's exactly what she wanted to do. They would believe her. They had to. She had been safe here for two years. She tried to free herself but he held her tighter.

"Be still," he commanded. "I'm trying not to hurt you, but if you keep this up you'll only hurt yourself."

Oh, no, he wasn't going to hurt her. A man never seemed to think that a little unwanted 'poking' hurt a woman. It was what they were made for, wasn't it? She struggled harder. She was not about to be used by any man, ever again. Suddenly she was swept off her feet and tossed onto the bed, the full weight of Tyrus Fortune on top of her, pinning her down, his hand still clamped over her mouth.

She could feel his hard length, but his elbows were propped on the bed on each side of her, keeping most of his weight from crushing her. She went limp. Maybe if he thought she had given up he would let down his guard and she could escape.

"I'm going to take my hand off your mouth," he said. "Just keep quiet."

Like hell, she thought. As soon as his fingers moved away she took a deep breath, but before she could scream he clamped his hand back across her mouth.

"So that's your game, is it? It won't work, you know. No one is going to force me to marry you just because they find us in bed together. Especially since you obviously came to my bed. I certainly didn't force my attentions on you in yours."

Her eyes widened. Was he insane? Then her brain began to work and she realized what was happening. She could smell the wine on his breath. He had mistakenly come to the wrong room, and the wrong conclusion. She struggled to free herself but he held her closer. Too close.

"Will you stop struggling!" It was a command, not a question.

Feeling him rise hard and long between her legs, she stilled instantly.

He took several deep breaths. "Now will you keep quiet if I let you go?" She managed to nod and he slowly took his hand away. When she didn't scream, he rolled off of her to lie face up beside her, taking slow, deep breaths and scrubbing his hand over his face.

"All right, now get out," he said, "and we'll pretend this never happened."

"You insufferable cad!" She kicked him in the side and began pushing him toward the edge of the bed with her feet. He was so surprised by her attack that he toppled over the edge and landed on the floor in an undignified heap.

He sat up, rubbing one shoulder. "You're insane!"

"You're the one in the wrong room," she countered.

He looked around. "It might be dark in here but I think I can recognize the room that—except for the last two years—I've slept in my whole life."

Now she understood what had happened! She started to laugh. She drew up her knees and hugged them, laughing harder.

"You really are insane," he grumbled, getting to his feet.

"Your room is next to this one," she explained.

Those fists were back on his hips. "I told you, this is my room. I'll thank you to get out of it."

"Out of your room, out of your house, and out of your life. That's what you'd like, isn't it, Mr. Tyrus Fortune?" She lifted her chin. "But I'll do none of them. Your mother gave me this room when I first came here. 'Tis mine now and I'll be keeping it, thank you. You'll find your things in the guest room next to this one. I prepared it for you myself. Now, if you don't mind, I'd like to get a wink or two before the sun comes up. I've a fine lot of work to be doing in the morning." With that she plopped back onto the pillows, pulled the sheet up and turned her back to him.

"Get back to sleep? I got the impression you were expecting someone, Miss Irish," he snarled at her.

She turned back toward him. "No, Mr. Fortune, I was not expecting anyone. What gave you the idea that I would welcome any man to my bed, seeing as how I'm not married?"

"Then who is this Paddy you were reaching for so eagerly?" he asked triumphantly.

The click of dog nails interrupted, they both looked down and saw Paddy outlined beside him wagging his tail.

"Oh," he said. "Oh, the dog."

She could imagine his face turning a bright red. It was surpris-

ing that it didn't light up the room. At least she had the good sense
not to laugh out loud as she heard him stomp across the room, grab
his clothes, and leave.

Ty woke the next morning to someone singing...in Gaelic if
he wasn't mistaken. He rubbed his face. Her, again. She was like a
monk's hair shirt, always there and always irritating. Did she have
to be so damned cheerful this early in the morning?

He sat up and looked around. He had expected to be gazing at
the familiar walls of his own room. Instead, he'd been packed off to
a guest room with furniture he didn't recognize.

She had prepared this room for him. A guest room. As if he
were the intruder. He wondered just how she had managed to
worm her way into taking over his room.

He thought of her there in his bed. She was certainly a handful. A nice handful. Even fighting him she had managed to get a
rather quick "rise" out of him. Just thinking about her writhing
beneath him last night woke a certain part of his anatomy he would
as soon remained ignorant of that particular little opportunist.

He got up and began opening drawers and doors, searching
for his clothes in the chest of drawers and armoire. They had been
neatly put away as if this was to be his room from now on.

This wasn't the homecoming he had envisioned. He felt like a
guest in his own home, first displaced from his seat at the table and
then from the room he had spent his life in. Displaced by an im-
pudent chit who wasn't even part of the family, who dared to wake
him up singing...in a language he didn't understand.

He took out the clothes he needed and--unlike his customary
conservative behavior--slammed the doors and drawers shut. He
washed, dressed, and headed down the stairs. He checked the living room. He had asked the servants to leave one of his chests on

the floor in front of the fireplace and there it was, just as he had instructed. At least something was going right.

He went in to breakfast, finding his mother just finishing.

She smiled as he went to greet her, bending to kiss her cheek. "You're a slug-abed this morning," she said.

He poured himself a cup of tea at the sideboard and placed a still warm biscuit on his plate along with a slice of ham. "I would have slept even later if I hadn't been awakened by Miss Irish singing at the top of her Gaelic lungs," he said, trying not to sound too peevish.

His mother smiled impishly. "Doesn't she have a lovely voice?"

He nearly choked on his tea. The quality of her voice hadn't been the point he was trying to make. But now that he thought about it, he had to admit that she did, indeed, have a clear, lilting soprano that seemed full of the joy of life. He wondered what the words she had sung meant. Probably something about putting a knife through his heart.

"I was surprised to find her ensconced in my room," he said, leaning forward on the table and looking at his mother with raised, questioning brows.

She pushed her plate to the side and leaned on the table as well. "You know about the fire that devastated Charles Town just after you left home?"

He nodded, wondering what that had to do with losing his room to this usurper.

"There were a lot of people without homes, without furniture. We had plenty. I put Irish in your room and gave away the furniture in the unused rooms to families in need. She's been there ever since. We had new furniture made for the guestrooms, including the one you're in. Do you like it?"

"Not as well as I would like my own place," he growled.

She shrugged and got up to pour herself more tea. "Well, I could hardly ask her to move out of the room that has been hers for the last two years, could I?"

He started to say that she was forcing him to move out the room that had been his all his life, but decided it would sound like childish whining. "The point, really, is why is she here at all? You know nothing about her, not even her name."

"Her name is Irish."

He gave an ungentlemanly--and uncharacteristic--snort.

She sat down and leaned forward to look directly into his eyes. "I know plenty about Irish. I know that she has been willing to take on any task I have asked of her, and many that I have not. I know that she is cheerful and sweet and kind. And I know that she has been a great deal of comfort to me."

"Comfort? Why would you need comforting from a stranger?"

"Think about it, Ty. With this war your father is gone privateering more often than he is at home. You were in London. Mariette and Alejandro now have their own place. Nate is always off, up or down the coast trading, and Matt tends to stay with his Indian friends for weeks at a time. Irish was here. I couldn't have run this place without her."

Ty looked down at the biscuit in his hand, wondering if *she* had made it, like she had made the rolls last night. He dropped it onto his plate. "Well, I am home now, Mother."

"For how long?" Her finger traced the edge of her teacup. "You have written time after time of wanting to start building your own place upriver."

"Fortune's Pride."

His mother smiled softly. "Your father had planned to build a house there."

Ty reached out and took her hand. "But he married you and

decided to live here instead."

She nodded. "And he said our son could build his home there."

Ty straightened. "And I will. I plan to start as soon as I can."

She pulled her hand away, folding it together with her other one. "You see? You will be gone and I will be alone again, at least until this war is over. For now, I have Irish."

"But you don't even know her real name. She must be hiding something."

"Aren't we all? Don't we all have secrets?"

He pushed his plate away, his appetite suddenly gone. "Perhaps we do, but they usually aren't dark enough for us to hide behind a false name. She's hiding something and you don't seem the least bit concerned about it."

His mother sat back, a look of surprise on her face. "Of course, I'm concerned. I worry about what burden that poor girl must be carrying. But I'm sure that when she knows, truly knows deep down that she can trust us, she will tell us whatever it is that we need to know."

Ty threw up his hands and rose, nearly knocking over his chair in the process. "It's not her burden I'm worried about. I'm concerned that whatever she's hiding might affect the well being of this family." He picked up the napkin that had fallen to the floor and threw it onto the table. "I know she's hiding something and somehow I'm going to find out just what it is."

Mrs. Fortune sat back with her teacup and watched Ty stomp out of the house. She nearly laughed out loud. She had never seen her son so worked up about anything before, so animated. The next few days and weeks might just prove to be very interesting.

He found Irish in the compound with several of the servant

women, between the two neat rows of houses where the plantation's workers lived. She was stirring one of two great steaming cauldrons.

He came to a halt in front of the cauldrons, and, with fists on hips glared at her, daring her to ignore him.

The other women noticed him at once, smiling and greeting him, "Welcome home, Master Fortune!" or "Nice to have you back Master Ty!" from some of the older women who had known him since his birth.

"Regina, how are those youngsters of yours?" he asked one black woman who came up to give him a hug.

"Jus' fine, jus' fine. Abby gettin' married in two weeks."

"Little Abby?" Ty remembered a scrawny, chocolate-colored girl with bare feet and a shy grin.

"Not so little no more." Regina chuckled. "Half the bucks hereabouts been beatin' down my door for the last year. Be glad to get her settled."

He shook his head. It was hard to believe the difference two years could make. "Who's the lucky fellow?"

"Maggie's son. You 'member Joe?"

"Of course, I remember Joe. He and Nate used to get into almost as much trouble as Matt and Mariette." He chuckled, remembering. "He'll make Abby a fine husband."

"I 'spect he will," Regina said nodding.

"What about Rex and Bill?"

"They both out in the fields today, workin'."

"Working?" Ty regarded the woman with surprise. "Aren't they a bit young?"

"They's thirteen and fourteen now. Plenty old enough to help earn their keep."

Ty shook his head. Two years ago they seemed like children playing in the dirt. Now they were working in the fields.

"Slave catchers come 'round couple days ago. Tried to say Rex is 'scaped from Mr. Salvus's plantation."

"But there are no slaves here!"

Regina nodded. "That's what we tol'em but they don't believe nobody 'til Miss Irish--she come out and she give'em a piece of her mind." Regina chuckled. "Ain't nobody can get as riled as dis here woman. Sent them slave catchers off fast."

Ty looked at Irish. She quickly glanced away but he knew she had been watching him, even if she was trying her best to ignore his presence now. He sauntered around the cauldron to stand at her back. Leaning down he spoke only to her. "Is that true, Irish?

Do you chase off any intruders you find threatening or offensive?"

She turned to look fully up at him. Her face was flushed from the heat of her work. She had again discarded her fichu and her sleeves were rolled up past her elbows. Her hair, wild and undisciplined, escaped from her mobcap in several places at once.

Anyone else would have looked disheveled. Irish looked like she had just come from some lover's bed. He clenched his teeth and tried not to remember just how she had felt beneath him last night in his bed.

She gave him the most coquettish grin he had ever seen on a daughter of Eve. She batted long lashes at him and widened hose green eyes innocently. "Why of course not, Mr. Tyrus Fortune." She poked him in the chest with her finger. "I let some intruders stay around just so I can torment them."

"Personally, I'm usually not so lenient with intruders."

She shrugged and a trickle of perspiration ran down her chest to hide in the cleavage that pushed above the top of the plain white stomacher she wore. "I guess it's that stiff-necked pride of yours."

"If I'm proud, it's because I have something to be proud of."

"Yes, it made itself quite evident last night." As soon as she said the words, her cheeks brightened further, but he had to give her credit. She didn't back down or stammer an apology.

He grinned. He had her at a disadvantage now. He bent closer to her, giving her no place to go to escape him, except into that steaming cauldron. "What are you up to? I want an answer and you're going to give me one. Now."

It gave him a pleasant feeling to see her squirm uncomfortably.

"I don't know what you mean." And this time her words did come out in a near stammer.

He bent even closer, narrowing his eyes and coming nose to nose with her. "Just what are you doing here?"

She gave him a big, innocent smile. "Why, Mr. Fortune, I'm doing laundry."

That took him by surprise. It was not the answer he'd expected. He had expected more hemming and hawing, excuses that he would rip to shreds. He had planned to trip her up with her own words, and find out just who she was and what secrets she held.

But she was not intimidated at all. Blast her, she was smiling!

"I can see you're doing laundry!" For God's sake, he was raising his voice. He never raised his voice. He clenched his teeth and drew a deep calming breath.

"Well, then," she said, again batting those lashes at him, "don't you think you'd better let us get on with it? After all, it's your shirts we have simmering there."

"Mine?"

She propped one hand on her hip. "After a month at sea don't you think they needed washing?"

"You're doing *my* laundry?"

"And who else do you think would be doing it?"

She turned away from him and pulled a shirt from the steaming water with the wooden paddle. Taking it gingerly with her fingers she let it cool a moment. She twisted it quickly to wring it out then tossed it into another cauldron of clear, cooler water to rinse. He saw her take something from her apron pocket. Something blue. He grabbed her hand just before she could toss it into the water.

"What's this? Are you trying to stain my shirts?"

Anger sparked dangerously in her eyes and she jerked her arm, trying to free her wrist. "It's bluing, you ass!"

"Bluing?"

"That's true, Master Ty," Regina said. "A little bluing in the rinse water make dem white shirts shine."

He felt like a fool. Of course. Bluing. He let go of her hand and she tossed it into the water. With a superior lifting of her brows she asked, "If there's nothing else?"

He backed away. "No, no, of course not."

It was only when he was halfway back to the house that he realized he had been bested again. He had not learned one thing about that woman. And she was still here.

Ty was the first one to the table at lunch time. He could have taken the chair beside his mother's, the chair where Irish had sat the night before--that was his traditional place. But somehow that seemed childish, to grab that seat before Irish came in. Besides, his mother was right. With his father away, Ty's place was at the head of the table.

Matt came in slipping a shirt over his head. Ty noticed the buckskins and moccasins his brother wore. He'd been hunting.

"Bag anything?" he asked even though he knew his brother never came home empty-handed.

Matt grinned. "A pair of rabbits and a deer."

"I suppose we'll have venison for dinner, then," Ty said.

Ty heard his mother and his sister Mariette coming down the

hall discussing baby clothes and diapers.

Alejandro came in just in time to help his wife to her seat. Ty noticed Alejandro's hand briefly touch Mariette's neck, then slide down her shoulder, before he took his own chair.

Irish came in with the first of the dishes of food, bringing a platter of ham. He noticed that she had at least tried to stuff her hair back into her mobcap, but it seemed determined to escape confinement. She had also taken time to tuck a fichu into her bodice. He pulled his gaze away from the place between her breasts where she would have tucked the ends of the fichu and saw her looking at him. He could feel himself grow warm but whether it was from embarrassment at having been caught staring, or from what he had been staring at, he wasn't sure. He looked away, grabbed his napkin and placed it in his lap.

Alejandro said grace and they began to eat. Ty wondered which of the dishes *she* had prepared. Everything was wonderful. He had to admit that the Irishwoman had done a superb job with the meals. If he only knew something about her other than that she could cook and wash clothes. And had a body that felt quite good writhing beneath him.

He gritted his teeth. He didn't need to think like that. Not about a woman who was hiding something in her past.

When the servants began clearing the table, Nate said, "I'm taking Mariette and Alejandro home this afternoon. Then I'm going back to Charles Town. I have a small shipment to run up to Williamsburg, but I'll be back in time for Abby and Joe's wedding."

"Before you go, I have some presents I brought back from London." Ty stood up. "My trunk is in the living room. Shall we gather there?"

As Alejandro helped Mariette struggle to her feet she patted her distended abdomen and said, "I hope you didn't forget to bring something for the little one. He kicks enough as it is. If he thinks his Uncle Ty forgot him..."

Uncle Ty. Ty's heart gave a little leap. *Uncle.* It sounded so wonderful he couldn't help smiling. "Of course I remembered. I brought something for everyone."

That was when his gaze again found Irish. Her eyes were shining, her lips smiling, and she almost skipped into the living room with the family. *Except her,* he thought. *I didn't bring anything for her.*

He had known she was living here, that the family seemed to think of her as one of them. But he hadn't. Certainly not when he was in London. All he had thought then was that some little tart had wormed her way into his family's life and home, and she didn't belong. He hadn't thought of her as a real person.

But as she settled expectantly on the floor beside Mariette's chair, he could see the anticipation on her face, her barely contained eagerness. She clasped her hands in her lap as if to keep them from tearing into that trunk. Then she looked up with a smile on her face and met his eyes.

That's when the joy faded from her face, when she realized that there would be nothing for her in that trunk. And that's when he felt like the worse kind of unfeeling cad.

She put on a braver front than he could. Her smile never wavered and she kept her place, her chin going up just a notch.

Clenching his teeth, Ty opened the trunk and began to distribute the gifts he had brought.

The first thing out of the box were fashion dolls for his mother and Mariette. They immediately began to exclaim over the latest style changes, and were joined by Irish from her position on the floor. He noticed that the sparkle was back in her eyes as she pointed out a feature on the dolls.

Bolts of fine material were next out of the trunk--silk, Indian muslin, Egyptian cotton--all in the same colors as the dolls' dresses. When he handed them to his mother and sister, he noticed that Irish also ran her hands longingly over the material, but when she held up one end of blue silk, she didn't hold it up to herself. She held it up to Mariette, exclaiming how wonderful it would look on her.

Ty knew his mother and sister would ask him about the latest styles and he had made note of what the ladies in London were wearing. From what he could see now, the dress Irish wore was sadly out of fashion. In fact, it looked a lot like it could be one of Mariette's castoffs. That, and her enthusiasm for the contents of his trunk, made him feel even worse.

Ty lifted a heavy box out of the trunk and handed it to Nate. Nate's jaw dropped and Ty knew his brother already suspected what was inside. Nate's hands trembled as he lifted the lid. It was one of the new sextants, and Ty could tell from the moment Nate's hands touched it that his brother would not need any instructions in its use. His eyes gleamed and his hands ran over it as lovingly as if it were a woman.

"Ty, I…" Nate was speechless.

"You couldn't have given him anything better," Matt said. "He's been drooling over the one Father bought for the last six months." Matt clapped Nate on the back. "Now maybe you can find your way around that big ocean out there!"

"It will certainly make navigating easier than using that old astrolab!" Nate tore his eyes off his new sextant to look up at Ty.

"I never expected anything like this. Thanks, Ty."

Ty nodded, happy that he had gone to the expense of buying the sextant.

For Matt there was a new hunting knife and musket. "And there's a whole trunk of beads and red cloth for your Indian friends, Matt. I think Nate stowed it in one of the sheds outside."

Ty handed Alejandro a packet of silver shoe buckles and coat buttons. "I also brought you a fine saddle," Ty said. "Mariette told me how you dote on your horses."

"And these are for the little one." Ty handed Mariette a silver cup, feeding spoon, and rattle, as well as some finely embroidered baby gowns.

As he pulled out each gift, Ty watched Irish. She seemed to be enjoying everything as much as if it were all for her, and he knew he had to give her something. Not just out of politeness and gentlemanly courtesy, but because he wanted to see her reaction.

He wanted to see her smile for herself.

But each gift he pulled out of the trunk was specifically for someone else. He couldn't have given her those baby things or the buttons or buckles. The bolts of cloth had already been given to his mother and sister. He couldn't very well say, *"Oh and some of that is for Irish."* Not now, anyway. There had to be something in here...

Then he spotted it. The sandalwood fan he had planned to give to his mother. It had just been a spur of the moment purchase, an afterthought, and something his mother didn't really need.

He handed the box to Irish. She turned with it in her hand to give it to Mariette, but he stayed her. "It's for you."

Her mouth dropped open and her eyes rounded. Then they narrowed as if she suspected that he was only teasing, that he would tell her he was only joking, that the gift was really for Mariette.

"It's for you. Really. Open it."

Irish placed the box on her lap. He could see the quick rise and fall of her chest, how she bit her lip as she caressed the box, almost as if afraid it would disappear.

"No one has ever given me a... I mean, except for Christmas..." She looked up at him and her eyes were beginning to fill with tears. But she hastily brushed them away and laughed. "Thank you."

Ty's heart constricted painfully. What kind of life had she had that she had never been given a present just for the sake of being given one? That she didn't even expect one when everyone else was receiving them?

"Don't thank me until you open it. You might not like it," he told her.

"Go ahead, Irish, open it," his mother said, placing a hand on her shoulder. Then she turned to Ty and mouthed a silent thank you.

Irish held the box tenderly a moment, running her hands over the brown wrapping. Then she tore it off and lifted the cover off the box. "Oh," she exclaimed as she gazed into the box. She reached inside and withdrew the fan. The scent of sandalwood filled the air. Quickly she held it up to Mariette and his mother to smell. Then she flicked it open, admiring the delicate filigree cut into each spoke.

"It's from India," he told her.

"So far away, from such an exotic place." She held the fan to her breasts. "Thank you. I will treasure it always."

Ty clenched his teeth. Such a little thing to treasure always. It made him want to give her emeralds to match her eyes. He pulled his gaze away from her. He was beginning to understand just a bit why his mother let her stay, even knowing so little about her.

"There's one more thing in here," Ty said, pulling out a small wooden chest. "And it's from India, too." He started to hand it to his mother, but changed his mind and placed it in Irish's lap, instead.

She started to shake her head in refusal but he stopped her. "It's really for all of us, but I thought you should open it since you seem to be in charge of the kitchen."

With a puzzled look, she opened the box. The scent of tea and spices filled the air and everyone laughed. Irish held one box up to smell. With a grin she glanced around at everyone. "Ginger! I can make gingerbread tonight."

Someone must have told her it's my favorite, Ty thought. Was it her way of thanking him?

Chapter Three

THE FORTUNE FAMILY AND IRISH SAT TALKING FOR A WHILE, passing around their new treasures for everyone to see. But Alejandro and Mariette soon excused themselves to pack their things for the brief upriver trip to their own home, and Nate went to ready his ship and try out his sextant. When Matt and Irish also left, Ty was alone with his mother.

"Thank you for making sure Irish had a present in that trunk, Ty," she said.

He shrugged. "I'm glad I had something to give her. She seemed pleased."

"She was. More than you can know."

"What do you know about her, Mother?"

She rolled her eyes. "Are you still worrying that bone?"

"I just want to know who she is, what she's doing here."

His mother sighed and leaned back in her chair. "You're right. We don't know very much about Irish. Mariette met her in St. Augustine when she went down there to rescue Matt.

"Irish had been enslaved by the Spanish and was not being very well treated," she continued. "But she helped Mariette while she was there, and helped them all escape."

Ty nodded. "Yes, you've told me all that in your letters."

She shrugged. "There isn't much more to tell. She only told us to call her Irish. We questioned her a few times, but she didn't seem to want to talk about her past, except to say that the ship carrying her to America had been taken by the Spanish and she had been sold into slavery. Mariette and I have talked about it and we believe, as you do, that she is running away from something, or someone. But we don't think she is a criminal, as you seem to. There's not a dishonest bone in her body. Besides, although the dress she was wearing when she came to Charles Town was in rags, it had once been quite fine. She must have once had money. Perhaps she is running from an abusive husband or attempting to escape a forced marriage."

"I might agree," Ty responded, "except that she said she had never had a present before. If she were rich at one time, wouldn't she have had presents?" Ty had another thought. "And she's been here for two years. Do you mean to tell me you or Mariette have never given her anything?"

His mother laughed. "Oh we've tried. She'll take Mariette's castoff clothing, but, except for a few Christmas gifts, she hasn't let us buy her anything of her own. She says we've given her enough already and insists on paying her own way. That alone should convince you that Irish is no criminal." She got up and stretched. "Too much pride for her own good, that girl." She looked down at her son with a twinkle in her eye. "Just like someone else I know." With that, she bent to kiss the top of his head and left.

Ty sat thinking about what his mother had told him. Maybe she was right. Maybe Irish was as innocent as a lamb. But somehow, he just had a niggling little feeling that there was more to the story. That she was hiding something more than an abusive husband in her past. Maybe he had been too harsh to think she might be a criminal, but he was still determined to find out just what Irish was hiding. With that thought in mind, he went in search of her.

Irish walked slowly up the stairs to her room, opening and closing the sandalwood fan. It was not only beautiful, but the spicy scent of it seemed to carry her away to exotic places. She ran her fingers over the delicate filigree. She had never owned anything so lovely. She could have bought something like this for herself now that she had a bit of coin, but she wanted to save every bit she could.

She fanned herself and danced a step or two as she went down the hall. *Wouldn't it be grand to use my new fan to flirt at a grand ball,* she thought. She brought the fan up to her face and pretended to hide coquettishly behind it as she batted her lashes at some wealthy planter. Then she snapped it shut. She wasn't going to a grand ball. She probably never would in her life. She ran her fingers over the fan once more before placing it back into its box to put away in a drawer.

It was just so delightful to have been given something like this as a gift. She hadn't expected anything at all out of that trunk. She had been prepared to take her joy from seeing what Ty had brought for everyone else. She had been totally surprised and touched when he had handed her the gift.

The Fortune family had been right about this oldest son. He might be a stiff-necked prig, more prim and proper and proud than any gentleman had a right to be, but he obviously loved his family dearly and knew them well. He had brought everyone just the right gifts. Nate couldn't have been more pleased with his sextant, and Matt with his musket. He had even remembered to bring a gift to the woman living with his family. Even though he disapproved of her being here, he had still remembered her.

She placed the fan inside one of her drawers. But why would he give her a fan? Did he really think it a proper gift to give to a woman he thought of as a mere servant, an intruder? Wouldn't he have thought that a new mobcap or apron would have been more appropriate?

Irish's eyes widened and she gripped the edge of the drawer. He hadn't brought the fan for her at all. He hadn't brought her anything! He had meant the fan for his mother or his sister. But being the proper gentleman, he must have felt he had to give her something since she was sitting right there with them.

All the joy of the gift drained out of her and she thought she might just cry for the first time since her arrest in Ireland. But then her strengths--anger and pride--came to the fore. She grabbed the fan and turned to stalk out of her room. She would fling it back in his insufferably proud face! She would... She came to a halt. Maybe the fan had been an afterthought, but he had thought of her. He could have let her sit there with no gift at all, but he hadn't.

She stood for a moment with the fan in her hand--debating. Then she turned and put it back into her drawer. It might be too fine a thing to give a "servant", but it was also too fine a thing for her to give up. She would accept it in the same spirit in which it was given. If he had felt nobly obliged to give it to her, she would nobly let him save face by accepting it, even if she never ever used it.

"By the saints!" Irish slammed the drawer shut and hurried out of the room. Thinking of gifts reminded her that it was just two weeks until Abby's wedding and she didn't have a gift for them, yet. She lifted her skirts and practically leaped down the stairs.

If she could get a bit of her money out of the box she kept locked in Mrs. Fortune's office and catch Nate before he left, he could get something for her in Williamsburg.

Mrs. Fortune's office was not large. The desk took up most of the space in the room. There were several drawers, some of them locked. Irish took her key out of the pocket in the back of her stomacher. Mrs. Fortune herself had given her the key to the small drawer on the left side of the desk so she would have a safe place to keep her money and her accounting, yet still have access to it any time.

Irish unlocked the drawer and took out her cash box. Most of her money was invested in Nate's shipping business, but she kept a bit of coin here for just such occasions as this. It was never easy to part with a single ha' penny and she seldom spent any on herself, but it would be a joy to give something to Abby and Joe. She took out several coins and recorded the amount in her book, then put it all away. She was just scooping up her money when her wrist was caught in a vise-like grip.

"You little thief!"

Irish looked up into the stormy face of Tyrus Fortune. His blue eyes had gone the gray of an overcast day, his nostrils flared, and his lips were pulled back in a snarl. It was the face of a man who would never believe she was innocent, the face of a man who had already made up his mind that she was guilty as charged.

She jerked her arm, trying to free it, but his grip was hard and fast.

He began prying at her fingers. "How much did you take?"

Panic seized her. She squeezed her fist as tight as she could. "It's mine!"

"Do you sneak in here and take money often?" he sneered.

"It's mine!" Fear had a grip on her as tight as his hand and she couldn't think of anything else to say. She only knew she had to free herself, get away. This couldn't be happening again. She was no thief. She had never stolen anything, yet she was forever being accused of theft. How many times would she have to be punished for something she had never done?

She refused to let the tears come. She could only hold on to what was hers and fight that unjust accusation once more. It all began to blur together, this accusation with that other one, strong hands upon her, dragging her away. She began to fight him, pounding on his rock hard chest with her free fist, kicking at his shins, struggling to free his grip on her wrist. Her chest tightened with fear and an inability to draw breath.

"Be still!" came his harsh command. But it only made her struggle harder.

Suddenly she was slammed into a corner of the room, his muscular body pressing against her. He had both her hands captive now and held them tight in one of his above her head. With his free hand he gripped her chin, turning her to face him. "Irish! Stop it! Be still! What's wrong with you?"

She tried once more to wrench away but she had no room to maneuver, no way to get free. Her breath came in quick, short gasps. They would put her in prison. Again. This time she would not get out.

"Irish! Look at me!"

She heard the words but she couldn't focus. "I'm not a thief. I'm not. I'm not. I'm not." She could only repeat the words she had said a hundred times before, words that meant nothing to those who had more reason to find her guilty than to find her innocent.

"And just whose money do you have in your hand?" a voice snarled.

She could not respond. She wasn't sure she could even fight anymore. What was the point? No one ever believed her. But then the thought came to her that this time she had proof. She had people who knew this money was hers. Taking a deep shuddering breath she opened her eyes.

Tyrus Fortune's accusing face was so close to hers that she could feel his breath upon her cheek. Tyrus Fortune...who wanted her gone, who would use this as an excuse to see that she was thrown out. She glared back at him. This time, she would stand her ground. This time, she would keep her place. This time, she had proof.

"I'm not a thief," she snarled at him. "I've never stolen anything in my life."

"Then whose money is this?"

His expression was almost a smirk, as if he thought he had her and knew it. But he was wrong. This time she had proof.

She lifted her chin. "It's mine, I told you. It's mine."

"Your money?" Her inquisitor sounded incredulous.

"I've earned it. 'Tis mine," she repeated adamantly.

"And just how did you earn it?" his voice was one shade away from being a sneer.

"Nate's shipping. Ask him. He'll tell you." She gave him a small triumphant smile.

He stood stock still for one, long, stunned moment then he let out his breath in a sudden whoosh. His grip on her hands loosened and his body slumped against her.

"My God, I've been a fool. Mariette did tell me in letters that you…" He looked away from her for a moment, then turned back to her. "Irish, I'm sorry…"

Now that he knew she was innocent, her panic drained from her and she had to clench her teeth to keep from shaking. They were clenched so tight, she couldn't answer him. All she could do was lift her chin a notch in righteous pride.

"Forgive me?" he asked.

She closed her eyes and turned her head away trying to calm herself. That was a mistake. It made her aware of the hard, lean length of him pressed against her, his thighs warm against hers, his chest pressing on her breasts. His hand, warm and firm, still held her wrists above her head, but its grip had loosened, feeling now like a tender embrace.

"Irish?"

She felt his other hand caress along the line of her jaw, urging her face back toward him. And then she felt his lips, so light, full, soft, and so very tenderly touching hers. It was a kiss of apology, a truce, but it sent a river of fire coursing through her, stopping her breath and speeding her heart.

But it was also a kiss from a man, who, but moments ago, had accused her of theft.

She tore her mouth away, jerked her hands free and shoved at his chest, anger rising to douse the fire. "How dare you!"

He moved back, lifting his open hands palm outward as if in surrender. "Irish, I--"

But she stalked him as he backed away, poking her finger into his chest with each step. "You sneer at me, you want me gone, you give me a gift out of pity, you accuse me of theft and now you dare to kiss me?"

"Pity?"

She paused in her tirade. She hadn't meant to say that, hadn't meant to let him know she knew why he had given her the fan.

But it was out now and she would not back down. "Aye. Don't think I didn't realize there was nothing for me in that grand trunk of yours. 'Twas a gift given from pity and nothing more. I should have thrown it back into your face."

"It wasn't pity, Irish."

"Hah!" She narrowed her eyes and propped her fists on her hips. "There'll be no kissing betwixt us, Tyrus Fortune. You've made your feelings about me plain enough. I might accept your pity present for the sake of your family, but I'll not be accepting your kisses."

His eyes narrowed, too, and he bent to glare right into her face. "It seems you were doing a bit more than just accepting my kisses a moment ago."

She opened her mouth to give him an angry denial, but with

a gasp, she realized he was right. It was but a brief moment between the touch of his lips and her anger, but that moment had been there, a moment when she had enjoyed and responded to that kiss.

"Hah!" he said, triumphantly giving her a quick nod and folding his arms across his chest.

She could think of no fit reply, so she pushed past him with a muttered, "Insufferable, arrogant peacock."

He caught her by the arm. "I'm not through with you. I want to know what you're hiding."

She gave him the most innocent smile she could, "Why Mister Fortune, what makes you think a simple woman like myself would be hiding anything?"

He pulled her closer to him. She could feel heat from his body, the strength in his hand, and her own response to his closeness. She was melting in his heat.

"Because you won't tell us anything about yourself," he gritted out through clenched teeth.

She tilted her head coquettishly. "There's a big difference between not telling something and hiding something." With that, she wrenched her arm free and swept through the door. Her anger fueled her down the hall, out the door and halfway to the dock. "Cad," she muttered. "Strutting popinjay!" But as her anger cooled, she thought of her response to his kiss, to his touch, to his very presence. She *had* enjoyed it. *Well, all right,* she told herself, *why shouldn't I enjoy a kiss from a handsome man with muscles like rock? A man with hair as black as the devil's own and eyes as sweetly blue as God's own heaven? What woman wouldn't?*

That didn't mean she would welcome any more of those kisses. Not from a man who was so suspicious of her. She drew a deep breath. All right again. He had reason to be suspicious of her. She was hiding something. But everyone else accepted the fact that she didn't want to talk about her past. Tyrus Fortune was just too determined to ferret out her secret. Her best choice was to avoid him as much as she could. And not to let him soften her up with kisses that could melt a marble saint.

Unfortunately, she thought, in the close confines of the Fortune home, with him underfoot every day, seeing him at dinner every night, and with him sleeping in the next room, that would not be easy.

Irish tucked some stray strands of hair back into her mobcap and straightened her bodice. She felt rumpled and disoriented by her encounter with Ty, and it went beyond the mere dishevelment of her appearance.

By the time she reached the dock, Mariette and Alejandro were just saying good-bye to Mrs. Fortune. Nate was securing their trunks on the deck for the brief upriver trip. Finishing his task, he came back to the dock to also say his farewells. Matt was there as well, his new hunting knife slung at his buckskin clad hip and his new musket comfortable in the crook of one elbow. He wore moccasins and carried a small leather beaded pack.

Matt turned to grin at her. She felt easy with Matt. He was always so calm and quiet, quick to smile, and never critical.

"Are you off on one of your trips, Matt?" she asked.

He nodded. "I promised a friend I'd help him build his house but I'll be back in time for Abby and Joe's wedding."

The way Matt was dressed for the trail, Irish was sure that friend was an Indian. And she knew he would make it back in time for the wedding. It was amazing how Matt could disappear into the wilderness for weeks at a time yet show up when something special was happening at home, like Ty's return from London. She squeezed his arm. "Be careful."

"I will." He leaned down to give her a quick kiss on the cheek, a kiss that could not have been more brotherly. How different from the kiss she had just gotten from his older brother! She loved Matt dearly, but his kiss was sweet and comforting. It did not rain fire.

Matt was looking over her shoulder and she turned to see a scowling Ty approaching, his eyes hooded, his mouth set and grim.

Ty didn't seem the least rumpled or disoriented from their encounter. His stock was still neatly tied with every pleat and fold in place. Matt looked from his older brother to her then slung one arm around her shoulders and pulled her close to his side. Ty's scowl deepened and she felt Matt chuckle deep in his chest. He bent to whisper in her ear. "Keep him guessing, Irish. Keep him off balance. It's the only way to handle him." He gave her a final squeeze and then went aboard the *Fortune*.

Handle him? She turned to look at Ty but he was saying his good-byes to Mariette, his hand resting beneath hers on her distended abdomen, feeling her baby kick. His look had softened, his mouth now relaxed, his lips parted in wonder. Mariette gasped and jerked with a sudden hard kick and then she laughed and so did Ty.

If Irish had thought this eldest Fortune sibling was handsome when he was scowling at her, her breath caught at how handsome he was when he laughed. His whole being seemed to light up. It looked like the sun had come out in the sky blue of his eyes, dispelling the gray.

He gave his sister a hug and shook hands with Alejandro and Nate, then stood beside his mother to watch them go aboard. Irish caught Nate's arm as he passed her. Pressing the coins into his hand she said, "Will you buy something for Abby and Joe for me in Williamsburg? Some linens, perhaps?"

Nate pocketed the money, agreeing to find something for the couple.

Then they were aboard. Nate and one other sailor set the sails and the little ship moved out into the river. He would take Mariette and Alejandro home, drop off Matt, then head back down river. He would not have time to stop again before he went to Williamsburg. But he would be back in plenty of time for the wedding. And so would the others.

Irish waved, feeling an ache as if it were her own family parting. She wished they were. She wished she were a part of this family. But no matter how welcome they made her feel, how much they included her, she was still just the intruder Ty accused her of being. Maybe it was time to find her own place. She had enough money to afford a small house in Charles Town. She could continue to invest in Nate's shipping business and her money would continue to grow.

She looked up at the house facing the river, that had been home to her for the last two years. She had been happy here. She had felt needed, especially during those times when the rest of the family was gone leaving Mrs. Fortune alone. But her son was home now. Irish was no longer needed, or wanted.

She sighed and headed back to the house behind Ty and his mother. No matter how adamant she had been with Ty that she would not give up her place, she decided that after Abby's wedding, she would leave.

After saying good-bye to his family, Ty walked with his mother into the house. She headed for her office and he went with her, leaning in the doorway as she sat down at her big desk and pulled out her account books. He couldn't believe that just a few minutes ago he had been kissing Irish right there in the corner. Kissing her and enjoying it, the little baggage!

He had meant the kiss as an apology, but it had turned out to be a lot more than that. It had been brief, but he had felt passion race through him. Passion and desire. Lust, pure and simple. Lust for a woman he knew nothing about, a woman who was hiding something that was most likely shameful. It had to be. And he should be ashamed of himself for kissing her. But he wasn't. Angry at himself, maybe, but not ashamed.

For one brief moment she had actually seemed so vulnerable. For one brief moment her claws had been sheathed and her thorny bristles gone. And that moment of weakness had sparked an answering weakness in him, a weakness that had made him want to hold and comfort and kiss her. But that kiss had ended up being something different than he had intended. Instead of comforting, it had stirred fires within him that he had been unaware of, fires that were not comforting at all, fires that he was decidedly uncomfortable with.

He watched his mother work for a few minutes, then he straightened. "I see you still take care of all the accounts."

She looked up at him and chuckled. "I enjoy it. Your father would rather be on the deck of a ship."

"Irish said that she has her own drawer and accounts in here."

She tapped the drawer Irish had pointed out. "I've been helping her learn to take care of her money and showing her how to keep her own books. She learns fast. And she's doing quite well with her investments, too."

"You've been good to her," he said.

She shrugged. "She's been good to me."

He stretched and tried to shrug off thoughts of that red haired vixen. "I think I'll ride over to Fortune's Pride, see how the crop is coming along." He had been home less than a day and had been taken up with visiting with his family. Now he was anxious to see the land again, to ride over the fields, to touch the soil, to smell the air. He had been confined to walking paved streets lined with brick buildings far too long.

His mother looked up and smiled. "I wondered how long it would take you to get out to the fields. I'm surprised it has taken you this long."

He grinned. "I wanted to visit with everyone, but I have been champing at the bit."

"Better take something to eat with you if you're going to be gone for a while. With just Irish and myself here, we eat early and rather informally."

"I will. I'll stop in the kitchen on my way out."

Ty changed quickly, pulling on old clothes and high riding boots, then he headed down to the kitchen.

The kitchen was a busy place with two women cutting up vegetables and a haunch of the deer Matt had brought in earlier that day for a venison stew. Face flushed with the heat, Irish was directing the women as well as wielding a knife herself. Strands of hair had once again escaped from her cap and in the heat of the kitchen she had once more discarded her fichu and rolled up her sleeves. The round fullness of her breasts seemed ready to escape their bonds. Why did she always have to look as if she had just risen from some lover's bed?

She looked up when he came in. She tilted her head and one side of her mouth quirked upward in a cocky grin. "And what can we be doin' for the master of the house?"

The other two women stopped what they were doing to give him wide grins. At one time or the other, all the household servants had welcomed him home yesterday or this morning, and he had remembered to bring each of them something. These two, Ruby and Dee-Dee, were sporting his gifts, new aprons and mobcaps with bright red ribbons. Their hair was tucked decently inside.

Irish wiped her hands on a wet towel and came around the table. "Is there something you need?"

"Yes." He watched, almost mesmerized as a trickle of sweat ran down her chest, right into the hollow between her breasts. Why couldn't she wear a fichu? Never mind that the other two women had also taken theirs off. It wasn't their breasts that drew his attention.

Irish propped her fists onto her hips. "And what would that be, Mister Fortune?"

He swallowed hard and forced his gaze upward to her face. But that didn't help a whole lot. There were her lips, full and parted, and tempting him with the sweetness he had all too briefly sampled. Her eyes. Surely he could look at her eyes and not be distracted by prurient thoughts. They were green and twinkling, as if she were laughing at him, or knew some amusing story she wasn't sharing. That sobered him a bit. He glared at her, forcing himself into his usual calm, stoic manner. "If it wouldn't be too much trouble, I'd like a lunch packed. I won't be back in time for dinner."

She turned to the women. "Ruby, would you cut a good slice from the ham in the smokehouse, please? Dee-Dee, could you bring in a bottle of ale?" The two women went to their appointed tasks and Irish picked up a knife and a loaf of bread, cutting thick slices.

"I see you're dressed for riding." Her words were casual, but he could hear the tension in them, as if she were trying as hard as he to pretend that kiss had never happened. That his accusation had never happened.

"Yes."

"I suppose you'll be taking Renegade?"

He chuckled thinking about his horse. "I visited him in the stable this morning, and took him a carrot. He seems well cared for and sassy as ever. I just hope he hasn't gone completely wild in the last two years."

The women returned with the ham and ale. Irish thanked them and began packing it into a leather traveling pouch along with the bread and a fried apple pie. "Renegade's a darlin' horse. I think you'll find him tame enough for even a fine gentleman like yourself to ride."

His brows went up. "You're familiar with my horse?"

She laughed. "Aye. Renegade and I have become fast friends."

He shook his head in disbelief. "Renegade? Are we talking about the same horse?"

"Ah, weel, now, he did take a bit of talkin' to before he let me ride him, but he took to me soon enough. Brazen devil. Loves to run full out, and that's a fact."

Ty was incredulous. "You *rode* him? No one can ride that horse but me."

"And me." She cocked her brows and tilted her head, giving him a cheeky grin.

"I don't believe it."

She handed him the packed traveling pouch and leaned back against the table, folding her arms under her breasts causing them to thrust upward. "I've always had a way with horses."

He put the basket down and leaned toward her, fists on hips. "You rode my horse?" He hadn't meant to raise his voice but it seemed to happen every time he was around this irritating piece of Irish skirt. She had ridden his horse? She had taken his room, his place at the table, and now she had ridden his horse? The horse only he had ever been able to ride?

She straightened away from the table and her fists also went to her hips as she squared off with him. "Well, somebody had to. He was too full of himself, by far." She leaned forward, narrowing her eyes at him. "Just like someone else, I'll not be namin'. If I hadn't ridden him for you he would have been ruined by the time you came home. And been too fat for his stall, as well. You should be thankin' me for the piece of work I did with that animal instead of caterwaulin' that somebody rode your own precious horse."

He clenched his teeth and took a deep, calming breath. "*You* rode Renegade?"

"Well now, I said I did, didn't I?"

He ran a hand down his face, realizing that she was right. That horse had to be ridden--and ridden often--or he forgot his manners altogether. He had worried about him while he was gone, hoping he wouldn't have gone so wild he would have to start all over with his training. Now, here was this bit of a thing telling him that she had ridden a horse with the hardest head he had ever encountered. Ridden him and kept him in training. Had she actually used the word 'tame'? If that was true, he supposed he should thank her. But he just couldn't believe it.

He grabbed up the lunch. He would soon find out just what, if anything, she had done with Renegade. "I just hope you haven't ruined him," he muttered ungraciously and stomped out.

Chapter Four

WHEN TY ENTERED THE STABLE, OLD MANGUS WAS mucking out one of the stalls. At this time of year every able-bodied worker was out in the fields weeding, hoeing, doing the back-breaking labor that was necessary to produce a good crop of rice. It was hard work, but they paid their workers well and expected a full day's work from them.

Mangus left off his chore to greet him and gave him a wide, nearly toothless grin. Looking him up and down, he set aside his shovel and headed for Renegade's stall. "I guess you be wantin' that rapscallion of yours saddled. I'll get him fixed up for you, Master Ty."

Ty grabbed the man's arm in alarm. Had the old man gone daft as well as toothless? Renegade would make short work of him. "I'll do it, Mangus."

Mangus chuckled and leaned against the door of the stall to watch.

Ty picked up Renegade's bridle and eased into the stall, holding the bridle out of the horse's sight.

"Ain't no cause to hide that bridle, Master Ty. That horse ain't gonna fight you none. Not after Miss Irish done got ahold of him."

Ty shot a glare at Mangus but decided to take the same pre-
cautions he always had with the stallion. Clucking quietly, he put
out a hand to touch the horse's back. Renegade turned toward him
with a soft whicker and nuzzled him--actually nuzzled him. In
amazement, Ty brought the bridle around and put it on. The horse
accepted the bit and bridle as if he were a lady's palfry. "Ain't Miss
Irish somethin'?" asked Mangus. "Cain't believe that's the same
horse, can you?"

Ty shook his head in agreement and took a quick look underneath the horse. He heard Mangus chuckle again. Surprisingly, the
stallion was still a stallion. But something certainly had changed.
Had Irish really tamed this horse all by herself? He put the saddle
on and led him out of the stall with no kicking, bucking, or biting.

He mounted while Renegade stood stock still for him. "If she
did this, then she certainly is something, Mangus."

Touching the brim of his hat in salute to the old man, he urged
the horse forward and set off down the road toward his plantation
with the most well-mannered horse that he had ever had beneath
him. Renegade kept to the pace Ty set, but he shook his head and
blew, snorting and prancing, clearly wanting to run. He was still
full of devilment. Whatever Irish had done to the animal, his spirit
had not been broken. Ty could not help laughing out loud. With
a whoop, he leaned forward in the saddle, swept off his hat and
smacked Renegade on the rump with it, giving him license to run
his heart out.

The horse did not slow all the way to Fortune's Pride. The road
was a blur. Ty had forgotten how fast he was. With his new manners, he might now be able to actually enter him in a race or two.

As Ty rode by the rice paddies at Fortune's Pride, the workers waved to him and called out greetings, many welcoming him
home. He stopped a time or two to speak to someone or to point

out a dike that needed repair. Once or twice he dismounted to feel the soil, running it through his fingers, touching the growing stalks of rice. But mostly he just enjoyed being home, breathing in the scents unique to this place, listening to the sounds, feeling the hot sun on his back. He had missed that most of all. England had too many gray days and chilling nights.

He had made a lot of good contacts in London, sat in the coffee houses and pubs and gotten acquainted with merchants and factors, learning their likes and dislikes and who to trust with selling his crops. But he was glad to be home, glad to be back to the soil.

When he reached the little rise overlooking the river where he planned to build his home, he dismounted and walked over the site. Here is where he would put down his roots, raise his children, and grow old. This view of the river was what he would see all his days. The windows of the living room would face just so, there would be a wide porch for sitting, the sheds and other buildings would be just beyond that line of trees.

The builder he had hired would be arriving any day. The walls would soon be rising. The land was rich and productive, the crop well-tended. All he needed was a wife to grace the halls, bear his children, and help him become a leader of Charles Town society.

He slapped his thigh with his hat. He would have to begin making the rounds of the plantations--visiting, getting to know what the prospects were, find out who had marriageable daughters. *Betsy Hall should be old enough to wed by now,* he thought, as well as several others who would have grown from skittish girls into young women in the last two years.

Loosening Renegade's saddle girth and hobbling the horse, he took out his lunch and sat on the grass to eat.

He pulled a deep breath and thought of the qualities he wanted in a woman. She would be gentle and kind, an outgoing hostess, and well-educated. He took a bite of the cheese Irish had packed for him and closed his eyes to picture what his future wife might look like. She would be slender with soft, full lips and sparkling, mischievous eyes and her red hair would…

His eyes snapped open. He looked down at the food spread beside him. It must be the lunch she had packed for him that made him picture her in his mind. As if he wanted a red-haired Irish termagant for a wife! He tossed down the cheese, his appetite suddenly gone.

He had wanted to think of that day when he would sit here at a fine table with his wife sedately beside him, but that Irishwoman had intruded again! His table, his bed, his horse, and now he had carried her to his future home in his thoughts. Would he never have any peace from her?

He gathered up the meal, put it back into his saddle bags, tightened Renegade's girth, and rode away, hard and fast.

Ty balanced the delicate teacup on his knee and wondered again just how he had gotten himself into this situation. When he had left Fortune's Pride he had given Renegade his head and let the horse run. When the horse had finally run his course, and began to slow of his own accord, snorting and blowing, Ty had found himself at the end of the lane that led to the Hall plantation. Thinking that it wouldn't hurt to stop by for a quick hello, he had guided Renagade down the lane and dismounted at the front steps. He'd thought he would talk to Betsy and wipe the image of red hair and green eyes from his mind.

He'd remembered Betsy as a quiet, pleasant girl. Her hair was a plain medium brown color always tucked up neatly in her cap, and her eyes were… Hmmm. He hadn't been able to remember what color her eyes were. But he'd known they weren't green.

A groom had appeared instantly to take Renegade's bridle and promised to cool the horse properly. Just as quickly, a servant had opened the front door to welcome him inside. He had been ushered inside the guest parlor, offered tea, and moments later Mrs. Hall had come bustling in smoothing her hand over a fresh stomacher, freshly donned, and pushing her two oldest daughters ahead of her into the room.

The three youngest Halls, all girls, had peeked at him from around the doorframe before Mrs. Hall had shooed them away and shut the door.

"Tyrus Fortune! We had no idea you were home again!" Mrs. Hall had held out a hand to him and dipped a quick curtsy nudging her daughters forward.

Betsy, at least he thought it was Betsy, had curtsied and given him a coquettish smile, complete with batting lashes.

"You remember Prudence, I'm sure," Mrs. Hall had said.

Ty had started in surprise, then realized she must be the second daughter. "Prudence," Ty repeated. "Of course, I remember Prudence." He'd turned to Prudence's sister. "And this must be Betsy."

He'd gotten the name right because Betsy had nodded and given him a soft, sweet smile. "Please sit down, Mr. Fortune," she'd said, her voice as soft and quiet as the rest of her.

He'd sat on a spindly chair that he'd hoped would hold his weight and a servant had brought a tea tray. Betsy had poured and done an admirable job, handing him the cupful that he now sat balancing uncomfortably on his knee, wondering awkwardly what to say next.

"How long have you been home, Mr. Fortune?" Mrs. Hall asked.

"Just since yesterday," he answered.

Her brows went up and she gave each of her daughters a

meaningful look before continuing. "And you came right over to see us! Have you, by any chance, been thinking of us while you were gone?"

Ty squirmed uncomfortably on his tiny seat. Actually, he hadn't given the Halls, or even Betsy, a single thought the last two years, but it would be impolite to say so now, especially if he wanted to win the girl's favor. But he could honestly say that he had been thinking of taking a wife when he returned home. He just hadn't thought in any specific way of any particular woman. He nodded his head. "Of course I have Mrs. Hall, and particularly of your lovely daughters."

Mrs. Hall beamed and gave the two girls another look. He noticed that Prudence nudged Betsy and stifled a giggle.

"You must tell us of your travels in England, Mr. Fortune," Betsy suggested.

"Yes, please!" Prudence said. "Have styles changed so very much? Are we hopelessly out of fashion?" She smoothed a hand over her gown, which, to Ty, did not seem any more out of style than anything else in the colony.

"I did bring some dolls home to my mother and sister," he answered.

"And they would let us see them?" Mrs. Hall asked, brightly.

"I'm sure they would," Ty responded.

"And could we come over tomorrow?" Prudence blurted out.

Betsy glared at her sister. "I'm sure that Mr. Fortune has better things to do than entertain ladies and show them fashion dolls this soon after his return home, Pru."

Sensible girl, Ty thought, but he noticed that she, too, turned hopeful eyes on him. How could he tell them not to come? "Yes, I'm sure tomorrow will be fine."

With that settled, they spoke of other things for a while. He told them about London and the sights he had seen. They told him about events and current gossip in the colony. When he rose to leave they begged him to stay to dinner, but by that time he felt suffocated by the surfeit of female attention. He had forgotten what a feminine household this was, with five daughters and no sons.

They walked him to the door, Mrs. Hall holding on to one of his arms and Prudence holding the other, with Betsy leading the way. His horse was brought and they stood waving kerchiefs as he rode away.

Riding back home, Ty took a deep breath, feeling like he had just clawed his way out of a bed piled high with goose down comforters and frothy pillows. He hadn't meant for his visit to result in a return invitation, but it was done now. Mrs. Hall must be ecstatic to think that she might have a possible husband dangling after one of her five daughters.

Ty shrugged. Maybe she did. He hadn't been able to speak much with Betsy, but she seemed a nice enough girl. She was well-mannered, quietly spoken. Restful. He could do worse. The thought of a red-haired termagant crossed his mind. *Yes,* he thought, *I could do a lot worse!*

The next afternoon the entire contingent of the Hall family descended on the Fortune household. There was such a flurry of skirts and petticoats and bonnets that Mr. Hall, even though he was a hale and hearty man, was nearly lost in the foamy sea of lace and ruffles.

Ty had warned his mother about the possible incursion so she and Irish had made sure there was plenty of hot tea on hand along with sweet biscuits and cakes. The fashion dolls were waiting for inspection along with the bolts of fabric Ty had brought home.

Ty's mother and Irish met the Hall's carriage. Mrs. Hall and Prudence were waving merrily as Mr. Hall brought the horses to a halt. Betsy smiled and nodded more sedately. Mr. Hall stepped down to help his wife and the two youngest out of the carriage. Ty helped Prudence and Betsy, each of them slipping him coy glances.

Ty noticed that Irish gave everyone warm embraces, then led the way into the living room where a burst of confusion over who was to sit where momentarily ensued. But at last everyone was settled, and Irish handed around the sweet biscuits and cakes while his mother poured tea.

The three youngest girls were seated on the couch in a row, each trying to be more grown up than the other, but Ty noticed the youngest--a girl of about nine or ten--eyeing the dolls. Irish must have noticed, too, because she handed one to her, pointing out some of the ruffles and a cap that looked a lot like the one the girl wore.

Irish handed the other doll to Mrs. Hall who "oohed" and "aahed" over it, turning it to examine it closely. Handing the doll to Prudence she asked about the bolts of material piled in the corner.

Irish brought one over for her to see.

"What a lovely color!" Mrs. Hall exclaimed. "Will you have it made into a gown like the doll's, Jesse?"

Mrs. Fortune shook her head. "That bolt is for Mariette. After she has had her baby, of course."

"I expect it won't be long now," Mrs. Hall said.

Mrs. Fortune laughed. "I can't believe I'm going to be a grandmother."

Mr. Hall bowed to her from his chair. "And I never saw a grandmother looking so young, my dear."

"Which bolt is for you?" Mrs. Hall asked.

"That one," Mrs. Fortune said, pointing out a deep red satin. Irish pulled it out and let a couple of yards spill to the floor to gasps of admiration from the Hall ladies.

"Which of the fabrics will you use for a gown, Irish?" Prudence asked. Mrs. Hall poked her daughter and gave her a quelling frown, but Prudence ignored her.

"Oh, none of these is quite my style," said Irish, brightly. She quirked a brow at him. "Ty didn't bring back a thing in a good Irish green."

"That gold one would be pretty on you, Irish," said the little girl who still held the doll.

Irish picked it up and draped a length of it across her. "You might be right, Meg. But somebody might think I'm a princess if I wore something this fine." She winked at the little girl. "I guess I'll just have to let Mariette have this one, too."

"I wouldn't mind looking like a princess," Meg said seriously. Irish bent to cup her chin. "I think you already do, Meg." She turned the girl's head to one side then the other as if studying her. "Yes, I do believe you look a good bit like a princess I once saw."

The girl's eyes widened. "A real princess?"

Irish nodded. "Better than a real princess." She leaned close to Meg. "She was one of the wee folk. A real fairy princess."

"And you *saw* her?"

Ty didn't think Meg's eyes could get any wider.

Irish shrugged. "I am from Ireland."

"Oh!"

Irish held out her hand. "Do you think we could let your mother see that doll for a bit?"

Meg gave the doll one last squeeze then handed it over to be passed around and inspected.

The women spoke about fashions for a while and Ty noticed the younger girls were beginning to squirm. As before Irish seemed to notice at the same time he did, because she said, "There are some new kittens out in the stable, and I could use some help checking up on them."

Mrs. Hall nudged Betsy. "Why don't all you young folks run along. Maybe Ty could show Betsy the gardens."

"I would love to, Mrs. Hall. I've had enough talk about fashion for now. A walk in the garden is just what I need." He offered Betsy an arm, and also one to Prudence.

Betsy accepted his invitation, but a tug to her sister's skirt by their mother, along with a quick negative shake of her head, made Prudence reconsider.

"I think I'd rather see the kittens," Prudence said, giving her sister a quick wink.

Ty watched Irish lead the four younger Hall daughters out of the room, while holding fast to Meg's hand and telling her that the kittens had just opened their eyes a couple of days ago. There was almost an unladylike skip to Irish's walk as if she were as anxious to see the kittens as Meg. Perhaps she was. Whatever was being discussed, from fashions to crops to the dangers of the impress gangs that roamed Charles Town's streets looking for men to kidnap into the king's navy, Irish seemed to show a keen interest.

Betsy, on the other hand, was quiet, almost to the point of being shy. Where Irish was exuberant and enthusiastic, every move Betsy made was graceful and controlled...ladylike. Her hand rested so lightly on his arm and she walked so quietly, he almost felt he had to look down to make sure she was really there. If it had been Irish beside him, she would not have gone unnoticed.

He frowned at himself. Why was he constantly comparing Betsy to Irish, anyway? He had a lovely lady on his arm, the day was glorious, and the garden quiet and secluded. That was where his thoughts should be. Not on some green-eyed hoyden.

The Fortune gardens were not extensive, but there were paths that wound between groups of shrubs and trees with secluded seats set throughout. They strolled along the entire curving length of the garden walk. Now they were headed back...and Betsy had still not uttered a word. Ty supposed conversation was up to him. He cleared his throat. "Would you care to sit for a while?" he asked.

She smiled prettily. "Yes, that would be nice."

He escorted her to one of the stone benches set back from the path. The seat was easily big enough for two and she sat at one end, smoothing her skirts to ensure he had room to sit.

"My brothers tell me that, with this war going on and the interruption of trade, a lot of the planters are worried about the price of rice this fall," he said.

"Do you think prices will fall or rise?" she asked.

He shrugged. "It depends on how many of his majesty's ships come to Charles Town needing provisions. That could easily send the price up in spite of the war causing difficulties with trade."

"I see," she said, noncommittally.

"What do you think?" he asked.

She bit her lip and lowered her gaze to her hands which were clenched in her lap. "I'm sure you must be right," she hedged.

That was clearly the proper answer to give to a gentleman if a lady wanted to impress him, thought Ty. But he was used to his mother and sister having their say about any matter that was broached in the household. And now that included Irish, too, who was always willing to chime in with an opinion.

"But what do you think?" he pressed her.

She twisted her hands before looking up at him. "I'm not sure. Papa never discusses business at home."

Well, of course not, Ty thought. *Very few men do,* he supposed. He searched his mind for another topic, one she would be certain to know about.

"It should be about time for the fair, isn't it? Please tell me I haven't missed it this year."

She brightened. "No, you haven't missed it. It starts just four days from today. I am so looking forward to it."

Ty leaned forward, intoxicated by her smile, so glad he had found a topic that pleased her. "What particularly are you looking forward to?"

"In the *Gazette* there was a notice advertising a group of players from London who will put on a short play." She stopped, her hand going shyly to her mouth. "I forget. You are so recently come from London that such a performance must seem very provincial to you."

He dared to lay a hand on hers, and though hers fluttered for a moment as if she would draw it away, she permitted him the liberty.

"Not at all," he assured her. "I look forward to it. For me, London was mostly schooling and business."

She looked up at him with shining eyes. "Then you will be there?"

"As I hope you will." And he meant what he said. It would be a pleasure to watch a play with her.

"I...I hope I will be able to go," she said hesitantly.

"And why would you not?"

"Papa is hoping he will find the time to take us to the fair, but we may not be able to stay long enough to see the play."

"Then perhaps you would consider allowing me to take you, Miss Hall."

That smile again. Ty felt as if he had been drinking.

"You are very kind, Mr. Fortune. I would enjoy it...so long as we are properly chaperoned."

He squeezed her hand. "I assure you we will be. My mother and Irish will both be going, and you can bring Prudence, if you wish." He hesitated a moment then dared to suggest, "Perhaps since we have been neighbors and friends all our lives, you could call me Ty?"

She laughed, a small light sound that delighted his ear. "I think that would be permitted. And you must call me Betsy."

She pulled her hand from his, perhaps thinking that he had held it long enough. "What will interest you at the Fair?" she asked.

He straightened. "I was thinking about racing my horse, Renegade."

Her hand went to her breast. "Isn't that dangerous?"

He chuckled. "Only if one is not careful. But with a horse like Renegade, I will be so far ahead of the rest, there should be no danger at all."

They talked a while of what they would see and do at the fair, then he took her back inside, promising to visit again the next day and make final arrangements for their outing. The other daughters had come in from the stable and were arguing the various merits of the four kittens. Mr. and Mrs. Hall were standing, ready to leave. Mrs. Hall gave Irish a big hug, inviting her to come and see them. Then they all piled into their carriage and were off.

"So you'll be taking Betsy to the fair?" Irish asked, as the Hall carriage pulled away.

"Yes, along with her sister, my mother, and you, as well, if you care to go."

She nodded absently. "And you're going to visit her again tomorrow?"

He turned to face her, wondering what her interest in his business was. "Yes, I plan to visit her again tomorrow. And if she's willing, we'll go for a ride."

Irish quirked a brow and gave him a lopsided smile, that was more of a smirk. "Then I suggest that you take the carriage because Betsy doesn't ride mounted." With that, she turned in a flounce of skirts and was gone.

The next afternoon, returning home from the Hall's, thinking about his quiet, pleasant drive with Betsy, Ty heard the thunder of hoofbeats coming fast from behind him. He pulled his carriage to the side of the road to allow the rider to pass, and was astounded to see Renegade charging toward him with a red-haired rider hunkered close to his neck.

Irish! And riding *his* stallion!

They flew past him with mane and tail and skirts flying. He could not help but admire her seat, the easy way she seemed to flow with each of the horse's movements. Holding the reins tightly, he stood to watch them. Irish gave a great joyous whoop as she passed. She could not have been more unladylike, whooping like that, her hair loosened and flying like the horse's mane--and yes, she was even riding astride. Renegade was running flat out, and Lord, that horse could run!

And how that woman could ride! He had never seen a more magnificent sight. His blood stirred just watching them. He grabbed his hat off and waved it overhead, giving Irish a great answering whoop.

He was sure to win that race at the fair. No one could beat a horse like that.

Taking his seat again, he slapped the reins over the more sedate carriage horse's rump and pulled back onto the road, a huge grin on his face and a lightness in his heart. That's when it hit him--Irish had been riding his horse without so much as a 'by your leave'. He would have something to say to her when he got back to the stable. He tried to scowl, but he felt too good, too certain of victory at the fair, too charged with the exuberance of seeing Irish ride like that.

He had been driving along. thinking pleasant thoughts about Betsy, about how sweet and ladylike she was, and how she had deferred to him in their topics of conversation. Betsy would never be caught riding astride like that. But, the thought also crept in, she would never stir his blood like that, either.

Well, hell, isn't that what I want? A quiet, tranquil life. Peaceful.

By the time he guided the carriage into the stable yard, Irish was out of the saddle and cooling Renegade, walking him in a large circle. Even pacing, both horse and woman seemed full of fire. Despite his run, Renegade was tossing his head and prancing. His coat gleamed. Irish's cheeks were flushed, her eyes shining, her red hair glinting in the sun as if she truly were on fire. Her cap, if she had even donned one that morning, was long gone, her hair wild and windblown. She looked like a woman just risen from a lover's bed. *But,* Ty thought, *she usually looks that way... to me.*

Handing over the carriage to Mangus, Ty joined her. He had meant to upbraid her for taking his horse without permission, but the joy of seeing her ride like that, seeing her now with her eyes bright from her ride, quite wiped away any annoyance he had felt.

"He's a fine fellow," Irish said, stroking the stallion's neck. Renegade nuzzled her and whickered.

"I can't believe he's the same horse I left here. He's as tame as a baby but still full of himself. What did you do to him?"

The horse bent his head, she scratched him fondly behind the ears and spoke as if only to him. "Well now, that's betwixt the two of us, isn't it Renegade?"

The horse snorted and bobbed his head as if agreeing with her, causing them both to laugh.

"And there's no way you'll tell me your secret?" Ty asked. The sudden guarded look on her face made him remember that she had more than one secret she was unwilling to share.

But she quickly pasted a mischievous smile in place and arched one brow at him. "I'm Irish. We Irish have always had a way with horses. Some of us more than others."

"And some of you are better at keeping secrets, too," he responded.

"Some of us have more reason than others to keep secrets," she snapped haughtily.

At least she was finally admitting that she did have secrets, he thought.

Ty decided to let the matter of her secrets drop for now and changed the subject. "Renegade's sure to win the race at the fair."

Irish nodded her agreement. "Tomorrow I won't ride him quite so hard or so far. He'll need some exercise but he should save himself for the race."

"I'll ride him tomorrow," Ty said.

"You?" He saw her dander rise, her free fist flying to one hip. "I'm the one who has been keeping him in shape, taking care of him, riding him every day."

"You're also the one who took my horse out without my permission."

"And what shape would he be in if I hadn't?" she snapped.

He fumed silently a moment, glaring at her, knowing she was right but unwilling to say it. "Well I'm home now, aren't I?"

"Aye, and off courting the minute your feet touch the sweet soil, leaving the poor lad here kicking his heels and wanting to stretch his legs."

"I am not neglecting my horse!"

Renegade gave a startled whinny, jerking his head up. Why did he always end up raising his voice whenever he was around her? For the horse's sake he lowered his voice, but his words still came out in an angry snarl. "And it's none of your business what I do with my time!"

"Nay. 'Tis your right to do as you please. I cannot fault you for courting Betsy. She's a fine girl."

"I'm glad you approve," he said sarcastically.

She shrugged. "She's every bit the fine lady."

"That she is!" he agreed emphatically.

"You could do worse."

"Aye," he snarled. "I could be courting *you!*"

Her head came up and he thought for just a moment that he saw hurt and a hidden vulnerability that he had no idea existed. He didn't know why he had said those words. The very thought of courting Irish was ludicrous. He wanted a lady. He wanted a calm and peaceful life. He didn't need a virago with secrets so dark she refused to even tell him her name, a termagant who set his blood to boiling.

But the hurt was gone from her face in an instant and she turned on him with fire in her eyes. "Courting me? You wouldn't know how!"

"And just what is so different about you?" he asked, as if he didn't know, as if he couldn't see the vast difference between her fire and Betsy's calm.

"I'm not some milk-and-water miss you can win with pleasant little carriage rides and a posy now and then."

"Oh, and just how would a man have to court you?"

She gave a coquettish little toss of her head. "When you figure it out, I might let you." Then she turned to lead Renegade inside the barn for a rubdown.

Irish began brushing the horse, keeping an eye on the doorway of the barn, hoping Ty didn't follow her. Why, oh why on God's green earth had she ever said she would let the likes of him court her? As if he would! The man had nothing but suspicion and contempt for her. Let him court the sweet and prim Betsy Hall if that's what he wanted.

She could see the two of them now, sitting by the evening fire, with Betsy placing delicate embroidery stitches in a kerchief and

Ty reading the *Gazette*, both of them dying of boredom. The image lightened her mood and caused her to chuckle.

The next morning, Irish was in the stable early when Ty came in. She was currying Renegade, his saddle and bridle close to hand.

He held out his hand for the curry comb. "I'll finish that."

She kept brushing. "'Tis no bother at all. I've done this every morning since you left home and abandoned such a fine animal."

Trying to control his outburst, he ground his teeth so hard they hurt. "I did not abandon my horse!"

She smoothed a hand over Renegade's back then walked to the other side to work there. "Oh, he had a good stall and plenty of feed, I'll grant you, but a horse like this needs companionship." As if to agree with her, Renegade whickered and turned his head to nudge her.

Ty leaned on the horse's back and looked at her. "If I have been remiss it is only in thanking you for caring for him while I was gone, and for teaching him some manners, as well. But I'm home now, the horse is mine, and I'll see to his care, as well as the riding of him."

She looked up at him. Her eyes were wide and wounded and one hand clenched Renegade's mane as if she would never let go. But the look was gone almost as quickly as it had come. If he had not been watching her at just the right moment, he would have missed it altogether. Her chin came up with a proud tilt. "I suppose now that the master is home, I'm no longer welcome in Renegade's stall? Does that include no longer giving him an occasional carrot and spending time with him?"

There was something about her tone that made him feel like he was taking away the only joy she had ever known. "You can do whatever you want with him, just as you've been doing, but I've only ridden him once since I came home. He'll have to get used to me again before I race him."

She seemed disappointed, Ty thought, but he knew he was right. No matter how well she had done with Renegade, she would not be the one riding him at the fair in two days.

"Aye. I suppose that would be best," she finally admitted. She stroked her hand down the horse's neck then reluctantly handed him the curry comb. But when he tried to take it she held on. "That does mean I can still ride the beast from time to time, doesn't it?"

He pulled the comb from her hand and began stroking the horse, smoothing his hand over him to make sure there were no burrs that would bother him when saddled. Irish retreated to one corner of the stall, watching him.

He felt like he had kicked a puppy. He cleared his throat, wanting to make things right with her. But Renegade did belong to him. He couldn't just let her have him. "I will need some help with Renegade," he said casually.

He saw her perk up a bit, but she tried to hide it.

"And I'm sure there will be a lot of days I just won't have the time to ride him." He glared at her so there would be no mistake. "But he's my horse and I'll decide what's best for him."

As if she had totally won whatever battle they were having, she sashayed back to Renegade. She looked across the horse's back at him. "I do believe you want what's best for Renegade, Tyrus Fortune. I just hope you know that I'm the best thing that ever happened to this horse!"

She patted the horse again and whispered in his ear, "I look forward to seeing you win." Then she was gone.

Chapter Five

IRISH COULDN'T HELP HERSELF. AS SOON AS TY LEFT ON RENEGADE, she went back to the stable yard to wait for their return, hoping that he didn't run the horse too far or too hard. It seemed like they had been gone too long already and she began to pace, then stood staring down the lane arms akimbo, fists on hips, unable to keep her foot from tapping impatiently.

At last she saw Renegade coming back, and she breathed a sigh of relief. Ty was keeping the stallion in check, not letting him have his head.

Ty slowed the horse to a walk and began cooling him off. She walked alongside them, taking hold of the stirrup and having to hurry to keep up with the horse's pace, his legs were so long.

"How far did you take him?"

"Just up to that old oak at the bend of the road and back."

She nodded in approval.

He grinned down at her. "I knew you'd skin me alive if I ran him any farther than that."

She started, thinking that once again he was being sarcastic with her, but when she looked up and saw his grin, she was surprised to realize that he was teasing her. She couldn't help grinning back. Would wonders never cease? The great, proud, prim Tyrus

Fortune making a near jest.

"You're right, Irish. I do want what's best for my horse. And I know good advice when I hear it, no matter where it comes from. You gave good advice when you said he shouldn't be run full out for the next couple of days. I kept him to a steady pace and kept him in check."

He was praising her? She swallowed hard and patted Renegade. Next thing she knew he'd be finding out the way to court her. She shook her head free of that thought. Tyrus Fortune would have none of the likes of her. As if she would have him if he would! *Stick to talking about horses and racing,* she told herself. *'Tis all you'll ever have in common with him.*

"'Tis good you ran him easy. He needs to be kept in shape but not worn out by running full tilt. Let him save it for the race," she said.

Ty dismounted and began leading Renegade in a slow walk, and she moved up to pace beside him.

"I wonder if Bill Townsend will be racing his bay mare again this year?" Ty said. "I've run against him three times and never beat him. Just once I'd like to win."

"He ran her last fall and last spring," Irish said.

"And won both times?"

She nodded. "But I heard this is the last time he'll enter her. He said he's going to win one more time and quit."

"But he won't win this time." He said, patting Renegade's neck. "We've got a new champion for sure."

When Renegade was cooled down, Ty took off the saddle and bridle, turned Renegade into his stall and picked up two brushes, handing one to her. In silent camaraderie they gave the horse a good going over, then walked side by side back to the house.

The next day, as Ty rode back to the stable after exercising Renegade, he found himself looking for that flash of red hair waiting by the stable doors. When he did not see her, he felt a strange sense of disappointment. She had been there to help saddle Renegade. She had lectured him all during the time they had brushed and saddled the horse about how to run him this morning. He had expected to see her when he returned. Savagely, he tamped down the disappointment. He should be glad that the interfering little harridan wasn't there.

He told himself he was disappointed on Renegade's behalf. He thought she was anxious to see and hear how the horse had run. It wasn't because he wanted to see how her eyes lit up when she ran an appraising hand over the horse, or when she approved the way he rode the stallion.

And then, suddenly, she was there, popping out from inside the stable, and it seemed like the sun had come out after a long, gray, London day. It was only because he had come to count on her expertise with Renegade, he told himself, that he was so glad to see her.

Irish propped her fists on her hips and began looking Renegade over with narrowed eyes, inspecting him for any harm.

Ty dismounted and began walking the horse. "He's fine, Irish. He ran well. He's in top form."

She nodded. "Aye, that he is. So long as you handle him the way I told you, he'll win tomorrow and that's for sure."

In his brief time back at home, watching her with the stallion, seeing what she had done with him, he had come to trust her abilities and instincts with horses. But he could not help but tease her just a bit now and then. It was so easy to set her hackles up. And then how the sparks would fly! Her eyes flashed, her hair seemed to take on new fire, and her cheeks flushed. Her whole body seemed to come to attention. Just as it had when he had kissed her. He shook his head, refusing to let his mind take that road.

Suppressing a grin, he tapped his chin thoughtfully with one finger. "Maybe I should just give him his head tomorrow. Let him run fast and hard all the way."

She rounded on him, her eyes blazing green fire. "You can't--"

He could not contain his laughter. He had to bend over, he was laughing so hard. He had not had a good laugh like this since— He couldn't remember when.

"Oh! You—you—" she spluttered to a halt. The corner of her mouth twitched. She turned away, but she couldn't help herself, either. She started to laugh, and a great hearty laugh it was.

Any other woman would have stomped away angry, her nose in the air. Irish might have secrets, but she could laugh at herself and take a joke. Without thinking about it, he slung one arm about her shoulders. "You are too easy to tease, Irish. I couldn't help myself."

She didn't have to tell him she forgave him. The way her body leaned into his told him. Her arm came around his waist as if they were very old friends.

"'Tis glad I am to hear you laugh, Tyrus. I was beginning to think you didn't know how."

He thought maybe he had forgotten, as well...until she had given him reason to remember. He bent and kissed her on the top of her head. It was meant only as a thank you, but when he felt her arm tighten about him, felt her stiffen, he straightened and pulled away. He didn't want their new found ease with each other to end because he had taken a liberty with her he never should have.

"We'd better see to Renegade," he said, and led the horse away into the stable.

On the way back to the house, Irish heard a hail from the dock where a small ship was just tying up.

"It's the *Merry Ann*," Ty said. "When Nate's gone with the *Fortune*, Papa's little river runner usually brings visitors upriver." He shielded his eyes with his hand and watched as a man jumped onto the dock. "It's my builder!"

Curious, she followed when Ty motioned for her to do so. Ty hurried down to the dock and wrung the hand of a man surrounded by trunks, boxes, and bags. "I didn't expect you for another week!"

"Apparently the winds were with us," the man said, clapping Ty familiarly on the back. Then the man looked up at her and his eyes widened, brightened, and he smiled. His smile seemed to come from his whole body, a body that was wiry and spare and full of life. His hair was a honey gold and his eyes were nearly as green as hers. They matched the green of his coat and the embroidery on his waistcoat. He held out both hands to take hers and she gave them to him gladly, unable to keep from laughing. "And who is this?" He asked Ty.

Ty looked down at their clasped hands and his smile fled. His brows came down and his mouth firmed into a straight line.

"This is Irish," Ty answered. "Irish, this is Charles Bowles. He has come from London to direct the building of my house."

Irish squeezed the hands that still held hers. "Mr. Bowles, welcome to Carolina."

One of Mr. Bowles's eyebrows quirked upward and he leaned close to her. "Irish? Nothing more?" Then he leaned closer and spoke in a near whisper, his eyes twinkling. "Do I detect a mystery here?"

She felt her cheeks flushing. Surely there wouldn't be someone else trying to delve into her secrets, and corner her into betraying herself.

Unexpectedly Ty came to her rescue. "There's no mystery, Bowles. She's from Ireland and everyone just calls her Irish." His words came out clipped and hard and Irish wondered if he were protecting her, or if he just didn't want anyone else to discover her secret before he did.

Mr. Bowles grinned knowingly at her and gave her a wink, but he spoke to Ty. "There's always a mystery whenever a beautiful woman is involved." Then he spoke to her. "But I'm willing to grant you your mystery so long as you grant me a smile and some time."

A knot seemed to ease within her and she gave Mr. Bowles her best smile. "That would be my pleasure, Mr. Bowles."

He blinked, looking offended. "Mr. Bowles? Nay, if I'm to call you Irish, you must call me Charlie." He turned to Ty. "And you as well, Ty. If we're to work together for the next year or two it takes to build this house of yours, I'd like it to be as the friends we became in London. I'll have none of this Mr. Bowles!"

Ty nodded. "Shall we go up to the house? I'll send someone down to bring up your things."

Charlie pulled Irish's arm through his and drew her close to his side as they headed toward the house. "So you are Irish, eh? Though anyone would know it just to have a look at you. My father is English, but my ma is pure shamrock. She has the red hair and green eyes of the breed, too, though not so green as yours. We've much in common, I would think."

Irish noticed that his pure, upper class English was melting into an Irish brogue as he spoke to her and it brought back a twinge of homesickness for the green island she had been wrenched from.

"Perhaps we do have things in common, Charlie. I can hear the Irish in your words. Do you speak the old tongue?"

"Gaelic?" He shook his head. "A few words only, more's the pity."

She felt a bit disappointed. It would have been good to speak it again after so long. But perhaps it was better this way. She was feeling the strong pull of friendship with Charlie Bowles. It would keep Tyrus Fortune at more of a distance, and keep him from prying into her secrets.

She glanced behind her and saw Ty following along, scowling at them both as if he resented her taking up with Charles so quickly and easily. What was it to him if she did? Surely, he could not be jealous! He was courting Betsy.

Upon reaching the house, Ty took Charlie to meet Mrs. Fortune. Irish called to Ruby to come help her prepare a guest room for Mr. Bowles, and she sent a couple of men down to bring up his things from the dock. Then she and Ruby went to the kitchen to finish making lunch.

Irish made sure an extra plate was set at the table for Charlie--right across from hers. When he had freshened up, he came in with Mrs. Fortune on his arm, charming her as readily as he did everyone else.

As they took their places at table, Irish said, "You know Charlie, you've arrived just in time."

"I have? In time for what?"

"Tomorrow's the fair."

They began to eat, chatting about the upcoming fair, all of them looking forward to it.

Chapter Six

SQUEALING AS IF IT WERE BEING SLAUGHTERED, A GREASED pig shot by her, and Irish barely had time to move out of the way before several young men came barreling after it. If it hadn't been for Charlie's hand holding tight to her arm, she might have fallen.

"I say there!" Charlie protested. But the boys were already gone and Irish was laughing. "I take it you are unharmed?"

She patted his arm reassuringly as she watched pig and boys disappear through the crowd, down the row of booths and around a corner. "I'm fine, but I pity the poor pig."

"That poor pig is leading them all a merry chase," Charlie said. "I doubt that he'll be caught before the fair is over."

"Don't underestimate us colonials, Charlie," Ty said. "We're a resourceful lot. One of those boys will find a way to catch it."

"They'll have to be resourceful to catch that pig. It's easily the biggest I've ever seen let loose at a fair," said Charlie.

"We don't do things halfway here," Ty said.

Irish looked around at the people. She loved the fair, but she was always worried, just as she was each time she went to Charles Town, whether someone from her past would happen to be there, recognize her, denounce her.

Irish watched Betsy smile up at Ty and nod in agreement...as she had nodded in agreement with every word out of his mouth the live long day. As if she didn't have a brain of her own.

Irish had been glad of Charlie's hand on her arm when that pig came by, but she didn't cling to him the way Betsy clung to Ty--as if she couldn't walk without him. Oh, there was nothing forward about the perfect Miss Hall. Heaven forbid! But she did constantly find ways of touching Ty--brushing against him, leaning close when someone led a horse or cow past them, using his arm for support to daintily step around droppings.

In a hundred small ways, Betsy continuingly kept Ty's attention on her. She was subtle, but Irish noticed that the woman never let Ty's eyes or thoughts stray from her for long without finding a way to bring them back to her. Sometimes it was a breathless little laugh, or an "Oh!" other times a gentle squeeze to his arm.

A dozen times that day Irish had had to grit her teeth and remind herself that--except for Renegade--she and Mr. Tyrus Fortune had nothing in common. Where, or upon whom, he chose to bestow his attention was nothing to her. If Betsy Hall was who he wanted, then they had her blessing. As she had told him, he could certainly do worse. She meant that. She really did.

She looked at them standing there, arm-in-arm, very much like a pair of fashion dolls. Even their clothes matched as if they had planned their outfits together. The soft blue of his coat matched her gown and the silver embroidery on his pearl gray waistcoat mirrored the stomacher she wore. Betsy's hair was not black like Ty's, but its medium brown color was certainly a better match to the family's than Irish's flaming red.

She glanced down at her own gown, its green slightly faded from innumerable washings. It was still good and serviceable, but it did not gleam with the new sheen that Betsy's did.

Irish put her arm through Charlie's, glad he was here with them, that she had someone who flirted with her with a merry twinkle in his eye. Mrs. Fortune's companionship was also wonderful, but Betsy had been commanding a lot of her attention today, as well.

"Shall we head over to the shooting range?" Charlie asked. "I've heard some remarkable things about the marksmanship of you colonials, and I'd like to see if it's true."

As they approached the shooting contest, Irish could see men clustered near the rope that had been strung at the line, looking over their weapons, comparing them to their rival's. There were local farmers lined up as well as some merchants and planters. There were even a few frontiersmen in buckskins cradling their long muskets. The targets looked small and far away to her, but then, she barely knew the rudiments of how to fire a gun.

Charlie slapped Ty on the back. "You know these men. Who should I put my money on?"

"Too bad Nate isn't here," Ty said proudly. "Nate has won every match he's entered since he was 14." He eyed the line of men and pointed out a tall frontiersman. "Seth's the only one who ever comes close to beating Nate."

"Is that right?" Charlie asked fishing in his pocket for some coins. "Maybe I'll place a bet or two, then."

The men lined up in groups of five with each man getting five shots. Then the next group took their turn.

Seth took his place on the line with his group and gave his full attention to his shooting. It took a while for most of the men to finish their five shots, but Seth finished quickly, smoothly loading then firing without seeming to aim. Yet he hit his target squarely every time. He was the clear winner in his group so he would have to shoot again later on against other winners.

Betsy flinched constantly at the noise, holding tightly to Ty's arm. He patted her hand soothingly and didn't seem to mind in the least holding her protectively close.

As Seth passed them, Charlie shook his hand, spoke a few words and clapped him on the back. "Well done! It seems you co-lonials know a thing or two about shooting."

Ty gave Seth a nod of approval. Even Betsy gave him a small, sweet smile. Irish thought Ty and Betsy acted like reigning royalty, graciously acknowledging Seth's skill. *Maybe they do deserve each other,* she thought. After half a day wandering around the fair she was beginning to feel wilted and sweaty and tired, but the two of them still looked as prim and proper and well-starched as they had that morning.

Charlie suggested that they find something to eat and they all made their way to a booth selling plates of food. Ty bought dinner for everyone then led Betsy to a bench, helping her to sit, handing her a plate, and making sure her drink was close to hand. Charlie found seats and carried Irish's plate for her, but he didn't fuss over her, and she was glad. She was not helpless and she didn't want to be treated like she was. Betsy, on the other hand, seemed to revel in Ty's attention to every minute detail.

Irish noticed that Betsy ate with the delicacy of a princess, never spilling a crumb or having to use her kerchief to wipe her mouth. Irish looked down at her own gown and brushed away some crumbs. She sighed. How did the woman do it? How did Ty?

After their meal, they walked along the line of booths and Charlie brought them to a stop beside a puppet show. Irish watched the antics of the puppets and couldn't help laughing out loud. At the end of the brief show, she clapped her hands and called out her approval, thoroughly enjoying herself...until she chanced to catch Ty frowning at her. Well, of course, he would frown at her, she thought, turning her gaze to the prim Betsy beside him, who was applauding politely with her small, slim hands. Her movements were ladylike, elegant and refined just like everything else about her. Like everything about Ty.

When a man from the show passed among them with a cup, Ty's contribution made the man smile and nod his thanks.

Mrs. Fortune suggested that they visit some of the booths selling lace and ribbons and buttons. She pulled out a small swatch of the cloth Ty had brought from London. "I want to find some ribbon to match this," she said. "And a bit of lace, too."

Mrs. Fortune and Betsy soon had their heads together at a booth. Betsy made several purchases, too. Irish quickly scanned the booths, making sure there was no one there who might have known her in Ireland. Not seeing anyone suspicious, she began looking at the items on display, gazing longingly at a cream silk stomacher embroidered with green vines and pink flowers, a fine lawn fichu that was feather light to the touch, kerchiefs trimmed in expensive French lace. She looked but she didn't buy. She was not about to spend her hard won coin on fripperies she did not need.

"You're lookin', but you're not buyin' darlin'," Charlie commented.

Mrs. Fortune looked up, smiled at her, and patted her cheek in a loving gesture. "Irish is saving her money," she said. "Let me buy you something, Irish. It would be small payment for all you do for us. What would you like?"

Irish backed away, shaking her head. She didn't want Mrs. Fortune buying her things as if she couldn't afford them herself. Just because she chose not to spend her money didn't mean she couldn't. "There's not a thing I'm needing," she said firmly.

"Now, darlin', just because a woman doesn't need anything is no reason they don't want something. Pick something out and let me buy it for you," Charlie said.

Irish put her hands on her hips. "I'll have none of it, Charlie.

I'll not have you buying me things. Nor you, Mrs. Fortune. I'm no pauper. I've money of my own if I want to spend it."

She tucked her arm into Charlie's and turned him toward another booth distracting Mrs. Fortune and Betsy, as well, by pointing out the gold and silver jewelry displayed there. They all spent some time gazing at those wares before moving down the row.

When they came to the last booth in the row Irish looked in, and gasping in horror, stepped back--right into the arms of Ty. He clasped her shoulders. "What is it, Irish?"

She could not take her eyes from the scene. Several Blacks were sitting chained in a pile of straw. One girl, barely beginning to blossom into womanhood stood in the center of the booth, head up, eyes blank as two men pawed her, and discussed her merits as if she couldn't see or hear them. A slave sale.

Irish felt smothered, trapped between the bargaining men and Ty's wall-like chest. She turned away from the scene, pushing at Ty, trying to get by, to get away. The others were hemming her in, peering past her at the slaves. Irish shoved down a rising panic, but she did not want to be here, did not want to see this.

"Let me by!" She shoved ineffectually at Ty's chest and he looked down at her with concern. He still held her captive by the shoulders and she tried to shrug him off, to get by him.

"What's wrong?" he asked.

She felt anger burning away the panic. "What's wrong? Can you not see for yourself?" She shoved again at him.

Mrs. Fortune tugged gently at her son's arm. "Let her pass, Ty."

Ty stepped aside and Irish pushed past him, walking quickly into the open air, breathing deeply. Feeling a hand on her shoulder she turned to find him there. "What is it, Irish? What's the matter?"

She noticed that the others had walked on a bit and were waiting a short distance away, giving them time to talk for a moment. "Did you not see the abomination going on in that booth?"

"You have been in the colony two years, Irish. Surely you've seen slave sales before. You can't walk down the streets of Charles Town without seeing them."

She rounded on him, hands on hips. "Aye, I've seen them. What's worse I've experienced them. I know what it feels like to be stood up in front of a crowd, your every flaw and merit flaunted and argued and bargained over."

Understanding seemed to dawn in his eyes. "When you were enslaved by the Spanish?"

She nodded and turned away. Even with the fair going on, where they stood at the end of the line of booths seemed incredibly private. Looking away from the throngs across the field where the horse race would be run later that day, she could almost imagine that they were alone here. Only the sounds of the fair intruded. The sounds and the touch of his hand, caressing her shoulder sympathetically.

"I can usually pass by those sales and look the other way, just like everyone else does," she said. "What else can I do? Slavery is a fact of life here. It's just…when it's a young girl like that…when I look into her eyes and know what she must be feeling because I've been in her place, I…" She took a deep breath and turned back to him. "I'm just glad that your grandfather was enslaved at one time and decided that your family would never own slaves."

He nodded. "It hasn't always been easy finding the labor to run the plantation, but I can't imagine being able to sell Mangus or Abby or one of her children."

Irish took a deep breath and rubbed her arms as if chilled. "I'm sorry. We should get back to the others."

She started to walk away but he stopped her. She turned and looked up at him.

"Never be sorry for having a kind heart, Irish."

Her head came up at his compliment. She swallowed hard. "Aye." Then she turned and went to join the others.

Charlie took her arm again, Ty took his mother's arm and Betsy latched on to his other.

"Isn't it about time for the foot race?" Mrs. Fortune asked.

"That it is, Mrs. Fortune," Charlie said. "I suspect you'll be wanting to see it since you put up the prize for it."

"What is the prize?" Betsy asked.

Mrs. Fortune smiled. "A silver serving tray and bowl. I've heard there are a lot of entries."

"And right after the foot race, Ty and Renegade are going to impress us all by winning the horse race!" Charlie said.

Ty grinned. "I hope you're right, Charlie. Mangus brought Renegade up early this morning and he's been taking his ease all day. He should be in fine form."

Charlie tucked his tongue into his cheek. "I hear there's a certain mare that's hard to beat."

"She'll have no chance against Renegade!" Ty and Irish exclaimed together.

Charlie held up his hands in surrender, laughing. "I hope not! I've placed a good size wager on that stallion."

There were indeed a record number of entries for the foot race. Boys as young as ten lined up at the start against men old enough to be grandfathers. Coats and hats were discarded on the ground or held by cheering supporters. Because Mrs. Fortune had put up the prize, the judges handed her the starting gun. She waited until everyone was crouched, ready to run, and watching her expectantly. Then she pointed the gun into the air, closed her eyes, and fired.

The line of racers charged down the field, some quickly sprinting ahead while just as many quickly fell behind. One man stumbled and fell and several others could not help blundering into him, tumbling over and piling up. One young man managed to leap over the pile and keep going to the cheers of the crowd.

The contestants ran to the end of the field then headed back, some falling so far behind that they gave up and leaned over, hands on knees, panting and heaving. Some even plopped down on the ground in the middle of the field to recover. By the time the rest came charging to the finish line, one young man was so far ahead that there was no longer any contest. He crossed the finish line and was immediately surrounded by his friends and family, thumping him on the back so hard they nearly knocked the panting youth to the ground. But finally he headed toward the judges and Mrs. Fortune to collect his prize.

Ty handed his mother the prize they had brought and stepped back. But just as she was finished presenting the award, a loud squeal rent the air, and the greased pig--followed by a group of boys--bolted from behind a booth and came barreling straight toward her. Judges, contestants and onlookers scrambled out of the way. A few hearty souls made a grab for the pig but it managed to elude their grasp.

Irish watched the pig head right for them, seemingly intent on running Mrs. Fortune into the ground. Betsy squealed almost as loudly as the pig and covered her face with her hands. Irish and Charlie started waving their arms and yelling, trying to distract the pig's headlong charge, but the rest of the crowd was already screaming so loudly their efforts were lost.

It was Ty who stepped in front of his mother at the last moment and took the full brunt of the charge. The pig careened off him and skittered away toward the woods, but the boys giving chase were not quite so nimble. They caromed into Ty, knocking him down and landing in a heap on top of him.

Amid apologies and laughter, the boys jumped up and took off after the pig again, leaving Ty lying in the dirt looking more crumpled than Irish had ever seen him. He sat up, running one hand over his hair and searching for his hat with the other. Someone handed it to him and he put it on, then straightened his stock.

Charlie stuck out a hand to help him to his feet, but when Ty tried to stand, he winced and sat back down.

"Are you all right?" Mrs. Fortune asked.

Ty tugged his waistcoat back into place, brushed dirt from his sleeve and looked up at them with a wry grin. "I'm fine. But my ankle isn't."

Irish and Mrs. Fortune immediately went down on their knees to examine his ankle. Betsy just stood there with a horrified look on her face and her hands over her mouth. Charlie was patting her comfortingly on the back as if she were the one who was injured.

Mrs. Fortune removed Ty's shoe and gently ran her hands over her son's ankle.

"Can you move your foot?" Irish asked.

Ty compliantly wiggled his toes and moved his foot.

His mother sat back with a sigh. "It doesn't seem to be broken, but you'll have to stay off of it for a few days. It's already beginning to swell."

Just then they heard the judges calling for contestants to bring their horses to the starting line for the race.

Mrs. Fortune looked at Ty. "And there won't be any racing for you, either. You can't ride with an injured ankle."

Chapter Seven

IRISH WATCHED TY TRY TO STRUGGLE TO HIS FEET.

"Renegade has to run that race," he said, wincing. "This is the last time Townsend is going to run his mare. He told me so himself this morning. Renegade's in top form today. He won't have any trouble beating Townsend's horse but this is the only chance he'll get."

Mrs. Fortune pushed her son back down. "If your horse races today, it won't be with you on his back. You'll have to find someone else to ride him."

Ty frowned and experimentally moved his foot back and forth a couple of times. Irish could tell he was forcing himself not to wince with the pain. "Maybe I could–"

"No!" she and his mother both voiced together, loud and with absolute finality.

"I agree, Ty," Charlie said. "I have a bit of cash that I'll lose if you forfeit that race, but I'd not like to see you riding in that condition."

Ty worked his foot once more then shook his head and leaned back with a sigh. Irish could tell he had given up the idea of trying to ride in the race today and she also sighed with relief.

Ty looked up at Charlie. "Do you think you could ride

Renegade?"

Charlie's eyes widened and he backed away shaking his head. "I do just fine in a carriage. I can ride astride if I'm forced to, but give me a gentle mount that's not going to go above a trot. I'm afraid I'm no good on the back of a horse."

Ty looked thoughtful a moment. "I wonder if Seth or one of the Mason boys could…"

Irish had heard enough. She stood up and placed her hands on her hips. "You know better than to think you can put a strange rider on a horse like that at the last minute, and expect him to win a race. Are you such a fool that you can't see the solution that's standing here facing you?"

All eyes turned toward her and every one of them looked puzzled.

She blew a stray strand of hair out of her eyes, in frustration, and glared down at him. "I can ride Renegade. And I can win that race." She knew all eyes would be on her if she raced, but she had not seen anyone suspicious all day. It was a chance she must take.

"You?" Charlie looked taken aback. "A wee slip of a girl like you ride that beast? And in a dangerous free for all race?"

Irish glared at him. "And why not?"

Mrs. Fortune stood up and laid her hand on Irish's arm. "We wouldn't want you to get hurt, Irish."

"Oh, Irish," Betsy said, her expression one of absolute horror. "You couldn't possibly do something so unladylike, could you?"

Irish's brows went up. "Maybe you couldn't, but I could. I can."

"Betsy's right," Ty said. "It wouldn't be proper."

Irish gave an unladylike snort. "Proper be damned! I can do it and there's no reason for me not to." She swung her gaze around at them and was pleased to see that Betsy was the only one who had seemed shocked at her words. Mrs. Fortune was even smiling at her.

But it was Ty who concerned her the most. Renegade was his horse. If he refused to let her race… He just sat there, looking at her thoughtfully, his lips pursed.

She squatted down beside him. "I know I can do this. You know I can, too. You've seen me ride Renegade. Besides, even if you hadn't hurt your ankle, I would have a better chance of winning than you."

"What?"

She saw his eyes narrow and thought maybe she had gone too far with that last statement. "It's true." She leaned closer to him, earnestly pleading her case as she ticked off her reasons on her fingers. "Every pound you add to a horse's back slows him down. I weigh a lot less than you do. He's used to me, even more than you now that you've been gone so long. I know that horse. I've watched him in the pasture with the other animals, seen how he never lets any of the other horses get ahead of him but won't make a move unless they nudge ahead of him. I know when to give him his head and when to slap his rump. I can do this!"

She watched Ty's eyes anxiously. He seemed to be torn, possibly even wavering. But finally he shook his head. "I can't let you ride, Irish. Betsy's right. It wouldn't be proper."

Irish jumped up, fists clenched at her sides. She gave Betsy a scorching glare that made the girl flinch as if actually burned. But her anger was all for the pompous Mr. Tyrus Fortune. "And just why isn't it proper?" she gritted out. "Is there a rule that says women can't race?"

Ty again began to try to struggle and finally made it to his feet, with a lot of help from his friend. Leaning on Charlie for support and standing on one foot, he hopped around to face her. "I don't know if there is a rule about women racing or not. But it just isn't done!"

She went nose-to-nose with him. "You mean it just hasn't been done before now!"

"That's right! And it's not going to start with my horse!"

They stood there, each leaning toward the other, glaring at each other, both with their fists and teeth clenched. She could see that he was not going to change his stubborn mind. Then she would just have to change it for him, now, wouldn't she? She spun on her heel and stomped off.

She found Mangus holding Renegade, patting him and looking anxiously for Ty to come get the horse. He had heard the call for the race and already had Renegade saddled and bridled and ready to go.

"Where's Master Ty?" Mangus was beaming with pride. "This boy is beggin' to be let loose. Been gettin' hard to hold him back. He's goin' to win today for sure!"

Irish began running her hands over the horse, adjusting the stirrups, doing a final inspection. "Ty hurt his ankle. He can't ride," she said. And without giving Mangus a chance to think, she took the reins, placed her hands on the saddle and said, "Boost me up."

The old man had helped her so often, he automatically cradled his hands together for her to step into. She was in the saddle before she saw his eyes widen and his mouth open to protest. "Miss Irish! You ain't thinkin' 'bout ridin' this here horse yourself, are you?"

She tucked her skirts in as best she could. "I'm not just thinking about it, Mangus. I'm doing it." It didn't take much encouragement to get Renegade going. She had to be firm with him to keep him to a walk. Mangus trotted alongside. "But Miss Irish, you can't do that!"

Giving Renegade a little more rein she trotted away, calling over her shoulder as she left Mangus behind, "Just watch me!"

All the other horses were already getting lined up for the start when Irish rode Renegade onto the field. The sidelines were crowded. It looked like everyone at the fair had come to watch the race. She wondered if Ty was there and if he had noticed her yet.

She wedged herself and Renegade into the middle of the line. If Ty did notice her, he would have to hobble all the way out to here to try and stop her. She hoped that even if he wanted to stop her, he would rather let her race than cause a scene. Besides, she had seen the look on his face when he had told her she couldn't race. He had wanted to let her. His stubborn pride just wouldn't let him. Well, she was taking the decision out of his hands.

As she pushed her way into the line, the rider to her right turned to protest. "Watch out, there!" Then his eyes widened and he looked her up and down, his mouth gaping open.

Other riders began to notice her, then. And suddenly there were hands grasping Renegade's bridle. Not Ty. It was two of the judges. "Here now, Miss! What do you think you're doing?"

Irish steadied Renegade and gave the judges the sweetest, most innocent smile she was capable of. She even batted her lashes at them a time or two. That really threw them off balance. "I'm lining up to race."

The judges seemed flabbergasted. One of them, a fat, red-faced man that reminded her a lot of the pig that had injured Ty, finally spluttered, "You can't race!"

She shrugged prettily. "And why not? This horse is quite properly entered."

The man's face turned even redder. "That's not the point!"

"Oh," she asked, tilting her head quizzically. "And just what point are you trying to make?"

The man huffed and puffed, "Why, that you are a woman!"

Irish nodded in agreement. "I'm quite aware of that fact, sir."

Horses down the line were beginning to snort and plunge. One or two broke away and had to be forced back to the line. It was getting harder and harder to keep over twenty well-conditioned, highly-strung horses in place. The riders were getting anxious, as well. If the race didn't start soon, there would be chaos.

The judge looked from side-to-side at the restless horses. "Women can't race!" With the anxiety and his anger, he was shouting now, further stirring up the horses.

Irish smiled. "Is that in the rules?"

The red-faced judge turned to the other judge for help, who simply shrugged.

"Let's go!" yelled one distressed rider who was having a hard time controlling his mount.

"Get this race started!" yelled another.

More and more riders, along with people in the crowd, began yelling for the race to begin.

"Let her ride," yelled a nearby rider. "No woman is going to beat a man, anyway!"

A chorus of agreement went up from the riders, as well as a hefty dose of laughter.

Irish took a moment to look over the crowd to see if Ty was there. He was. And the look he was giving her made her gulp. Now she understood what Mariette and Nate and Matt had told her about their older brother. As children, they had often rethought ideas of mischief as soon as Ty's name was even mentioned.

She looked away and held up her head. She was not going to be cowed by Tyrus Fortune. She was not doing anything wrong. This was something he should have suggested himself. She shouldn't have had to take matters into her own hands. But now that she had, she was not about to quit until she had run this race. She would face Ty and his anger later. For now, she had a race to run and she forced her mind to that task.

The two judges looked at each other and shrugged then hurried to the stand set up for them. As soon as the riders were able to get their restless mounts in some semblance of a line, one of the judges fired a gun into the air, starting the race.

With whoops of joy from the riders, the horses sprang from the starting line and the crowd began screaming louder than ever, urging on their favorites. Many of the riders were already applying the crop to their mounts, trying to take—and keep—the lead.

Irish was not going to allow herself, or Renegade, be swept up in the excitement of the moment. Bent over the horse's neck, she kept a tight rein on him. Let the others wear themselves out at the beginning. The race was nearly a mile. Most of them did not have the stamina to keep up that pace for so long. They would begin dropping back, faltering. That's when she and Renegade would know which horse it was they really had to beat. Those others were not important and she would not let Renegade waste his energy trying to outrun them all. Let them defeat themselves.

Her father had taught her that the race was not always to the swift. There was also strategy involved. A wise rider took advantage of her horse's strengths, as well as his weaknesses.

Although she was keeping Renegade to a steady pace they began to pass the horses who had made a fast start but did not have the stamina to finish. They neared the half-mile marker, a huge live oak tree. There were only a handful of horses still ahead of them. Townsend's bay mare was one of them.

As they closed on the tree, Irish kept Renegade to the outside. She and Ty had walked the course this morning and she knew that there were some exposed roots close to the tree that could trip up a galloping horse. Keeping a close eye on that bay mare, Irish noticed that Townsend also knew about those roots, because he also swung wide of the tree. One horse and rider were not so wise. His horse tripped badly enough to lose his stride, and be left behind as Townsend and Irish swept by.

There were only three horses ahead of her as they made the turn and headed back toward the finish line. These were the horses she and Renegade had to beat. The others who had fallen behind, all foam-flecked and weary, were no longer important. None of them was going to suddenly make a fast break and take the lead at the end. Only those three ahead now need be of any concern.

All the riders now steered their horses to the outside of the course, and Irish knew why. There was a low spot just ahead where the ground was wet and soft. She and Ty had found it this morning. She had planned to skim just along the outside of it and then race for home. But apparently the others had seen it, too. Townsend's mare swept by the soggy spot neck-and-neck with another horse. She had allowed Renegade to gain on the third horse and now that horse and rider crowded them, forcing her to the outside.

Once clear of that spot, the field was firm and flat all the way to the finish. It was time to let these nags know just who they were racing against.

It took very little urging from her for Renegade to pass the third horse. Renegade's nose was almost to the horse's withers when the rider abruptly tried to bring his horse in front, attempting to cut them off. But he had waited too long. Renegade was easily able to hold his ground and push ahead.

They were coming up fast on the two lead horses. Townsend's mare was ahead with the second horse close on her right. Irish guided Renegade to Townsend's left. His was the horse Renegade had to beat and it was time for Renegade to understand that, as well.

With the field now open before them, Irish felt Renegade surge forward. He was not about to let any other horse ahead of him now that she was giving him a chance. He ran neck-and-neck with Townsend's mare for a few strides, then pulled slightly ahead.

The finish line was coming up. Irish knew this horse. He would not give up the lead, but he would be content to win by a nose. Just being ahead was good enough for Renegade. She could feel his exhilaration as he kept just slightly ahead of the mare.

But Irish didn't want to win by just a nose. She didn't want there to be any chance that the race would be contested in any way. She had to be the clear winner. She let Renegade have his way until they were nearing the finish line then she gave him a good smack on the rump with her crop, letting him know it was time to quit fooling around and to run full out.

Renegade responded with that reserve of power and speed she knew he had. They surged forward, finishing nearly a full length ahead of Townsend.

Irish slowed Renegade and turned him back toward the judges to receive her prize. As soon as Renegade had won, the crowd had grown strangely quiet, as if amazed that Townsend's mare had been beaten—and by a horse ridden by a woman.

Townsend trotted up on his mare and stopped. He leaned his crossed arms on the pommel of his saddle and looked her and Renegade up and down, shaking his head. But there was an admiring smile on his face, and when she rode up next to him, he held out his hand in congratulations.

There was almost dead silence from the crowd. But when she put her hand in his and they shook, the crowd went wild, surging forward to gather around the two horses.

Irish steadied Renegade. He was not used to this many strangers around him and she was not sure what he would do. But the horse surprised her. For most of his life he had fought grooms and riders, and anyone else who had gotten too close. But she had been working with him for nearly two years, gentling him, bringing him carrots, dragging in every person on the plantation she could find to pat him and bring him treats, trying to teach him that people were not so bad. Now he seemed to have learned that lesson. He was willingly accepting the many hands that reached out to pat his neck or rump. He even nudged a few pockets looking for a handout.

Irish wondered where Ty was and what he thought of his horse winning without him as its rider. And what did he think of her? Would he be so angry that he would ban her from ever riding Renegade again? Would he ask her to leave the plantation? She shook her head, not wanting thoughts of his scowling face to spoil this moment, not wanting to think of how much better this moment would be if he were here and smiling.

She pushed back several straggling strands of hair that had come down, tucking them up into her cap, and refused to look for Ty in the crowd. She would have to face him soon enough.

The judges were pushing their way through the crowd, along with the rotund merchant who had put up a fine saddle and bridle as first prize, and pair of spurs and a saddle blanket as second prize. The heavy, red-faced judge finally managed to clear an area in front of Renegade. He glared at her then turned to Bill Townsend with a regretful smile, and reached up to shake his hand.

"Sorry, Bill," the judge said. "I thought sure you and this mare would win again."

Townsend glanced at Irish and gave her a wink. "I thought so, too, Mr. Markham. Maybe we'll have better luck this fall."

"Thought this was going to be your last race, Bill?" one of the losing riders called.

Townsend laughed. "I thought so, too. But I can't let this pretty lady beat me without giving it one more try."

The judge harrumphed. "Don't know as we'll be letting a woman race next time, Bill. Got to have rules about this sort of thing."

Irish saw the other judge nodding his agreement and felt like lashing out at both of them. But if this was to be her last race, she was not going to let them spoil it for her. Even if they disqualified her from future races, she and Renegade had won this one.

The merchant presented Bill with his prizes and then they turned toward her with the saddle and bridle. The heavy judge again glared at her and put out a hand to stop the merchant. "That prize rightfully belongs to the owner of the horse. Where's Tyrus Fortune?"

"He's right here!" Irish heard Charlie call from the crowd. "But you'll have to make way for him. He's injured."

Irish saw the crowd parting as Ty made his way forward, supported on one side by Charlie and on the other by his friend, Seth, who had shot so well. Mrs. Fortune and Betsy followed close behind with a broadly grinning Mangus bringing up the rear.

Irish couldn't see Ty's face. He had his head down, carefully picking his way as he hopped on one foot between his two supporters. She slid down from Renegade's back and came forward to meet him. Her stomach might be growing lumps in it as she thought about what he might say, but she was going to meet him on even turf and stand her ground.

Mangus hurried around the group and took Renegade's reins from her. "You won, Miss Irish! You won!" The old stablehand clapped Renegade on the neck. "You earned your oats today, Renegade!"

Irish grinned. At least someone was happy for her, and proud of what she and Renegade had done, she thought. But when she caught Mrs. Fortune's gaze, she was smiling, too, and Irish's heart lightened. Betsy seemed completely unsure of what to do. She seemed to have been caught up at least a little in the excitement of the race and seeing Ty's horse win. But when Betsy looked at Irish, her expression was one of bewilderment, as if she wasn't quite sure whether to congratulate her or keep her distance in order to avoid being tainted with the impropriety of what Irish had done.

Just then, Ty came to a halt and raised his eyes to hers, and all other faces faded into unimportance... He was grinning. Oh, he was trying hard not to. The grin was only teasing the corners of his lips and he was trying hard to scowl at her, and be the staid and proper Mr. Tyrus Fortune, but the grin was there. It went all the way to his eyes.

She thought her heart would burst with happiness, and just a little relief. She took a step toward him, wanting nothing more than to throw her arms around his neck in a jubilant hug. But the scowl that was warring with his grin stopped her. It would not do to push the prim Mr. Fortune too far or he just might give her the dressing down right here and now that she expected him to give her later on in private. She contented herself with tossing him a smug, triumphant smile.

Mrs. Fortune, however, took her hand and squeezed it, and leaned forward to give her cheek a kiss. "Congratulations, Irish."

With Mrs. Fortune's words, Betsy stopped her wavering enough to at least give Irish a nod and also congratulate her.

Charlie looked like he'd like to scoop her up and twirl her around, and if he wasn't supporting Ty she was sure he would have done just that. But Ty would never do something so inappropriate, she was certain.

The heavy judge looked down at Ty's ankle. "I can see now why you didn't ride your horse yourself, Mr. Fortune, but how could you allow a woman to take your place?"

Ty's looked directly at her. "I would not trust Renegade to anyone else, Mr. Markham."

Irish's jaw dropped.

The judge spluttered. "But a woman! The committee will look into the rules before the fall races. You can be sure of that!"

"It would be a shame to change the rules now," Ty said looking around at the other riders. "Some of these fellows just might want a rematch this fall."

Mr. Markham harrumphed, gave Irish a final glare, then

stepped aside for the merchant to present the prize.

The merchant stepped up to Ty. "Congratulations, Mr. Fortune!" he said, wringing Ty's hand as an assistant held the saddle and bridle up for everyone to see.

The crowd cheered and then dozens of people pushed forward to shake Ty's hand and offer their congratulations.

Irish turned to Mangus. "See that he's properly cooled down, will you, Mangus?"

"That I will, Miss Irish!" The old man led the horse away and Irish gave Renegade a last pat on the rump as he left.

The crowd began to thin, heading off to other attractions now that the race was over.

Irish watched as the last few people shook Ty's hand. Standing there on one leg, even being propped up by Seth and Charlie, was beginning to take its toll on him. She pushed her way up to him, cutting off several people. "Mr. Fortune needs to sit down and prop up that ankle," she said.

"I believe you're right, Irish," Mrs. Fortune agreed, looking down at her son's ankle.

"I'm fine," Ty protested, but Irish could tell that his protest was half-hearted.

"We need to get you home," Irish said.

"We've yet to see the play," Ty answered. And it seemed that he deliberately turned from her to smile at Betsy. "I did promise to take you to see that play."

Irish propped her hand on her hips. "I think Betsy will understand that you need to get home and off your feet."

Betsy looked from Irish to the palisade where people were already lining up to go in to see the play. Lifting her chin she looked back to Ty. "I'm sure Irish is right, Ty. It might be best for you to get home."

He reached for Betsy's hand and lifted it to his lips. "We will go to the play," he said firmly. Then, looking sternly at Irish and his mother he said, "Just get me in there. I'll be seated and I promise to keep my ankle propped up through the whole performance. Then we'll go home."

Irish and Mrs. Fortune both sighed, and, knowing he would not change his mind, they nodded their reluctant agreement.

Irish heard Betsy give a sigh as well, albeit a happy one, and they all headed for the makeshift theater. Once they were inside, Irish pulled a bench close enough for Ty to prop up his ankle and Betsy sat beside him.

Chapter Eight

THE FOLLOWING MORNING, TY WATCHED IRISH COMING out of the stable tucking more of that marvelous hair of hers back into her cap. Her face was flushed from her ride and her skirts wrinkled from being hiked up so she could mount astride. Why did her disheveled condition always make him think of bedding her? He could feel himself filling with the wanting of her now, just watching her walk toward him.

She had tucked her fichu in but he could still see the swell of her breasts, and he remembered the feel of them pressed against him that night beneath him in bed, firm yet soft, yielding--unlike the rest of her prickly personality. She was a woman who would never give an inch unless she gave her all. Mayhap that was what was so enticing about her. She challenged a man every step of the way, but the man who would eventually win her would win her completely.

Watching her ride this morning was almost as thrilling as it had been to see her win that race yesterday. It was hard to gaze at her now, coming toward him, without feeling that thrill all over again. Thrilling was not what he needed to be feeling with Irish. He was not about to let himself feel anything about a woman he knew nothing about. He tamped down his feelings with a fierce scowl.

He could not help but admire the way she rode, though. "That was quite a ride," he said.

Immediately, her fists came to her hips and she met his scowl with one of her own. "I know you told me not to ride in that race but Renegade couldn't have won with anyone else on his back. And he had to run yesterday. With horses you never know if they'll be at their best on the day of a race. Sometimes you just can't race them for one reason or another. Renegade was in top form and rearing to go. I knew he could win. I had to give him that chance. And if you are going to chastise me for that, then you are a fool, Tyrus Fortune. And as for a woman riding in a horse race--"

He started to laugh and she spluttered to a stop.

But he couldn't help himself. She looked so kissable when she was riled up. And it was so very easy to get her riled. Indeed, he seemed to have a knack for it.

"I meant today's ride," he said. "I was watching from the up-stairs window when you and Renegade had that little duel in the lane." It had been more than a duel. Renegade had pranced around fighting the bit, wanting his head. He had danced sideways and even bucked a bit. Ty had been afraid for a moment that the horse was going to throw her and take off. He had grabbed his crutch and hurried down the stairs as fast as he could, but by the time he had reached the front porch, Irish had let Renegade know who was boss and they were cantering down the drive. His heart had not quit pounding for a quarter hour. And it wasn't from the exertion of hobbling down the stairs faster than any sane man on crutches should have. As if there was anything he could have done to help in his condition anyway.

She blew a strand of hair out of her eyes and then she quirked a bit of a smile. "Aye, well, he was full of himself today. Winning a race can give a horse like that airs that he needn't be having. But we soon got things settled betwixt us."

He nodded. "How was the new saddle?"

Her brow went up. "Well now, that's something you'll have to find out for yourself when you're up to it, Mr. Fortune."

It was his turn to be surprised. She didn't seem to think anything about appropriating his horse. He thought sure she would have used the new saddle, especially since it was her training and riding of Renegade that had won it. "You didn't use it today?"

She propped one fist on her hip and tilted her head quizzically at him. "Now you saw me ride in and you saw me dismount, and you saw me cooling that beast down, and you're telling me you never noticed that he was wearing the same saddle he always wears?"

No, he thought with surprise, he hadn't noticed. He had been too busy watching her. He had noticed the mud spattered on those shapely calves of hers. He had noticed the wild tresses flying in the wind and how she had tried vainly to contain them. He had noticed the sway of her backside as she walked Renegade to cool him. But he hadn't noticed the saddle.

She laughed then. "Now isn't that just like a man? Never noticing things."

"I notice things," he said, and even to himself he sounded defensive.

She arched one brow. "Like saddles?"

He let his gaze sweep over her, from her mob cap that was sitting askew on that blaze of glory she called hair, to the fichu that had not been tucked in properly on one side and was gaping wide enough to show a fine swell of breast, to the fist still propped at her narrow waist to... "Oh, I notice things, Irish. I notice things."

She froze, then turned the most delightful shade of red.

He chuckled, then bent to pick up a muslin wrapped parcel he had set on the edge of a feeding trough. He held it out to her.

She looked at him suspiciously, eyes narrowed. "What's

that?"

He shoved it toward her. "Open it and see."

As if not completely trusting him, she gingerly took the parcel and turned a water bucket upside down to sit on. Placing the parcel on her lap she unwrapped it. He watched her face eagerly.

Irish's eyes grew wide and her mouth dropped open when she saw what was in the parcel. "Oh!" she said. She looked up at him. "For me?"

Her face was full of wonderment and he thought her eyes were welling up just a bit. She looked back at the things he had bought her, running her fingers lovingly over the embroidery on the very stomacher she had seemed to yearn for at the fair. She held up the lawn fichu between them. It was so fine he could see her expression through it. Folded and tucked into the stomacher, it would not be so transparent, he thought, but it would lie softly against her skin.

She lifted the stomacher next, tracing over the delicate embroidery, feeling inside the pocket on its back. Then carefully she rewrapped the items and stood, holding it out to him.

"I cannot accept them," she said, lifting her head proudly, her chin at a determined angle.

Stubborn wench! Proud, stubborn wench. His mother was right about her. She was too proud for her own good. He knew she could have afforded to buy the things for herself, but she hadn't and he had bought them to give to her. And he wanted her to have them. He wondered what it was costing her to refuse the gifts and how he could change her mind.

"And just why can't you accept them?" he asked.

"Besides the fact that they are far too personal for a man to give to a lady?" she asked sarcastically.

He blinked. Too personal? As much as his mother had drilled the gentlemanly proprieties into him, the fact that a stomacher and a fichu were rather personal items that a gentleman certainly would not give a lady had not even entered his mind. He had simply seen her admiring those things, knew she wanted them, and wanted her to have them. What had this Irishwoman done to him to so muddle his thinking? And still he wanted her to have the damned things. And he wanted to be the one to give them to her.

He cleared his throat and thought hastily. "They're um...they're not gifts."

A light seemed to go out within her, but within half a moment an angry fire was blazing in her eyes. "So I'm to pay you for them?" She thrust the package at him, ramming it into his midrift so hard as to almost knock the wind out of him. "I told you yesterday I can buy for myself what I want and need."

He grabbed her wrist before she could stomp away. "You misunderstand."

"And just what is it I'm misunderstanding?" She jerked her wrist but he held it tightly.

"It's payment."

She jerked her wrist harder this time, nearly succeeding in getting loose. Her eyes were fully ablaze now and her cheeks flaming. "And just what am I supposed to do for this payment, Mr. Tyrus Fortune? No lady takes that kind of payment from a gentleman unless she is no lady at all."

He pulled her close, nose-to-nose and eye-to-eye and spoke softly. "It's for winning the race."

Once again her jaw dropped, and while she was momentarily speechless he continued. "I wanted you to have something for winning the race yesterday. It's tradition to pay the rider something."

The fight went out of her immediately. "For winning the race?"

"Yes," he said, slowly letting her go, not wanting to but allowing her wrist and hand to slide free of his. He wanted to clasp her to him, not release her. Her hand was not soft like Betsy's. It was firm and strong and he wanted nothing more than to keep holding it, to pull her to him and hold the rest of her. But he let her go. "Yes, for winning the race."

"I thought you said it was highly improper that I rode in that race."

He grinned. "And so it was. 'Twas not something I could allow at all. But since you took the bit between your teeth, so to speak, what can I do but thank you. It was a superb feat of horsemanship."

She straightened away from him, clutching the package to her, and her face shone with satisfaction. "This is my rider's fee?"

She looked so vulnerable just then, so full of a delicate pride that he could shatter with just a word, that he wanted to take her in his arms and shelter her. But he knew she would not accept that, and with this blasted crutch, she might just end up supporting him more than he supported her.

He nodded. "Your rider's fee." He tapped his crutch. "And I expect you to keep that horse in good shape while I'm incapacitated."

She smiled, but he could see her batting her lashes to keep tears at bay. She would be too proud to cry in front of him. "I will," she said. And with a toss of her head she added, "And after you're better too!"

He laughed. The little scamp! They began walking back to the house together, he hobbling along on his crutches and she clutching her "payment". And for once they were not fighting.

"Ah, that was a fine meal," Charlie said that evening, slapping his belly in appreciation. "You've a rare fine talent, Irish." He pushed back his plate and leaned onto the table, and looked straight across at her. "And when would you like to marry me?"

Irish just laughed.

Ty looked over at her. She had been laughing the whole meal. At every flirtatious remark Charlie made. And there had been a lot of them. The two of them had had a fine time of it.

Charlie had complimented her biscuits, he had praised the sweet potato casserole, he had lauded the ham and beans. Then he had started getting personal--eulogizing her eyes, the blush on her cheeks, her hair.

He had flirted outrageously with Ty's mother, too, telling her that he had mistaken her for a girl when he had first arrived, her figure was so slim and trim. He had complimented her hair, still dark, and told her how the red of her gown brought out the color in her cheeks. None of that had bothered Ty. It was just harmless flirtation.

It was when the man turned his attention to Irish that Ty's stomach began to clench, his teeth began to clench, and he found it very hard to keep his fists from clenching, too. Maybe it was because Irish seemed to be taking Charlie's flirtation more to heart. Did she believe every word that man was saying to her?

Ty wiped his mouth with his napkin and looked at her again. Hmmm. Maybe she did believe Charlie. Why not? Everything he said about her was true. Her eyes did look like emeralds, her hair did put a warm winter fire to shame, she did have skin like cream.

Ty was not sure he could have said those things to Irish even if he had wanted to. They may be true, but somehow the comparisons seemed too commonplace, the words too inadequate. They were shallow blandishments at best and he hoped she would not be taken in by Charlie's charm.

But why should he care if she were taken in? She was nothing to him. If she wanted to hang onto Charlie's every word, let her. Let her lean forward with that eager light in her eyes and give him a view of décolletage that the builder was lapping up like a starving dog.

Ty threw his napkin on the table and stood up so abruptly that he nearly overturned his chair. "I'm ready for some good port," he said pointedly to Charlie. "Would you like to join me?"

Charlie gave him a negligent wave of his hand. "Nay, you go ahead, Ty. I think I'll stay here with the ladies while they finish their tea."

Ty felt like grabbing a handful of Charlie's shirt and dragging him away. He had offered the port as an excuse to lure Charlie from the table, away from Irish, but now Ty could not just sit back down. He swallowed the growl rising in his throat and grabbed his crutch to seek out his port. Alone.

In the living room Ty poured himself a healthy draught of port and tossed it back. The mellow wine seemed like gall and burned like vinegar in his stomach. He could hear Charlie regaling the ladies with some tale about one of his ancestors who had tried his hand as a highwayman on a dare from his friends.

Too bad the man had managed to escape being caught, Ty thought. *Charlie might not be here now, dallying with the affections of an innocent young woman.*

He slammed down his glass and limped over to where he had left his crutch. Perhaps he would just go to bed early. Nate should be back tomorrow. Maybe he could take Charlie upriver to the site where Ty would build his home. It would be good to get the man out of the house, and it was high time they began to get down to the business of building his house.

Yes, he thought. *Tomorrow Nate and Charie and I will sail upriver.* Away from the house and away from laughing Irish eyes that were too easily being taken in by this courtly charmer.

Nate arrived back home early the next morning. He gave Irish the set of fine linen sheets and some towels he had bought for her to give to Abby and Joe at their wedding. There was even a bit of change left over which she gladly pocketed.

By late morning he was ready to sail up to the site where Ty would build his house. Mrs. Fortune suggested to Irish that they go, as well, and take a picnic lunch with them.

She helped Irish carry the baskets of food she had prepared down to the dock and place them aboard the Fortune. Charlie and Ty were already there, and Ty turned with surprise when they reached the dock.

"You're going with us?" he asked.

His mother glanced up at the sky. "It looks like a fine day for a sail. Irish and I thought we'd go see the site, too, and hear what Charlie thinks of the spot you've chosen."

Charlie beamed and held out both hands to Irish.

She couldn't help but feel warmed by his welcoming smile. It was so much better than the scowl on Ty's face. She couldn't understand why he didn't seem to want his mother and her to come along, but that was just too bad. It had taken Mrs. Fortune several minutes to convince her to leave her work and the wedding plans she was helping with, but his mother wanted her along, so she was going even if the look on Ty's face could have soured milk.

Pointedly, she turned her back to Ty and gave Charlie one of her best smiles.

"You've brightened the day by coming along!" Charlie exclaimed. "I only hope you won't be bored by all the talk of house plans and building."

"That's true," Ty said. "It might be boring for you. Are you sure you want to go?"

Mrs. Fortune laughed. "And just who do you think has been supervising the firing of the brick for that house of yours, and making sure the timber was cut and cured properly? Irish and I have a vested interest in seeing just what is to be done with all that brick and timber."

Ty looked from his mother to her and she thought he might be about to strangle on something, before Mrs. Fortune took her son's arm and stepped up onto the gangplank.

Ty had no choice but to help his mother aboard Nate's little ship, and Charlie offered her a hand with the dash of a practiced courtier.

"It's not all that far to Fortune's Pride," Irish told Charlie. "We could have ridden there easily except for Ty's ankle."

Once they were settled aboard, Nate unfurled the sails and, with Ty's help, headed the little ship upriver.

There was a fair wind and it was not long before they rounded the bend to the site Ty had chosen for his house. The land sloped upward from the river to a slight rise. Irish gazed up at the site. She had been here often in the last two years with Mrs. Fortune or Nate or Matt. She thought Ty was right. It would be the perfect setting for a fine and imposing house.

A small dock had already been built. Nate tied up his ship and they all headed up the hill, Charlie carrying copies of the house plans.

Irish noticed that Charlie's eyes were shining as he took in the site, but Ty's eyes shone with pride as he looked around.

"What do you think, Charlie?" Ty asked.

"'Tis a fine place, Ty. You chose it well."

Ty gave Charlie a wry smile. "I agree it's a fine site, but I didn't choose it. My father did. He was going to build a house here, but decided not to." He glanced at his mother. "He decided to fix up Mother's place and live there instead."

Charlie looked out over the river. "Fortune's Pride. It won't just be your pride. It will be the most imposing house on the river. It will be a marker for travelers. They'll say, 'There's Fortune's Pride.

Just two more hours 'til we get home.' Or 'There's Fortune's Pride, we're almost to Charles Town.'" Charlie turned to Ty. "Thank you for letting me be part of the grand plan."

Ty gripped Charlie's shoulder. "I've seen your work in England. I can't think of anyone I'd rather have build my house."

Charlie swallowed hard and looked away for a moment. Then he turned back, all business. "Let's take a look at this brick the ladies have made while you've been gone."

The brick was stacked nearby and they walked over to it. Charlie hefted one, looking it over carefully, scraping at it with his penknife, clinking it against another. He nodded and pronounced the brick sound. "Some of the best I've seen," he said. "You ladies did a fine job."

Charlie pulled Irish into a one-armed hug. "She can cook, she can ride like the wind, she can make bricks, and she's beautiful. What more could a man want in a woman? When did you say you were going to marry me?"

Irish pushed away from him, laughing, loving his teasing, embarrassed by his overt compliments, yet pleased by them, too. But she noticed that Ty was not so pleased by Charlie's jests. The scowl on his face was almost thunderous. She arched her brows at him and tossed her head, turning back to Charlie.

"We didn't actually make it ourselves, Charlie," Mrs. Fortune said, laughing.

"Let me show you the lumber, Charlie," Ty said, drawing the man away from them. Ty and Charlie and Nate went to check out the lumber while Irish helped Mrs. Fortune set out the lunch. When the men returned they sat to eat, and--of course--Charlie managed to sit beside Irish.

She laughed at one of his jokes after another, let him hand her extra food, fill her cup, ask if she were too hot. It was nice to be pampered by a man, she thought. By anyone. It was nice to be fawned over and made the center of someone's attention. Not that Charlie didn't give a lot of attention to Mrs. Fortune, as well.

But she knew it was all only harmless flirtation, though it was so much nicer than the glares Ty was throwing her way. Why was he in such poor humor, anyway? He didn't want her. She could just imagine him dancing with glee when she told him she was leaving. So why did he scowl so ferociously every time she smiled at Charlie?

While Irish and Mrs. Fortune put away the remains of their luncheon, Ty and Charlie paced out the approximate outlines of the house, and placed markers where Ty wanted them. Then it was time to go.

Nate helped his mother aboard and Charlie helped Irish, and she could feel Ty's scowls behind her with every touch of Charlie's hand on her arm or at the small of her back. Ty hobbled aboard and they set off for home, this time with Mrs. Fortune at the tiller.

At Charlie's look of surprise, she laughed. "I come from a sailing family and married into a sailing family. Why should it surprise you that I can handle a tiller or hoist a sail?"

Mrs. Fortune and Nate sailed them home while Irish sat between Charlie and Ty, each of them vying for her attention. It was a new and heady experience and she took full delight in it, smiling at each man equally.

What a shame such pleasure as this couldn't last, she sighed to herself, and resolved to enjoy every minute.

The next day the whole plantation was busy with preparations for the wedding that evening. Several of the women were making special dishes to bring in their own homes, and Irish was supervising the main kitchen. Matt had arrived back home the day before with six fat geese in hand, and a girl was basting and turning them as they roasted over the fire.

There were platters of ham and dishes of sweet potatoes and corn. And of course, as always, there was rice that had been grown on the plantation. Women brought rice flavored with onion and garlic, they brought it mixed with vegetables, they brought it baked with eggs and cheese, and they brought heaping mounds of it fresh, fluffy and plain.

Once the food was ready to serve and the bride proclaimed ready, Irish dashed up to her room to dress in her best gown. It was one Mariette had given her and it was so green it reminded Irish of the home she had been forced to leave. Her new stomacher would look well with it, she thought, as well as her new fichu.

There was not much she could do with her hair, though, with its frizzy curls that were almost as kinky of Abby's black hair. The red mass seemed determined to escape any pins, caps, or combs she tried to subdue it with. With a shrug she pinned it up as well as she could and left her room to go to the wedding, holding the fan Ty had given her in one hand.

Ty was just coming out of his room next to hers and when he saw her, he halted with his hand on the knob of his door, not moving except for his eyes as he looked her over. She saw him swallow hard and his eyes seemed to darken.

She felt herself growing warm beneath his gaze. So intense was his inspection of her it was almost like being back on that Spanish auction block, as if he were examining her for every flaw, for every attribute. But unlike the auction, it was not fear she felt, but a strange growing warmth. Her heart began beating faster and her lungs seemed to strain for air.

Although he did not say anything, he must have found her appearance at least satisfactory for he absently closed his door and, with a slight bow, offered her his arm as if from a gentleman to a lady.

Surprised at his arm proffered in such a manner, she was about to make some acerbic comment but then mentally shrugged, deciding that if he wanted to treat her like a lady for once, she could at least accept this temporary truce, take his arm, and act the part. She knew how to be a lady. He might not think of her as one, but then, he didn't know anything about her. He didn't know how she had grown up or what her background was. It was time to let Mr. Tyrus Fortune know that she had the manners and demeanor of a countess if she chose to use them.

Snapping her fan open she fanned her cheeks then placed the fan before her face, peeking coyly over the top of it as she dropped into a deep curtsy. Rising, she took his arm and they made their way down the hall to the stairs. His gait was rough with his injured foot and his crutch, but she noticed that he was now able to put a bit of weight on his foot.

He had to let go of her arm to negotiate the stairs with his crutch and she needed room with her panniers holding out her skirt. She went ahead of him and when she was about halfway down the stairs, Charlie appeared at the bottom.

Charlie's jaw dropped when he saw her, his fists went to his hips, and he actually gave an appreciative whistle as he openly looked her up and down. He grinned broadly at her and reached to take her hand as she reached the last step. She thought she heard a low growl from behind her, but she ignored it.

"You will put every other woman here to shame, Irish, including the bride." He turned her around and the gleam in his eyes showed his appreciation. "You would sparkle in the court of St. James. I've not seen a lady there to compare to what I see here before me."

As if she truly were at court, Irish tapped him lightly on the arm with her fan, a chiding gesture. "You are a flatterer, Charlie."

He leaned close to her. "I do tend to have a keen appreciation for the ladies, but I do not flatter. If I tell you something, you can believe it is the truth." He straightened. "Besides, with you there is no need at all to stretch the truth, or even bend it."

Charlie turned to Ty who had at last made his way down the steps. "You tell her, Ty. You must agree with me. Any man with eyes in his head would have to agree with me. Doesn't she shine like a jewel?"

Irish thought Ty's teeth would crack, his jaw was clenched so hard. "You needn't put words in my mouth for me, Charlie. I can tell Irish what I think of her myself."

Charlie looked back and forth between the two of them, but Irish saw only Ty looking at her. He might have said that Charlie didn't need to tell him what to say, but he remained silent. He didn't have to say anything. She could see a hunger in his eyes that matched her own. He wanted her. But that didn't mean he thought she was pretty or intelligent or a good person. It only meant that he wanted her.

And God help her, she wanted him.

She tore her gaze away, pasted on a happy smile, and took Charlie's arm. "Shall we go to a wedding, Charlie?"

Charlie gave Ty a smug grin and led Irish away.

Irish smiled and chatted absently with Charlie, but her mind was whirling. How could she be attracted to Tyrus Fortune? Not just attracted, she thought, she wanted him. Really wanted him. Her whole body seemed to be pulled toward his. Her breasts seemed to be aching and she felt like her feminine parts were warming, melting, opening, all in anticipation and yearning. She could feel the blood rushing to her cheeks and neck. It seem as if every drop was rushing to her skin, warming it, flushing it, making it tingle with a need to be touched...by Ty.

She could hear him behind her with his crutch--step, clomp, step, clomp. Was he feeling this same way she was? Were his lips swelling with a need to kiss? Were his hands tingling, wanting to touch her as she wanted to touch him? By the saints! She felt like a piece of dry kindling with a flame stalking her.

This was not good. If she gave in to these feelings she would be consumed, used up, and discarded. She could not let that happen.

But she could recognize a weakness within herself when she thought of Ty, a weakness that could be her undoing. She could only hope that he was more of a gentleman than she was a lady. With his prim, proper, starched demeanor, maybe he would have more control than she did. Maybe the very part of him that she wanted to shake loose was the part that would save her from herself. She hoped so. The way she was feeling right now, she couldn't trust herself.

Charlie held the door open for her and she stepped outside. She had to leave. Not just the house right now–she had to leave the Fortune plantation. She took a deep breath as they headed down the path to the workers' homes where the wedding would take place. She had told herself she needed to leave as soon as she saw Ty step off the *Fortune*, the day he returned home. Now, she would have to do it. She could not stay under the same roof with him.

It was too dangerous.

Chapter Nine

TY FOLLOWED CHARLIE AND IRISH DOWN THE PATH, watching the enticing sway of her backside with apprecia- tion. It was a bit difficult to discern her true shape with the panniers she wore, but he had seen her without them often enough to know exactly what was beneath the wires and hoops and miles of material. The panniers made her waist look even smaller and he longed to measure its span with his hands. He wanted to caress upwards to that fragile ribcage to the swell of her breasts. He wanted to...

He gritted his teeth and forced himself to look away before what he wanted became all too apparent beneath the cloth of his breeches.

She held easily to Charlie's arm and she was smiling at him, laughing with him, sharing who knew what jests and secrets with him. As much as he liked Charlie and admired his work, right now he felt like punching the man in the nose.

When they came to the end of the path, Ty noticed that the small open ground between the rows of houses had been trans- formed by Abby's family and friends. Lanterns were hung from every door to be lit later for the dancing. Bunches of flowers were placed every few feet and a small bower of vines and flowers, where the wedding would take place, had been set up in front of Joe's house. Several long tables were filled with the food and plates and drinks. Several girls had been assigned to stand beside them with palmetto fans to keep off the flies.

There was no sign of the bride yet, but the groom and two of his friends, including Nate, stood by the bower, nervously shifting from foot to foot. Nate kept gripping Joe on the shoulder and saying something to him and Ty could only hope it was something encouraging and not dire warnings about the married state.

"I take it the man next to Nate is the happy groom," said Charlie, "but why is the bower in front of that house? It seems to me it would have been better to put it there in the center."

"Joe and Abby wanted to include some traditions from their African heritage," Irish answered. "Regina explained it to me. In Africa the bride is brought to the man's house for the ceremony, so the bower is in front of Joe's house."

Charlie looked surprised. "Joe and Abby were born in Africa?"

Irish shook her head. "They were both born here, but Joe's parents are from Africa and Abby's grandparents are."

Just then the door of Regina's house opened and Abby and her parents stepped out. Immediately several musicians began beating out an intoxicating rhythm on large and small drums.

The bright colors of Abby's dress, in green and gold, looked African, but the style was English. Ty thought she looked regal as she walked toward Joe.

Joe came forward to meet her carrying several packages that he presented to Abby's parents and to some of her other family.

"What's he doing?" Charlie asked.

"Bride price," Ty answered.

"You mean he has to pay for her?" Charlie was incredulous.

"Is that so different than the English system of dowries?" Ty asked.

"Actually," Irish said, "Regina told me it's called *lobella* and it isn't exactly payment. He is giving gifts to the people Abby told him to give them to, in order to prove to her relatives that he is wealthy enough to care for her."

Once Regina and her husband accepted the gifts, the drumming stopped and the couple stepped under the bower, where they exchanged their vows in front of a minister. When the final "I do's" were spoken, the crowd cheered and threw rice.

The newlywed couple walked around the crowd greeting and thanking their friends for coming to the wedding and for the gifts they had brought. Then the food was served.

At Irish's insistence, Ty sat on a bench and she brought him a plate then Charlie sat beside him to eat. Ty watched Irish make her way around the crowd, nibbling on her own plate of food while she chatted and laughed with everyone. He wished she would come back to him and give him just one of those smiles.

"She's a lovely lass, isn't she?" Charlie said sighing. "I've half a mind to quit teasing her about marrying me and ask her in earnest."

Ty nearly choked on the ale he was drinking but that was not the cause of the near panic he felt. Charlie and Irish? He looked from one to the other. Surely the man wasn't serious. He'd known her less than a week.

Ty shoved a forkful of ham into his mouth. Well, he hadn't known her much longer than that himself, and he was ready to punch Charlie for even thinking about asking Irish to marry him. How could she affect him so strongly?

It seemed he had been coming unhinged ever since he stepped off the *Fortune* and met her. He couldn't stop thinking about her, especially tonight. He had never seen her looking so tantalizing. Or had he? He thought of that night when he had held her close beneath him in her bed. He had been angered thinking she had come to his room just to entice him, but he had been more than just a little aroused nonetheless.

And the day she won the race there had been such a glow about her he had wanted to scoop her up and kiss her all over, kiss every bit of her flushed skin. He hadn't, of course. It wouldn't have been the least bit proper. But he had wanted to. He had never wanted to do anything so improper before in his life.

With Irish, he seemed to want to do everything improper.

Just watching her now made him want to take her arm, pull her into the bushes and kiss her until her mind reeled as badly as his was reeling. He felt like he was coming apart, piece by proper piece, and if he didn't take his eyes off her soon, he would be too tempted by far to keep from doing something very improper indeed.

Yet for the life of him, he couldn't stop watching. Especially when the food was put away, the music for the dancing began, and she began to sway in time to it.

Good lord! Did no one else notice the sensuality of her movements? It was all too easy to imagine her moving like that beneath him, naked on cool sheets, the flame of her hair licking at the pillows, her arms reaching up to him.

A man began calling for couples to form up a reel. Abruptly Charlie stood up. He grinned down at Ty and said, "Excuse me, Ty. I think I'll ask Miss Irish to dance." Then he winked. "In fact, Old Boy, I'll take your turn with her as well, seein' as how you're a bit laid up at the moment."

Ty gritted his teeth. Did the man have to smile like such a cocky dolt? He must not realize how close he was coming to getting his face punched in.

He watched Charlie give Irish a small bow and offer his arm. She accepted it with a smile and they took their place in the line. Did she have to be so eager to dance with the man? Why couldn't she at least look at him as if she wanted to dance with him? Did she have to give all her attention, all her smiles to Charlie?

He watched as she circled, as she skipped down the line to the end, how Charlie swung her about. He had never understood the meaning of the phrase "light on her feet" until he saw Irish dance. Her feet seemed to skim the earth. She seemed to be flying. There was such joy in her that it seemed to lift her right off the ground--along with his heart. He couldn't help but feel her joy as she flung her head back and laughed.

And he resented each touch of Charlie's hand on her arm, or at her waist. He wanted it to be his hand and his alone that touched her. He could feel a tingle in his fingertips straining toward that smooth flushed flesh. He fisted his hands and forced himself to look away, but he could not help looking back.

When that dance ended Irish and Charlie were laughing and breathless, and Charlie pulled her close into a quick hug. Ty jumped to his feet, grabbing for his crutch, but then he forced himself to sit back down. It was just a quick meaningless hug, for goodness sake. There was nothing to it, he told himself, then wondered why he felt a bitterness coil inside him as he watched them. *Because I want it to be me dancing with her. I want it to be me swept up in the heat of the moment and scooping her up in a hug no matter how improper it may be.*

Matt danced with Irish next, then Nate, then Charlie again. The three men took turns squiring Irish and his mother around the beaten compound. The music, English fiddles and oboes, were accompanied by African drums pounding out a sensual rhythm that seemed to heat Ty's blood, sending it surging through his veins. That and the sight of Irish swaying, laughing, her hair tumbling about her shoulders, made him want her as he had never wanted anything in his life.

He tapped his foot thoughtfully with his crutch. He may not

be able to dance with her himself right now, but she was wearing his gifts, and it was as if, whether she knew it or not, she had accepted that she was his. The fichu and the stomacher marked her as his. The fan dangling from her wrist marked her as his. His.

Ty watched Irish dance every dance. Occasionally someone would come and sit by him and they would talk a while, but he kept her in view all the time. It was as if he were afraid she would disappear if he took his eyes off her.

He laughed to himself. When he had first returned home, all he'd wanted was for her to disappear, to be gone from his life, from this plantation, from his room, from his table. Now the thought of Irish not being here gave him a feeling of empty restlessness.

Ty saw his mother heading toward him and moved over to make room for her on the bench.

She sat down with a big, "Whew!"

"Getting too old for all that dancing?" Ty asked playfully.

She smacked him on the thigh and laughed. "At least I can still dance!"

They sat watching the couples for a few moments, then Ty said, "You were right about Irish."

His mother merely cocked a brow at him, encouraging him to continue.

He shrugged. "I mean, she must be good company for you here."

She nodded. "And a big help."

"She seems to do more than her share," he agreed. "Maybe I was hasty in wanting her gone."

His mother smiled. "I thought you might come around. Irish has a way of winning hearts."

Irish placed a hand on Charlie's arm and leaned close to him, and Ty narrowed his eyes. They were waiting for the next dance to begin and to Ty she seemed to be flirting with the man. A hard knot formed in his gut as he watched Charlie respond to what Irish was saying, and casually place a claiming hand at her waist. Ty felt like growling.

"Yes, I can see that," he said, hating the fact that his words came out sounding very much like that growl.

His mother smiled and patted his arm. "There will be other chances to dance with her, Ty."

He nodded his agreement, but secretly he wondered if that were true. Charlie was an attractive man. A bit thin, with a nose that was a little too big, but attractive, nonetheless. He was not wealthy, but he had more than adequate means and he was a talented builder. And he was charming, too. He could easily seduce an unwary maid. Or maybe he would find himself deciding to be more serious the next time he mentioned marriage to Irish.

Ty could not think of a single reason why a woman would not accept an offer from Charlie. Irish could certainly do worse. She was old enough to be wanting a home of her own, a family. He was not going to offer that to Irish. He knew the kind of woman he wanted to marry and build a life with, and it was not an unknown Irish woman who rode in horse races against men, with her skirts hiked up and her hair flying. A woman who showed little care for the proprieties of upper class life in Charles Town colony.

He wanted Irish, but he could never have her. He would not offer her marriage and he would not take a woman any other way. It wasn't right. He would just have to bypass that tempting little morsel. She would be better off with Charlie.

And he would be better off with Betsy.

Ty thought of Betsy attending a wedding like this on her parents' plantation. She would not dance like Irish and his mother were doing, he was sure. Betsy's family probably would not even stay very long. They would be intruders at such a celebration because their workers were slaves. He had been a frequent visitor to the Hall plantation all his life. Their slaves were well treated, but they were still slaves. Betsy would probably not feel very comfortable at a lively party like this one, where whites and blacks accepted each other as free people, so he hadn't invited her tonight.

He wondered if she would grow accustomed to free, hired workers rather than slaves if they were to marry. Irish certainly seemed to have no problem with it. Nor did Charlie. Maybe Irish and Charlie would suit each other very well.

At that thought, a feeling of alarm filled him. Alarm and something else. Possessiveness? He shook his head. No. Certainly not. He wanted her, but only in the way a man wants a woman. It was certainly no more than that. And those feelings could certainly come to no more than they were now--thoughts and feelings.

Suddenly his mother patted his knee. "I think I'll turn in. This celebration is bound to go on into the wee hours. I just hope no one shivarees the newlyweds."

Ty chuckled. "I think Nate and Matt promised Joe to watch out that no one kidnaps the bride, and with the party going on most of the night, Joe and Abby will have plenty of chances to slip away."

She leaned close to him. "Where are they spending their wedding night? They'll have no peace at all if they plan to stay in Joe's cabin."

"Nate told me they're going to use that old cabin at the edge of Fortune's Pride. If anyone plans to shivaree them, or bang pot lids and drums outside Joe's cabin, they won't be there."

She nodded, smiled once more at the crowd, and left.

Ty turned back to watch the dancing. Joe and Abby seemed to glow in each other's presence. They danced, they looked, they touched, promises of their night to come.

Ty envied them their joy. Would he find such joy in his bride when he wed? He thought of Betsy, but her image wavered, replaced by red hair and sparkling green eyes, and a mischievous grin.

He tried again to think of Betsy as his bride, but all he could think of was her lying quiet and submissive in his bed. He glanced at Irish. Most of her hair had tumbled down, perspiration sheened her face and dampened her new fichu. She seemed to sparkle all over. She would never lie meek and submissive in a marriage bed.

He remembered her body beneath his that first night home. Tender, slim, but full of fire. Full of passion. Just as her kiss had been full of passion. Irish would fill a man's every dream in bed. He frowned. Unfortunately, she would be just as willful and unmanageable out of bed. But maybe she would be worth it.

He tried to squelch that thought but the sight of her dancing made it impossible. He stood up to ease the fullness in his breeches, and leaned on his crutch.

He tested his ankle, gingerly placing his weight on his foot. It hurt. But could he manage one dance tonight? Just one? With Irish.

Keeping his foot up to spare his ankle as much as possible, he hobbled toward the couples, his eye on Irish. The dance was ending and he hurried toward her to claim the next dance, to claim her before Charlie again took her.

When he touched her arm, she turned away from Charlie and looked up at him with surprise. Then she smiled. Ty thought he had never seen a smile so beguiling, so enticing, so inviting. Her lips were lush and full. He was mesmerized by them. He started to bend down to kiss them but remembered where he was, and that kissing Irish was not something he could ever allow himself to do. But he could dance with her...for as long as his ankle held up, at least.

He held out his arm to her. "Dance?"

She looked down at his ankle. He was still supporting himself on his crutch.

He handed the crutch to Charlie. "I think I can make it through at least one reel," he said.

She looked doubtful but he pulled her arm through his and led her to the end of the forming line. She stood opposite him, her red hair and creamy skin standing out like a bright jewel in the long, dark line. Then the music started and she held out her arms to him, just like he had been thinking of her earlier.

He reached for her, taking her hands in his. Her hands were firm and strong, the palms, not calloused, but work toughened. Capable hands. Hands that could easily share life's work and burdens.

They came together then moved apart, he, bowing, she, curtsying, then he took her in an embrace to circle around. Her waist was delicate for a woman who seemed so strong. Reluctantly he let his hands slide away from her as they moved back into place to form an arch. As the head couple skipped down the line beneath their uplifted hands, Ty looked into Irish's eyes and felt his mouth go dry.

Each movement, each touch to her hand or waist or shoulder seemed to inflame him. The pain in his ankle was forgotten until he came down on it just a bit too hard and a pain shot up his leg nearly causing him to fall. But Irish was there immediately, supporting him, helping him to ignominiously limp from the line.

His ankle had only held up for half a dance and he might suffer a few days longer because of his indulgence, but it had been worth it.

She took him back to his bench and fussed over him, finding something to prop his foot on and getting him something to drink. Then she sat down beside him.

"I shouldn't have let you dance with me like that," she said. "I knew your ankle wasn't healed enough yet."

His heart warmed at her concern. "It was my choice, Irish. I couldn't bear seeing all that dancing and not try at least one." *With you,* he added to himself. *I wouldn't have used that ankle to dance with anyone else.*

She laughed. "I can understand. I love to dance. I don't think I could sit by and not dance even if I had two bad ankles."

Charlie came over to join them, handing Ty and Irish each a piece of wedding cake. "How's our patient?"

"He's going to suffer a few extra days because he couldn't resist dancing," Irish said.

Charlie gave Irish a look that Ty was sure was similar to the way he, himself, had been looking at her all evening--as if he wanted to drag her into the bushes and tear off her clothes. He clenched his teeth. He didn't want Charlie looking at her that way.

Charlie reached for her hand. "It wasn't just the dancing that made Ty risk that ankle, I'm sure, Irish. It was you. How could any man watch you dance and not want to dance with you?"

"Charlie, you're going to turn my head with all your flattery!" she laughed, but as she looked back and forth between the two of them, her laughter died and her lips parted in a soft, "Oh!" It was as if she realized that for once Charlie was serious, and that both men were looking at her the same way.

Ty was charmed by the blush that traveled down her cheeks and along her neck, and to what he could see of her chest and one lovely rounded breast. He glanced at Charlie and noticed that his gaze was taking the same route. Although he could not fault the man, his hackles still rose, and he wanted nothing more than to pull Irish's hand from Charlie's and claim her for his own.

The musicians finished the reel and put their instruments down to take a break, all but one fiddler. He tucked his fiddle under his chin and struck up a lively tune. Irish and Charlie looked at each other with matching grins and gleaming eyes.

"An Irish jig!" they exclaimed together.

With only a quick nod to Ty they jumped up, still holding hands, and hurried to the center of the compound. There, they kicked up their heels in one of the liveliest, most frantic dances Ty had ever seen. Their feet seemed to fly. Irish had grabbed two handfuls of skirt, hiking it up almost to her knees.

Her legs seemed to beat her petticoats into a lacy froth, her hair tumbling even more wildly. Her fichu came completely loose on one side and Irish pulled it free, waving it above her head like a banner.

Ty had never seen such indecorous behavior from a woman. Nor had he ever seen one so lovely, so appealing, so enticing. Her passion, as well as two very shapely ankles and calves, was on display for everyone to see. By the time the dance ended, he was again standing, leaning heavily on his crutch, but standing, leaning toward her, drawn toward her. His heart was beating so hard it could have been him out there dancing with her instead of Charlie.

As the last strains of the music died, the crowd burst into cheers and applause. Irish and Charlie stood in the center of the crowd looking at each other, grinning happily and panting from their exertions. Ty had never wished more fiercely that he could have been the one to dance that jig with her, that he could have let himself go enough to kick up his heels with her and not mind that it was not quite proper...that he could have been the one grinning happily at her having shared that exciting experience with her.

It *had* been exciting.

Ty wished he could kiss those lush lips, those flushed cheeks, those heaving breasts that were now half-exposed with her fichu hanging limply from her hand. He shifted his weight. He was not hanging limply, that was for certain.

Then she turned toward him and their gazes met. Her lips parted softly and she took a step toward him. He forced himself not to reach for her, but he need not have concerned himself.

Charlie touched her arm and she turned back, and Ty's anger rose within him. He glared at his builder, but the man seemed oblivious to him.

Ty's hand fisted. *I'd also be oblivious to everyone else around me if she were smiling at me like that,* he thought. He wanted her to look at him again. And he wanted Charlie out of the way, gone, vanished.

He looked on with envy gnawing at him as everyone continued to talk to Charlie and Irish, complimenting them on their dance, commenting on how good they looked together. As if they were a couple already promised and bound together! *But they aren't,* he wanted to shout. *They aren't!*

But as the music began again, everyone urged Charlie and Irish to dance again. They treated them like they belonged together. And why not? They did look good out there, dancing, damn it.

"You're looking a tad shaky, Old Man," Nate said, walking up to him with Matt.

Ty glared at his brothers, but Nate was right. He was feeling more than a tad shaky and very little of it could be accounted for by his injured ankle.

Matt took his elbow. "You look like you could use some rest. Would you like us to take you back to the house?"

"I'm fine," he insisted, but he did let his brother help him to sit back down. But Matt was wrong. It wasn't rest he needed. He needed to punch Charlie in his stupidly grinning face. And he needed a sound ankle to dance on with a wild Irish hoyden.

"Irish sure looks like she's having one fine time," Nate commented.

"Charlie's a great fellow," Matt said. "She looks happy."

"Aye," Nate agreed. "And it's about time." He sighed. "She sure is beautiful."

Matt laughed softly. "I thought you were over her, Little

Brother."

Nate blushed and shrugged, then said to Ty, "I have to admit I had high hopes for Irish and me there for a while. She let me down easy, though, and I have gotten over it, but I can still say how beautiful she is, can't I?"

Matt reached over to clap Nate on the knee. "Why not? It certainly is true. Although," he turned to Ty, "you should have seen her when we first brought her home from Saint Augustine." He shook his head.

"What?" Ty asked.

Matt leaned forward, resting his arms on his legs. "She'd had a rough time of it with the Spanish. She was skinny as a bean pole and had bruises on her face and arms. She was wearing the same dress she had been captured in six months earlier." He sighed. "She sure has filled out nicely."

"Not you, too!" Ty said. "I can understand a youngster like Nate falling for a beaten down waif, but I'm surprised at you, Matt."

Matt grinned. "Well, she does have an ability for worming her way into a man's heart. Although," he made a negligent gesture with one hand, "I think I care for her more like a sister."

Nate laughed. "I guess you're still pining for that Frenchie who dumped you."

It was Matt's turn to look a bit abashed. "Yeah." He watched Charlie and Irish while they executed an enthusiastic turn. "I'm just glad to see her happy. Maybe you're right, Nate. It is about time she found someone to love and marry. Charlie's a great fellow."

"Better than that John Edwards who was hanging around here for a while," said Nate.

Ty's brows went up. "John Edwards? The tavern owner from Goose Creek?"

Matt nodded. "Him and dozens of others. She's turned them

all down. She hardly ever goes into Charles Town but when she does, men start finding reasons to come out here and visit."

Dozens? He straightened, feeling something surge within him as if those men were all here now and he needed to fend them all off at once.

"Well, I'm glad you hired Charlie, Ty. He's a fine fellow. He'll make Irish happy," said Nate.

Matt nodded. "Yep. Fine fellow. Make any woman a fine husband."

"Just because he's a great fellow doesn't mean he's right for Irish," Ty said tightly.

He saw Nate and Matt exchange a knowing look. He glared first at one, then the other. "It's not like that!"

They just laughed and Matt arched one maddening brow, like he always did when he knew something the rest of them didn't. It just made Ty angrier.

"Think what you like, then!" He reached for his crutch and got to his feet.

"I don't think I'd try dancing on that ankle again," Matt said. Ty could hear the teasing tone in his voice and it seemed to fuel his anger more for some reason. Maybe because he knew he couldn't dance with Irish again.

Turning, he hobbled back toward the big house, muttering over his shoulder to his brothers, "I'm going to bed. It's late."

Ty left the sounds of the celebration behind him, the sound of the music and the sight of Irish dancing with Charlie, and the farther away he got, the angrier he got.

By the time he hobbled up the stairs, he didn't know which he wanted to do more--punch Charlie or shake Irish until the rest of her hair tumbled down. *Or kiss her,* he thought. But he shoved that thought down.

He went into his room and took off his coat, waistcoat and

shoes. He removed the stock from around his neck and flung it into a chair. Disgusted with his uncharacteristic action, he hopped over to the chair, picked up the stock and put it away.

He pulled his shirt out of his breeches and then sat on the chair to take off his socks. He glanced out the window. He could see the beginning of the path that led to the compound but he couldn't see the cabins from here. He shoved the window up a bit. He could hear the music, though it was faint.

He wasn't as tired as he'd thought and he sat there just listening to the music. But then he began imagining Irish dancing with Charlie and the things he saw in his imagination were far worse than what he had actually seen. Charlie pulling Irish close in a dance, Charlie caressing her back in a turn, and worst of all, Irish returning Charlie's smile, returning his caresses, pushing herself close to him.

His hand fisted on his knee and he stared at the path, waiting for them to come back to the house, wondering how long it would be. And the longer he watched and waited, the angrier he became.

It was after the big clock downstairs had chimed midnight when he saw Matt and Mangus making their way along the path, laughing and talking. Ty knew those two wouldn't leave until the party was well over, so where were Irish and Charlie? Impatiently he drummed his fingers on the padded arm of the chair. He heard Matt enter the house and make his way to his room, and still Charlie and Irish did not appear.

The big clock chimed again at the quarter hour and again at the half hour before Ty finally spied them. The moon was big and bright and it was easy to see that Charlie had his arm around her waist and that she was not protesting one bit.

Charlie pulled her to a halt and turned her toward him. Moonlight and shadows danced in her hair and lit her face. She was smiling softly at Charlie, and, apparently encouraged, he pulled her closer. Ty nearly came up out of his seat. What was the man doing? He wanted to beat on the window, to tell him to leave Irish alone, but he told himself it was none of his business what Irish and Charlie did.

That was when Charlie kissed her.

Chapter Ten

TY GRIPPED THE WINDOWSILL, HIS KNUCKLES TURNING WHITE. Charlie was kissing Irish, and she was not pulling away or turning her cheek to him. Indeed, she seemed to be relishing the kiss, leaning into him, her hands moving up to rest on his shoulders.

I shouldn't be watching this, Ty told himself, but he could not tear his eyes away. He felt as if Irish was squeezing his heart, instead of Charlie's shoulder. He wasn't sure he could draw a complete breath.

His eyes narrowed, watching that kiss. Already they were moving apart. It was not the kind of kiss he would have given Irish if he were down there in the moonlight with her. Even from here he could tell it had not curled her toes. But her hands had slid down Charlie's arms and now rested in his as they faced each other, talking.

What are they talking about, Ty wondered. She didn't seem to be raking Charlie over the coals as she had him when he had kissed her. Hell, she had damn near flayed the hide off of him. But she was down there smiling at Charlie like a love struck girl!

What if Charlie had really asked her to marry him? Good lord! What if she had accepted?

He blinked. What was she doing now, leaning forward, going

up on tiptoe? She was lifting her face for another kiss, damn it! And Charlie obliged, curse him! But this kiss was almost chaste, on the cheek. What was the matter with the man? He was standing in the moonlight with a beautiful, lush, ripe woman and he kisses her on the cheek?

Holding hands they began to walk toward the house and Ty jumped up and began to pace, in spite of the pain it caused him. He rubbed a hand over his chest but it could not rub away the feeling of a lance lodged in his heart.

Had she accepted a proposal of marriage down there? Is that what that was all about? She couldn't want Charlie. Not after that insipid kiss. Did she think that sharing a marriage bed would be any better than that with Charlie? Is that all she wanted?

Ty had given her that one other kiss, but she had been upset then. Maybe she didn't know what kissing was really all about. His lips curled up into a wicked grin. Maybe she needed someone to show her.

Charlie's room was downstairs and when Ty heard her footsteps on the stairs, he stalked to the door of his room and flung it open. It banged against the wall but he didn't care.

Irish looked up at him with wide, startled eyes. Slowly she stepped up that last stair and paused, looking at him. Her lips parted softly and her breath seemed to quicken. She had tucked her fichu neatly back into her bodice, but her hair, now tumbling wildly about her shoulders from her dancing, eliminated any look of innocence the fichu might have given.

In spite of that hair, she didn't look like a woman who had just been kissed. But she soon will, Ty thought, leering at her.

"I thought you would be asleep by now," she said, glancing briefly down at his ankle. Her gaze took in his state of undress. "Or did I wake you?"

"I'm not such an invalid as that, Irish," he said, moving out into the hall, blocking her way.

"Of course not," she stammered. "I just thought..."

"I saw that kiss Charlie gave you."

She glanced into his room at the window overlooking the path from the compound. Her nostrils flared and she straightened, her fists going to her hips. "You were spying on me?"

He chuckled. Now here was the fire he had come to expect from his Irish. Charlie must be quite some wet blanket to have put it out for a while. But it was reignited now.

He took a fistful of fichu and pulled her toward him. "It didn't seem like much of a kiss to me," he told her.

She looked up at him with a challenge in her eyes. "And do you think you can do better?"

"I could do better than that when I was fifteen. And you deserve better."

"You're arrogant if you think..."

"Shh," he said. "Tell me that if you still believe it after I kiss you properly."

With that he bent to kiss her. He was encouraged that she let him. Perhaps Charlie had not proposed after all. Or maybe she just wanted to compare kisses to be sure Charlie was who and what she wanted. Then let her try and compare. He would give her something incomparable.

He knew he could do it, too. He had seen Charlie's kiss. Even from his window he could tell that it had not inflamed her. If it had, she wouldn't be here now with him waiting for his kiss. The one kiss they had shared in his mother's office, brief as it was, as much as she had protested his impertinence, had affected her far more than Charlie's.

Her lips were soft but, unlike other women he had kissed, Irish's lips were not yielding. They were giving. So different, so exciting, so very like Irish to give as good as she got, to take as much as she gave. His blood surged within him.

With one hand still fisted in her fichu and the other at the small of her back he pulled her closer. His mouth worked on hers and she did not resist him.

Her arms went up around his neck. They did not stop to merely clasp his shoulders. They went all the way around his neck, tightening, urging him to deepen the kiss. He did not hesitate.

One of her hands tugged at the ribbon binding his hair, pulling it loose. As his tongue plunged into her mouth, her fingers plunged into his hair.

He ran his hand up along her spine, along the slim column of her nape and splayed his fingers into her hair, pulling out her pins, letting them clink one by one onto the floor. The rest of that glorious, unruly mane toppled into his hand and he sifted it through his fingers, vaguely wondering why the fiery mass didn't singe him.

Letting go of the fichu he caressed her neck, then slid his hand down her throat to her collarbone, inching toward her shoulder until he encountered the fichu. How often he had scowled when she had indecorously discarded it. He had given her this one. Now he wished it gone to Hades.

He tugged at the fichu, pulling it handful by handful out of her bodice. The soft, lacy material seemed to bunch and grow, tangling in his fingers. Why was he having so much trouble ridding her of it when it seemed to come loose and undone at her slightest movement during the day? Finally, he felt the end slip free and he pulled at it, sliding it from her neck and tossing it aside.

At last his fingers touched the soft, round fullness of her breast mounded up above her bodice and stomacher. For days that rich abundance had tempted him, making his fingers itch to touch it. Every time he had seen Irish working in the kitchen, riding Renegade, bringing platters of food to the table, these breasts, rarely covered by a fichu, had enticed him. Now at last they were his.

Or half his. Most of them were still covered by her bodice.

While he worked his way into her mouth with his tongue, he worked his fingers down into her bodice.

He paused a moment to relish the feel of her hands on him. Irish played with his hair with one hand, combing her spread fingers through it then twisting one strand after another around a finger, gently tugging, letting go, winding another strand. Her other hand played at his nape, working seductively beneath his shirt, splaying on his upper back.

He groaned as she caressed his back in kneading swirls, clutching at him when he deepened the kiss. She pressed herself against him as if she couldn't get enough of him, as if she couldn't get close enough. He felt her one thigh against his. Her other thigh pressed closer to him, between his legs, and what was there responded fully. He thrilled to her soft, hungry moans, moans that urgently asked for more, which he was all too eager to give.

His attention went back to that breast still trapped inside her bodice. She usually seemed to come apart at the most inopportune times, nearly tumbling free of her bodice as she worked. So why the hell was he having such a devil of a time freeing it now?

At last his fingers curved around her fullness, lifting it, pulling it free. He thumbed the crest and he thought she was going to climb right on top of him. His ankle nearly gave way beneath him and he had to lean against the wall to hold her weight, slight though it was. His free hand slid down her back and over her rump to hold and support her, lifting her more firmly against him.

He was losing his mind. His senses were reeling. Never had he experienced such passion from a woman. And never had his body responded so strongly. All he could think of was her lips on his, the heat of her mouth, the sweet tang of the taste of her, her breast now finally his, her round bottom fitting so perfectly into his hand, the jointure of her thighs against him causing him to swell to painful urgency.

All he could hear was her breathy, "umm's" as if he were something she was feasting on. He wanted to feast on her. He tore his mouth away from hers to kiss the breast his fingers had freed. And that was when he heard the whistled sea chantey.

It was a soft, quiet whistle, but it was coming closer. Then he heard a step on the stairs. Nate!

Irish must have heard him, too, coming up to bed, for she stiffened and he heard her gasp. He felt it, as well. The warm breast in his hand jumped with it, but he couldn't take time to enjoy it. Irish wouldn't want Nate to catch them here in the darkness together. Already his footsteps were on the third or fourth stair.

There was only time for one thing. He jerked her into his room, bending quickly to snatch her fichu he had tossed aside. Then he closed his door, holding the knob and releasing it slowly to avoid making any noise.

He heard her take a breath but he clamped a hand over her mouth and pulled her to him to quiet her. She relaxed into him and nodded and he removed his hand, finding a much more pleasant resting place for it on her backside.

They stood like that in his room, in a shaft of moonlight, scarcely daring to breathe as they listened to Nate's footsteps come down the hall, the chantey still sounding softly.

"It's Nate, isn't it?" she asked in a barely heard whisper.

He nodded. "It's a good thing it wasn't Matt," he answered. "We wouldn't have known he was there until he tapped us on the shoulder."

Nate's footsteps halted outside Ty's door and Irish's eyes grew round with fright. Ty knew she was thinking the same thing he was. What if Nate knocked on his door and wanted a brotherly chat? He reassured her with a squeeze and a smile. If Nate wanted a talk, he'd take him downstairs, giving Irish an opportunity to escape to her room.

But it wasn't a talk Nate wanted. He was doing something out there in the hall. They listened, puzzled, then Irish groaned and leaned her head against his chest. "He's picking up my pins. The ones you took out of my hair."

Ty stifled a chuckle. "I imagine he is. Nate always likes things ship shape and tidy, as he says." "Those are my pins!" she whispered. "I don't have that many and I need them."

He grinned. "Shall I go out there and tell him to give them to me?"

She punched him lightly in the chest. "Don't you dare!" She groaned again, and though he knew it was a groan of frustration at possibly losing her pins, he could easily imagine it as a groan of passion and his body could not help responding.

He lifted her chin and smiled down at her. "I'm sure you can get your pins back from Nate tomorrow."

"Oh, of course," she said dryly. "I'll just go up to him and say, Oh, by the way, Nate, I lost my hairpins in the hall last night while Ty was kissing me into insanity. I heard you picking them up while I was hiding in Ty's room with his tongue in my mouth. Could you please return them?"

He could not help but chuckle. He brushed hair back from her face, hair no longer confined by the damnable pins that were now all over the upstairs hallway. "Did I really kiss you into insanity, Irish?"

She tweaked the hair on his chest. "Don't be so smug. You seemed to be losing a bit of control yourself."

He kissed her forehead where he had pushed back her hair. "Not completely, but I've never come so close."

He heard Nate's door open and his brother's whistling grow fainter then stop altogether when he closed his door.

Irish slumped against him with a sigh. "I suppose we should

be thankful Nate came along."

He growled. "I'm not so sure about that." He pulled her closer and bent again to kiss her but she turned her head and pushed away, leaving him feeling strangely bereft.

"I am." She pulled her fichu from his hand and turned toward the door.

"Irish." He laid a hand on her shoulder.

She shrugged him off and reached for the knob to open the door. He placed his hand flat on the door, holding it closed. She turned to look up at him questioningly.

"I'm not sorry about what happened."

She leaned her head back against the door. "How will I ever face Nate again?"

"Nate doesn't know anything, Irish."

"He found my hairpins!" she nearly wailed.

"I'm sure he'll return them to you tomorrow."

She groaned. "And what am I supposed to say when he does?"

He could not help but finger her hair again, touching it gently, tickling her chin with it. "You just say thank you."

She started to respond. Something scathing, he was sure. But he stopped her with a finger across her lips. He smiled. "Irish, you are always coming undone, losing hairpins, your fichu. He won't think anything about finding a few of your pins after the way you were dancing tonight."

She grasped a fistful of his shirt and let her hand slide down its loose folds. "It seems you've come a bit undone tonight yourself, Ty." She smiled. "I've never seen you looking better."

Surprised that anyone could think he looked better this way than all tucked up and properly put together, he had no chance to reply before she was out the door and down the hall to her own room.

Irish twirled into her room and shut the door, leaning back against it. Nate had almost discovered her climbing all over Ty. How could she have let herself lose control like that? A smile played about her lips. She wasn't the only one who had lost control. She had never seen Ty so mussed, so masculine, so appealing.

She looked down at his hair ribbon that she still held in her hand. Tonight was the first time she had seen his hair loose, falling about his shoulders in thick black waves. She had done that to him and he had allowed her, had seemed to relish the feel of her fingers sifting through his hair. The sight of him with his stock gone and his shirt undone, hanging loose, standing there in the hall had surprised her. But it had also excited her more than he ever had when all starched and proper.

She had told him she had never seen him looking better, and how true that was. Tyrus Fortune needed to quit being so stuffy. She tossed her fichu onto a chair. And maybe she needed to make more effort to keep herself put together. She chuckled.

She had certainly come undone tonight. She had never experienced anything like Ty's kiss. He had been right. He had done better than Charlie. Charlie's kiss had been sweet, but it hadn't been a kiss that made her wild. She hadn't been kissed into insanity as she had by Ty.

And it had been insanity, she thought. She walked across the room to her window. It was next to Ty's and looked out on much the same scene. How would she have felt if she had seen Ty kissing Betsy down there on the path? Her fist curled into the drapes. She would have hated it. She would have wanted to kiss him until Betsy's kiss was not even a memory. Was that why he had kissed her tonight? Why would he care who she kissed? Obviously he did. Was he beginning to care for her?

She ran her hands down the embroidered stomacher he had given her. She had accepted his reason that it was for winning the race, but she had not been fooled. That may have been part of the reason he had given it to her, but deep inside she knew it was because he just wanted to give her a gift. And she had wanted to accept that gift.

She unpinned the stomacher and laid it in a drawer. Ty was beginning to care for her. What was she going to do about that?

Charlie had been easy to put off. When he had kissed her he had told her that he wanted to court her, but she had told him she only wanted to be friends. And that was true. She really liked Charlie, but his kiss had done nothing for her. She could smile and be friends with him.

But she could not do that with Ty. His kiss had taught her that. She could not tell him she only wanted to be friends. He would know better. She would know better. She could not be around him and not fall into his arms any time he opened them. What would happen the next time? What if there had been no Nate to interrupt them?

She ran her hands down her body. She still ached for Ty. She wanted him. She wanted his touch. She wanted to touch him. She wanted more than just his coat and waistcoat off of him. She plunged her splayed fingers into her hair, lifted her head and wanted to cry out in frustration. She had wondered how she could face Nate the next day. How on God's green earth was she going to look Ty in the eye tomorrow? How could she sit at the same table with him without wanting to climb across it and into his lap? How could she pass him in the hall, brush his shoulder with hers without pulling him to her?

She couldn't and she knew it. He felt it, too. There would be no avoiding him, their shared feelings. And they were feelings that could come to naught. Even if Ty was not courting Betsy, there could be nothing between this rich Fortune and her. Not with his pride and her secrets.

But it was those secrets more than anything that would keep her from Ty. She could never tell him the truth about herself. If she did, she would lose him for certain, but more than that--he would scorn her. And she could not allow their relationship to deepen without being honest with him.

She had to let him go. And since she could not do that, she had to get away from him before she did something foolish.

Well! She planted her fists on her hips and looked around the room. She had already decided that it was time to get her own place. Now she would have to act. Nate would probably be going back to Charles Town tomorrow to pick up some cargo. She would go with him. She could stay at the Fortune's town house until she could find a place to rent.

With the decision made, Irish began to pull her clothes out of the chest of drawers. There was a valise in the armoire and she fetched it and began stuffing her things into it. She didn't have all that much, but she would probably need a small trunk for all of it. She would get everything ready and in the morning pack the rest, and tell Mrs. Fortune she was leaving.

It would be hard to leave the woman who had been like a mother to her, but she would see her at times. The family would be moving into their town house in another week. By then she would have her own place and could see Mrs. Fortune, and the rest of the family, any time she liked. It wasn't as if she would never see them again. So why did she feel so weepy?

It's because I'll always be alone, she thought. It wasn't this family she was fleeing. It was Ty. It was a relationship she could never have with any man, but especially not with the proud, proper Tyrus Fortune...and all because of her secrets.

She had had dreams of a future, dreams of happiness with a

husband and children. When Mariette had rescued her from the Spanish, she had thought she would be able to start a new life and have that happiness. But now she knew she could never have that life because she could never marry a man without being totally honest with him. And honesty was the one thing she could not give. It was too dangerous.

She finished gathering her things, packing a few more into the valise and stacking the rest neatly until morning when she would get a trunk from the attic. By tomorrow afternoon she would be in Charles Town...and alone for the rest of her life.

Irish's eyes snapped open to the sound of a tapping at her door, Paddy whining, and Mrs. Fortune calling her name. She sat up. The room was still dark. She had no idea what time it was but something must be wrong.

"Coming!" she called, jumping up and padding to the door.

Mrs. Fortune was fully dressed in traveling clothes, complete with hat and a light shawl. A valise sat at her feet. Nate was just coming out of his room. He was also dressed but still rubbing the sleep from his eyes.

Mrs. Fortune must have knocked on Ty's door just moments before she knocked on Irish's because he was standing there looking delicious with his hair still loose, his feet bare, just tying the sash of his robe. She could see the chest hair that she had tweaked just hours ago and it brought a blush rushing to her cheeks. Matt had also been awakened and stood with the rest of the family, obviously naked beneath a blanket he had hastily wrapped about himself and looking very much like his Indian friends.

They all looked to Mrs. Fortune to explain this pre-dawn awakening. It was clear that nothing could be too much amiss. She was grinning.

"A messenger just arrived. Mariette's in labor. Nate's going to take me upriver. I just wanted to let you know, before I left."

Ty ran a hand through his hair. "It's not even dawn yet, Mother. It will be dark on the river."

"I know every inch of that river, Ty. We'll be fine," Nate said, puffing up proudly.

Matt chuckled. "Besides, dawn isn't that far off. It will be light enough to navigate by the time you get the *Fortune's* sails up and under way."

It always amazed Irish how Matt always knew what time of day or night it was.

"Matt's right, Ty. There's no need to worry," their mother said. "I'll send word as soon as Mariette's had that grandchild of mine."

"I'll get ready and go with you." Ty started to turn back to his room.

"No, no," Mrs. Fortune said. "That's not necessary, and you want to start on that house of yours."

"I'll go," Matt said. "I was planning to head up that way back to the Yadkin."

She nodded. "All right." She went onto tiptoe to kiss Ty on the cheek. "You go on back to bed. Irish, if you'll walk out with us there's a couple of things I want to tell you."

Irish nodded and went back inside her room to put on her slippers and a wrap. By the time she returned, Matt and Ty were back in their rooms and Nate had gone ahead to prepare his ship. Mrs. Fortune linked her arm through Irish's and they walked down the stairs together.

"Irish, there are a few things I'd like you to take care of while I'm gone. If I can, I want to stay with Mariette for the next two weeks. I've kept a small valise packed but I'll need a few more of my things. If you'll pack some clothes up for me and send them, I would appreciate it."

"Of course, Mrs. Fortune," Irish said, patting the older woman's hand.

"You'll be in charge here for a while, Irish. I'm counting on you."

Irish stopped, surprised. "Me?"

Mrs. Fortune nodded, concern in her eyes. "I do hope you don't mind the extra work, but it will just be until I return. There's no one else. Matt is going to be gone again. Nate has a cargo to pick up tomorrow that just won't wait, and Ty is going to be busy with building his house."

"I...I...of course I'll do what I can, Mrs. Fortune. You know that."

She gave a sigh of relief. "I knew I could count on you, Irish. Now the dikes up on the north field need to be checked. Matt said they looked like they needed attention. And old Pete, you know who I mean, that crazy old man who lives in that shack up there, might need a little food. And Sarah will be calving any day now, and that cow always has a hard time. You might want to check on her. And—"

Irish squeezed Mrs. Fortune's hands reassuringly. "I know. Don't worry about a thing. If there's any problem, I'll send word or make Ty take time to help me."

They were almost to the dock and Mrs. Fortune stopped once more. "There's one more thing."

Irish nodded for her to go on.

"Take care of Ty." She sighed deeply. "Once he gets started with that house of his he'll forget to eat unless someone reminds him. He can be so single-minded, that one." She leaned closer. "Take him some lunch to the building site and make sure he stays off that ankle and—"

"Mother! Come on aboard! We're ready!" Nate called.

Matt came swinging by with a leather pouch slung over his

deerskin-clad shoulder. Grinning, he took his mother's arm, pull-ing her along with him down the dock. "Come on, Mother. Irish can handle things but Mariette's baby won't wait."

"Don't worry, Mrs. Fortune!" Irish called as Matt hustled his mother aboard, and helped Nate and another sailor set the sails.

She said the words but her heart sank. She couldn't leave as she had planned.

She turned to go back to the house. Matt had been right. It was getting light. She yawned. She'd had precious little sleep but it was time to start the day. She looked up and came to a halt. Ty was standing in the door waving to his mother. When he saw Irish, he slowly lowered his arm and waited for her. Together they went back inside and to the stairs.

She tried hard not to touch him, tried not to be so very con-scious of his presence behind her as she went up the stairs. She was almost to her room when he took her arm.

"Irish," he said softly.

She turned toward him, acutely aware that they stood there alone, in their nightclothes, just inches from a bedroom door. She tried hard not to look at him but it didn't matter. She would always remember how he had looked when he had come from his room, sleep tousled, wrapping his red robe about him with bare feet and chest showing.

"We—I need to get dressed." She pulled away from him, quickly went into her room and closed her door.

Her clothes were still stacked, ready to pack, ready to leave. But she wasn't leaving.

She would still be here facing Ty every day. And now it would be worse. Mrs. Fortune was gone, as well as Matt and Nate. Thank goodness Charlie was still here. Maybe that would make being in this house with Ty bearable--eating at the same table, sleeping in the room next to his, brushing shoulders as they passed in the halls.

Maybe having Charlie here would keep her out of Ty's bed. Although it hadn't kept her from kissing him in the hall. Nothing could have kept her from kissing him in the hall, but she could hope that the next time Ty took her by the arm she would find a way to resist flinging herself into his arms.

As she put on her clothes she found one way to help her resist Ty. She crossed her fichu over her breasts and tucked it in thoroughly. Then she put on an apron and made sure the pins went all the way through--apron, bodice, and fichu. No one was going to pull her fichu out and seek her flesh again. She was going to stay as tucked up and pinned down as she could.

Finished dressing, she put her hand to her hair and sighed. Nate had not returned her hairpins and she didn't have enough left to contain this mess. She reached for her brush and saw Ty's ribbon lying there beside her few pins. The very one she had pulled from his hair last night. She picked it up and ran it through her fingers, and a wicked grin lit her face. He was responsible for the loss of her pins. She would just appropriate his ribbon.

Brushing her hair back she divided it into three parts and quickly made a braid, weaving the ribbon into the last part and then tying it off. Just dare him to ask for it back! The ribbon was hers. At least until she got her pins.

She took hold of the knob of her door and paused. Ty would be down there at breakfast. And Charlie. How was she going to face them? One of them she had turned down and the other she had practically torn his clothes off at his merest touch.

She squared her shoulders. She couldn't hide in here all day. She had to face them sooner or later. She would act normally.

She would laugh and smile and take Renegade out for a ride. And she would keep Tyrus Fortune at a very long arm's length. What happened in the hall last night could not happen again.

Paddy whined and looked up at her. She bent to scratch his

ears. "You're right. I'm being a coward." With that she yanked open the door and followed Paddy's clicking paws downstairs to the kitchen to begin breakfast.

Chapter Eleven

STEAMING COFFEE WAS SITTING ON THE SIDEBOARD WHEN Ty came limping down to breakfast. Charlie was already helping himself to some. The builder lifted his cup in salute and took a sip.

"Quite a night, wasn't it?" Charlie said.

It was, indeed, Ty thought, remembering the softness of Irish's breast in his hand. *You may have kissed her, Old Boy, but it was me she kissed back.* "Yes," Ty answered. "Quite a celebration."

Charlie sat down, leaning back in his chair with a faraway look in his eyes. "That Irish is certainly a sweet thing."

Ty almost choked on his coffee. Sweet? Irish? Had they kissed the same woman? Sweet? Intoxicating, yes! Full of tang and spice, definitely! Inflammatory, absolutely! But hardly sweet. Sweet was a word he would apply to...well...Betsy. Sweet, placid, steady, Betsy.

"Sweet. Of course," Ty responded, not even sure Charlie heard him, he was so far off in his imagination.

But Charlie must have heard him, must had heard the sarcasm in his voice, too, because he plunked the front two legs of his chair back down, leaned forward and rested his cup on the table, cupping his hand around it.

Ty again recalled the warm breast his own hand had cupped

the night before.

"You don't like her much, do you?" Charlie asked.

If Charlie thought he was going to answer no to that question, the man was an idiot. He was not going to leave a clear field to a woman who deserved a whole lot more than Charlie Bowles. Charlie was a fine fellow, but from what he'd witnessed of that kiss last night, Irish deserved more. Hadn't he told her just that? Hadn't he given her more?

"I like her just fine," he said curtly. Maybe too well. What was he doing kissing one of the women in his household in the middle of the night? And if Irish deserved better than what Charlie could give her, she also deserved better than what he would have given her. Hadn't he already decided that he had no intention of marrying her? So what did that leave?

"Doesn't seem like it, from all the snipping and snapping you two do at each other," Charlie muttered.

Ty took another sip of coffee. *Another reason I don't need to be chasing that particular piece of tail,* he told himself, even if it was one of the nicest he had ever seen—or felt.

"Where's your lovely mother, and the rest of the clan, this morning?" Charlie asked.

Ty grinned. "Nate took them upriver to Mariette's. She's having her baby. I might be an uncle by now."

The dining room door burst open and Irish led Ruby into the room, both carrying steaming platters--eggs and ham and biscuits and gravy, from the look and smell of it.

He glanced up at Irish but she wouldn't meet his eyes. But she certainly had plenty of smiles for Charlie. She set her platter down in front of Ty but for once there was not one bit of cleavage in sight. She was wrapped up in that damned fichu tighter than an Egyptian mummy. He lifted his gaze from that delectable spot and of course now she was looking at him, and she had seen exactly where his attention had been.

He cleared his throat and scooped some of the eggs onto his plate. "Good morning, Irish." He nodded to Ruby as she set her platter down.

Ruby went back to the kitchen but Irish turned to pull out her chair. That was when he saw what was holding her unruly hair in place—his ribbon! He gripped his fork. The little tart! Wearing his ribbon like some kind of trophy!

He was about to dip into the eggs for a bit more when she practically snatched the platter out from under his hand and proffered it to Charlie...with the sweetest smile he had ever seen on her lips.

Ty grabbed a couple of biscuits before she could shove that plate down the table to Charlie, as well. Maybe that smile was why Charlie had the idiocy to call Irish sweet. She was certainly being sweet to Charlie.

His eyes narrowed as he wondered just why she was being so sweet to Charlie. What was she up to?

"Have some ham, Charlie," she said. "And another biscuit. You said you liked them so I made them this morning."

Charlie reached out to lightly pinch her cheek as if she was a child. "Ye're a darlin', you are, Irish." He grinned at Ty. "Isn't she a grand lass, Ty?"

Ty noticed that Charlie's Irish accent seemed to deepen when he was around Irish. Was he doing it on purpose, Ty wondered. "Oh, aye, she's a grand lass," he agreed, putting on a bit of brogue himself.

Irish and Charlie burst into laughter.

Ty harrumphed. "Well, I'm Irish, too," he said defensively. "At least in part."

Charlie and Irish began talking about Ireland then, describing to each other her green hills and bright seas in rhapsodic terms as if neither of them had ever seen it. Ty threw down his napkin and stood up. "If you're ready to go, Charlie, I'd like to have my house built sometime in this decade."

Charlie tore his attention away from Irish. "And how are we to get to the site today, Ty? Nate's gone with his ship."

"I'll have Mangus hitch up the carriage. It will take longer to get there, but at least I can still drive even with this ankle."

"Then I'm ready when you are." Charlie nodded and stood up, giving Irish a buss on the cheek. Ty wanted to leap across the table and strangle him, especially when she didn't object to the kiss but just smiled at the man.

"If you'll excuse us, Irish," he said. The little baggage merely nodded at him as regally as a queen, then got up and began clearing the table, dismissing him out of hand.

The moment Ty and Charlie left the room, Irish dropped back into her seat, with the dishes still in her hand. She just had to get her bearings and calm herself a bit to be sure her legs would carry her all the way to the kitchen. It had been nearly impossible to pretend indifference with Ty, but she had no choice. One of them had to be sane, and it didn't look like he was going to be the one, not with the way he had been looking at her, eyeing her now covered cleavage.

Charlie was so much easier to deal with. They understood one another. He had readily agreed to just be friends. She didn't think he was more than half-serious about that proposal last night, anyway. She was glad that he could still flirt with her this morning, still share a laugh and a memory or two about Ireland, even though she'd had to be very careful about what she said. She didn't want to give away any information about her past, her family, her real name, or exactly where she was from. With Charlie that was easy.

She just let him do most of the talking.

Ty was going to be a little more difficult, she could tell. She just didn't know what was going on behind that scowling face. Did he still think of her as an intruder and want her gone from this house?

She wished she could be gone. She had planned to be gone. But until Mrs. Fortune returned, she would have to stay. Hopefully, Charlie's presence would keep her from jumping into Ty's lap and demanding another thorough kissing, in spite of that scowl.

She set the platters back on the table, idly brushing some biscuit crumbs around on the tablecloth. Why had he kissed her anyway if he wanted her gone so badly? Did he think he could frighten her into running?

No, that kiss was not meant as intimidation. She touched her lips. He wanted her as much as she wanted him. It was up to her to make sure that nothing like that ever happened again between them. She couldn't have a relationship with Ty--or any man- -without telling him the truth about herself, and that was something she couldn't do.

When they returned home that evening, Charlie was rubbing his hands together in anticipation of another good meal. Yet all Ty could think was that he would have to face another dinner watching Charlie fawn all over Irish, while she lapped it up like a kitten with a bowl of cream.

Ty was surprised to find Ruby and Dee-Dee putting the food on the table with no sign of Irish.

"She's down at the barn," Ruby told him. "That cow decided it was time for her calf to be born, but she's having a hard time. Irish has been down there all afternoon."

"Sarah?" Ty asked.

Ruby nodded as she set a bowl of mashed potatoes on the table. "Sarah is Mrs. Fortune's favorite milk cow." She giggled. "Mine, too. That cow gives the best milk. But she always did have trouble having her babies." She shook her head. "That girl's plumb tuckered out trying to save that calf, but she won't give up."

"Irish?" Charlie asked, incredulously.

"And what does Irish think she can do? Where's Sally?" Ty asked.

"Sally went up to Miss Mariette's last week. Ain't nobody knows more about deliverin' anything than Sally," Ruby said. "But she ain't here."

"So Irish thinks she can take Sally's place?" What was she trying to do, Ty wondered, take over completely? Did she think she could do everything around here?

He threw down his napkin. "You go ahead and eat, Charlie. I'm going to see that Irish doesn't ruin a perfectly good cow."

Charlie chuckled. "I'm certain Irish knows what she's doing or she wouldn't be doing it."

Ty wasn't so sure. He stomped out and headed down to the barn.

Ty opened the barn door, and couldn't believe the scene that greeted him. Sarah, the cow, was lying down in the straw, her sides heaving. Every so often she would give a low mournful bawl. Irish was face down on the floor with her arm up in the cow. Two men were there with her, one holding the cow's head and the other hovering beside Irish, offering advice.

Irish pulled her arm free and turned over looking more exhausted than the cow.

"What the hell are you doing?" Ty demanded, moving to stand over her, arms akimbo.

Irish didn't bother getting up. Her skirts had hiked up above her knees and her fichu had been discarded, her hair had worked loose from its braid and his ribbon, and she had straw and muck all over her. "Trying to save Sarah's calf," she said. He could hear the fatigue in her voice but also more than a little defiance.

"Can't you let someone else do that?"

She shook her head. "No one else can."

Ty looked back and forth at the two men, big brawny twins, both of whom were good stout farm workers who knew a thing or two about cows. "And just why not?"

"Sally's not here."

"I know that, but that doesn't mean you have to take her place. Just what do you know about cows, anyway?"

"Shh!" Irish scolded him, pushing herself up and her skirts down. "Keep quiet. You'll upset Sarah and she needs to be calm right now."

He rolled his eyes and threw up his hands in exasperation. "Will you just get out of here and let Paul and Silas take care of Sarah?"

The two men looked at each other and then at Irish to explain. "They can't," she said.

"And just why not?" Ty asked, keeping his voice low.

"Oh, you're right. I don't know a whole lot about cows. I've mostly been around horses, seen a lot of them born, but I never knew much about cows. But it doesn't seem to be too different and Paul and Silas are telling me what to do," she explained.

He nodded, "But why do you have to be the one with your arm in there and your face in the muck?"

She held out her arm. "There's not a lot of room to maneuver in there, and their arms are too short to do a whole lot of good."

Ty looked at the twins' arms. Irish was right. They had big, bulky muscles, but their arms were shorter than hers by four or five inches. "Very well, but surely there are other men on this plantation who have arms that are long enough?"

"Oh I'm sure there are, but how many of them have experience birthing a cow?" she said. "But if you want to take the time to try to find one, go right ahead. I'd rather try to save this calf."

The anger drained from him. He nodded. "What can I do to help?"

"Nothing," she answered. "The calf's head is turned. Sarah is trying to push it out neck first and it just won't work. I'm trying to get hold of the calf's jaw and pull it around. Every time I just about have it, she has another contraction and I have to let go."

Ty nodded, trying to think. He had seen his share of farm animals born. What could she do to get hold of that calf and hang on during a contraction? Just then, Paul, holding Sarah's lead, stood up and stretched, twirling the rope.

"Give me a length of rope!" Ty said.

Silas handed him a slender rope and Ty tied a loop in one end. He handed it to Irish. "See if you can get that around the calf's jaw."

Her eyes lit with understanding and she grabbed the rope. Soaping her arm to ease its passage she again lay on the floor and pushed her arm up into the cow with the rope in hand. It took her several tries and he could see how Sarah's powerful contractions must hurt Irish's arm, but she held on, forcing her way back after each one.

At last she looked up at Ty with a gleam in her eyes. "I've got it!"

Keeping tension on the rope, Ty pulled steadily while she pushed the calf back far enough to get the head around. After that it was just moments before the calf slipped out of the cow.

Ty just stood there stunned for a moment, then he started grinning. He had seen a lot of animals born but this was the first time he had actually helped. It was an exhilarating feeling. He looked at Irish and knew she felt the same way. They stood together gazing down at the calf, watched as Sarah got up and begin to lick her calf clean, watched the calf take its first hesitant steps and begin its search for food.

He glanced at Irish.

She was the most rumpled, disreputable looking woman he had ever seen but the light in her eyes, the glow on her cheeks, the soft smile on her lips, the pride of accomplishment about her made her beautiful in that moment.

He could feel the silly grin on his own face as he watched the calf nurse for the first time. He had always enjoyed seeing horses or cows born, but somehow, this one was special, maybe because he had helped in a small way, been a part of this birth.

He continued to gaze at Irish and she looked up from watching the calf.

He wanted to scoop her up into his arms and twirl her around until they were both falling down dizzy. He wanted to kiss those glowing cheeks and run his hands through her mussed hair. He wanted to lay her back down in that straw and hike her skirts back up and run his hands up those shapely legs. He wanted her and he wanted her now. He wanted her to be his and he wanted to claim her...but of course he didn't. He even took a step toward her before he stopped himself, clenching his fists to keep his hands off her.

She seemed to lean toward him as if in anticipation of his touch but when he stopped, she averted her face. She was not for him, he was not the one for her, and they both knew it.

It was Silas who broke the spell between them by slapping Sarah on the rump with a hearty chuckle. "Guess we better give this new heifer a name," he said to Irish.

She turned to Ty. "Do you want to name her?"

He touched the soft, still damp back of the new calf. "You did most of the work bringing her into the world. The privilege of naming it should be yours."

She grinned impishly at him from the other side of the calf. "Let's call her Desiree."

Desiree--French for desire. The hoyden had exactly named what was between them. Something they both knew they could never give in to. "Rather pretentious for a calf, isn't it?"

"That's a good name," Silas disagreed. "But maybe Master Ty's right 'bout it bein' too much for such a little thing." He looked down at the calf. "How 'bout we just call her Dezzie?"

A little thing? Maybe the calf was little, but the desire he was feeling was anything but. He thought it was going to consume him. "Yes," he agreed. "Dezzie is just right. Dezzie it is."

"'Scuse us, Miss Irish," Paul said. "Supper be waitin' and I'm mighty hungry."

Ty let out a breath. "You're right, Paul. My supper is waiting as well. Irish?"

She ran her hands self-consciously down the front of her apron, now hopelessly stained. "You go ahead, Ty. I think I'll get cleaned up and then just have a plate in the kitchen."

He nodded, reluctant to leave her. At the last, he just couldn't. He held out his hand to her. "Come along. I'll walk you back to the house."

She looked at his hand as if he were offering her the world, but then squared her shoulders and clasped her hands behind her. "Thank you," she said and preceded him out of the barn and up the path back toward the house where they parted ways--he to his dinner and she to her room.

Irish toweled her hair dry as she picked at the food Ruby had brought her on a tray. She had decided that the only way she would feel clean was to get into the big tub that was kept in a small room off the kitchen. Ruby had helped her fill it and Irish had indulged herself in a long soak.

She had finally given up the idea of banishing Ty from her thoughts. It had been hard enough not to take the hand he had held out to her down at the barn. It had been hard not to throw herself into his arms, straw, muck, and all. She chuckled. Wouldn't the starched, always perfectly groomed Tyrus Fortune have just loved having a filthy Irishwoman he scorned on the best of days fling her dirty self at him, soiling his starched, crisp clothes?

She began combing out the tangles in her hair. Actually, she thought, for a moment it had seemed that he might have welcomed her into his arms, the way he had looked at her, taken a step toward her. She snorted at herself. That was ludicrous. She was imagining things.

But she was sure she had not been imagining the desire that surged between them. What devil had prompted her to name that calf Desiree? Good lord, she might as well have propositioned Ty right there in front of Paul and Silas.

If she hadn't been so filthy and he so clean, she just might have given in to the pull she had felt between them. Thank goodness the two farmhands--and copious amounts of filth--had been there. No, she refused to let herself descend into anymore "if only's". She could not have Ty and he would not want more than a tumble with her if she could.

She finished combing her hair and gathered her things together on a bench. Her wrap lay there but she would put that on after Ruby helped her dump the bath water from the tub. She pulled open the door and began to call, "Ruby, I'm ready to..."

She came to a halt. It was not Ruby waiting for her in the kitchen, but Ty.

Except for a single candle the kitchen was dark, and except for Ty, the kitchen was deserted. He was sitting on a bench by the table but rose when she opened the door. Her breath caught at the sight

of him dimly lit by the candle. He was apparently waiting for his
own bath because he wore only his robe and slippers. A towel and
comb lay beside him.

The light from her own candle behind her flowed out to join
his, and she realized just how little she had on. Not enough. She
needed more between her and Ty than just a thin, cotton shift and
desire. The width of the Atlantic Ocean might do it.

She clutched at the neck of her shift but there was nothing
she could pull around her. She backed into the bathing chamber,
feeling for her robe. "Ruby was going to stay and help me dump
the bathwater."

"I sent Ruby to bed," he said. His voice seemed raspy and he
cleared his throat. Much of his face was in shadow, but she could
tell that he was looking at her, that his jaw was clenching. "I told
her I would take care of it."

"That was very kind of you."

Her searching fingers found the bench, began to feel along its
length for her robe while she pretended to a casual indifference she
was far from feeling. She needed that robe. His eyes were in deep
shadow but she could feel their pressure on her, touching her neck
and waist and breasts. She glanced down at herself and gulped.
Good Lord! She had never noticed before just how thin this shift
was. She could see the pink of her nipples showing through the
thin, slightly dampened material. And if she could see them... She
glanced up. Oh, yes, that's exactly where he was looking.

She switched from trying to gather the material close about
her to pulling it away. That didn't help. Then it gaped at the neck
giving him a different view. She gave up any pretense of noncha-
lance and whirled and grabbed her robe, slinging it around her.
She jabbed her arms wildly at the sleeves but couldn't seem to find
them. She had grabbed the hem, not the neck. She had it upside
down. She struggled with the mass of material but it seemed to be

fighting her.

"Here," Ty said.

She glanced up to find him standing in front of her. He took the robe from her hands, shook it out and held it out for her.

She lifted her chin, determined not to let him notice just how much she was trembling. She put her arms into the sleeves of the robe and it was like stepping back into his embrace. His heat and scent wafted over her, a scent that was becoming all too familiar, all too enticing, all too addictive.

Standing behind her, he adjusted her robe onto her shoulders and wrapped it around her, along with his arms. But she danced away from that dangerous embrace, bending to get her brush and comb and the clothes she had removed. "I'll just leave you to your bath, then," she said as she headed quickly out the door.

"Irish," he called and she halted, her breath gone.

This shouldn't be this hard. He's just a man. An extremely handsome, virile man whose kisses made her toes curl, but just a man. She turned back toward him. "Yes?" she answered, proud that her voice did not betray just how shaky she felt.

"I..." He was reaching for her. His fingers brushed her cheek. She closed her eyes.

Then she felt his hand snatched away. Her eyes flew open to see him straighten, to see him look away, rubbing that hand with the other as if it had been burnt.

"Good night," he said, abruptly.

She backed out of the room, her things clutched tightly to her. "Good night." She glanced toward the big kettle over the well-banked fire. "I'm sure there's plenty of hot water left."

"Yes," he answered. "There is."

She backed farther away, past the table where his candle still flamed, past the cabinet, to the door. "If you're sure you don't need anything else?" *Fool! Of course he doesn't need anything else, especially not you.*

"No, I have everything I need," he said.

Yes, he does, she thought. *He is handsome and wealthy, he has a wonderful family, and he has the ideal woman all picked out to marry. He has everything he needs.*

She turned and fled down the hall and up the stairs to her room.

Ty watched Irish leave. Ruby had left plenty of hot water for him, but right now he was thinking that what he needed was cold water, and lots of it. He dumped Irish's bathwater and he recognized the spicy scent of calendula wafting up from the water. He could have guessed that Irish was not the kind of woman to use the sweet scent of lavender or rose oil in her bath.

He had to get his mind off her.

He began filling the tub for his own bath. Betsy was who he planned to marry. She was who he should be thinking of, not the pale pink nipples that had peeked so enticingly at him from beneath Irish's thin shift. Not the slender length of bare ankle and calf he had seen, nor the dark triangle at the jointure of her thighs that the dampened material had revealed.

He shook his head. Betsy. He tried to picture Betsy. She was… No, she did not have red hair, damn it! And her eyes weren't green, either.

Ty stepped into the tub and sank into the water, trying to remember. Blue. Betsy's eyes were blue. Weren't they? He dunked his head and began scrubbing his hair. Betsy's hair was brown. That, he remembered. It had just been a while since he had seen her. That's why he couldn't remember the color of her eyes. Tomorrow he'd go see her. He'd smile and they would laugh together, and the sight of her sweet… The sight of her sweet…something or other would

wipe the picture of a red-haired, green-eyed keeper-of- secrets completely out of his mind.

Irish was still awake. She heard Ty come down the hall and go
into his room. In the darkness she looked at the wall that separated
her room from his. She could hear him moving around, putting
his things away. She couldn't hear them, but she could well imagine the creak of the ropes when he got into bed, the rustle of the
sheets as he slid between them. She shut her eyes, but she could
still imagine it—still imagine him--all too well. His long, lean legs,
his muscled chest with the dark, springy hair she had glimpsed at
the vee of his robe, and felt when he had kissed her, and when his
body had lain across hers right here in this very bed the first night
he had come home.

This was his bed. She had wondered what the brother who was
off studying in England was like. From the descriptions Mariette
and Matt and Nate had given her she had pictured a stiff, tyrannical man. Ty, the tyrant they had called him as children.

But they also had a great love for their older brother. Now she
knew why.

Ty was stiff, but he was not unyielding. They had called him
tyrannical, but that was a child's view. If he was demanding, it
seemed that it was himself he demanded the most from, as if he
should be the one to set the example for proper behavior and he
dare not fall.

Irish kicked at the covers, tossing them aside. It might be good
for Ty to fail at something, to have a bit of a fall, she thought, to
dent that stubborn pride of his just a bit. Then he might find out
that no one—not even he-—ould constantly meet the impossibly
high standards he set.

She flipped over and punched her pillow. Well good old Betsy wasn't going to pull him down. Not that paragon. She hated to think what the pair of them would be like in another ten years. All Betsy would do is prop him up, stiffen him up even more. And she didn't mean that one certain part of him, either.

Then she began to wonder if Betsy stirred him *that* way. They had seemed the perfect lord and lady at the fair. If there was any passion there, Irish hadn't seen it. When he looked at Betsy it didn't seem to affect her in the least, not the way one of his looks could melt Irish's insides. Maybe Betsy was just better at hiding what she felt than Irish was. But if she had had to place a wager on it, she would have said that Betsy's cool demeanor went all the way through. Ty's glances, his touches, his smile had not melted anything.

But then, she hadn't seen Ty give Betsy one of those smoldering *I-could-eat-you-alive* looks that he gave her every time their paths crossed. Ty seemed to be courting Betsy. Did he think passion was not necessary to a good marriage? Or did he simply think that all passion was beneath him? She chuckled at that last thought. Beneath him is exactly where passion should lie. Where she would like to lie.

No, she thought. No. She was leaving just as soon as Mrs. Fortune came back. There could never be anything at all between Ty and her except a distant friendship. Let him have his Betsy. Let him have his cool, dispassionate marriage bed. And please, God, give me the strength not to pull him down on top of me and be that passion beneath him. Because beneath him was the only place she could have in Ty's life. Beneath him in passion, perhaps, but also beneath him socially, beneath him in proper behavior, and beneath him in wealth. All those things could be true and she could still find happiness with Ty if they didn't matter to him. But they did.

In his eyes, she would never be his equal and that was the only thing that mattered.

Chapter Twelve

Irish and Ty and Charlie were just sitting down to breakfast the next morning when Nate burst through the door, and strutted across the room to the table as if he were lord of the morning.

Ty jumped up from his place, showing the most excitement she had ever seen in him. "How is Mariette?"

Irish could not help but laugh out loud. "From the size of the grin on Nate's face, Ty, I would assume that all is well."

Ty leaned on the table, glaring across at his younger brother. "Well? Is she all right? Don't just stand there grinning like a fool, Nate, tell us what happened."

Nate struck a proud pose. "That's *Uncle* Nate, if you please."

"So she had the baby?" Ty asked.

"Yep." With a wicked grin Nate turned to fill a plate.

Ty pounded the table with his fist making the silverware jump. "Then tell us about it. How is Mariette?"

"I'll be going on down to Charles Town in a little while in case anyone needs anything," Nate said over his shoulder.

"Blast you, you nincompoop!" Ty thundered. "Are you going to tell us about Mariette or not?"

Nate turned with his plate in hand and held up an admonishing finger. "That's *Uncle* Nincompoop, if you please."

Irish had to hold her sides she was now laughing so hard. Nate was bursting to tell them the news but he just had to torment his brother first. Ty might put on a stern, polished exterior, but when it came to his family, he obviously cared deeply. Nate knew just how to rile his oh, so proper brother.

"Oh, Nate, er, Uncle Nate," she said. "Do sit down and tell us all the news."

With her plea, he turned and set his plate on the table, pulled out a chair, and sat down, his face alight with happiness. He grinned up at Ty. "Mariette's fine. It was a long labor, but Sally said that's normal the first time."

He popped open a biscuit and slathered butter on it as if finished with his story but Irish could see the twinkle in his eyes, and that he was biting his lip to keep from telling the rest.

"So what did she have?" Ty bent over the table and Irish thought Nate had better tell Ty now or his brother just might leap across the table and strangle the details out of him.

Nate knew Ty's limit, too. He put down the knife and biscuit. "Well, you know Alejandro wanted a son?"

They nodded.

He leaned back in his chair. "Alejandro's happy."

"A boy!" Ty crowed, sitting down with a goofy look on his face.

Irish shook her head. "Poor Mrs. Fortune. She was so hoping for another girl in her family."

"Oh, Mama's quite happy," Nate said.

She smiled. "I'm sure she is, Uncle Nate, so long as Mariette and the baby are doing fine."

"No," he said, "I mean, Mama's happy because Mariette had a girl."

Ty was back on his feet. "I thought you said she had a boy?"

Nate grinned broadly. "She did."

It took a moment for the implication to sink in, then Irish and Charlie and Ty all exclaimed together, "Twins?"

Irish didn't think it was possible for anyone to grin any broader, but Nate did. He nodded. "Twins," he confirmed.

"How marvelous!" Charlie said.

"Well, I'll be!" Irish thought of Mariette with her very own babies. Two of them!

Ty sat down and leaned his head back and laughed, a rich full laughter. "Twins! Serves her right. I hope those two little rascals give her just as much trouble as she and Matt gave everyone."

Irish leaned forward. "What do they look like? Are they strong? What did she name them?"

Nate shrugged. "They look like babies. Red, wrinkled, and from the sound of their screams, they have strong lungs if nothing else. Sally said they were a bit small because they were twins and a little early, but that they're both fine. Ryan has dark hair and eyes like his father but Rachel's eyes might be blue. Sally said baby's eyes can change, but it looks like she might have blue eyes."

"Rachel and Ryan," Ty said quietly, a soft smile on his lips.

Irish thought she might have the same melting look on her own face. Babies. Somehow they could tug at the heart of every woman and weaken the strongest of men. If Ty could look like this at the birth of his niece and nephew, how would he react to the birth of his own babies? It was something she would never see, now would she?

Ty slapped the table. "I'm going up there." He arched a brow at Nate. "You're not the only new uncle around here."

"I can't take you up there today, Ty," Nate said. "I've got a cargo waiting for me in Charles Town that I should have picked up yesterday."

"That's all right, Nate," Ty said. "I'll take the carriage. I wanted to go see Miss Hall today, anyway. The Hall plantation is on the way."

Irish picked up a biscuit and bit into it. It tasted like sawdust. What difference did it make to her that he was going to see Betsy?

"If you're off to your sister's for the day, Ty," said Charlie, "I think I'll take Nate up on his offer of a ride into Charles Town. There are some supplies I need to order and I need to hire a few more workers."

"I'll be ready to leave in an hour," Nate told him. "Irish, do you want to go, or do you need anything?"

She shook her head. "No, I have to tend some things here. Maybe when you return you can take me up there to see the twins."

Nate grinned. "I'll just be three or four days. Then I'll come get you. Just wait 'til you see them!"

"I'll be on pins and needles until then," she answered, grinning. She glanced at Ty. He was gazing at her, but when he saw her look at him, he turned away, tossed down his napkin, and stood up.

"I might be a while. I expect to have lunch with the Halls," he said, and it seemed to Irish that he was speaking only to her, as if he wanted to let her know that Betsy was who he wanted and who he would have.

She refused to let him see how much that hurt. After all, what he was doing--where he was going--was for the best, and they both knew it. She tossed her head and gave him a bright smile. "Say hello to Betsy for me." And then, bedeviled, she batted her lashes and added, "I'm sure the two of you will have a proper good time."

She thought she could actually hear the grinding of his teeth. He turned and she watched him limp away from the table, his ankle now healed enough to need only a cane.

Charlie and Nate also excused themselves from the table, Nate saying something about his ship and Charlie to go pack for his trip. That's when she realized that she and Ty would be alone together in the house for the next two or three nights.

Heaven help her.

Except for a light in the dining room, the house was dark and quiet when Ty returned home that evening. He freshened up in the deserted kitchen then went through the house to the dining room, hoping that a plate had been left for him. Irish sat alone at the big table, a single candle reflecting off the gleaming surface and turning her skin to pale gold.

She looked up when he entered, a forkful of food poised halfway to her mouth. She set the fork back on her plate, her hand reaching up to pull her robe close about her, but not before he had had an enticing glimpse of her creamy skin and the low cut nightgown she wore.

She tightened the sash at her waist and tossed her head proudly, her mane of glory not quite tamed by the braid that lay down her back. "I didn't think you would be returning since it is so late."

At first he was not sure he could speak, she was so beautiful sitting there in dishabille. He had tried hard all day to get her out of his mind, but it had not worked.

On his way to Betsy's this morning Irish had thundered by him on Renegade, her skirts and hair flying, giving him a glimpse of shapely leg to take with him to the Hall plantation. That glimpse had haunted his entire visit with Betsy. Betsy's eyes were a blue-gray, he had noted, but he couldn't help comparing them to a pair of brightly sparkling green ones.

Betsy was so quiet, answering his questions softly, seldom offering her own opinion, but if she did and he disagreed with her, she meekly submitted to him. What would it be like to live with a woman who never stood up to him, never crossed him? Would it be blissful peace or baleful boredom? He was beginning to fear it would be the latter. Every soft, sweet word from Betsy's mouth had made him think of the fiery exchanges he had had with Irish--fiery, but exhilarating.

Then he had kissed Betsy. She had allowed the kiss, but had remained cool, composed, almost detached. When he had tried to deepen the kiss, to find some fire there, she had politely pushed him away. She had not blushed at his advances. She had not been in a dither. She had not been angry. Or breathless.

"I thought about staying at Mariette's," he answered. "But the chaos there was beyond belief."

Leaning heavily on his cane he could not help but wince as he limped toward the table.

Irish jumped up and hurried over to him, placing a hand beneath his elbow. "You need to get off that ankle," she said, pulling out a chair with the other hand and pushing him into it. "You push yourself too much. You need to let that ankle heal."

"I'll be fine," he said. "I don't need you fussing over me." But he had to admit to himself that he did rather like it. Betsy hadn't fussed over him. She had been sweet and kind, but she hadn't fussed. She had asked about his ankle, but not insisted that he stay off of it when he had told her it was fine. They had taken a stroll about the garden.

"Have you eaten?" she asked.

He shook his head.

"I'll get you a plate." She disappeared into the kitchen.

It was late, his ankle hurt him, and he was tired. Taking a cue from Irish's state of undress, he took off his Steinkirk and shrugged out of his jacket.

Several minutes later she returned with a tray for him. The plate was heaped with enough food for two men and there were thick slices of bread on another, a bowl of soup, and tea. She set it all before him with no more than a raised brow at the sight of him at the table without a coat, and then returned to her place at the other end of the table. He thought that even if they were married for years, he and Betsy would never sit alone at a table at night relaxed this way.

"Now tell me about those twins," she said.

He frowned, looking at the distance between them. With his good leg he kicked the chair next to him away from the table. "Move down here."

Her eyes widened and she glanced around as if very much aware of how alone they were.

"I'm not going to bite," he told her. "I just don't want to shout."

Her head came up proudly and her shoulders straightened. He suppressed a chuckle--she appeared as if she were preparing to enter the lion's den.

But his Irish was not about to back down from any challenge. She got up and moved her plate, bringing the candle closer, as well. He frowned at himself. *His* Irish? When did she become *his?*

"The twins?" she urged.

"They were a handful," he said, chuckling. "One or the other of them was either wet, hungry, or crying the whole time I was there. Mariette used to call *me* a tyrant. Those two little babies have got everyone in that house running to take care of them."

Irish was eating automatically, but her eyes were wide with wonder as she listened intently to him. Suddenly he realized how eager he had been to get home and tell her about Mariette's twins.

"Did you hold them?"

He scoffed at the idea and shook his head.

Her mouth dropped open as if she couldn't believe anyone could be around babies and not hold them. He had to laugh.

"I'm teasing you. Of course I held them." He held up his left arm. "Where do you think I got this spot on my sleeve?" He was surprised at himself that for once, a stain on his clothes did not bother him.

"What are they like?" she asked. "Other than wet, hungry, or crying, that is."

"Ryan is the bigger of the two and was born first, but Rachel is the queen of the crib, I think. I do believe her eyes are going to be blue. Her hair is black as sin and curly. She's going to tie every heart in the county in knots when she's older."

She leaned her cheek into her hand and sighed. "I love babies," she said with a faraway, wistful look.

He could well imagine Irish with her own babies. They would have her red curly hair and they would squall louder than the twins. "You'll have some of your own someday," he said.

She jerked upright, and began to busy herself pushing food around on her plate, as if running from the idea. It made him wonder why she didn't have children already, why she wasn't married. She was certainly old enough, and it wasn't from lack of suitors. Did it have something to do with how she hid everything about her past from them?

"Why aren't you married, Irish?" he asked softly.

Her chin went up. "Why aren't you?"

He scowled, noting how she had again evaded a question about herself by turning it back on him. "That's—"

"None of my business?" she answered for him. She leaned toward him with a too sweet smile. "Oh, I forgot. You have a plan in mind. The lovely Miss Betsy, right?" She stabbed at a piece of venison with a vengeance that belied her smile. "Do tell me how the courtship is coming along."

He refused to answer her baiting, jabbing at his own venison.

She tsk-tsked at him. "Not so good, hmm?"

He gripped his fork as if it were a weapon. "At least she is open and honest with me," he threw at her, "which is more than I can say for you."

"But it isn't me you're courting, is it?" She tossed her fork down into her half-full plate and stood up, beginning to gather her dishes.

He grabbed her wrist before she could escape. "Do you want it to be?"

She wrenched free and began to stomp away, her dishes left on the table. "Don't delude yourself."

He shoved back his chair and grabbed his cane to limp after her. "I don't have to delude myself. You're deluding me enough."

She swung around to face him. "I've never lied to you."

He towered over her, feeling thunderous. "Haven't you?"

Her fists went to her hips and her chin jutted out. "Name one lie I've told you. Go ahead. Just one."

"You said…you…" He stumbled to a halt.

"Ha!" she threw at him and headed for the stairs.

He went after her, catching her by the hem of her robe half way up the stairs. "You've lied by omission," he threw at her triumphantly.

"And just what have I omitted?"

"Everything!"

Having no answer to that she jerked her robe free and stomped on up the remaining steps with him fast at her heels. He caught her again just outside her bedroom door, snagging her arm and spinning her around and up against the wall. He trapped her there, placing a blockading arm between her and her room, then leaned into her.

"Who are you?" he demanded. "From what I've seen of you—your carriage, your fine manners, your speech—you're no common trollop, so just who are you?"

There was fire in her eyes and the color had drained from her skin but she was undaunted. She lifted her chin. "Molly Malone, Maggie Magee, Moira O'Malley," she sneered. "Pick one. I'll answer to it."

"I don't want some common Irish name. I want to know yours. I want to know *you*." He narrowed his eyes, watching her there, up against the wall and still defiant. She was so beautiful she took his breath away. His breath and his good sense. He let go of his cane, allowing it to clatter to the floor to reach up and take her chin into his hand, to turn her face up to his.

He had left his dinner practically untouched, but it was a different kind of hunger he was feeling now and he knew exactly where he could find sustenance. His mouth devoured hers and she allowed it. She answered, not with a polite pushing away when he plunged into her mouth with his tongue, but with a hunger of her own, strong enough to match his, and he knew that tonight he would at last know Irish--in the oldest way men have known women throughout the ages.

Chapter Thirteen

At the first touch of Ty's lips on hers, the anger drained out of Irish and all she wanted was more of that touch. Yes, she wanted him to court her. But she knew that nothing could ever come of it because she could never let him know who she was.

But just for now, just for a while, couldn't she enjoy his kisses, revel in his touch? Glory in giving herself to this man?

She'd had plenty of suitors in the last two years but few of them had interested her, and none of them had made her feel like throwing caution to the four winds, and herself into their arms. Not until Ty. There may never be another after him. For once she was going to take what life offered and take it while she could.

She lifted her arms and slid them around his waist to hold on to what she could have of him.

She would be leaving soon and Ty could go back to courting Betsy. For surely he would want that saint gracing the halls of the fine home he was building, and not some Irish woman with a name she dared not say aloud. She would wish them well. Her heart would be breaking but she would not let Ty know that about her, either.

His kiss was magically melting her insides and his hands began to work their sorcery on her back as he pulled her closer to him. He molded her body to his, breast to chest, belly to belly, thigh to thigh. She could feel the swell of him against her, proof that the melting he was doing to her was affecting him in quite another way.

Her hands were busy gathering every scrap of sensation they could, running over his back and shoulders. His body was magnificent with hard sculpted muscles. She could tell that even through the fabric of his waistcoat and shirt. What wonders would she discover once her fingers found flesh?

His hands had found her buttocks and hers answered in kind, and they both pulled each other closer there. She could feel herself opening in anticipation. She felt his buttocks flex and tighten as her fingers dug into them. Ty's had been especially nice to look at. Now she was gaining a more intimate knowledge of them. She never knew a man's buttocks could feel so good.

But she wanted flesh to touch and to taste. She slipped her hands up between them and began working at the buttons of his waistcoat, pulling at the tail of his shirt until at last she found what she was looking for, warm flesh, firm and hard against her hand. The ridges of his flat belly enticed her as she slid her hands upward.

His hands were just as busy, searching just as hard, opening the front of her robe, pushing it to the edges of her shoulders. She helped him by shrugging out of it, letting it fall to the floor behind her.

His fingers traced along the neckline of her chemise as if searching for a way inside. At last he nudged it off one shoulder, pushed it downward, skimmed his fingers down the slope of her breast and found the peak. Her indrawn breath seemed to spur him to new endeavors. His fingers slid to the underside of her breast to lift it as he bent to take the tip into his mouth.

She could not help but gasp in surprise. She had not known that that part of herself, in his hand or in his mouth, could become an instrument of such exquisite pleasure. Her fingers stopped, her breath stopped as she simply stood there in amazement. At last she said the only thing she was capable of, a simple, "Oh!" of wonder.

She felt rather than heard his chuckle and it pleased her to know that he seemed to be enjoying what he was doing to her as much as she was. Then her thoughts turned to another path. Was there a place on him that could give him pleasure like this? If so, she was going to find it. Later. In a few minutes. Her fingers on his chest turned to claws and she clutched at him. His head came up with a quick gasp and she knew she had found that place. Were his breasts as sensitive as hers?

Finding his nipples she pinched them lightly. Oh yes. He wouldn't have gasped like that and stood stock still waiting for her to continue if she hadn't given him pleasure. It was her turn to chuckle. She wanted to throw her head back and laugh out loud.

But he was more impatient than she. With one arm he drew her close. The other slid down her body to the jointure of her thighs to press and play. There was *more?* She opened to him and his hand plunged between her legs sending searing sheets of pleasure upward, outward, inward. Oh yes, there was more. And more. She was weak with more.

There was only one place this could lead and she began to nudge him toward it. Inching backward, toward her door, she felt behind her, finding the doorframe, the door, and at last the latch. She opened the door, pushed it open, all while feeling so weak-kneed she wasn't sure she could stand.

By this time she was not the only one headed for the bed. It was an erotic dance between them, and now he was leading, urging her across the floor. She felt the edge of the high bed against her hip and he lifted her up to sit there while his fingers pulled at her chemise, trying to find their way beyond it and back to that nest between her thighs. She reached up to push aside his waistcoat and he took a moment to let her pull it down his arms and banish it to the floor.

She scooted back onto the bed and he followed. Four clatters announced the discarding of two pairs of shoes and she lay back, pulling him down on top of her. She felt him loosening his breeches and she reached to help him slide them down, her hands at last touching his bare behind. She pulled him to her until he rested against her, his thighs between hers.

That was when they heard the sound. A clicking sound, then a snuffle, coming into the room. Irish relaxed. She knew exactly what it was. But Ty started to jump up.

She grabbed him by the shirt. "It's just my dog, Paddy," she told him. "He was sleeping downstairs and just came up."

They heard the dog settle down on the rug beside the bed with a heavy sigh.

"Irish, I'm sorry."

"Sorry? For what?" She felt him begin to move away.

"For this! How can we do this? I must have been out of my mind." He smiled at her and caressed her cheek. "I was out of my mind. Touching you just once seems to do that to me. But I cannot take your virginity like this."

Her virginity? He was concerned about her virginity? How could he even think of a thing like that right now? How could he even *think?* All she could do was want. If it was only her damned virginity he was worried about she could solve that problem easily enough and they could get back to exploring those wonders she never knew existed.

She grabbed a fistful of his shirt and yanked him back down to her, nose-to-nose. "Do you really think that a woman captured on the high seas by Spanish privateers and sold into slavery for six months could actually still be a virgin?"

Even in this dim light she could see the shock on his face, a shock that turned to tenderness and sympathy. "You were...?"

"Yes. More than once. Now can we..."

"Irish, I'm so sorry. I didn't know."

She lifted her head to look directly into his eyes. "I don't want you feeling sorry for me. Not now. God, not now, Ty. I only want you to feel. Feel me. Let me feel you. You are giving me something right now I never knew existed, such pleasure and glory I think I might die from it. But if I don't die, then this will have gone a long way to wiping out some of the horrors of the past."

He rested his forehead on hers for a long moment, then raised his head to kiss her sweetly on the cheek before rolling off her and off the bed.

She felt bereft, betrayed. Could he not accept what had happened to her? Did he consider her "soiled goods" and unfit for him even though it was no fault of her own? She knew now that hearts really could break. She turned her head into the pillow and tried to hold back the sobs.

Chapter Fourteen

SHE FELT HIS HAND ON HER SHOULDER AND TRIED TO SHRUG it off.

"Irish, I'm not abandoning you," he said. "I just wanted to do this right."

She turned to see him stripping off his breeches and socks and shirt. His clothes were coming off, not going on. He wasn't abandoning her. And he was beautiful. Maybe that was not the right word to use for a man, but it was the right word to use for this man.

He sat down beside her. "I will be as tender with you as any man could be, Irish."

She was as close to tears then as she had ever been, even in midst of the horror of that Spanish ship. On the ship she had been angry. Now she felt a healing beginning to flow into her. "I know," she said. "I know. You couldn't be anything else."

Gently he caressed her face, kissing in the wake of his trailing fingers, her forehead, her cheeks, her eyes, her lips. His hand trailed down the column of her throat, along her collarbone and down pushing her chemise with it. She lifted her hips for him to slide it on down her legs and off.

He trailed the fingers of one hand lightly down her body from face to breast to stomach, to her thigh, and then her toes, and she could feel the wonder in his touch, as if every bit of her were precious. Lightly, so lightly, he ran his fingertips over her again and again, touching her everywhere. Then he used his hands to touch her, running them over her, not just her breasts, but every part, down her arms and legs, her sides, her feet. She was beginning to feel lethargic, relaxed.

Then he touched her breast and her lethargy melted away, her body again coming to full alert.

He bent to kiss her then, all over, running his tongue over parts of her that she never knew would be stirred by such an action.

Lying down beside her, his attention went back to her breasts, one then the other as if he were trying to decide which he preferred. He lifted his head to look down at her and she lifted her hands to his head to urge him back to her breasts. Her fingers played with his hair, loosening the ribbon that held it, pulling it free.

Propping himself up on his elbow, he stopped what he was about to look at her, lit by shafts of moonlight. "Are you stealing another hair ribbon?" he asked, and she could hear the teasing laughter in his voice.

She shrugged. "I never did get my hairpins back."

He bent to nibble at her ear. "I will buy you a whole case."

"No," she said.

"No?"

She shook her head. "I don't want you buying me things. I don't want anything from you except this."

"This I will be glad to give you," he answered and lifted himself over her, pushing her knees apart to nest between them.

He reached down between their bodies to cup her, splaying his fingers into her most intimate place. She felt an embarrassment at how she was melting there, how her moisture was draining from her, how his touch only exacerbated her melting. But his groan reassured her that he found only pleasure in her readiness for him.

He caressed her and she thought she would come up off the bed, gasping for the breath that the shock of pleasure took from her. There was more. More and more and more. So much she was not sure she could contain it.

His hand left her and she felt him position himself and could not help but stiffen in fear. He paused and looked at her.

"Irish?" he asked. "Are you all right?"

She shook away her fear. This was Ty. She clutched at his buttocks, straining to pull him closer, to force him to enter her. "I won't be if you don't finish what you've started!"

Giving an evil little chuckle he entered her, but not far enough. He pulled away and she clawed at his backside, lifting her hips up, trying to keep him in her. But he eluded her. Again he thrust forward, entering further, then backing away, again and again, teasing, tormenting until she was nearly frantic. Then, at last, in one long thrust, he entered her fully and rested against her, not moving for long moments.

He was hard and warm and wonderful within her. He filled her completely. That warmth within her seemed to flow to all parts of her body making her want even more.

Ty kissed her, thrusting his tongue into her mouth the same way he was thrusting into her, with the same rhythm. She answered that rhythm, that thrusting with her own tongue, with the lifting of her hips to meet him. Then the spasms came, harder and harder, causing her to throw her head back, gasping shallow breaths while he held her tightly, pressing hard against her until she was almost done. Then she felt him within her, fast and hard, bringing on more of her own pleasure before they both were done, sated, fulfilled, panting.

One of his hands went behind her head and he played with her braid. Then he chuckled. "We have to do this again," he said.

"Again?" she asked weakly. How could he even think about doing this again right now?

He chuckled. "I said I wanted to do this right for you."

"I can't imagine anything more right. I can't imagine feeling any better. I can't think how another time could possibly compare to this. I–"

He kissed her, stopping her. "You certainly do bolster a man up."

"Oh! So you were just hoping for compliments on your performance, were you?"

"No, there really is something I missed."

"What?"

He pulled her braid from under her and tickled the end of her nose with it. "I wanted to loosen your hair."

She laughed. "That's all?"

He shrugged. "I had to think of some excuse to do this again. Now that I've had a taste of you, do you think I can just walk away?"

She turned her face away for a moment to gather her thoughts. Yes, she had expected him to just walk away. It was Betsy he wanted, wasn't it? The perfect Betsy who would be the perfect hostess for him...his equal in Charles Town society. He did not want an unknown Irish woman cluttering up his future. But maybe it wasn't his whole future he meant. Maybe he wanted only a few days of her before he had enough. Fine. That was just fine with her. She was leaving anyway. He didn't know it yet, but she was sure he would be relieved when he saw the last of her sail away to Charles Town.

"I doubt that you could walk away even if you wanted to," she said. "That ankle of yours still seems to be giving you some trouble."

He laughed. "Imp. You know what I mean."

She wasn't sure she did know what he meant but she just

shrugged.

He wrapped her braid around his hand. "But I think it's time you told me something about yourself, who you are."

Good lord, but the man was persistent! "I would think that after what we just did that you would know quite a lot about me."

"I know that you are a woman whose great passion would surpass any man's wildest dreams. I know that you respond to my touch with the same enthusiasm you have for everything you do. I know that you stir my own passions in a way that no other woman has ever done." He looked down at her as if hungry for that more of her that she could never give him. "But I don't even know your name."

She wished she could tell him. She wished she could confess everything to him. She wished she could tell him something. But she didn't want to see that expression on his face turn to abhorrence. She didn't want his pride torn between what was now between them and his upright standing in the community.

She wanted him to stay right where he was forever. She wanted to stay right there under him, cradling him between her thighs and being cradled in his arms in return, but she had to distract him somehow. She pushed at his chest to get him off her, wiggling as if she were uncomfortable.

Immediately he lifted himself and moved to lie beside her. She stretched and forced a big yawn, turning her back and snuggling down under the sheet.

Sighing, he pulled the sheet up over them both.

It was not long before she was sure he was asleep. She could hear his quiet breathing and feel the even rise and fall of his chest.

"Kathleen," she whispered. "My name is Kathleen."

She was sure she had not spoken loudly enough for him to hear, but he must have heard her because he put his arm around her and pulled her close. His face was against her shoulder and she felt him smile.

The next morning Irish awoke to a warm contentment curled against Ty's back. He stretched and turned to her, nuzzling into the curve of her neck. Birds were busy singing in the live oaks and she could feel warm streaks of sunlight across the bed.

Her eyes flew open. Sunlight? Had she really slept that long? A big yawn was rudely interrupted when she remembered what day it was. Oh no! Hastily she began kicking free of the covers, shoving at Ty's arm across her trying to get up.

With a muffled "mmm" he pulled her back to him, his hand brushing her breast. Her breath caught and her whole body seemed to come to attention, but she shoved those feelings aside along with his searching hand.

"Ty! Wake up!"

With the urging of one arched brow, one of his eyes came half-open and she could see his unspoken question.

"You have to get back to your own room! This is wash day."

She managed to slide out from under his arm and out of the bed. She began to gather clothes, sorting his from hers. By this time he was well awake with his head propped on one elbow watching her every movement, a grin on his face. She tossed his clothes to him and began to dress.

She had her chemise on and her stockings and petticoat, and was reaching for her gown when she noticed that he was still watching her. "Ty, you have to get up!"

"I would much rather lie here watching you," he said languidly.

She pulled on her gown and shoved his clothes closer to him.

"There's no time. Dee-dee always comes up to strip the beds on wash day. If she finds you in here…"

He rolled out of bed, clothes in hand, and was already sliding his arms into his shirt like a soldier rousted and ready for battle.

In moments he had his breeches on and the rest of his clothes and shoes in his hand, and heading for the door. He paused just long enough to kiss her lightly, then he peeked out the door before slipping out of her room.

She ran to the door, catching him. "Ty! Don't forget to muss your bed so that--"

He turned, his shirt loose and flowing about him. She was stopped by his hand beneath her chin, lifting her face to his for another kiss. His long dark hair swept forward, brushing her cheek. "I'll take care of it," he promised and his thumb skimmed across her lips in a parting caress.

Irish turned back into her room, her lips still tingling from his touch. She washed and finished dressing, then began pulling the linens from her own bed. She felt a pang of guilt when she saw the stains on the sheets. What she and Ty had done last night was wrong. But, God help her, she was not sorry. Gathering the sheets and her soiled clothes into a bundle she hurried down the stairs to help prepare breakfast. She met Dee-dee just starting up the stairs.

Irish ate a hurried breakfast in the kitchen and let Ruby take something into the dining room for Ty. Besides getting a late start on her day's work, she didn't think she could sit down to a civilized meal with him just yet.

By noon the wash was done and drying, Irish had exercised Renegade and visited old Pete, taking him a basket of food as Mrs. Fortune had asked her, and done a dozen other things. She was returning to the house when she saw Ty in the workers' compound.

The workers were already work-stained and sweaty, but Ty looked like he had just stepped out of his room after a good bath.

How did he do it? she wondered. She had seen him out earlier walking the dikes with one of the overseers, checking them for leaks and soundness, and later sending off a crew to weed one of the fields.

As Irish helped Ruby gather in the dry laundry she watched Ty with the men. For a few minutes they seemed to have nothing better to do than swap stories and clap each other on the back. Then Ty asked a few questions and the men started talking. Ty stood with hands clasped behind him, head slightly bowed as he listened intently to what the men had to say, their listing of things that needed repair, a roof here, a door there, or a broken step. He walked around the compound with them and they pointed out several things that needed to be done.

With a few curt instructions Ty sent the men in various directions and by the time she and Ruby had finished folding the laundry into baskets, ladders were already going up and hammers were already pounding.

Ty turned from the repairs he had set in motion to see Irish watching him. She quickly went back to her work, pretending an indifference to his presence. Did she not feel the heat of his desire from all the way across the compound? It should have been scorching her, charring the edges of her apron, singeing the ends of her hair, stirring the passions he knew she possessed. But she went about her work as calmly as ever. Did she not feel it, too? Was she unaffected by what they had experienced together the night before? Or worse, had she determined that there would be no repetition of it?

His hands clenched and he actually took a step in her direction before he stopped himself. He watched her efficient directing of the servants in their work and saw how she was not loath to plunge in and help wherever an extra pair of hands was needed.

He could not help but smile inwardly when she paused a moment to tuck several long loose strands of hair back into her cap. Then, in the age-old way of a woman who is aware of male eyes upon her, she smoothed the hair at her nape, brushing it upward into her cap before she bent to take up one of the baskets of laundry to carry it into the house. Her swinging gait and swaying hips gave further evidence that she knew he was watching her, and that she was not opposed to his watching.

She *would* be his again tonight. And best of all, he knew something about her no one else in the colony knew. He knew her name.

His mother had been right. He just had to wait until Irish trusted him. Then she would tell him the rest. Until then, he would be patient until she was ready.

With Mrs. Fortune gone there was more than enough to keep Irish busy, and to keep her from thinking about another night alone in the house with Ty. But by the time she was setting the table for supper that was all she could think about.

She managed to find a few minutes to wash up and don a clean gown before facing him at the table. She was sure he would show up as immaculately groomed as he always did and she didn't want to look any more disreputable than she could help.

She pulled her hair back as neatly and sleekly as she could, trying her best to tame the curly wisps that constantly escaped confinement. When she and Dee-dee had tidied the upstairs rooms that afternoon, Irish had found her pins in a neat pile on Nate's chest of drawers and was indeed glad to have them back. She shoved the last pin into place and coiled both of Ty's hair ribbons together beside her brush to return to him later.

He was waiting for her when she entered the dining room and he was, as she had come to expect of him, elegantly dressed with not a wrinkle to be seen anywhere from the coat that lay smoothly over his wide shoulders, down the cream colored waistcoat that matched the breeches that fit snugly over hip and thigh, and to his polished buckled shoes.

The table was gleaming with candlelight and that light cast a warm glow over his face, but it seemed to pale in comparison to the glow that lit his eyes when he saw her, and that glow seeped deep down inside her, warming her more surely than any candle ever could. She managed to smile in response to that glow in his eyes and not throw herself into his arms to beg him to forego supper and take her straight to bed.

She nodded a regal thank you when he held her chair for her, noticing that her place had been moved next to his again while she was upstairs, and she caught her breath. In spite of their rather formal dress and the careful placement of china and crystal, this meal would be far from formal. Not with her sitting so close beside him. Not with the way his hand lingered on her shoulder, caressing her skin before sliding away.

"You are looking lovely this evening, Irish," he said as he took his own place. He grinned at her. "I see you found your hairpins."

Unconsciously her hand went to her nape, to where her hair had been pinned up, where strands of it even now had escaped to trail down her neck. "Yes," she said.

He had called her Irish. She had wondered all day whether or not he had heard her whisper her name to him last night. Perhaps he hadn't heard her after all.

Silently they filled their plates from the bowls set on the table. Afterward, even though she had helped prepare the meal, she wasn't sure she could have said what they ate. She would only remember Ty, the way he looked at her, the gleam in his eyes, how their fingers touched each time she passed him a bowl or he handed her a dish.

She put a bite of something or other into her mouth, because that was what she was supposed to be doing. She watched his dexterous use of his knife and fork, the movements of his hands and fingers, so strong yet capable of the most tender touch. His fingers stilled and she looked up at his face. He was looking at her as if he, too, would prefer to just push his plate away and pull her to him.

She swallowed hard, needing to break the silence that lingered between them. "I want to thank you for getting those repairs going in the compound today," she said. "I really have been meaning to get to them, but there always seems to be so many other things I need to do first." She smiled up at him with a false brightness. "And I doubt that I could have gotten things moving half so fast as you did."

His fingers tightened around the stem of his wineglass. "That wasn't something you should have had to do anyway, Irish, nor my mother. My father has been gone entirely too much lately. Nate and Matt are never here."

Her brows went up. It was the first time she had heard any member of this family criticize another.

He tossed back a healthy drink of wine and set his glass down. "Hell, I've been gone too long, too."

She laid a hand on his arm intending it as a comforting gesture. But she felt the hard muscles beneath the cotton coat and pulled her hand away, fisting it in her lap. "You've been at school," she said. "Nate is busy building up his business. Matt brings in a lot of furs trading with the Indians and he keeps the lumber business going. Your father is fighting a war."

He waved a hand negligently in the air. "I know, I know. But there's always a war. He's given enough to England. It's time for him to come home to his family."

"Your mother tells me he has brought in several rich prizes."

Ty nodded in acquiescence. "He has done very well for our

family, but I think we would all prefer that he come home."

"You're just worried about your mother, Ty. But she thrives on running this plantation. You know that."

He nodded. "That is very true, but we all need to give her more help than we do." He reached over to tip up her chin. "Thank God she has you here. I've seen how much of the burden you handle."

She swallowed hard and looked away, unable to face him. Unable to tell him that she would be leaving soon. She didn't want to go. But she had to. Before she lost any more of her heart to him and told him things about herself she couldn't let anyone know.

She forced down a few more bites and noticed that he did the same, trying to think of some way to lighten the mood.

"Privateering seems to run in your family from what everyone tells me."

He put down his fork, shoved his plate away and leaned toward her. "Not just mine, it seems."

She looked up at him questioningly.

"They all wrote to tell me how you helped capture that Spanish warship."

She put down her own fork and also leaned on the table. "I played a very small role in that encounter, believe me. It wasn't me wielding swords and pistols. That was your family."

He grinned and leaned closer. "We're true privateers, one and all." He took her hand and lifted it to nibble at her fingers. "Did they also tell you that piracy runs in the family, too?"

"I have heard that story."

"It's true, you know."

I believe it, she thought. He was stealing her heart even now as well as her good sense. Why else was she going to allow him to take her to bed again this night? Allow it? Good lord, she was going to insist on it.

Neither of them had eaten that much but supper was over for

them both and she knew it. She had told Ruby and Dee-dee that they could go as soon as the meal was served. She and Ty had the house to themselves. She looked at him sitting there and she could tell that he wanted her. He just wasn't sure that she wanted him. It was time to let him know.

Leaning toward him she lifted her chin, let her eyelids drift half-closed, and parted her lips in invitation. He was not slow in responding. His mouth claimed hers and he was pulling her closer before her eyes could even close completely. She wanted to be closer to him. Apparently he wanted the same thing for he rose from his chair, his lips still clinging to hers and pulled her up against him.

His hands gripped her shoulders and his mouth trailed kisses down her throat. She tilted her head back to allow him access but his hands came up to pull her mouth back to his. His fingers splayed into her hair and the barely restrained strands began to tumble down as he began pulling the pins out, letting them drop onto the floor, the table, the chair.

He pulled far enough away from her to look at her, to sift her now loosened hair through his fingers. She felt so shaky she thought she would have more trouble walking up the stairs than he would with his bad ankle.

"You've loosened my hair," she barely managed to whisper.

He must not have been capable of speech at all, right then, for he merely nodded as he played with her hair, laying it over her shoulders then pushing it back, combing his fingers down its long length, letting a strand curl about his hand as he watched the candlelight gleam on its surface.

Watching him she thought she might not ever be able to speak again either, but she managed to say, "I suppose this means that tonight you plan to do things right?"

"Maybe not," he said. "I might just always find some way to not get things right."

"And why is that?"

He grinned. "So that I will always have an excuse to try again."

She could scarcely breathe. "Always?"

"Always," he confirmed, and his mouth claimed hers again before she could say anything more.

Always, she thought as she savored the taste of him. *Always.* Maybe it was just talk. Men did that. It didn't necessarily mean anything. It couldn't. She was leaving. He was courting Betsy. This brief time alone with him was only a temporary situation. She knew that. Surely he did, too. But she pushed those thoughts aside. It was temporary but she intended to enjoy it fully while it was here. She slid her hands inside his coat, feeling the warmth of him, feeling the sleek smoothness of the silk back of his waistcoat. She pressed herself against him.

He pulled back and took a deep shuddering breath. "I wasn't sure you would want this again. I was worried that you wouldn't, that you would sneer at me and scorn me and push me away, that you would blame me for seducing you."

She shook her head. "There's no blame, here, Ty. I wanted you last night and I want you tonight. Let's not waste any more time. Take me upstairs now and love me."

He laughed, but his laugh was shaky with desire. He reached over to pick up the cane that leaned against his chair. "As much as I would like to do just that, Irish, as much as I would love to scoop you up into my arms and carry you upstairs and lay you across my bed"--he tapped his bad ankle with the tip of the cane--"I'm afraid that tonight you'll have to walk."

She twirled away from him and looked back at him coyly over her shoulder. "I won't mind at all so long as you follow me."

"Follow?" She saw the bright sheen flaming in his eyes, the flaring of his nostrils, the sharp intake of his breath, as he looked at her. "If you don't get up those stairs right this moment I will have you on the floor here and now."

Laughing she picked up her skirts and fairly flew up the stairs.

Chapter Fifteen

I N SPITE OF HIS INJURED ANKLE TY WAS NOT FAR BEHIND HER
going up the stairs. He snatched at her skirts but she jerked
them from his grasp. At the top of the stairs she relented, turning to him to let him catch her, to lean down to him for his kiss,
reaching to caress his cheek, his neck, sliding her hands along his
shoulders beneath his coat to push it off him. It fell behind him on
the stairs as he came up to her. He stood a step below her and as
she lifted her head for him to kiss her neck, his hand slid under her
skirt, skimming upward over ankle and calf to knee.

Not here, she thought. *Not here on the hard stairs. I want you in
my bed pillowed in soft down.* She moved backward away from him
along the hall, drawing him along with her, her mouth still clinging to his. She began loosening clothes. By the time she reached
her room she was tossing aside her apron and shrugging out of her
gown and he was helping her, his fingers nimble at the ties to her
bodice. She wasn't sure where or when she had lost her fichu, but
right now she didn't much care, either.

Ty alternately helped her with her undressing and hindered
it by stopping to caress whatever body part was currently being
uncovered, a shoulder, an arm, a breast. That last caused quite a
delay as he brought her breathless against him, waiting for the next

light pinching of her nipple, the next teasing tickle of his fingers. It came, again and again and she began to feel that there would be nothing left of her but a damp puddle on the floor as she melted into oblivion.

Then he was gone, moving away from her and she groaned in protest, reaching for him, pulling him back to her.

"I want to light a candle," he whispered against her temple. "I want to see you this time. I want to see every curve and swell of your body. I want to see the light mingling with the flame of your hair as it streams over your pillow. I don't want to miss any of you, any of this."

Mutely, humbled by his words, she nodded her head. *Yes*, she thought, *I want to see you, too.* She let go of him and stepped back against the bed while he felt on her nightstand for flint and steel and candle. She heard the zing of stone on steel, saw the sparks fly between them, and watched the candle ignite to flame.

She looked down at herself now more than half-undressed, her clothes strewn across the floor. Other than his missing hair ribbon and coat, Ty was still clad. The light played along the loose folds of his shirtsleeves and at the ruffles at wrist and neck. She reached out to trail her fingers down his still buttoned waistcoat, noting how it fit so smoothly over his torso. "You are not playing fair, Tyrus Fortune," she said.

He merely arched his brows questioningly while his gaze played over her, touching her as warmly as the light from the candle's flame.

"You have on far more than I do. I demand the removal of something before this goes any further."

He lowered his head with a wicked grin and reached up to unfasten his Steinkirk from about his neck. He tossed it over his shoulder toward a chair but missed. "Satisfied?"

She returned his grin with one of her own. "Not yet, but I

soon hope to be."

His brows shot up and he chuckled. "Soon? I think not, my lovely one. We have all night."

She leaned back against the high bed deliberately twisting to entice him with her exposed breast. She let out a great mock sigh. "I suppose that's how long this is going to take if you keep dawdling."

Ty reached out to snag her to him with an arm about her waist. "Dawdling, am I? I think it's the other way 'round. I have nearly undressed you, but you have been too busy enjoying it to do the like for me."

A thrill went through her at the thought of undressing him, button by button. She sighed heavily as if a chore awaited her and reached out to unbutton the top button of his waistcoat. "How do men always manage to turn things around so that it is ever the woman who is to blame?"

He caught her hand and lifted it to kiss each of her fingers. "I suppose I must accept at least some of the blame in this instance," he said, giving her a teasing grin. "I was giving you such pleasure that you could think of nothing else."

She had to laugh. "Such arrogance." She undid the second button.

He looked down to watch her progress as she slipped the third button from its hole. He started to help her but she pushed his hands away, finishing the job in her own good time. Slowly. Very slowly. Letting the backs of her fingers skim down his body as she worked her way down the row of buttons. She slowed more on each button until she was sure he was even more frustrated than she was. When she heard him groan, she looked up at him with a coy grin. "You did say you wanted this to last all night, didn't you?"

In one quick motion he shrugged out of his waistcoat, lifted her onto the bed, kicked off his shoes and lay down beside her.

"Witch," he snarled. "Now I know why so many red-haired tempt-resses met their end at the stake."

With that he bent to take her breast into his mouth causing her to writhe and clutch at his hair. It was difficult, but she managed to grit out, "You still have too many clothes on."

He lifted his head. "As do you, my lovely one. A situation we can easily remedy." He pushed her chemise further down her body and she lifted her hips to be rid of it, along with her petticoats. When he moved aside to remove her clothes she pulled his shirt tail out and began working at the fastenings of his breeches. She ran her hands inside the waist of them and pushed them down as her hands reveled in the feel of the warm flesh of his backside.

When his manhood sprang free of its confinement, she looked at it, now swollen with his desire for her, dripping with his need. For a moment she was back on that Spanish ship, those sailors taking her. But the moment was fleeting. She was not on her back on a hard deck, she was not being held down, she was not being forced against her will. This was Ty, who even now, she was sure, would get up, go to his room and leave her alone if that was what she wanted.

She looked up into his face.

He must have seen her hesitancy because he also paused. "Are you all right?"

Quickly, she nodded.

He cupped her face and looked down at her intently. "I would never hurt you. If I do anything you don't like…"

She smiled. "I didn't know there was anything you could do that I wouldn't like."

He returned her smile. "I hope that is true. I want only to please you."

"And I want to please you," she said.

"You do. With every writhe of pleasure, with every little moan, with every button you undo, you give pleasure to me." He laughed. "Simply lying here allowing me to touch you gives me pleasure."

"Allowing you to touch me?" She took his hand and placed it on her breast. "I thought I was demanding it."

He laughed, then, too. "That also gives me pleasure." He settled himself between her thighs, pressing against her. "Great pleasure."

She felt him against her and she felt herself opening for him, inviting him inside her. He must have felt her response because he took a deep breath. "It is so hard to wait," he said. "I want you now."

Lifting her hips to press even more firmly against him she said, "This doesn't *have* to take all night, does it?"

"Now?" he asked.

"Now," she responded.

He positioned himself and entered her then, sliding in slowly. She could see in the gritting of his teeth and the pained expression on his face the effort it cost him not to just plunge into her. It made her love him even more.

Love? She gasped, her jaw dropping and she went still.

He froze. "Are you all right? I didn't hurt you, did I?"

Only a spear through the heart, she thought, forcing a smile and shaking her head. How could she have let this happen, she wondered. He was not hers to love. But then, could she have done this with anyone she did not love? How could she have fooled herself into thinking she could?

She loved him. She loved Tyrus Fortune, the wealthy son of a tidewater plantation owner. A man who owned his own plantation and who was even now building a mansion to bring a bride to. A bride who could do him proud, who could stand by his side as an equal in Charles Town society. He would never want a... He would never want her. Not beyond this.

She looked up at him. The candlelight sculpted his face into warm light and cool shadow, sharp angles and hard planes. A proud face. But there was no pride in his blue eyes as he looked at her. If she didn't know better, she could almost convince herself he was looking at her with love.

He bent then to kiss her, softly, tenderly, lightly. "Kathleen," he whispered and it was her turn to freeze. But he only chuckled easily as he kissed her again on chin and cheeks.

He had heard her last night after all. She was not sure she could breathe. She lifted her hand and placed a finger across his lips. "Don't," she said. "Don't call me that."

"Why not?"

She tried hard to keep from shaking in fear. "It's..." She couldn't say "dangerous," not out loud, not to him. "Just don't."

He looked down at her, his face serious. "You gave me that name here in this bed and here in this bed I will use it because that is who you truly are. Here I want naught between us but truth. I will know you here as Kathleen as I know your body with mine."

"But—"

He shushed her protest with a shake of his head. "I know not the reason you do not want your name known to others, Kathleen, but you have entrusted it to me and I will not betray you. And I am content to wait for you to trust me enough to give me the rest of it, as well as your reasons for keeping it secret. Until you give me leave, your secrets will go no further than this. This I pledge to you with my sacred honor."

His sacred honor? She could expect no higher pledge than that from any man. That he would offer that to her humbled her be-yond reason. But then, she thought, she was already beyond reason when she took him to her bed last night, when she told him her name, when she thought she could make love with him without loving him.

She wanted to pull him down to her then with a whispered,

"I love you," and seal her pledge with a kiss. But she could not do that. She could only give him the kiss. And she did.

He returned her kiss and thrust within her, thrusting again and again, bringing them both to sweet completion.

Afterward she lay beside him, enjoying the feel of his arm about her as his fingers played with her hair, knowing that, in spite of what he had said, this was not for "always." This was not even for very long. They had one more night before Nate and Charlie returned. He could not come to her room with others in the house, with his brother right across the hall. Then in a few more days, Mrs. Fortune would return, and she would be gone. Ty would not protest because he would understand that it was for the best.

Only her heart would protest because it would be torn in two, with half of it remaining forever his whether he knew it or not.

He sighed contentedly and shifted her closer to him. "Did I get it right this time? Please say no so I have an excuse to try again."

"Neither of us seems to need an excuse," she said.

"I certainly don't," he answered, nuzzling his face into her hair. "Your hair fascinates me," he said.

"It's wild and unmanageable."

"It has fascinated me since I first saw it."

"You didn't seem fascinated by my hair or anything else about me when you first met me. I thought you were going to order me out of the house that very day."

"I thought about it. I did want you gone. But yet, I think I have wanted you ever since I saw you standing there on the dock when I came home. I could just never admit it to myself."

She smiled, thinking that was the day she began wanting him as well. "Is that why you were so angry with me?"

"Perhaps," he admitted. "But it was more than that. I thought you were an adventuress, an interloper preying on my family."

"And what do you think now?"

He let one of her curls twine about his finger. "I think I have never seen anyone give so much of themselves and ask so little in return."

She shrugged. "I only try to do my share."

"My mother depends on you a great deal."

"But you're home now. And your father should be back soon, too."

"We'll still need you, Kathleen. Always."

She did not respond and she could soon feel him breathing the deep, steady breath of sleep. Always. He had said it again. But it was not for always. Not for them.

The next morning Irish reluctantly tore herself from Ty's arms and urged him back to his own room before Dee-dee or Ruby could come looking for her, wondering why she wasn't in the kitchen as usual.

When Irish did manage to get to the kitchen, tucking the last strands of her hair into her cap, Ruby was just pulling a pan of biscuits from the oven. That was when she noticed her hair pins in a neat pile on top of her neatly folded fichu which was laid on Ty's coat. The coat she had taken off of him halfway up the stairs the night before.

Ruby just looked from the pile to Irish with a suppressed smile and set the biscuits on the worktable. "You and Master Ty going to starve yourselves to death if you don't eat more supper," she said. "Not much missing off either plate the last two nights, far as I could tell."

Irish tried, without avail, to avoid blushing. She could feel the heat of it up into the roots of her hair and down to her breasts Ty had been kissing but moments before. She should have cleaned up the supper dishes. It wasn't like her to leave her messes for Ruby. But dishes had been the last thing on her mind the last two nights. "I guess we've both just been too tired to eat," she said lamely.

Ruby pursed her lips. "Mmmhum. You have been looking just a mite peaked the last two days. Maybe you need to spend more time in bed. Sleeping."

Irish started to make some excuse, to say something, but what could she say? Ruby just gave a low chuckle and turned away to tend the bacon frying on a spider over the fire.

That night she and Ty did not make it up the stairs. Ty took her there halfway up the steps, the hard ridges against her back going unnoticed until they were done. The fourth night Nate and Charlie had still not returned and that night, she and Ty did not even make it out of the dinning room but fell into each other's arms among the legs of table and chairs. At least that time her back was well padded by the thick carpet.

When Charlie's blithe hale greeted them the next morning, Irish smiled at him and Nate, but she felt a deep pang of disappointment. Her little sojourn into paradise was over.

That afternoon Nate took them all up to Alejandro's and Mariette's to see the babies. She was surprised to see how easily Ty handled the twins, patting a back or rubbing a tummy to put one or the other to sleep. Mariette looked tired but radiant with happiness. Alejandro acted like he had invented the whole idea of babies the way he strutted around so proudly.

The sight of the tiny babies rendered Irish speechless. When she was allowed to hold Rachel she could only look down at the dark hair and soft creamy skin with awe, touching her with reverence. Then Rachel opened her eyes and looked up at her, and she had to smile. "You all told me her eyes were blue. You didn't tell me they were such a clear bright turquoise blue."

Ty caught Alejandro's eye. "I guess I'd better start practicing my fencing. It looks like it will take both of us to fight off every young buck in the colony when this one comes of age!"

Irish thought about the babies all the way back home, wishing that husband, home, and children could be in her future.

Talk at supper that night was about the twins for a while. But she found it hard to sit the length of the table away from Ty, again unable to touch his hand or lean forward for his kiss or caress. She only hoped that Charlie and Nate were oblivious to the looks he sent her from his end of the table. And she could only hope that the longing she felt was not obvious on her face.

It was over. There could be nothing more between them. Ruby had easily made the connection to the right conclusion. She didn't want Nate or Charlie making that same discovery. It was over. It had to be.

Ty asked Nate for news from Charles Town and she cursed herself for being glad just to be able to hear his voice, to be in the same room with him.

Nate hunched forward to lean on the table, his face serious. "Two English warships are in town. Our factor has sold them some of our rice."

Ty put down his fork and also leaned onto the table, his gaze intense. "From the look of you, I take it there's more which isn't so good."

Nate nodded. "They've sent press gangs into town, twice now. The trouble is, the *Eagle* is in port, too, and nearly ready to sail. I told my sailors to stay close to home until the warships clear the harbor. I don't want my ship to be caught short-handed."

"I take it these press gangs are a real problem with you colonials?" Charlie asked.

"We've complained time and again to ship captains, to the admiralty, to parliament itself, to no avail," Nate said. "They take our sailors and press them into service whenever they find themselves shorthanded. It doesn't help that their men sometimes jump ship to take berths on American ships."

"And why would they do that?" Charlie asked.

Nate grinned. "Conditions are a lot better on our ships. And the pay, too."

"Especially on your ships, Nate," Irish said. "You pay well."

"That's because I want the best for my ships and I demand the best from the men who sail them, but this impressment by the king's navy must stop."

They talked about the problems with the navy for a while and then Nate pushed back his chair and stretched. "Well, after dodging press gangs and that visit with the twins I'm for bed."

Charlie got up as well. "It will be an early morning. I want to be on the building site before those men get there. Nate already unloaded the extra supplies." He leaned down to chuck Irish under the chin. "That's why we were a day late, Darlin'. I hope you didn't miss me too much."

She cocked her head and gave him a teasing grin. "Were you gone, then?"

Charlie clutched his chest. "Ah, lass, you wound me to the core!"

She laughed and stood to begin gathering dishes. Ruby would find nothing to tsk-tsk over in the morning. Nate and Charlie left to go to their rooms, but Ty just sat there. She didn't look at him. She couldn't. If she did she would walk over and fling herself into his lap. But she could feel him watching her, waiting for her to come close.

She gathered the dishes at the end of the table away from him and headed for the kitchen. Hopefully, he would be gone by the time she came back.

"Irish." He said her name so softly she almost didn't hear him. But she stopped in the doorway, dishes in both hands, stopped, waiting for more, for anything from him, knowing that she shouldn't--she couldn't--respond. If only her body could believe what her mind was telling it. But her body was telling her that he was there behind her. She could feel him. And her traitorous body was beginning to respond to him with every part--heart, and breasts, and between her thighs.

"I have to get these dishes cleaned up."

He touched her shoulder and that touch went all the way through her. Her body began to exult, to sing. It wasn't listening to her, only to his touch. She felt his fingers skim up toward her nape, tease up her neck and tug gently at some loose strands of hair. "The dishes can wait, Irish. I'm not sure I can."

If he didn't stop what he was doing, or if she couldn't find the strength to walk away, she was going to drop the dishes she held to turn into his embrace, and let Ruby think what she would. When the dishes began to rattle in her shaking hands she managed to step away from him, turning to face him, to keep him at bay with the dishes between them.

"I have to clean this up, Ty. I always do. Except for the last three nights. And you know why that was." She took a deep breath. "And so does Ruby."

"Ruby knows? What did she say?"

She looked at Ty aghast. The wretch was grinning. She felt like throwing the dishes at him. She had to grip them tighter just as she had to clench her teeth to keep from shouting at him. Wasn't it just like a man to want the world to know he could add another notch to his bedpost?

She leaned toward him with narrowed eyes and gritted out, "What does it matter what she said, Ty? She *knows*."

She started to turn back to the doorway but he stopped her with a hand on her arm and turned her back toward him. "How could she know anything, Irish?"

Of course, a man wouldn't think about the obvious clues they had left. She ticked them off for him. "Because I always clear the dinner dishes. Because I don't usually leave a trail of hairpins from the dining room to my room. Because you don't usually leave your coat on the stairs." She stopped and took a breath, and then stated firmly. "I'm cleaning up these dishes tonight like I always do."

He leaned over the dishes in her hands and kissed her lightly on the forehead. "I'll help." She didn't want his help.

She wanted him to go to bed and leave her alone. She wanted this time alone to return to her nightly routine so she could emphasize to her body that her brief affair with Ty was over. "Leave them, Ty. I'll do them. You go on to bed," she said, but he had already picked up his dishes.

He stepped toward her, dishes in hand. "We'll get them done faster together. I don't want to wait any longer than I have to, to have you beneath me again."

"It doesn't matter how fast the dishes get done, you'll not find me beneath you at the end of it!"

He was so stunned by that pronouncement that she was halfway down the hall to the kitchen before he caught up to her, managing in spite of his ankle to get around in front of her to bring her to a halt. "What does that mean?" he demanded.

She tried twice to go around him but he blocked her way. Giving up going around him, she faced him. It was so hard to stand there with him but inches away and not reach out to him, touch him. He was so close, in fact, that she could feel the heat of him, feel his breath on her cheek, see the consternation and hurt in his eyes. Her exasperation with him drained away. "It's over, Ty," she said softly. "It's over."

He backed her up against the wall but then looked at the dishes in his hands as if he had forgotten they were there. He looked around and found a small table nearby. Keeping her trapped, he reached over and set the dishes on the table, then took her shoulders in his hands. She couldn't push him away. Not without dropping the dishes she still held. But she could turn her head and she did. But wherever she turned he moved within her line of sight until she gave up and just looked at him, accepting the fact that he was not going to let her go until he had asked her why, until she had explained her reasons to him, or at least some reason he would accept.

"This isn't over, Irish. We've just begun."

She shook her head but he ignored her. He leaned into her, forcing her to hold the dishes out away from them. He pressed against her and she savored the hard feel of him along the length of her, breast, hip, and thigh. Then he kissed her and she could not help but accept his kiss. And, God help her, to kiss him back. She grew weak with that kiss. Her knees felt like they would give way beneath her and the dishes began to rattle in her hands.

Somehow, without breaking the kiss, Ty managed to take the dishes from her left hand and set them on the table, then those from her right. There was nothing left to fill her hands with except him, and gleefully she did just that. She slid them around his waist into that secret place between coat and man where only a woman intimate enough with that man might venture. It was filled with his warmth. It was filled with him. And now it was also filled with her.

Chapter Sixteen

ONCE MORE SHE WAS IN HIS ARMS AND HE WAS IN HERS. It was a place she thought would never be hers again. It wasn't hers. In the midst of his intoxicating kiss and his hands now clutching her backside and pressing her ever closer to him, she was barely able to remind herself of that. He was going to marry Betsy and raise boring little pillars of the community. So why was he here in the hallway kissing her? More importantly, why was she allowing him? Because, she had to admit to herself, when Ty was within touching-distance she had very little resistance. He only had to touch her and she threw self-control to the winds.

One of them had to gather some of that self-control or they would find themselves naked on the hall floor just a few feet away from Charlie's door. It was a wonder he hadn't heard them and come out already. This had to stop. Ty had to stop kissing her. He had to stop caressing her back. He had to stop—oh my! Just a few moments more. Then she would push him away. Or maybe she wouldn't. Maybe she couldn't. She wasn't sure she had enough breath and strength left to even push away the *thought* of pushing him away. If Ty wasn't pressing her up against the wall she would have slithered to the floor by now. He had melted her very bones with that kiss. There would be nothing left of her when he was done.

He was pulling her skirt up, inching it higher and higher up her thigh until his fingers found flesh. He lifted her leg and pulled her closer to him, her skirt bunched between them. Her body knew what was coming and she felt herself opening for him, wanting him, wanting that sweet thrusting. He did not leave her wanting. He opened his breeches and found her, lifting her higher against the wall to ease his entry. And then she was riding him, feeling tension build within her, building until she thought she would cry out loud for relief. But she could only moan into his mouth as his kiss deepened in matching thrusts until that tension snapped, leaving her pulsing, and causing him to spill his seed within her.

He broke the kiss and she leaned her head back against the wall. Panting, he leaned his forehead against hers, until his panting became gasps and then turned into a soft, quiet chuckle. "Wouldn't this have been a lot easier in a bed?"

"I told you, you aren't going to get me into your bed again."

He chuckled again. "So you did. That's how we wound up against a wall."

She was beginning to regain some breath. And with it came a returning strength. "You'll not have me against a wall again, either, Tyrus Fortune."

His brows shot up and he grinned. "So I'll have to keep finding new and interesting places, is that it? I think I can come up with a few."

She pushed at his chest and he eased out of her, releasing her, letting her skirt fall between them.

"No, Ty," she said, shaking out her skirts. "I mean there can be no more of this between us."

He smoothed a hand down her skirt. "Good. I'd much rather do this naked."

She gave a huff and pushed him away from her. "Are you being deliberately obtuse?" She picked up the pile of dishes. "It's over." She headed for the kitchen.

They bumped into each other as she came back out of the kitchen with a tray to finish clearing the table. She went around him and he followed her around the table as she placed dishes on the tray.

"Is it because Nate and Charlie are back? Are you afraid someone besides Ruby will find out?"

She stopped what she was doing and turned to face him, noting that for once the impeccable Ty was slightly rumpled. Because of her. Because of what they had just done together. It almost made her smile. Nothing else had done that to him. "No. It's because we never should have let this happen in the first place and you know it."

He took her by the shoulders but she shrugged off his hands. "Why not? It's something we both wanted."

"And now we've gotten what we wanted, and it's over." She turned back to her work, placing the last of the dishes on the tray.

"Just like that?"

She picked up the tray and tilted her head. "Just like that."

"But why?"

She started back to the kitchen but he took the tray from her and placed it back on the table. Then he stood before her with fists on hips, demanding an answer.

She leaned forward, poking him in the chest with one finger. "Because you are going to marry Betsy and raise perfect little children together, that's why."

He blinked at her and she thought he looked completely surprised. "Who said I was going to marry Betsy?"

She rolled her eyes and gave a huff. "You did." He was so stunned that she managed to pick up the tray and make it back to the kitchen with it before he caught up to her again.

He had come almost at a run and slid to a halt beside her, fists on hips. "When did I ever say I was going to marry Betsy?"

She rounded on him and her fists also came to sit on her hips. "That day you came home from courting her and said what a wonderful wife she was going to make."

He looked blank for a moment and then laughed. "I remember now. I meant she would make a wonderful wife for someone. Not for me. She would bore me to death. I don't want to marry Betsy and, as you put it, raise perfect little children. I want to marry you and raise little red-headed hellions."

She felt panic begin to rise but she pushed it down as she backed away from him, her hands palm outward as if to fend him off. "No. Oh, no."

He caught her by the shoulders and pulled her to him, grinning down at her. "No? Why not?"

She sought wildly for something to say to him. Anything to convince him that he really did not want to marry her. Anything but the truth. And then she realized that Ty really didn't want to marry her. He was just feeling some honor bound duty to marry the woman he had just "ruined." Had been "ruining" for the last three nights.

When she spoke she tried to sound calm and logical. That was the way to convince Tyrus Fortune. "Ty, you don't want to marry me."

"Of course I do." He laughed and tenderly brushed her hair back from her forehead.

Even that casual touch made her want to close her eyes and snuggle into his arms. She would never be able to talk coolly with him standing so close. She pulled away from him and walked to the other side of the kitchen work table and, placing her hands on the table, leaned toward him. "Ty, think about this. You want a wife in that palace you're building who is your equal in Charles Town society. A wife who will be a grand hostess for the balls and fetes you will have. A wife who–"

He pounded the table between them once. "Do you think I don't know my own mind?"

She straightened. "Perhaps you don't because I am not the kind of wife you said you wanted when you came home from England."

"No, you're not," he agreed, crossing his arms. "But you're the wife I want now."

"Ty," she said softly, stepping back up to the table, "don't think you have to marry me because of what we've done together the last three nights. You know I was no virgin even that first time. You have not dishonored me or ruined me. I will not let you marry me out of duty."

"Damn it, Irish, duty has nothing to do with it!"

"Desire, then. Lust. Because marriage never entered your mind until I told you our little affair was over."

Again she could see that stunned look on his face. She was right. It was lust. She had just been a woman close at hand who was willing. No, more than willing. A woman who had practically dragged him into her bed. But she would not let Ty make the mistake of marrying her. She might have dragged him into her bed, but she would not drag him down in society by allowing him to marry her, because sometime, someone would come along who had known her in Ireland. Then the accusations would ring out, and Ty and his whole family would be shamed. How would he feel about his wife then?

While she still had enough resolve, she marched out of the kitchen and up to her room leaving him standing there.

Too stunned to move, Ty watched Irish walked away from

him. He had just asked her to marry him and she had refused. He had to admit that she was right--he had not planned to ask her right here and now, but he had thought of it. He grimaced. And up until now, every time he had thought about it, he had thought it was a bad idea. So why had he blurted out a proposal? Was she right? Was it only lust motivating him? She certainly wasn't the kind of woman he had had in mind for a wife when he first came home.

He smoothed a hand down his chest and, surprised at the unusually rumpled feel of his clothes, looked down at himself. His shirt was pulled out of his breeches and was loose and hanging, his Steinkirk was askew, his waistcoat had two buttons undone, and he had refastened his breeches wrong. This was what she did to him.

He couldn't imagine ever getting this rumpled with Betsy. He grinned. He also couldn't imagine Betsy ever letting him have her up against a wall or under the dining room table. There was certainly something to be said for an improper woman doing improper things.

All right, so he hadn't thought seriously about marriage to Irish until just a few moments ago, but now that he was thinking about it, it seemed like a fine idea. He was growing hard again just thinking about her. But it wasn't just lust that made him want to marry her. If he really thought about it logically, Irish would make a fine wife.

Just look at how she practically ran this plantation. His mother depended on her for a lot more than just companionship.

He began straightening his clothing. She could cook, too. Her biscuits alone were worth marrying her for. Her rolls and stew weren't bad, either, yet she was equally able to delegate tasks. The servants all seemed to worship her. She worked well with them and didn't act like she was better than they were, the way a lot of women did. She didn't mind plunging in and actually helping, either. She would never be a decorative but useless wife, whining over imagined ills.

He limped back to the dining room to find his cane, and that reminded him of how Irish had ridden Renegade in the race. What other woman in the colony would have done that? What other woman would have been able to tame that beast in the first place? With her talent with horses and with Renegade at stud, they could raise a fine lot of horses.

He headed down the hall to the stairs. Yes, now that he thought about it, Irish would make him a great wife. She might be a little rough around the edges, but she was a beautiful woman. A good maid could tame her hair and a good seamstress could make clothes for her that would make her shine in any setting. She hadn't bought clothes for herself even though he knew now that she could afford to. She was not a spendthrift. Another fine attribute in a wife. But of course, as his wife, he would be sure she had fine clothes.

He stopped with his hand on the banister and his foot on the first step trying to imagine Irish with her hair tamed and wearing fine clothing. He shook his head. He couldn't. But he could well imagine her at the governor's ball with her hair coming loose, making every man who gazed at her think about taking her to bed. That wild hair was part of who she was. But she could have the clothes. She deserved them, even though she could probably put every woman to shame at a fine gathering with just her smile.

Yes, now that he thought about it, Irish would make a fine wife. He would tell her so and ask her again to marry him.

But over the next few days, Ty found no chance to talk to Irish alone. When he was not off at the worksite, she suddenly seemed especially adept at eluding him. If she was around, so was Nate or Charlie, or both. After supper each night she excused herself and locked herself in her room. Ruby stayed late to clear and wash the dishes.

He suspected that was Irish's doing because Ruby arched her brows at him as if she disapproved of something he had done. He wanted to shout at her that he hadn't done anything and if Irish would just sit still for five minutes he would make it all right with her.

Finally, he decided it would take a bit of sneaky guile to get her alone. So the next night when she stood up to excuse herself from the table, he said, "I stopped by the stable on my way into the house and it looked like Renegade was a bit lame."

She whirled on him. "Lame? And you didn't tell me until now?" She shoved her chair in and headed out of the house.

Thank goodness his ankle was better. He was able to catch up to her halfway to the stable. "I don't think it's bad, Irish. Mangus looked at the leg but didn't see anything wrong. I thought it could wait until you had eaten."

"He still needs to be checked," she shot at him.

"I agree. That's why I wanted you to look at him."

That earned him a genuine smile from her although she still looked worried as they entered the stable.

Renegade whickered when they came up to his stall and stretched out his head toward them both looking for apples.

"Where's Mangus?" Irish muttered. "If there's something wrong with Renegade, he should be here."

"I knew you'd be coming out to check Renegade so I told Mangus to go on home. We could get him if he were needed." She nodded absently and Ty sighed with relief that she accepted his story. Well, it was true...mostly. He had certainly sent Mangus home. He had come by the stable to make sure that the old man would be well gone before Irish came out here. He didn't want to be interrupted when he proposed.

Gad, he'd never dreamed he would propose in a stable. But with Irish, he couldn't think of a better place. He just couldn't see her dressed in satin, sitting idle in the parlor while he knelt on one knee.

She was already in Renegade's stall running her hands down the horse's legs.

"Let me just check that right foreleg," Ty said, pulling out a small stone he had hidden in his pocket and surreptitiously palming it. Grabbing a hoof pick he lifted Renegade's hoof and picked at it a moment then lifted the stone. "Here's the problem," he said.

Irish gave a grateful sigh and slapped Renegade on the neck. Ty watched as she led the horse around the stall just to make sure he was all right, feeling just a little bad at deceiving her. *Maybe,* he thought, *when we've been wed twenty or thirty years and are sitting by the fire one evening, I'll confess what I've done. Maybe by then she will laugh at it but more likely she'll still be the fiery temptress she is now. She'll likely prop those fists on her hips and scold me like a shrew.* He almost laughed out loud thinking of it.

But Irish was leaving Renegade's stall and if he didn't ask her to marry him now, they might never have those twenty or thirty years.

"Irish, there's something I wanted to say," he began.

She stopped and Renegade came up to nudge her in the back, inadvertently shoving her toward him. *Good boy!* Ty thought. *I need all the help I can get with this one.*

He took advantage of her closeness to him and guided her out of the stall and out of the stable and into the moonlight. He wasn't going to propose in a parlor, but he could at least take advantage of the moonlight.

He stopped and she looked up at him suspiciously, eyes narrowed. He took her by the arms and faced her squarely. "Irish, I want you to marry me."

She tried to pull away but he wouldn't let her. "Just listen," he said. "I want to marry you, Irish. You. I know all the things I said about a proper wife and society but you are the woman I want. I've seen how you helped to organize Abby's wedding. I'm sure you could do as well with a ball or a house party. You are gracious and smiling and make everyone comfortable. You would make a wonderful hostess."

Her eyes narrowed further and she pursed her mouth, nodding her head. "So I'd make a good hostess for you?"

"Yes! And as for feeling duty bound to marry you because of... because of..."

"Because you think you ruined me?"

"Well, I don't think you're ruined, exactly, Irish. It doesn't matter. I'm sure any man would be glad to have you. And I'm one of them."

She nodded again, but he noticed that she didn't seem to be warming to the idea of marriage. In fact, her jaw seemed to be clenched as if she were ready to lambaste him but was holding back.

He hurried on. "You accused me of wanting you because I lust after you. That, I will have to admit, is true. I do lust after you. I want you constantly. I think about you constantly. I want you in my bed every night. But is that such a bad thing? I would hate to think of marrying someone I didn't lust after." He paused and stood up straight. "So, Irish, will you marry me?"

She looked at him for a long moment and he thought she looked like she was trying not to shout at him, although he couldn't understand why she would. After all, he had just proposed marriage.

"Now let me see if I have this right." She held up one finger. "I can organize a wedding so I would make a good hostess for you." Another finger came up. "I'm ruined, but not exactly ruined, but you'd have me anyway." A third finger came up. "And it would be convenient to marry someone you also happen to lust after." That's when her fists went to her hips and he knew he was in trouble. "With a proposal like that, how could a woman possibly refuse? Hmmm. Maybe just by saying 'no'." She gave a humph and turned away and headed for the house.

Ty stood there, stunned. That seemed to happen a lot to him when he was dealing with Irish. He just never knew what she would say or do next, or why she would say or do it. What had just happened? He had expected her to accept his proposal. What had he said wrong? She had thrown his proposal in his face and practically run back to the house.

Any other woman would have been thrilled to accept a proposal of marriage from him. He knew his own worth. And it wasn't just measured in acres of land and fine clothes and money, although a lot of women would have been happy with the wealth no matter what kind of man came attached to it. But then, Irish wasn't any other woman. And that was precisely why he wanted her.

He began walking back to the house, no longer needing to lean much on his cane. Why wouldn't she accept his proposal?

He thought he had negated all her objections very logically. Obviously she didn't see things the same way he did. He sighed and paused to look up at the moon for inspiration. He should have been looking up at that moon with Irish in his arms, with her arms around him close under his coat. He grinned thinking of the way she liked to snuggle inside his coat and wished she were there now. He missed her.

He missed the way they worked together and fought together, and for the last three nights he had missed the way they loved together. He stopped stock still suddenly realizing what had been missing from his proposal. He hadn't said anything about love.

Women wanted that, needed that. Hell, men did, too.

Good God, did he love Irish?

He did lean heavily on his cane then, nearly staggered by that thought. If love meant caring for another person, wanting them and missing them when they weren't around, wanting to touch them, sleep with them, be with them, then yes, he loved Irish. It wasn't just lust. He was sure of that. Yes, the lust was there, thank goodness, but he loved her, too. He should have told her he loved her when he proposed, and he would have if he had realized it then.

He grinned and set off down the path toward the house at a jaunty gait in spite of the slight twinge in his ankle. Then he nearly stumbled when another thought stuck him. He loved Irish, but did she love him? Maybe that was why she had turned down his proposal!

He thought of how she had responded to him, the looks she had given him across the table during the three days of bliss they had shared. Irish would never have let him into her bed if she hadn't loved him. In her bed, under the table, up against the wall, on the stairs. Irish had too much pride to just let a man--any man--take her the way he had unless she did love him.

He went on to the house, whistling a jolly tune. Tomorrow he would let Irish know that he loved her. He would let her know in all the ways a man lets a woman know he loves her. Tomorrow he would start to court her. And the next time he proposed, she would accept because he would not fail to tell her he loved her.

Irish paced agitatedly back and forth across her bedroom. Paddy looked up from his bed on the floor and whined at her, and she stopped her pacing to squat down and pat the dog. "What am I going to do, Paddy?"

He licked her hand and settled down to enjoy her attention.

"Ty proposed to me! And, God help me, I wish I could have accepted."

Paddy gave a contented sigh as she scratched behind his ears.

Irish sighed, too, and rose to get ready for bed. She couldn't marry Ty. She could never marry anyone so prominent in society. She might eventually have been able to marry some inconspicuous farmer or tradesman. But now even that path was barred to her because she knew she loved Ty and that that would never change. She couldn't marry Ty and she wouldn't marry anyone else.

Ty and his family were just too prominent in society for her to risk marriage to him. Everyone would know who she was. And eventually, someone would come along who had known her in Ireland, who knew what had happened to her. At the pinnacle of Charles Town society, there would be no place for her to hide. She couldn't risk it. Not for herself, nor for the shame and possible legal complications it could bring down upon Ty and perhaps the whole family.

Mrs. Fortune would be home in less than a week. Then Irish would pack her bags and be gone. Ty would eventually marry Betsy or some other planter's daughter and move into his fine home.

She would find a way to continue to make money and keep herself hidden away in some quiet place in the country. If she ever went to town and saw Ty, she would drink in the sight of him and then turn away before he could see her. She swallowed hard and promised herself that she would never shed even one small tear over any of it. It was what she had to do. She had no choice if she was going to remain free.

She bit her lip as she slipped into bed. Had freedom ever been purchased at such a cost?

The next morning Irish nearly tripped over a bunch of flowers that had been laid before her door. She knelt to pick them up, lifting them to her nose to take in the fragrance of roses she recognized from Mrs. Fortune's garden.

The roses did not gladden her heart. They were a sign that Ty had not given up. He had proposed and he had not accepted her refusal.

When she went into the dining room, stiff and armored against any smiles or touches Ty might give her, she was surprised to find only Charlie there.

"Ty rousted his little brother from bed at dawn this morning," Charlie told her. "Said he had some business to take care of in Charles Town. They'll be back this afternoon."

With a sigh of relief and a sweet smile to Charlie, she sat down to enjoy her meal. But she found that she missed having Ty there. She missed being able to hear him, see him, feel his presence, watch him enjoy the food she had made. She gritted her teeth and forced herself not to even look in the direction of his empty chair. She might as well start getting used to not having him in her life.

When Ty and Nate returned, they stopped only long enough to pick up Charlie, then head up river to the building site. She was in the workers compound and didn't even see him. *Good,* she told herself. *Good.* The less she saw of Tyrus Fortune, the easier it would be to keep him at a distance. The easier it would be to leave.

That evening at supper, he was dressed even more elegantly than usual. He wore a stock tonight and it was frothy with lace, as were the ruffles at his wrists. His dark blue coat fit smoothly over his broad shoulders and his silver shoe buckles gleamed. She felt even more dowdy by comparison. She brushed ineffectually at a large greasy stain on her skirt where the roast beef had spattered her in the kitchen. It was a dress that would have been discarded long ago if she hadn't been trying so hard to save every penny she could.

He rose and bowed to her as politely as if she were the queen and gallantly held her chair for her. Her heart couldn't help but give a betraying flutter when he leaned over her, lightly touching her shoulder before he took his own seat.

Ruby was standing there watching it all with a wryly lifted brow, but she held her tongue as she finished serving them.

She saw Charlie's and Nate's brows go up too, but thankfully, neither of them said anything about Ty's unusually courteous treatment of her. But her eyes narrowed suspiciously as she wondered just what he was up to. If he thought he could charm her into accepting his proposal, he was wrong. Charm had nothing to do with it. She already loved him. She would accept him gladly if she could. She would have to let him know that courting her was a waste of his time.

She gave her full attention to Nate and to Charlie, asking Nate about the cargo for the *Eagle* and when she would put to sea again, and asking Charlie about the progress on Ty's home.

Ty didn't say anything but he was smiling and watching her every time she slipped a glance his way. When Ruby came in to gather the dishes, she stood to excuse herself from the table, to go and hide in her room, coward that she was. It wouldn't be much longer, she told herself. Mrs. Fortune would be back in another few days.

But tonight Ty rose with her and walked down the hall just behind her. At the bottom of the stairs he took her by the arm. "Walk outside with me, Irish."

She started to pull away, to go on up those stairs, but he said, "Just a walk in the garden. Nothing more."

Still she hesitated, thinking of being out in that garden with him, in the dark, alone. She suppressed a shiver of anticipation. She couldn't allow herself to walk with him anywhere. She knew how susceptible she was to his touch, to his very presence. Already she was growing warm with desire just thinking about it, just feeling his hand on her arm. She shook her head no and pulled away from him. It felt as if she was pulling herself in two to do it, but she started up the stairs.

He stopped her on the fourth step with a soft, "What are you afraid of, Irish?"

She turned to face him, her fists going to her hips. "I'm not afraid. I just don't see any point to it."

"It's a beautiful night. You can't shut yourself up in your room alone every evening."

No, she thought, *just for a few more evenings. Then I'll be gone.* "I have mending to do."

He stepped up to the third step, just one below her, coming nose-to-nose with her before she could escape him. "You don't have anything to do that can't be done by one of the servants. You're avoiding me."

She leaned down until their noses very nearly touched. "Yes, I'm avoiding you. Do you think I don't know what would happen out there in the dark with you?"

He grinned.

They heard someone humming and looked down to see Ruby passing by with a tray full of dishes headed for the kitchen. She acted like she hadn't seen them, but Irish knew her humming was just her way of letting them know she was there.

"Come outside with me, Irish," Ty whispered. "I just want to talk."

"No!"

He took her arm before she could escape him. "Very well, shall we just talk here where Ruby and Dee-dee, and anyone else can come by?"

He was going to ask her to marry him again. She just knew it. Neither of them wanted that conversation overheard by half the people in the house. But she didn't trust herself to be alone with him, either.

"I promise I won't touch you, Irish."

She looked down pointedly at his hand still holding her arm and he took it away. He lifted both hands up, palm outward in a gesture of surrender.

She sighed, knowing that she would have to let him have his say, and then she would have to tell him no again. She gave a quick nod and followed him out the door and around the side of the house to the garden.

They walked all the way to the end of the path before either of them said a word. She was glad that he was keeping his word. He hadn't touched her at all, not even a hand at her back to guide her. But she could feel him beside her, and hear the crunch of the crushed shell walk beneath their feet.

At the end of the path he stopped and turned to her and she waited for him to speak. Shadows and moonlight played over his face and she had never wanted him to kiss her more than she did right now, right here. But he had promised not to touch her and she knew he would keep that promise unless she released him from it.

He looked down a moment and she was sure he was gathering his words, trying to find just the right ones to persuade her.

Then he looked into her eyes and she felt as if he were touching her very soul.

"I want to marry you, Irish. I want us to live and love and grow old together knee deep in grandchildren. You said I didn't know my own mind, but I do. When I came home I wanted to build a fine home and marry a woman who could stand beside me in Charles Town society. I wanted someone to raise my children. I still want that and I could have it with any number of women, but I want it with you. You give me joy. You make me forget to tuck in my shirt. You make me insane. You give me balance.

"We fight, but with you it's never hurtful. I feel like I'm finally alive. When I am with you I want to be touching you, kissing you, holding you. And when we are apart I miss you and think about you. I love you, Irish." He held out his hand and she saw the ring he held. There was a large center stone surrounded by what must be diamonds but it was too dark to tell for sure. "An emerald, Irish, for your eyes. Will you marry me?"

For once in her life she couldn't help the tears that streamed down her face. For once, someone had touched that place deep within her that she thought no one could ever find. Ty had not had to find that place. She had tucked him in there herself and she knew that he would always be a part of her. And that made it even harder to tell him no.

She bent her head, knowing now that he had made Nate take him to Charles Town this morning just to buy that ring for her. She couldn't look at him and say the words she had to say to protect them both from her past. "I can't, Ty. Please don't ask me again."

"I will ask you again, Irish. I'll ask again and again and again until you say yes because I know you love me, too. You don't have to say it for me to know it's true. I see it in your eyes when you look at me, I felt it in your body when you gave yourself to me, and I see it now in the tears you're shedding."

She swiped at the telltale tears with the back of her hand and straightened her head to look him in the eyes. "It doesn't matter, Ty. I can't marry you. I won't marry you. You will have to be satisfied with friendship."

"Friendship?" He shook his head, disbelief in his eyes. "Do you really think we can just have friendship between us now?"

"That's all I can offer you."

She could see his teeth clench. "That's not enough."

"I can't give you anything else, Ty."

"Can't? Or won't?" He shoved the ring back into his pocket. "Then there can't be anything between us. I can't see you every day, live in the same house, breathe the same air and not have more from you than friendship. It's marriage, or it's nothing."

She turned her head away, unable to look at him when she cut the final bond between them. "If that's the way it has to be, then so be it."

She could feel him still standing there. She could hear the shuddering intake of his breath. She knew he was waiting for her to take back her words, to throw herself into his arms. But she had to be strong. She would not be the ruination of him and his family.

There was a pain somewhere inside her where her heart should be but she felt as if she had just cut it out and thrown it down onto the crushed shell to let it die at his feet. He waited for a long time, but finally, he turned and she could hear the anger in his stride as he left her.

Chapter Seventeen

TY WASN'T AT BREAKFAST THE NEXT MORNING AND NEITHER was Charlie. Nate was there, though, and he smiled brightly at her when she came in. "Ty and Charlie took the carriage up to the building site," he said.

Irish sat down but she didn't think she could eat anything. She hadn't slept at all the whole night through. She had done some crying, though. More than she had ever done since…since Ireland. She had heard Ty pacing for a while in his room next to hers, but then he must have managed to sleep. She hoped so. Her eyes felt like someone had rolled them in hot sand then stuck them back in her head.

Ruby was just setting out a plate of eggs, but Irish just shook her head and pushed her plate away, only taking a cup of tea.

"Neither one of them men ate a thing before they left," Ruby said. "Charlie wanted to, but Master Ty he just growled at him and told him to quit wasting time or his house would never get built. So they took off out of here and didn't even take no lunch with them like they usually do." She glared at Irish as if it was her fault and she was probably right. "I'll make up a basket and you can take it to them."

Irish looked at Nate but he shook his head. "I have to see to the final loading of the *Eagle*. There are two English warships in the harbor. I want to get my ship out of here on the evening tide and well away from both of them. I don't want either of them catching the *Eagle* at sea and taking any of my men."

Sighing, she nodded. "Pack the lunch, Ruby. I'll take it to them. I'll ride Renegade up there."

She would have to face Ty sooner or later. It might as well be this morning. She knew he had left early to avoid seeing her, but she hoped that he would allow them to at least be amicable.

Later that morning Ruby handed her the basket she had packed and Irish set off to Fortune's Pride. Charlie was not in sight when she arrived but Ty was, and a pang of guilt shot through her. She had never seen Ty look less than perfect, but he did this morning. His stock was slightly crooked as if he had tied it in haste and without looking in the mirror, his queue was not as neatly tied as usual, and there was a smudge on his sleeve. Was it because of her? He looked up at her approach and he didn't appear to have slept much, either.

He gave her a tight smile and nodded his head politely as he would have to any stranger who would happen by.

Because of the lunch basket she held in front of her she had not been able to let Renegade run like he wanted and he was in a feisty mood, especially now that she had stopped altogether. He kept prancing around and urging her to give him his head.

She dismounted and tied him to a tree where he would be able to graze, hoping that would content him for the time it would take to deliver the lunch.

She carried the basket to where Ty waited beside a stack of brick. "I brought you and Charlie some lunch," she said, holding the basket up for him to see.

"Thank you," he said coolly. "I'm sure Charlie will appreciate it."

Charlie would appreciate it. Not him. She set the basket on the ground and leaned against the chest high stack of bricks, looking across the pile at him standing stiffly on the other side. She toyed with one of the bricks, its surface red and rough against her fingers, wanting him to say something, to smile at her. She didn't want things to be this way between them. Why couldn't they be friends?

"You're angry, aren't you?" she asked.

He nodded politely then looked away from her. "If you'll excuse me, I have to get back to work."

She slammed a brick down against the others making a dull clank. "You're not making this easy for me, Ty!"

He turned to face her across the stack of bricks. "What do you want from me?"

"I thought we could at least be friends."

He shook his head. "I told you I don't think that will work."

"Why not?"

He leaned against the stack on his side, his fingers white-knuckled from the strength of his grip on the edge of the pile. "Do you think I can look at you every day, smile at you, laugh with you, and never be able to touch you, to know I will never have you beneath me again? What do you think I'm made of, Irish?"

"Do you think it's any easier for me?"

His gaze traveled up and down her, but instead of being warmed by it as she usually was, she felt like she had been struck. "It must be. Here you are insisting on friendship like there was never anything at all between us."

"Oh there's something between us, Ty." She set a brick between them, then another on top of it. "You're building a wall between us that I can't seem to knock down."

He set one of the bricks off her pile. "I'm not the one building walls, here, Irish."

She put the brick back. "Oh, yes, you are. And you're too proud to admit it. Your pride is hurt so now you're trying to build a wall to keep me out."

He slammed two more bricks onto the pile so hard chips flew. "You accuse me of building walls, Irish, but the wall you've built around yourself is so high no one can get in and you won't let anything out." He leaned over their little wall to look her directly in the eyes. "What are you hiding behind your wall, Irish? What is it that is so terrible that you won't let anyone know who you are?"

Her breath came out in a whoosh and she stood there trying to find something to say. But she dared not say the one thing he wanted to hear. She couldn't tell him who she was. "That's why you won't marry me, isn't it? Your terrible secret." He piled two more bricks up between them. "Until you can trust me enough to tell me what is wrong, there can never be anything more between us... except walls." With that, he turned and walked away.

She watched him go and was glad she had the bricks to lean against for support. He did not look back even though she watched him for a long time, and she knew he meant what he said.

He was right. She had said it to herself. She could not marry anyone she could not trust with her secret. It wouldn't be right. But how could she tell him? She looked at the little brick wall they had built between them. He was right. It was not nearly as strong or as tall as the wall she had surrounded herself with. But what else could she do?

Lifting her chin she walked back to Renegade and mounted. She would make sure to avoid Ty until Mrs. Fortune returned and she could leave. It shouldn't be difficult. He was trying to avoid her just as hard.

Nate brought Mrs. Fortune back home the next afternoon and

Irish decided it was time to leave. Now. Today. Before Ty returned home this evening and she had to face another dinner made even more awkward with his mother sitting there wondering why Irish and her son were not speaking to each other--were not even looking at each other.

Maybe he was right. It was too hard to be so close and only be friends, especially now that they had tasted each other, and knew what more there could be between them.

So she had bid farewell to a tearful Mrs. Fortune who made her promise to stay in the Fortune's town house until she found a place of her own.

"You stay there as long as you want to, Irish," Mrs. Fortune had said as Irish boarded Nate's little ship for the brief trip to Charles Town. "And I hope you are still there when we all come next week for Ruth Townsend's wedding."

Irish waved until Mrs. Fortune was out of sight. She watched the last of the house disappear as they rounded a bend in the river and wondered if she would ever see it again. She had been happy there. Safe. It had only been when she had accompanied the family into town that she had worried someone from her past might see her, and the accusations would fly. Now she was heading back to town--this time alone.

A week passed while she scanned the papers for any advertisements of property outside of town she might be able to afford. She talked to merchants and bankers asking about property, but nothing seemed available right now that would meet her needs, and suit her pocketbook.

She had hoped she would find someplace before the family came to town but they were due to arrive today and she had found nothing. She peeked out the tiny window of the attic room she had moved her things into. With the whole family coming, including Mariette and the twins, every room would be needed, so Irish did not remain in her usual room. Besides, that room, too, had been Ty's. She didn't want to impose on him or the family any more than she had to. No matter how much Mrs. Fortune insisted that she was part of the family, she knew that was not true.

She bent to shove her small trunk under the narrow bed. The room was normally used only by visitors' servants, so it was bare of decoration with only a small chest and the bed. There wasn't even a rug. But in the heat of summer, she wouldn't need one. However, it did have a window that overlooked the street, even though the ceiling slanted down on one side and she had to be careful not to bump her head.

Irish glanced out the window again, watching for the family. Watching for Ty. No matter how many times she had scolded herself for wanting to see him again, she found herself looking for his form, his face, on half the men passing three stories below on the street. Her pulse would race until the man came close enough for her to realize that he was too tall or too heavy or too poorly dressed to be Ty.

She was still gazing out the window when she spied a man walking by who made her breath catch, but this time it wasn't because she thought it was Ty. She had not gotten much of a look at the fellow but he had strongly resembled...her brother. Unconsciously she clutched at her fichu as if she could stop her heart from pounding. *You're just overwrought because you expect to see Ty,* she told herself.

She sat on the bed, gripping the edge of the mattress. It couldn't be Ian. Not here. Not in Charles Town. Ian was in Ireland.

Taking a deep breath, she muttered one of Nate's favorite phrases, "Steady as she goes." She always worried about running into someone from her past when she was in Charles Town. There were always so many ships coming in to port--who knew who they might bring? But was it possible? Had one of them brought Ian to Charles Town?

She shook her head in denial. Surely she was just imagining things. After more than two years it was unlikely that anyone was still looking for her. No, she was safe. She had to be. But the sounds of people calling out and the rattle of a carriage still startled her, until she realized that it must be the family arriving.

Jumping up, she looked down in time to see the Fortune carriage door opened by one of the town servants, and then Ty was stepping down into the street just below her. He was here and she drank in the sight of him, even though she could see little more than the top of his tri-corn. She scarcely noticed Mariette and Mrs. Fortune each holding one of the twins, or Alejandro. Nate and Matt were driving a wagon loaded with the family's belongings.

Alejandro and Ty began helping the servants unload trunks and Irish knew she should go down and help the family get settled. She stood and for a moment tried hard to calm herself. The family wouldn't be staying more than a week. Surely she could live within reach of Ty that long without dying.

Lifting her chin she marched down the stairs. To her dismay, the first person to look up and see her was Ty. His eyes widened and he looked her up and down, as if he were as hungry for her as she was for him. But then his mouth tightened into a hard line and he merely nodded an acknowledgement of her presence. She managed to meet his gaze without flinching, nodding her head to him, as well.

There was utter chaos in the entry with trunks and baskets and babies and baby beds being hauled in. Mrs. Fortune and Mariette were directing the servants which room to take things to. Servants seemed more interested in seeing and holding the babies than in putting things away, and Mariette seemed pleased to show them off. One of the babies started to cry and that woke the other who started to cry, too, and that, more than anything, got the servants moving.

Irish stopped near the bottom of the stairs, her hand on the curved wooden banister and Ty right before her.

"I thought you would be gone by now," he said, but his tone did not carry the harshness the scowl on his face did.

"I hoped to be. I'll find my own place as soon as I can. Meantime, I'll try not to intrude any more than I have to."

They looked for a long moment into each other's eyes but there didn't seem to be anything else to say. She edged past him and plunged into the chaos helping the servants get everything sorted and put away.

After that, she tried to stay out of Ty's way. She took a tray up to her room for supper. But she just couldn't stay away from the babies. Neither could anyone else. There were always servants holding the babies when their other duties were not pressing. Or one of Mariette's brothers. Irish managed to get to hold each of the twins a time or two the next day, always making sure Ty was not around first.

That afternoon Mariette asked her to go with her and the babies for a walk. They strolled down Church Street each holding an infant with a servant trailing behind. They could hardly get down the block for so many people, friends and strangers alike, stopping them to look at the twins.

The next morning Irish ran a few errands for Mrs. Fortune, and walked with Mariette and the babies again, and at noon she was just sitting down in her room with a tray when there was a tap at her door. She was surprised to find Mrs. Fortune standing there.

"May I come in?"

Irish stood aside and Mrs. Fortune came into the tiny room.. There wasn't a chair, so she sat on the bed and patted the spot next to her. Irish sat down beside her. Mrs. Fortune came straight to the point. "Why haven't you been eating with the family, Irish? And why are you hiding up here?"

Feeling a bit uneasy at Mrs. Fortune's directness, she shrugged. "It's crowded in the house with everyone here."

Mrs. Fortune crossed her arms. "That explains why you moved to this room but it doesn't explain why you're missing from our table."

"I don't want to intrude."

Mrs. Fortune reached over and took her hand. "Irish, darling, you are not an intrusion. You are part of this family."

She shook her head. "Not really. I appreciate all you've done for me, but I need to find my own place."

Mrs. Fortune pursed her lips and looked at her through narrowed eyes. "It's that son of mine, isn't it?"

Irish didn't say anything. What could she say? But she felt the telltale warmth of a blush spreading across her face.

Placing her hand on Irish's arm, Mrs. Fortune leaned close. "Please don't let whatever it is between you and Ty stand between you and the rest of this family. You have been too dear to us. We want you to continue to be a part of this family. And I speak for Mariette and Matt and Nate, as well as myself."

"Thank you, Mrs. Fortune." She hugged the older woman and received a warm hug in return.

Mrs. Fortune stood up. "Now come along and have lunch with us."

She couldn't. Not yet. She needed some time to prepare before she faced Ty at that table. "I've already brought up a tray--but I'll come down for dinner tonight."

Mrs. Fortune looked at her a moment then nodded. "I'll take that as a promise." Smiling she left.

That afternoon Mrs. Fortune asked Irish to run a couple of

errands for her. She was just a block from the house when a man stepped out of a side street directly in front of her, barring her way.

"I just knew you'd land on your feet. You always do."

Irish felt the blood drain from her face and she clutched the packages she held to keep from shaking. All her worst fears surged within her. She had imagined this happening, had hoped it wouldn't...but now it had.

She hadn't imagined seeing her brother two days ago, after all. He really was here. And somehow she would have to deal with him.

"Hello, Ian," she said coolly, surprised at how steady her voice sounded when she was shaking so hard inside. Maybe it was all those times she had imagined what she would do if he--or someone from her past–really did show up.

"Not a very warm greetin' for yer own flesh and blood, now is it, me girl?"

"How did you find me?"

"The ship they put you on was bound for Charles Town. I figured you'd be here somewhere. But it took you long enough to show up. I been here nigh on to three weeks now searchin' for you." His voice had changed from a snarl to a complaining whine. "Been askin' lots of folks about you, too, but nobody seemed to know you. But I figured if you was here you'd be where the gentry lives. I knew it would take some rich nabob to buy you. That's why I been hangin' around."

"Go away and leave me alone," she snapped, and tried to push past him.

But he snared her arm, gripping it so tightly it hurt. "Now is that any way to treat me after I come all this way lookin' for you?"

She tried to pull her arm free, but he jerked her close to his side. She could smell the whiskey on his breath, his unwashed body. He never had much coin but he could always manage to find enough to slake his thirst.

"I have to go, Ian."

He grinned. "Got you on a tight leash, have they? I been watching you parade up and down with them babies, and runnin' errands for them."

"Let me go!" she whispered, afraid of being noticed by a passerby.

"We gots to talk, Kathleen."

A stab of fear shot though her to hear her name spoken so casually, and on the street in broad daylight, no less! But her brother must not know what had happened to her after she was transported. "I have nothing to say to you!"

She tried again to free herself but he pulled her even closer, shoving his face into hers. "Either you meet me and talk, or I'll come calling. Right up to the front door of that big, fine house, and demand to see me sister."

Anger and fear swirled within her. Her brother could easily destroy all that she had worked so hard for in the last two years, expose her, possibly get her sent to prison. She gave him a quick nod of acquiescence.

He grinned and loosened his grip on her arm. "Tonight. After dark. Johnny's Tavern. You'll be sorry if you don't show up."

Ian let her go then and swaggered off, whistling a jolly tune as if he didn't have a care in the world. She gritted her teeth. Well, he didn't. It was her who had always had to deal with his mistakes and flaws. She rubbed her arm where he had held her. Now she would have to give him whatever he had come for and get rid of him before she lost everything all over again.

That evening Irish hurried down the street not liking this part of town and wanting to get back to the house. The streets were full of sailors from a newly docked English war ship and the men on shore leave eyed her, and called out to her. But she ignored them.

When she arrived at Johnny's Tavern, she was surprised that any man would ask a woman to come to such a disreputable place, especially when that woman was his sister. But Ian had never cared much for her reputation or safety, only for what she could give him, or do for him. She was glad she had worn old clothes and brought a dark shawl to cover her head.

The door of the tavern stood open to catch the last of the evening breeze. But there had been too many years accumulation of smoke and ale, vomit and rancid bodies for any breeze to ever freshen the smell.

Irish edged inside, stepping carefully over a rough wooden floor littered with broken glass, tobacco ashes, and other leavings, and looked around, trying to find Ian through the thick haze of smoke inside. Johnny's was evidently a popular place and every table was full of uniformed sailors and rough laborers, many with blowsy women with nearly exposed breasts and shortened skirts sitting on their laps.

Suddenly Irish's arm was snagged and she was jerked around. "'Bout time you got here," Ian snarled. He shoved her down onto a rickety wooden bench at a table so littered with food scraps Irish thought it probably had never been cleaned. He settled into his seat across from her and pulled a mug of ale to him and took a deep drink. Wiping his mouth with the back of one hand he looked her up and down and smirked. "I'd offer you a drink, but I remember how particular you always was. You probably wouldn't drink it anyways. Besides, I'm a little strapped for cash right now."

"You always were," she stated flatly, sitting straight and folding her hands in her lap.

He laughed and sat back, throwing one arm over the back

of his chair. "I likes me comforts, that's true," he said. "And that brings me to why I'm here."

Irish gripped the pocket she had tied around her waist under her skirt before she came. She had known he would want money and she had come prepared to buy him off. She hoped she had brought enough to keep him out of her way until she could find some place to live where he might not find her again. Maybe she would even buy passage to another colony. Anywhere she would be safe.

She only glared at him, waiting for him to continue.

He hunched forward again, his mug within the folds of his arms on the table and leaned close to her. "Ah, lass, times were hard without you."

She was not about to soften with sympathy. "Was it any harder than the life of slavery I was condemned to because of you?" she asked coldly.

He waved a hand in the air as if all that was past and forgotten. Maybe he had forgiven and forgotten but she had not.

"You don't seem to be so bad off." He looked her up and down. "Though yer masters don't seem to clothe you as well as most of the other servants I been seein' comin' and goin' from that fine house. Now why is that, I wonder?"

She didn't need him asking too many questions. It was to her advantage that he believe she was an indentured servant in the Fortune home, bought and paid for on the auction block. If he knew the truth, he could expose her. "What do you want, Ian?" she asked, cutting short his questions.

"Ah, lass, yer're hard," he complained.

"What do you want, Ian?"

He cleared his throat and wiped his mouth. At least it seemed that he found it a little bit difficult to ask his sister for money. "There wasn't much left for me in Ireland and as I said, I'm a bit low on coin."

"In other words you had made too many enemies to stay there." She leaned forward to glare into his eyes. "Then how did you manage to pay for your passage? Fares are not cheap, Ian. What did you do? Steal the money?"

He managed to look offended, putting a hand to his chest. "Nothing so low as that, Kathleen."

She winced at his use of her name in a public place but could not berate him without raising his suspicions.

He shrugged. "I knew a thing or two about the ship captain's past dealings is all."

"Smuggling."

"He was more than happy to help me on my way."

"You threatened him with exposure." She nodded in understanding, knowing he would do the same thing to her if he found out about her. The blood they shared between them would make no difference to Ian.

"Aye, weel, I'm here now, ain't I, lass?" He gave her a grin. "And glad I am to see you once again. I could always count on you for a shilling or two."

"Is that what you want now, Ian? A shilling or two?"

He squirmed. "Well, with this war and all, expenses are a mite higher, especially here in the colonies." He held up a hand to make her let him continue. "I knows you're but a servant what don't get paid, but I know you, Kathleen. Money always seems to find its way to you."

She leaned toward him and spoke as if instructing a child. "I work for it, Ian. It's something anyone can do."

He waved a hand and continued as if he hadn't heard. "But I could use more than a shilling or two, Darlin'. I got me just a few wee debts."

Her eyes narrowed. "Gambling."

He just shrugged and grinned at her, laying his hand palm up on the table and wiggling his fingers waiting for her to place her hard earned coin in it.

Suppressing a sigh she pulled out the money she had brought and placed it in his hand. His eyes widened at the amount and immediately his fist closed over it, and he put it in his pocket.

Grinning broadly now he waved to the barmaid to come fill his empty mug and Irish pulled her shawl further forward on her face, not wanting to be seen. The maid must have served Ian before because she held out her hand for the money before she poured his ale.

Gritting her teeth, Irish noticed that Ian gave the girl far more than the price of his drink and swatted her appreciatively on the bottom as she walked away. At that rate, she thought, the money she gave him would not last long. She stood to leave but he grabbed her hand. "Don't rush off, Darlin'!"

She shook off his hand and walked away. She couldn't wait to get away from the sight and smell of the tavern, and to put Ian from her mind for at least the few days that her money would last him.

Halfway to the door, she turned to look back to make sure Ian was not coming after her, and ran into a rock-solid male chest. She gasped and started to apologize but the man grasped her by the shoulders.

"Irish?"

Irish gasped with alarm then sagged with relief. "Nate! I'm glad to see you!" And she was, she realized. Nate would make sure she got home safely before some drunken sailor accosted her.

"What are you doing here?" he asked. Still holding her by the shoulders he leaned back to look her over as if something might be wrong with her. "Who is that man you were with?"

"I..." She looked back to Ian who was looking their way, grinning amicably and nodding to them both as if they were old acquaintances. There was no explanation she could give for being in this part of town and she certainly did not want to either explain or introduce Ian, so she simply shrugged.

Nate studied her through narrowed eyes for a moment but didn't press her to explain why she was there. "Would you like me to see you home?"

Breathing a sigh of relief, she nodded. He pulled her arm through his and started walking back the way he had come. "Not a very pleasant part of town to take a stroll," he said.

"Not pleasant at all," she agreed. "What are you doing here?"

"I'm going around to the taverns to find our sailors and warn them to go home. There's a war ship newly docked this evening and I don't want any of our men "pressed" into the royal navy."

"I thought the *Eagle* sailed a few days ago."

"It did but there are still two other Fortune family ships in port."

Irish looked up at Nate with a start. "What about yourself? What if they take you?"

He laughed, but she could tell it wasn't totally free of worry. "They usually don't start impressing men until the last day or two in port. After they've rounded up every man of their own, that's when they go out to find a few to fill out the ranks. Usually they grab men in their cups and tell them the next day, after they've sobered up, that they've enlisted."

"I thought they grabbed any able-bodied man they could find?"

Nate shook his head. "Only when they're desperate. And with this war, they too often do get a bit desperate for sailors."

They walked in silence the rest of the way. Nate saw her inside and started back down the street.

"Nate," she called after him, "be careful."

Giving her a jaunty salute, he went on his way.

Chapter Eighteen

ALL THE TALK AT LUNCH THE NEXT DAY WAS ABOUT THE BALL the family was attending that evening. Irish listened but didn't participate in the discussion since she did not plan to go. She allowed herself a quick glance to the other end of the table where Ty sat and their gazes met. They both froze for a moment and she thought she could see as much longing in his eyes as she felt.

She tore her gaze away. No matter how she felt, it was certain that she could not marry Ty now, not with her brother here. Ian was always on the lookout for a way to make quick easy money. It would only be a matter of time before he figured out the truth of her situation here. Then she would be subjected to blackmail of the worst sort. She had to get far from Charles Town as soon as she could. One of those Fortune ships in the harbor now would surely be leaving again within a week or so.

"Of course Irish is going tonight, aren't you, Irish?"

Irish jumped at Mariette's question. She shook her head. "No. I hadn't planned to go."

"But my dear, you must," Mrs. Fortune said. "I don't want to be the only female from this household going."

"What about Mariette?"

Mariette laughed. "I already have two dance partners named Rachel and Ryan. I just don't want to leave the twins that long so soon. And besides," she said, patting her belly, "I still don't fit into my ball gowns, yet."

"Well, that's another problem for me," Irish said to Mrs. Fortune. "I don't have a ball gown."

Mrs. Fortune grinned triumphantly. "I knew that and I knew you'd try to use that as an excuse not to go, even though I know how much you love to dance." She threw a glance at Mariette. "Mariette brought one of her gowns for you to wear tonight. It will fit you just fine."

Irish just sat there with her mouth hanging open not knowing what to say.

"It's a beautiful emerald green, too," Mariette added. "It will look wonderful with your hair and eyes."

Mrs. Fortune patted her arm. "It's settled then! Nate and Matt will ride in the carriage with us and Ty…"

"I'll be walking over to the Hall's, and will accompany them to the ball," Ty said, looking pointedly at Irish.

She looked away from him feeling like he had just stabbed her in the heart. She tried to tell herself that Betsy would make him a fine wife. But she didn't believe it and she didn't think he did, either. The evening would be a difficult one watching Ty dance with Betsy, knowing that she could never have him, never again experience his embrace. She felt like one of those sailors impressed into service in the navy. She felt trapped. She lifted her head. It was just one evening. She would get through it. And she would smile and enjoy every dance!

Suddenly Matt startled them all by jumping up from his chair and running to the window.

"What is it, Matt?" Ty asked, already on his feet along with Nate and Alejandro.

Matt didn't answer but ran out of the house to return a few moments later. "Someone was out there," he said.

"Maybe it was one of the servants," Mrs. Fortune suggested.

He shook his head. "He's gone now. But whoever it was was there for some time."

"What did he look like?" Alejandro asked.

Matt shook his head again. "I didn't see him, just a movement outside the window. The plants there had been trampled by a man's boots, but the man was gone."

"I wonder what he could have wanted," Mrs. Fortune said.

A band was tightening about Irish's chest. She didn't have to wonder who it was and what he wanted. It was Ian. She was sure. It was just the kind of thing he would do to spy on her. She had less time than she thought to get out of Charles Town.

The orchestra was very good and the food wonderful, but Irish was not enjoying the ball nearly as much as she had enjoyed Abby's wedding. It was not easy to watch Ty dance every dance with Betsy or her sister, or other young and beautiful women. Not that she didn't have her own share of partners. But there was only one partner she truly wanted and he was the one she could not have. But realizing that, accepting that, didn't stop her heart from breaking every time she saw Ty put his arm about Betsy's waist or take her hands in the steps of a reel.

Betsy, as usual, was smiling sweetly and Irish wished she could at least dislike the girl, but except for the fact that she was in Ty's arms, there was nothing to dislike. She might be a bit insipid, but Betsy was good and sweet and proper. In short, all the things Irish wasn't.

Matt, for once, had put off his buckskins and moccasins for formal dress, but he had loosened his stock and looked like he wished he were out in the woods instead of in a Charles Town ballroom.

Mrs. Fortune seemed to be enjoying herself, and had her choice of partners, though she had chosen to sit down for a bit.

Irish sat down beside her thinking the woman did seem a bit wistful, though, and was sure she was missing her husband. She kept touching the necklace her husband had given her, a string of emeralds set in gold.

Irish tried to focus on the conversation with Mrs. Fortune and Betsy's sister, Prudence, but her gaze and her thoughts kept turning back to where Ty was dancing with Betsy. They made a fine looking pair, he with his silver silk coat and her with a gown nearly the same color. It was as if they had planned to wear matching outfits. Betsy had worn an outfit that matched Ty's to the fair, too, which made Irish wonder if Betsy had a spy in the Fortune household who told her what Ty was going to wear so she could dress accordingly. Then she dismissed the thought. Not proper, sweet Betsy.

Irish glanced sideways at Betsy's mother who was sitting there looking more than smug. No, not her either. The Halls were just too upright and open for subterfuge. But Mrs. Hall certainly seemed pleased with the attention Ty was giving her daughter, which, considering the wealth and influence of the Fortune family, and the handsomeness of her daughter's suitor, that was to be expected.

Suddenly Ty caught Irish looking at him and she quickly averted her eyes. But it was too late. She was sure he had seen her watching him. Using the fan he had given her she fanned herself and peeked over its edge. He wasn't looking at her now. He was giving his complete attention to Betsy, leaning close to her with a captivating smile on those sensuous lips. Lips Irish had tasted but which she would never taste again. Had Betsy had a taste of them as well? Irish snapped her fan closed and gripped it tightly in her hand. So what if she had? If Ty married Betsy, she would taste far more than his lips. Then she had to stifle a giggle. No, not Betsy. She couldn't imagine Betsy ever tasting the parts of Ty that she had. Or, for that matter, allowing him to taste parts of her that Irish had more than enjoyed having him taste.

At that thought she had to fan herself again. It was a thought she would have to put away, wrapped in silken splendor and tucked far back in her mind, to be taken out only on rare occasions like a fine and delicate treasure.

The dance finished with a grand bowing of the partners to each other, and when Irish saw Betsy sink into a deep graceful curt-sey with Ty bowing over her hand, they looked so perfect together she thought they could be models for Meissen figurines. Then they straightened and headed toward her.

Well, not quite toward her. Ty led Betsy to a seat next to her sister and Betsy opened her fan and began to fan herself languidly, enough to stir the air but certainly not enough to muss her still perfectly piled and curled hair.

Douglass Townsend, a lawyer and long time friend of the fam-ily came over. He nodded and smiled at Irish and the Fortunes then asked permission to sit beside Betsy and began to talk with her, his pale blond head bent close to Betsy's.

The orchestra director announced an alamand and couples be-gan forming squares for the dance. Ruth Townsend and her fiancé came up to them. "We need two more couples for our square," she said looking around their group.

Standing before Betsy, Ty gave Irish a long, clenched-jawed look. Then he turned back to Betsy and gave her a smile that would have left Irish melting into a puddle at his feet, but which seemed to have left the perfectly poised Betsy, well, still perfectly poised.

"Betsy?" Ty said holding out his arm.

She cast a quick glance toward Douglass then gave Ty a sweet smile, placing one hand delicately on her chest as if out of breath.

"I think I would like to sit for just a bit, Ty, if you don't mind."

Prudence jumped up and took Ty's proffered arm. "I'd love to do the alamand, Ty." Then she grabbed Irish's hand. "You and Matt can be partners, Irish. That will complete the square."

Matt arched a questioning brow at Irish and she glanced up at Ty. All evening she had managed to avoid being in the same square or opposite him in a reel, but now he was giving her a challenging look as if he had known what she was doing. Her chin came up. She might die a little bit each time he touched her in the dance, but she was not going to back down from him, or anyone. Placing a hand on Matt's arm she stood and led all of them onto the dance floor.

Irish and Matt took their place for the dance across from Ty and Prudence. Irish wiped suddenly damp palms on her kerchief then tucked it back into her bodice. She looked up to see Ty looking at where she was tucking it. She took her time then, stuffing it slowly into the crevasse between her breasts, trailing her fingers down her stomacher. His gaze followed with an intensity that made her grow even warmer than the heat of the ballroom warranted. In moments he would be touching her, his hand at her waist or touching her hand. Why had she allowed herself to get talked into this?

She lifted her chin and straightened her shoulders. Why not? She loved to dance and she was not going to live her life avoiding any possible chance encounter with one very handsome and desirable Tyrus Fortune. And if she had to leave the colony because of her brother, this dance would give her something to always remember. She was going to savor every touch, every look.

The music started and the four couples began going through the steps. Whenever she took Ty's hand in the alamand, he gave her fingers an extra squeeze. Whenever he had to circle with her, his hand did not rest lightly on her waist but kneaded or slid upward, daringly close to the underside of her breast in so public a place. He never took his eyes off her. And his gaze was so intense, his brows drawn together, shadowing his eyes, making them look deeper, darker, like two black coals ready to burst into flame. Already she felt scorched. It wasn't just the heat of the ball room and her dancing that was making her cheeks feel hot, making her feel like every organ within her was melting into slush.

She wondered if he was deliberately reminding her of what she was throwing away, or if he just wanted her as much as she wanted him and was doing something about it. The answer came near the end of the dance when he circled with her once more. His hand slipped downward, the edge of his hand just resting on the top edge of the curve of her buttocks.

He bent down close to her, his lips so close to her ear that she could feel the breath of him touching her neck, finding all those places he had kissed, reminding her anew of what they had shared so briefly. She tried not to respond to him but her body had been well-trained to his touch and it sprang to life. Her breathing quickened, her lips parted of their own accord, and she could not help leaning closer to him.

"Your body hasn't forgotten me, Irish. I am as imprinted on it as you are on mine. Remember that as you walk away." With that he let her go and finished the last steps of the dance swinging Prudence in a circle that caused the girl to squeal with laughter.

Irish wasn't sure how she got back to Mrs. Fortune and her chair, but she knew that she couldn't have done it without leaning heavily on Matt's arm. She refused to look at Ty again. She couldn't. When she managed to get some strength back into her legs she stood up. "I'm going to get some air."

"I'll go with you," Matt said. "It's stuffy in here."

The two of them fetched lemonade, then went to stand by the open door that led into the garden, trying to catch a bit of a breeze. Irish looked out into the darkness for a moment, fanning herself, until she realized that she was using the fan Ty had given her. She snapped it closed and dropped it to let it dangle from her wrist.

Mrs. Fortune joined them, fanning herself with one hand and fingering her necklace with the other. They turned toward the door when they heard the sound of new arrivals.

"It's the captain of the English war ship and his wife," Matt said.

Mrs. Fortune craned her neck to see. "Mrs. Townsend met them yesterday. She told me that the captain is the second son of the Earl of Rochester." She leaned closer to Matt and Irish and whispered, "Mrs. Townsend also told me that his wife is a merchant's daughter and not very attractive, but was able to snare Captain Woodford because of her money."

Matt turned back from the door and made a face. "Mrs. Townsend is right. The captain's wife is certainly no beauty with that long nose and—" Mrs. Fortune punched her son's arm and he chuckled. "But with money and a connection to the nobility, they're sure to be the toast of the town while they're here." He said, tossing back the last of his lemonade, not at all impressed with the new arrivals.

Irish's eyes widened in horror. No, it couldn't be! She looked around Matt's broad shoulders to see Captain and Mrs. Woodford and then clutched his arm for support. It really was Amanda Collins, now Mrs. Woodford, who stood amidst a throng of people waiting to greet her. The very same Amanda Collins who had accused her of theft and gotten her transported for life. What would Amanda do if she saw her here? Unless Amanda asked, she would not know that Irish had never been sold, never served a day of her sentence, unless she would count the six months Irish was a slave of the Spanish.

But knowing Amanda, she *would* ask and she would find out, especially if she happened to see her former hired companion in a fine dress, in the company of a prominent family, dancing in a grand Charles Town ballroom. Just what she would do then Irish had no way of knowing, but she couldn't risk finding out. She could not let that woman see her. Amanda was just petty and spiteful enough to make sure Irish was turned over to the law to be sold for her "crime", as she was supposed to have been.

Irish looked around wildly, wondering how she could make her escape.

"Irish, darling," Mrs. Fortune said, "are you feeling all right? I've never seen you looking so pale. You look as if you are about to faint."

Irish seized on what Mrs. Fortune had said. "You're right, I don't feel very well. I really would like to go home." She began edging toward the open door behind her, keeping the fan Ty had given her up before her face. "I'll just slip out this way. Please make my apologies to the Townsends."

Before Irish could escape, however, Mrs. Fortune caught her arm. "You can't go home alone, my dear. Matt, would you see Irish home?"

Gratefully, not feeling at all that sure that her knees wouldn't give way beneath her, Irish took Matt's arm and he escorted her home.

Ty saw Irish talking to Matt and his mother, then disappear out the door to the garden with Matt. She seemed to be in some haste to leave the dance for some reason, and just when the captain of the war ship and his wife were arriving. All the other women seemed to be hurrying toward the new arrivals, anxious to make their acquaintance. He had to suppress a smile. Wasn't it just like his Irish not to be impressed with someone because of wealth or connections. His Irish? He shook his head. She wasn't his. She had made that clear. Or tried to.

The smile he had tried to suppress made its way to the corners of his lips, lifting them. No, she was his. She just wouldn't admit it. He had felt her tremble each time he had touched her in the measures of the dance. He had seen the quickened rise and fall of her chest and her pulse throbbing wildly at her throat. She wanted him as much as he wanted her. If only she would trust him enough to tell him what was keeping her from him. Surely they could find some solution. Together.

Prudence was tugging at his arm and urging him forward for an introduction to the captain and his wife. Betsy was already half-way across the room, her arm through Douglass's, with the most animated smile on her face he had yet seen.

He sighed and led Prudence over for her introduction.

It was late when the ball ended. No one had wanted to leave before the Woodfords. And that couple, especially Mrs. Woodford, seemed quite pleased with their reception by Charles Town society. They had been inundated with invitations, including one from Ty's own mother. Mrs. Woodford had left with a beatific smile on her homely face.

As Ty walked Betsy home, she held his arm so lightly he could almost believe she wasn't there. She was a lovely, sweet girl, he thought. He wanted to get married sometime and as he had told Irish, he could do worse than marrying Betsy. Then why did he keep thinking about Irish? He had imagined how Irish would look at a ball with her hair in disarray and her cheeks warm and flushed, and that was just how she had looked tonight. And he couldn't help but compare her appearance with the way she had looked right after they had made love on the dining room floor—the images were disturbingly the same. Had every other man in that ballroom gazed at her and imagined her just rising from a passion driven bout in bed? Maybe that was why she'd had a partner for every dance.

He ground his teeth. Irritating wench! Why couldn't she admit that they were right for each other?

"This is where I live, Ty." Betsy gently tugged at his arm to halt him, pulling him out of his reverie. So wrapped up in thoughts of Irish, he *had* forgotten Betsy was there.

Is this what his life with Betsy would be like? A wisp of a wife scarcely making her presence evident? He turned to face her and she gave him one of her sweet smiles, and he wondered if he could ever break through her cool reserve, if there was warmth and passion hidden beneath her calm exterior. There was one way to find out.

He opened the gate and led her not to her door, but into the privacy of the garden. He pulled her close and bent his head to kiss her, but at the last moment she turned her head, so that his kiss landed on her cheek. No passion there, he thought, but he persevered, turning her face to his with a hand on her chin. Then he claimed her lips.

She stiffened at the first touch of his lips on hers, but she did not fight him. Nor did she kiss him back. Betsy kept her lips tightly closed, her mouth pursed, like a child. It was like kissing a fencepost. This must be her first kiss, he thought, because she certainly didn't know how to go about it. That somehow pleased him, but he was still trying to find some response, some spark to let him know that passion was there somewhere.

It had not been hard to find the passion in Irish. She exuded it. She glowed with it. Her passion seemed to jump out and grab him. The first time he had even touched her, let alone kiss her, he had felt drenched in passion, both his and hers. There had been none of this cool, detached touching of lips like he was finding with Betsy. Yet Irish was able to keep her passion in check, too, the way she was rebuffing him and trying to keep him at bay. It was still there, though. He had felt it, seen it, each time he had touched her on that dance floor this evening.

Putting his arms around Betsy, Ty sought for a better angle of attack, but Betsy's whole body felt stiff and fearful. What the hell did she think he was going to do, anyway?

"Relax, Betsy," he said. "I just want to kiss you."

He could feel her relax, but he could also tell that it was a conscious effort on her part to do as he asked. He must be going about this all wrong because she just didn't seem to be enjoying it.

He tried again, and this time tried a more indirect approach, kissing her cheeks lightly, kissing her chin, then the corners of her lips before he again tried to claim her lips. She still held her lips tightly closed, but it wasn't as bad as before. Tentatively, he touched her lips with the tip of his tongue and she allowed it, but did not respond. He stood kissing her like that for a few moments, lightly, lightly, teasing and tempting, but she remained cool and unresponsive, simply allowing him the liberties. And suddenly he realized that neither of them was enjoying this.

He lifted his head and held her at arms length. She stood still, looking up at him with wide eyes. Had she ever closed them, he wondered? He didn't know because he had closed his, even though it hadn't helped one bit.

She lifted one hand to touch her lips, seemingly amazed, as if to say, *"Is that it? Is that all there is to kissing?"* He wanted to tell her that it wasn't. That with the right person, this kissing thing could be wildfire and could lead you to places you never thought you would ever go.

With the right person.

With Irish.

For him the right person was Irish. He had kissed a lot of women and there had been varying degrees of passion, but none was so right as when he kissed Irish. And that stubborn wench was denying both of them what should rightfully be theirs.

He sighed, looking down at Betsy. What was he going to do with her? He couldn't marry her now. He had known real passion, real wanting. He admired Betsy, but he couldn't marry her.

He let his arms drop, giving an uneasy laugh. What did one say to a very properly brought up young lady who would probably be expecting a marriage proposal at this point? He had called on her several times and had kissed her in a dark, private garden, after all.

"Betsy, I—"

But before he could say anything more, she blurted out, "Ty, I don't think this is going to work."

He blinked, surprised. Betsy had never interrupted him, or anyone else that he knew of. And she certainly had never spoken so strongly or directly. He nodded his head for her to continue.

She placed one hand on his arm, suddenly shy, sweet Betsy again, struggling to find the words for what she wanted to say. "Ty, I admire you and your family tremendously, but I just don't think there's anything...I mean, you haven't yet made your intentions clear, but...I don't..."

He took her hand and squeezed it. "I think I know what you mean, Betsy." He smiled. "You want to end this before I make a fool of myself and offer you a proposal you would have to reject."

She sighed and her shoulders slumped in relief. "Exactly."

"But you would like for us to remain friends."

She bit her lip uncertainly. "Could we?"

He smiled, greatly relieved. "We can. We should." He squeezed her hand again then bent and gave her a chaste kiss of friendship on the forehead.

As Ty walked back to his home he realized that for a man who had been turned down by two women in a matter of days, he was feeling extraordinarily lighthearted. Well, he hadn't actually proposed to Betsy, but he was happy about the outcome at any rate.

Now he just had to figure out a way to deal with Irish.

When he had come home, he had thought he wanted a quiet, genteel but submissive wife. A wife he could live with in peace and quiet and raise rice and children. Irish was hot tempered, hot blooded, anything but submissive, and sure to wreak havoc with any thoughts he had of having a quiet, peaceful life. She stirred him within and without, she made him look at his own future with anticipation, and she made him feel alive. She would bring a great deal of chaos into his life. He might have to forego a bit of the dignity he had cultivated along with any thought of propriety, but she would also bring him a great deal of laughter, love, and adventure.

He chuckled out loud, causing a passing gentleman to raise his brows at him and veer wide around him. Maybe there was more of his pirate grandfather in him, and less of his merchant-minded forebears, than he had thought.

There was just one problem to overcome. She had turned him down. But if he could just ferret out her secret, perhaps—just perhaps—she would have him after all. He had been hurt by her refusal of him and even more hurt by her lack of trust in him. He had tried to salve his wounds by returning to his courtship of Betsy. It hadn't worked. Now he knew that it was Irish he wanted and it was Irish he would have.

If he thought she really didn't want him, he would let her go, no matter how much pain it caused him. But he knew better. Her reaction to his touch during the dance told him she still wanted him. He grinned tightly. He was determined. She would be his.

Irish read the advertisement in the *Gazette* again. A small house and property were for sale near Williamsburg. It sounded perfect. She would have to borrow some money, but with her investments in Fortune Shipping, she should have no problem paying it off. It was out of the colony, but not so far that she couldn't visit sometimes. Nate was always running up to Williamsburg for one thing or another. She took out ink, pen, and paper and wrote a quick note to the address given. She would take this to the family shipping office today and send it.

On her way out the door she noticed Mrs. Fortune's necklace lying on a hall table and smiled. She was always leaving jewelry there.

She was only a block up the street when her arm was roughly grabbed.

"Seems you ain't no servant, after all, are ye?"

"Ian!" He was hurting her where he held her arm and she was shaking from the fright he had given her. Angrily, she wrenched free and walked on, but he kept pace beside her.

She gave him a quick sideways glance and noticed that his clothes looked like he had slept in them. They were stained and his stockings were gray and mud-spattered. His stock was a limp rag and his tricorn battered. He bent close to her ear and whispered, but loudly enough for anyone passing close to have heard. "They don't let servants eat at the table with 'em. Not even here in the colonies."

Irish nodded to a couple of impeccably dressed passing women, acquaintances of the Fortune family she had helped entertain a time or two. They looked from her to Ian with raised brows but smiled wanly and nodded to her. She was sure the news of her walking down the street with such a disreputable man would soon reach the Fortune household.

She turned to glare at Ian. "So it was you sneaking around and spying outside the window. It's just like you, Ian."

He shrugged. "I finds out things that way. Things you wouldn't of told me yerself."

"I see no reason to tell you anything, Ian. I gave you the money you asked for. Now leave me alone."

"That's just what I was goin' to do, Kathleen."

Her heart sped to a quicker beat but she tried not to let him see her fear when he used her given name so casually. He could so easily ruin all she had worked for. And if he realized it, his demands would be unending. As calmly and as casually as she could, she said, "Everyone here calls me Irish, Ian. You might as well do the same."

"I found that out, 'Irish', when I went askin' for ye and nobody seemed to know who I was talking about. Then I said, 'That redhaired Irish girl what lives with the Fortune family.' Then everybody knew who you was, and they gave me an earful, they did."

"Fine, Ian. Now if you'll excuse me, I have an errand to run." She tried to walk away from him but he caught up to her and snagged her arm again, holding her close.

"Don't go runnin' off, Darlin'. We do have things to talk about."

She stopped halfway across Church Street with carriages and wagons passing on either side of them. "We have nothing to talk about, Ian. I want you to leave me alone." Then she made a dash for the other side of the street. But he wasn't about to let her go, and he managed to keep pace with her.

"Folks told me how the ship you was on got captured by the Spanish, and how you helped rescue Matthew Fortune. The family couldn't do enough for you after that. I seen you last night in that fine gown going to that fancy ball." He nodded his head sagely. "No, me gal, you ain't no servant in that house. You done good for yourself. But then you always did. And here I am barely makin' it."

Irish could feel Ian circling like a vulture and fear plucked at her heart. Just how much did he know? All she could do was brave it out and hope she could bluff him into leaving her alone just long enough for her to get away from Charles Town. If she could just put him off for another day or two she could get to Williamsburg before he knew she was gone. If she asked the Fortunes not to tell anyone where she was, they would abide by her wishes, she was sure. So for now, she felt safe enough to snap at him, "Then get a job, Ian."

He put a hand to his chest as if she had wounded him. "Now Darlin', why should I do that when me dear sister has got more than enough for the both of us?"

She frowned. "Just because the Fortunes treat me well doesn't mean I have money to spare, Ian."

He grinned slyly. "But you could get it, now couldn't you?"

She cocked her head. "And just why would I want to do that?"

"Why, to help out your poor, destitute brother," he said.

She merely snorted.

"Or if that don't move your heart"–he squeezed her arm painfully–"maybe you'd do it to keep me from telling them folks what I know about you."

"You don't know any more than anybody else does, Ian. You can't threaten me."

"You mean that you told them fancy folks you're running from the law?"

She came to a halt, scarcely able to breathe. Then, realizing how much stopping like that was admitting to Ian, she went on. But her brother was sharp. Lazy, but sharp, and he went on like a dog with a bone in its teeth.

"Didn't think I'd figure it out, did you?" He chuckled. "But I put two and two together. If your ship got captured by the Spanish, then you never got sold as a transportee, did you? And if you never got sold, then you didn't serve the sentence you got." He scratched his head as if trying to remember just what that sentence was, but she was sure it was as clear and fresh in his mind as it was in hers. "A *lifetime* transportee, weren't you? Don't that mean you would be sold as an indentured servant for *life?*"

He pushed his face up close to hers for emphasis. "In other words, to be no better than a slave for the rest of your life! Yet here you are, a heroine rescuing the Fortunes from the Spanish, and traipsing around to fine balls with no mention that you were a condemned felon."

Irish shoved down her rising panic. Showing fear to a jackal like her brother only made him braver. Besides, she would soon be gone from here. Williamsburg would not be far enough to go, she now realized, but she would ask Nate to take her there. Then she would go someplace else from there. Ian wouldn't track her down again. But for now, she had to placate him somewhat.

"Very well, Ian. I'll meet you at that tavern again tomorrow tonight with more money."

He straightened and grinned hugely, now patting the arm he had previously so sorely abused. "That's me girl. I knew I could count on you." He tipped his grimy, battered hat to her and sauntered off down the street, whistling a tuneless air.

Irish clutched the letter she had written. It was worthless now. She wasn't going to be buying that little piece of property in Williamsburg. But she could go to the Fortune Shipping office and ask Nate if any Fortune ship would be leaving port soon, and if she could sail on it. At this point it didn't make any difference where, just as long as it was away from Ian.

She realized that her brother had distracted her so much she had passed the street she needed, so she turned around and retraced her steps, heading for the office.

Chapter Nineteen

IRISH RETURNED HOME IMMEDIATELY AFTER TALKING TO NATE. One of the Fortune ships was set to sail to Boston on the morning tide, he had informed her, and she was welcome to go. He had been puzzled and saddened by her sudden departure, but had agreed not to tell anyone where she had gone. She had planned to tell the rest of the family after supper that night that she was leaving.

Although she knew she could no longer live with the Fortunes and be in such close proximity to Ty, she had thought she would at least be living near Charles Town. Even if she could never marry him, she had thought she could at least see him once in a while. She could have caught a glimpse of him on the street or at a fair. But her brother had ruined all that. Now, she would never be able to return to Charles Town. She would have to disappear completely. She would stay in Boston long enough for Nate to transfer her funds from his shipping company, then she would leave and never see the Fortunes again.

Irish swiped at an angry tear with the back of her hand. She had always been strong. It was she who had found employment after Ian's father had died, leaving them with very little after his debts were paid. She would have to be strong again.

She was just packing the last of her things into a small trunk when a maid tapped lightly on her door to inform her that she had a caller.

"A caller?" Irish shook her head wondering who would come to call on her. "Who is it, Daphne?"

The girl shrugged and wrinkled her nose. "Don't know, Miss Irish. But he shore don't look like the sort we ought to be havin' in this house! I didn't let him in the parlor. I made him wait in the hall." With that, the girl flounced back down the stairs, clearly insulted to have whoever it was standing in the Fortune's front hall.

There was only one person who would come to the house looking for her that would fit a description of disreputable. Ian.

She wadded the fichu she had in her hand and threw it down then slammed the lid to the trunk. How dare he invade this home with his demands!

Fists clenched, she hurried down the stairs and stomped across the front hall to face her brother. He turned, eyes widening and hands raised, palm up.

"Now, Kathle—er, Irish, darlin', get that fire out of your eye," he said, backing up.

She charged straight at him, stopping only when she came nose to nose with him. "Get out of here," she growled. "You have no business coming here."

He gave a nervous chuckle. "I just thought I'd save you the trouble of meeting me tonight. You can give me the money now."

Hands on hips, Irish leaned toward him. "Why are you really here, Ian?"

He shed his subservient demeanor like a snake sheds its skin. His mouth tightened and his eyes narrowed and hardened. "I followed you this morning. You went to a shipping office, didn't you? I figured you're trying to skip out on me, so I come here to make sure you give me a little something before you leave, darlin', or I just might have to find some officer of the law and fill his ear."

"Hah! You getting cozy with an officer of the law? I doubt it. You have too much to hide yourself to go seeking out trouble." She crossed her arms triumphantly, knowing she was right. The last thing he would chance was to make himself known to the law. "Now you can just leave and meet me tonight as we planned."

Ian grabbed her arm, jerking her close. "I'll not be fobbed off, 'Irish'. I want me money now, or these fine folks will find out just what kind of vermin they're harboring under their very roof!"

She wrenched her arm free. "You won't tell them anything, Ian. At least not until you've bled me a little more. Otherwise, you'd have nothing to threaten me with. Now get out."

He started toward her again and she began backing up. He had just grabbed her again and was shaking her when the front door opened. It was Nate, and he reacted immediately, grabbing her brother from behind with one arm around his throat, the other pulling one of his arms behind his back. Ian struggled but there was no escaping Nate's iron grip built by years hauling up sails and anchors, while the only thing Ian had lifted was a mug of ale.

"Who is this, Irish?" Nate asked. "And what do you want done with him?"

Irish gave Ian a threatening glare and her brother kept quiet, knowing that to speak was to end the possibility of getting cash from his sister.

"He was just leaving, Nate," Irish said. "Just show him out." She glared at her brother again. "I'm sure he won't be back."

She opened the door, Nate shoved Ian outside, and Irish slammed it and locked it. She leaned against it for a moment, trying to still the trembling inside until she was able to turn and face Nate.

"Are you all right?" he asked.

She nodded. "Thank you, Nate," she said, trying to think of

how to explain her brother. She could think of nothing so she simply said, "Maybe it would be best if we didn't mention this to the others?"

He looked at her uncertainly a moment, then shrugged. "Whatever you say, Irish. But if you're in any kind of trouble…" he let the words trail off, giving her a chance to confide in him.

But how could she? There was nothing she could confide without condemning herself. She shook her head. "I'll be all right." She laid a hand on his arm. "Thank you."

Nate looked at her a long moment, giving her time to change her mind, then went on into the house. Irish peeked out a window. There was no sign of Ian, but she knew he would not go far. And if she didn't meet him tonight, there was no telling what he would do—if she were still here. But she would not be here and she had no intention of meeting Ian.

It was later that day, nearly dinner time, that the Halls came to call. Irish had been hovering near the door all day in case Ian decided to come back in spite of her unspoken threats, so it was she who answered the door.

Mrs. Hall came breezing in as quickly as her short round form would allow, followed by Prudence and Betsy. With them, paying close attention to Betsy, was Douglass Townsend.

"We've just been out shopping for a wedding present for Ruth," Mrs. Hall said, fanning herself briskly, "and thought we'd stop and pay a call." She leaned close to Irish. "Isn't Douglass being such a darling to help us find just the right gift for his sister?"

Irish agreed that he was, but wondered if the tall, blond lawyer might not have another reason for escorting the Halls about town, from the way he was looking at Betsy. When she turned to greet him, she knew there was another reason the instant his face reddened. Betsy was hanging on his arm and looking up at him with something in her eyes Irish hadn't seen there when the girl was with Ty. Suddenly, in spite of all her other worries, Irish's heart felt lighter.

She had always liked Douglass, from the time she had met him escaping from the Spanish in Saint Augustine. If he and Betsy could find happiness together, she would be happy for them...for more than one reason. She greeted Douglass with a warm smile.

"Please come into the parlor and sit down," Irish said. "I'll have Daphne bring you some refreshments while I go find Mrs. Fortune."

Irish didn't have far to go to find Mrs. Fortune. After settling the Halls and speaking to Daphne in the kitchen, she found Mrs. Fortune standing in the front hall, tapping her chin with one finger and looking quite puzzled.

"Irish, dear, have you seen my necklace? The gold and emerald one. I was sure I left it here on the hall table last night when we came home from the ball. A careless habit of mine, I know, but now I can't find the necklace anywhere. I've already asked Daphne and she checked with the other servants." She shook her head. "I'm sure they would have brought it to me or put it away upstairs, but it isn't there and no one knows anything about it." She bent to look under the table.

Irish didn't need to look for the necklace to know where it was. It had been on that table this morning before she'd gone out. And had probably still been there just before Ian had come to 'call'. Ian had taken it. She knew it. Panic threatened to overcome her. *Not again,* she thought, *not again.* Hadn't her brother caused her enough grief?

Taking a deep, cleansing breath she pulled herself together. *No,* she decided, *not again.* This time it would be different. This time she would not take the blame for Ian's thievery. This time she would not go after Ian alone, bringing back the stolen item in her pocket to be taken as evidence of her guilt. This time she would take someone with her to confront her brother. Nate or Matt, whichever one she could find. This time, he would not get away with it. She would not take the blame. Ian might retaliate by telling everyone how she had eluded the law. She might still end up being sold for that other time, but so be it. This time, she was not going to let Ian use her, even if it meant that they both ended up in prison.

Forcing her voice to a calmness she did not feel, Irish said, "We have company, Mrs. Fortune. The Halls are in the parlor. Why don't you go on in and visit with them. I'll find your necklace."

Mrs. Fortune patted her arm. "Thank you, my dear."

Irish put her hands to her mouth to keep herself from screaming with anger and frustration. She turned in all directions not knowing which direction to go first. She looked at the stairs, wondering where Matt and Nate were. Were they at home or had they gone out? Her heart kept trying to tell her to find Ty. Ty would take care of this. Ty could be trusted. But how could she turn to him now when she had not trusted him with her secrets before?

Just then she heard Matt's voice and glanced up to see him and Ty coming down the stairs. They appeared to be on their way out, with tricorns under their arms. Matt was dressed casually, as he usually was, with a coat but no waistcoat, his stock wrapped and tied loosely, and moccasins on his feet. Ty was impeccable from his stiffly starched Steinkirk to his silk stockings and polished buckle shoes.

The two of them halted on the bottom step when she came toward them. Then Ty stepped down and took her hands in his, looking with alarm into her eyes. "Irish, what's wrong?"

It felt wonderful to feel his hands holding hers again. Somehow his very presence, his touch, gave her the confidence to go on. She swallowed hard wondering how little she could get by telling them.

"Your mother's necklace is missing," she said. "The gold and emerald one your father gave her."

Ty's shoulders relaxed a bit and he smiled. *He doesn't understand,* she thought. *He thinks it's just a matter of looking behind a couch or under the bed.* But it was so much more. It was the whole life she had built for herself that was at stake.

Matt stepped down and walked over to the hall table. "She left it here last night. She's always leaving her jewelry here."

"It will turn up somewhere," Ty said. "Maybe Daphne or one of the other servants put it in a safer place. Ask them."

Thinking her problem solved she could see him retreating back behind his wall, stepping back from her, dropping her hands. He gestured to Matt and started toward the door.

"Your mother already asked the servants about it. It's not going to turn up, Ty. A man stole it this morning."

He turned back to her, his eyebrows raised.

"Matt! Ty! I thought I heard male voices out here." Douglass came into the hall, hand extended in greeting to the two brothers. "I was about to drown in a sea of feminine talk of ribbons and weddings and–" He halted, looking from one to the other of them and seeing their serious faces. He let his hand drop. "Is something wrong? What can I do to help?"

Matt and Ty nodded toward her and Douglass turned to her, his forehead furrowed with concern.

"A man stole Mrs. Fortune's necklace late this morning. You know the one. She wore it to the ball last night," Irish said.

Douglass nodded. "A man? What man? And how do you know he stole the necklace?"

She couldn't help but smile at the way Douglass's law trained mind worked, asking for proof of the theft.

"I'm sure, Douglass. I know this man. I know what he's like.

And he was here in the hallway just minutes after I had seen the necklace there on the table. Nate was here. He saw him, too."

Ty passed a wordless command to Matt with a glance and a quick nod of his head toward the stairs.

"I'll get him," Matt said, amicably, and took the stairs two at a time, his moccasined feet making no sound.

"Who was this man, Irish?" Ty asked.

Thankfully Matt returned before she could answer, with Nate clattering along at his heels.

Ty turned to Nate. "Irish said you saw the man who was here with her today?"

Nate looked to Irish, silently asking permission to tell his brothers about Ian, since he had agreed not to mention him. She nodded and he said, "Thoroughly disreputable type. I tossed him out on his ear."

"He stole your mother's necklace," Irish said.

Nate took a wide spread stance and clasped his hands behind his back as if he were in command on board his ship. "Then let's go find him."

The men nodded their agreement but Ty looked at Irish. "You said you knew this man. Just who is he? And what was he doing in this house?"

Irish bit her lip. This was the part she had been dreading, but it was unavoidable. She squared her shoulders and lifted her chin. "His name is Ian and he's my brother."

Several male brows shot up. Matt straightened from where he was leaning against the stair banister and stood beside Nate, folding his arms across his chest. "He's not much of a brother if he would steal from the family you're living with."

"It's not the first time," she said, then bit her lip, feeling ashamed for Ian and wishing she had not spoken.

Nate gave them a lowering glare. "I say we find him and wale the tar out of him."

"I'll kill him," Ty growled, looking at her with such protective intensity that she wanted to put her arms around him under his coat as she had done in the past, and bask in the warm security she had always found in his arms. But that was over now. She folded her arms and hugged herself instead.

Matt gave an evil little grin. "I can think of several things that we could do to him a lot worse than a thrashing or a killing."

"What we really need to do is bring him to justice," said Douglass, "especially if he is a repeat offender."

Ty brought them back to practicalities. "We need to find him first." He looked at Irish. "Do you know where he might be?"

She nodded. "He's been spending a lot of time at Johnny's Tavern. I was supposed to meet him there in a couple of hours."

Ty clapped his tricorn on his head. "We'll need weapons. Nate, you're the only one who knows what this fellow looks like, so we'll depend on you to point him out."

Douglass stopped them with a raised hand. "There's another possibility. That necklace is quite valuable, as I recall. Irish's brother may be out there right now trying to sell it."

"You're right, Douglass," Ty said, "but I have no idea where a scoundrel would go to sell ill gotten goods."

"I know all the best places for that sort of dealings," Douglass said, his pale face turning bright red.

Matt grinned. "You? The honest, upright Charles Town attorney? Seems there's a whole side of you we never knew about."

Douglass shrugged. "I might be honest and upright, but many of my clients are not. They tell me things."

Nate clapped Douglass on the back. "Then we should split up. We can cover more ground that way and find this rogue faster."

"Except that you're the only one who knows what he looks like," Matt said.

Irish propped her hands on her hips. "You're forgetting about me. I know what he looks like."

Douglass protested instantly. "We can't let you go to these unsavory places, Irish! Besides, it might come to a brawl. It wouldn't be safe."

"Ian is my brother. I feel responsible. I'm going to find him and I hope someone will come along with me, because I just might need some muscle," she glared at each one of them, daring them to dissuade her.

A small grin kicked up one corner of Ty's mouth and she thought he was actually looking at her with some small measure of pride. "She's right." He held up a hand to stave off their protests. "Nate, you go with Douglass to those places he knows. Matt, you come with Irish and me to Johnny's. Let's arm ourselves and Irish can find a shawl or something to cover up that hair of hers and conceal as much of her face as she can." He actually tipped her chin up with one finger. "We don't want to have to fight off every man jack out there who might want to claim her for his own."

"I'll need to see the Halls home," Douglass said to Nate as they disbursed to their various tasks, "but we can do that on the way."

Irish was soon walking back to Johnny's Tavern, feeling considerably safer this time with Ty on one side and Matt on the other. They both had pistols tucked into the top of their breeches. Matt had added a type of long knife preferred by his Indian friends. Ty had buckled on a sword.

"Make sure you don't trip over that thing," Matt said to Ty with a grin.

Ty just arched a brow at his brother and adjusted the coat he had changed into to accommodate the weapon. The coat was plain, brown, and serviceable, with a slit on the side for quick access to the sword. The sword itself appeared well used. Irish could tell by the worn hilt and the scratches on the plain scabbard that it was certainly not just for ceremony and show.

"Ian was not supposed to meet me for a while, yet," she said. "He may not be at the tavern yet even if he does intend to meet me." "Do you think he might not show up?" Matt asked.

She shrugged. "If he's managed to sell the necklace for a good price, he may be celebrating some place. But knowing Ian, if he thinks he can squeeze a few more shillings out of me, he'll be there."

"He's done this often?" Ty asked, his brows lowering.

She nodded.

"Bloody bastard," she heard him mutter.

The tavern was as smoke filled and reeking as the last time she had been there and the occupants just as rowdy. She glanced up at Ty and saw his nostrils flare and his jaw clench as he looked around.

"Is he here?"

Seeing the murderous look on his face she almost hoped Ian didn't show up. But, sheltered between the two men, she stepped farther inside and looked around for her brother. "He's not here."

Matt touched her elbow to guide her across the room. "Then we'll order a round of ale, which I doubt any of us will actually be brave enough to drink, and wait."

They found a table in one corner with only two occupants, both of whom were well into their cups and not likely to strike up a conversation. Ty pulled out a chair facing the door for her, and she sat down. He sat near the two drunks and pretended to be one of them. "Your brother might not join you if he realizes you're not alone." Matt took up a position nearby, leaning against the wall with his head lowered and his hat pulled low.

A barmaid swayed her ample hips to a halt beside Ty and gave him a leering, gap-toothed grin. Leaning forward to display the great swell of her bosom, she asked, "What can I get for you?"

Ty ordered a round of ale for them, including his two table companions in the order. When the barmaid brought the ale, the two at the end of the table happily exchanged empty mugs for full. "We won't be needing anything more," Ty told the barmaid and gave her several extra coins that she tucked into the top of her stomacher with a smile.

And then they waited.

Although Irish kept her shawl forward, concealing herself as best she could, a couple of men started to approach her, but were warded off by the ominous glare in Ty's eyes.

After more than an hour Irish was beginning to think her brother was not coming, but then she saw him, standing in the doorway spraddle-legged and belligerent, the way he usually looked when he'd had a few too many pints. She glanced at Ty and then up to Matt, giving each of them a nod and feeling very glad that they were with her.

Other than to return a slight nod, neither of the men moved, but she could sense a coiling of tension within them like a snake ready to strike.

Irish pushed her shawl back from her face just enough for Ian to spot her and head her way. He swaggered toward her, his coat thrown back and his thumbs hooked into the armholes of his waistcoat, a triumphant grin on his face.

He sat down across from her, right next to Ty, and Matt immediately sat down on his other side, pinning him between them.

"'Ere now! Give a bloke room!" Ian said, trying to elbow the two brothers to make room on the bench.

They gave him a bit of space but still kept close, not wanting their quarry to bolt. They had agreed ahead of time to let Irish get what she could from him, maybe even get the necklace back before they stepped in with more high pressure persuasion.

Ian reached over and pulled her now quite warm ale to him

and took a long drink. Then, wiping his mouth with the back of one hand he belched loudly and smacked his lips. "Thanks, darlin', for having that ready for me. I was feeling a bit parched."

She leaned forward, glaring at him. "I want that necklace back."

His hand moved down to cover his coat pocket just for a moment as if checking to make sure his booty was still there and Irish felt a wave a relief. He hadn't sold it yet.

"Now, what necklace would that be, darlin'?" He tried to appear casual, but she could see the nervous tic in his cheek before he took another drink.

"You know perfectly well which necklace I mean, Ian!" She tried not to raise her voice, but she was so angry with her brother it was hard not to.

Ian grinned smugly and leaned on his elbows, the ale cradled in his hands. "Now, Kathleen, what would you be wantin' that necklace for? Remember the last time I let you talk me into returning a necklace to you? You wouldn't want that to happen again, now would you?"

She tried not to glance at Matt or Ty. "I can assure you that won't happen again." She held out her hand for the necklace but her brother just laughed.

"Aren't you supposed to be giving me something?"

Good lord, she had forgotten to bring money. Maybe if she had brought him some, he would have returned the necklace. But she had nothing to trade for it.

Ian polished off the ale and slammed the mug down on the table. "Well, me girl, if you've nothing to give me, we've nothing more to say." He grinned and patted his coat pocket where Irish supposed the necklace was. "Until the next time I need a bit of cash, that is."

He stood up to leave but both Fortune men rose with him,

and they were no longer trying to hide their faces from him. Ian looked from one to the other and Irish could tell when recognition dawned. Even in the dimly lit tavern, she could see her brother turn white.

"You may not have anything more to say," Ty said to Ian, "but we do." He nudged him with the muzzle of a pistol, holding it so Ian could see it plainly but the other patrons could not. "Outside."

Ian turned to her and she had never seen such a venomous look on anyone's face before. "You've betrayed me, girl! Yer own flesh and blood! How could you?" he snarled at her.

Ty shut him up by grabbing a fistful of his coat and shoving him toward the door. Matt gripped Ian's arm, and Irish followed along behind them.

Ty turned once they were on the street to make certain Irish was with them, then hustled her brother along to the end of the block. They paused long enough for Matt to pull their mother's necklace out of Ian's pocket and put it in his own. Then the two brothers nudged him along.

Irish caught up to walk beside them. "Where are you going to do with him?"

Matt grinned. "I can think of a few interesting things, but I doubt that Ty would permit it."

"You spend entirely too much time with your Indian friends," Ty said, but he was grinning.

"You have the necklace back," Irish said. "Can't you just let him go?"

Ty looked at her aghast. "After what he's done to you?"

"Listen to the little lady, gents," Ian wailed, nearly stumbling. But the brothers kept him moving at a brisk pace. Ian looked from one to the other. "As she said, you have the necklace back. No harm done, now is there?"

Matt and Ty did not reply. But Ian was not finished trying to weasel out of his predicament. "I was just helping Kathleen, here, out a bit, seein' as how she's me sister, and all."

Ty still had hold of the back of his coat and he gave him a shake. "Extorting money and stealing is how you help your sister?"

"But I didn't steal nothin'. Kathleen gave that necklace to me when I come to the house this morning. She told me to sell it and split the money with her. I didn't know she'd stolen it, swear to God I didn't."

Ty jerked Ian to a halt, swung him around to face him and then socked him hard in the jaw with his fist. Ian would have gone sprawling if Matt hadn't been holding on to him. "You despicable piece of trash. Do you really think we would believe that Irish would steal from us?"

Ian rubbed his jaw with one hand and pointed at her with the other. "She's just got you all fooled. She's probably been stealing from you all along. I seen her last night in that fine gown. How else would somebody like her get something like that?"

Ty's fist was still clenched and he threatened Ian with it. "If you want to keep your teeth, I suggest you stop maligning Irish. In fact, it might be best for you to keep quiet unless we ask you a direct question." Ty nodded to Matt and they resumed their pace, dragging a more and more reluctant Ian along.

They walked in silence for a block farther until Ian found the courage to ask, "What are you going to do with me?"

"I'm not sure, yet," Ty answered. "It depends on your sister. But for now, we have a nice snug room for you in the cellar."

"You're going to let Kathleen decide my fate?" Ian sounded surprised.

"Seems fitting to me," Ty said. "She's the one you've wronged the most."

Ian craned his neck to look at her and gave her his most winning grin. It wilted just a bit when she did not return it. "Now Kathleen, you know I've always been good to you. You won't let this little incident come between us, now will you? You tell these here gents to let me go since there's been no harm done."

Irish could scarcely stomach Ian's lies. Good to her? She wished she could ball up her fist and punch him as hard as Ty had.

"Shut up," Matt snarled and twisted Ian's arm until he winced.

They were at the house now and the two men took him around to the back and in through the kitchen. Daphne was there and watched them with wide eyes.

"Bring a chamber pot and a jug of water, Daphne," Ty snapped. They opened the cellar door and pulled Ian down the steps so fast he would have fallen if they hadn't been holding him up.

Daphne found a jug and filled it with water. Irish took it from her along with the chamber pot, and followed the men into the cellar.

Matt opened the door to a small storage room and shoved Ian inside, and Irish handed him the water and pot. Ian stood staring at them, too stunned to speak or protest. Ty pulled her out of the room, and Matt shut and locked the door.

"Shall I go find the constable?" Matt asked.

Ty shook his head then looked at her. "Not until Irish and I have had a little talk," he said. Then he glanced at Matt and added, "Privately."

Chapter Twenty

IRISH WATCHED MATT HEAD BACK UP THE STAIRS AND FELT AS IF a band were tightening around her chest. The moment she had dreaded was here. She had put off leaving just a bit too long and now she would have to tell Ty everything. Either that or he would thrash it out of Ian.

No, Ty wouldn't have to lay a hand on Ian. Her brother would be all too glad to tell Ty everything he knew, especially if he thought he could gain his freedom by talking. She would rather tell him herself. Who knew what kind of twist Ian would put on the tale?

But when Ty turned that intense, expectant gaze of his back to her, she found herself backing up until she came up against a sack of rice. He waited a moment then took her arm.

Glancing at the door to the storage room, he said, "Let's go outside."

All the way up the stairs and out into the garden, Ty did not loosen his grip on her arm. She felt as much a prisoner as Ian. Did he think she was going to bolt and run? She certainly felt like it, but she knew there was no place for her to go. Her only hope was that once her story was told, he would keep her secret and let her leave the colony.

The garden at the Fortunes' town home was small but well

cared for. Ty led her down the oyster shell walk to a quiet place at the back where he turned her to face him, and at last let go of her arm.

"You and your brother don't seem to have very much in common."

Irish clutched her hands together at her waist. "He's not really my brother."

Ty merely raised one questioning brow.

"You want to know it all, don't you?"

"Everything."

She sighed and sat down on a stone bench. He clasped his hands behind him and stood waiting.

"My father is the Earl of Staunton."

Ty's right brow went up but he didn't say anything. He merely nodded for her to continue.

"Unfortunately, he never married my mother. She was a lady, the great granddaughter of a duke, but our family was nearly destitute. By the time she found out she was expecting, the earl had already wed another. My mother married the first man who would have her. That man was a neighbor who raised horses. He was Ian's father. His wife had just died and he needed a mother for his son."

"What made Ian take up a life of debauchery and crime?"

"His father always did love a pint or two and Ian took up after him. When my mother died…"

"They drank."

She nodded. "All the time. Ian's father died shortly after my mother. We had nothing. I found a job as a companion to Amanda Collins, the woman who is now Captain Woodford's wife."

"And Ian stole a necklace from her."

She stood up and began to pace back and forth. "He came to the house every week. At first it was just for money. Then things started disappearing. Little, unimportant things at first. But I soon realized it was Ian who was taking them."

Irish turned to face him, lifting her chin. "I confronted him about the thievery and he admitted it. I warned him to stop, but on one of his visits he took the necklace. It was too valuable not to be missed."

She bit her lip. This was harder than she thought. But she had started this, and she would finish. "That day Captain Woodford had come to call. Not on Amanda, but on me. She had been flirting with him, hoping for a proposal. It would be a triumph for her, a mere merchant's daughter to wed into the aristocracy, even if he was a second son. She had always been jealous of me, I think, for being an earl's daughter, even if that connection was never openly acknowledged.

"Amanda and I are about the same size so I had been standing in for her for a fitting for a new ball gown. Ian had just left when Captain Woodford arrived. The captain is a good man, but I felt nothing for him and had just told him so when Amanda came home and found us together. He was only kissing me goodbye and on the cheek, but she was furious.

"It was only a few minutes later that she noticed her necklace was missing. I knew immediately where it was and went after Ian. I took most of the money I had saved and gave it to him in exchange for the necklace, but when I returned Amanda was waiting with the constable. They found the necklace in my pocket, of course, and immediately assumed I had stolen it.

"Amanda then noticed some of the other missing pieces. A small enameled box, a Chinese vase, a crystal bowl. Enough to condemn me. She wouldn't listen to explanations because she wanted me gone, far enough away that I would not jeopardize her chances with Captain Woodford. I was arrested immediately. She didn't even wait for me to change clothes. That's why I was wearing such a fine dress when Mariette met me, even though it was in rags by then. My trial was a farce. The judge was a friend of the Collins family. I was sentenced to be transported and sold into servitude for the rest of my life. But the ship carrying me to Charles Town was captured by the Spanish. You know the rest."

"And your brother never came forward," Ty said, his voice grim.

She shook her head.

"Bastard," he muttered.

She shrugged and gave him a small smile. "Actually, that would be me."

He acknowledged her attempt at humor with a quirk of his lips, then asked, "That's all?"

She looked at him with amazement. "Isn't that enough?"

It was his turn to shrug. "Is that the only reason you wouldn't marry me?"

"Isn't that enough of a reason?"

"I was imagining far worse ones."

"Such as?"

"That you had accidentally murdered someone, or that you were running from an abusive spouse, or"–he paused slightly before adding–"that you just didn't want to marry me."

A lump formed in her throat because he had said 'accidentally.' He did trust her. "Oh, Ty," she stepped toward him, putting her hands on his arms. "I want to marry you. Nothing would make me happier. I would marry you if I could."

He grinned and pulled her close. "Then you're saying yes?"

"I can't marry you, Ty. If I were ever caught, your family could be implicated for harboring a fugitive. And as your wife, I would be found easily if anyone is still looking. I can't take that chance for either of our sakes."

That's when he started to laugh.

She pulled away and her fists went to her hips. "I'd like you to tell me what's so funny about this?"

He didn't answer. He just kept laughing. But he did pull her into his arms and began to kiss her with a smile still on his lips.

For once she was able to withstand his assault and wrenched away from him again. "You don't seem to understand my predicament here, Ty. My brother has found me. He knows the whole story. If he tells what he knows, and I'm sure he will if he thinks he can profit from it, then I will be arrested. I could be publicly whipped and I would certainly be put on the block and sold. For life, Ty. For life! I was a slave for six months in Spanish St. Augustine and I don't ever want be a slave again."

He gave her a gentle smile. "You won't be, Irish."

She sighed with relief. "Then you'll help me get away? Will you keep Ian until I can get out of the colony?"

He shook his head. "You're the one who doesn't understand. You don't have to go anywhere. Don't you know how wealthy and how powerful this family is?"

"You are still not above the law, Ty."

"No, but I have an idea of how we can work within the law. I'll have to talk to Douglass, with your permission, of course."

She bit her lip uncertainly.

Ty's expression became serious, all humor gone. "Will you trust me with this or not, Irish?"

She had carried this fear with her for two years. It was hard to suddenly trust someone else with her secret, but when she looked into his eyes she knew two things. If she didn't tear down the wall he had accused her of building around herself, if she couldn't set aside her pride and let him in, there could never be anything between them. And second, she could not think of anyone she would trust more than she would trust Ty. She had already trusted him with her secret. How could she not trust him further?

"Yes," she said, simply, "Yes."

But that was all she needed to say. He enfolded her in his arms and held her as if she were the most precious thing in his life. She wedged her arms beneath his coat and around his waist and reveled in being in his embrace, in finally feeling like she had found a safe haven, in being home.

He kissed her hair. "I'm going to take that yes of yours to mean that you will marry me as soon as this little problem is settled. This time I'm not going to let you go."

They started and jumped apart when they heard Matt clearing his throat. He was standing less than a yard from them and Irish marveled anew at how he could move so quietly, even over an oyster shell path.

"Douglass is back," he said. "He's had a bit of a tussle with a press gang. A tussle Nate seems to have lost."

"They took Nate?" Ty snapped.

At Matt's grim nod Ty said, "Woodford's *Lady Margaret* is the only warship in the harbor right now, and they're not set to sail for several days yet. Why would they be rounding up men now?"

"Nate said too many sailors realized it was wise to disappear for a day or two just before a vessel sailed. Press gangs are starting sooner."

They had already started walking toward the house, with Ty once more holding onto her arm. But this time she did not feel like a prisoner. She felt like he only wanted her close and just perhaps, she thought, he was holding onto her for his own comfort, that her presence was giving him support in dealing with this new calamity.

Douglass was sitting in the parlor holding a cool cloth to his jaw when they joined him. Except for when he had just escaped from the Spanish, Irish had never seen him looking so disreputable. Buttons were missing from his waistcoat, his clothing was awry and smudged, and his coat sleeve torn. And the clothes themselves were not Douglass's usual style. They were old and worn, something a servant might wear.

The three of them pulled up chairs beside Douglass and Ty asked, "Are you all right?"

Douglass worked his jaw and rubbed it with one hand. "I'll have a sore jaw in the morning but other than that, I fared better than Nate."

At Ty's look of alarm, Douglass held up a hand and continued, "I'm sure he's fine, but between us, we gave them such a hard time that in the end, they could only take one of us."

"I'm surprised that they would have the audacity to attack obvious gentlemen on the street," Ty said.

Douglass held out his arms to display his clothing. "As you can see, we didn't exactly look like gentlemen. I suggested to Nate that it might be better if we didn't go into the rather unsavory locations we were headed looking like we wanted to be robbed. He changed into some of his working sailor togs."

Ty slapped his thighs. "Well, we'll go down to the *Lady Margaret* in the morning and get Nate."

"It might not be so easy, Ty," Matt said, "I'm sure he won't sign the articles, but that doesn't mean someone won't sign for him."

"It should be easy enough to prove it isn't his signature," Douglass said.

Matt shook his head. "We aren't dealing with a logical court of law, Douglass. The navy's got him and they're not going to let him go just because we go down there and plead his case. There's a war on and they're desperate for men."

Ty stood up and began to pace. "We can't just let them take him!"

"They're not going to sail without a full complement of men," Matt said quietly.

They looked at each other silently for a moment, each with his own thoughts. Irish gasped when an idea came to her. "Ian!"

The men looked at her waiting for her to continue.

"We can trade Ian for Nate." She jumped up, excited with her idea, and looked from Matt to Douglass and then to Ty. "You said I could decide what to do with my brother. For once, maybe he can be of some use."

"The life of a sailor in his majesty's navy is not an easy one," Ty said.

"But I've also heard that it's been good for many an errant lad," she insisted. "And for Ian, it might just furnish the structure and discipline he needs. At least it's better than a hanging, which is what Ian is headed for if he continues down the road he's on."

"Pardon me, Irish, dear," Douglass said, "but why would the captain give up a hale and hearty sailor like Nate for, begging your pardon, an untrained ne'r-do-well?"

Ty nodded in agreement.

Irish bit her lip trying desperately to think of some other inducement they could offer Captain Woodford when she spotted Mrs. Fortune's fan lying on a side table. It was the same fan she had taken to the ball where she had met the Woodford's.

She turned to the men with a triumphant smile. "I know what will convince Captain Woodford to make the exchange."

"Welcome aboard, Mr. Fortune, Mr. Townsend." Captain Woodford held out a thin, fine hand smothered in a froth of lace and shook Ty's and Douglass's hands, then motioned for them to follow him down to his cabin.

Ty glanced quickly over the side where Matt was guarding Ian in a boat rowed by four hefty sailors from Fortune ships.

Matt looked up and grinned. Ian, somewhat the worse for

wear after his night in the storeroom, was still scowling.

He hadn't liked the choices Douglass and the Fortune brothers had presented him with last night, Ty thought, but joining the king's navy was far preferable to hanging for theft.

Captain Woodford was tall enough that he had to stoop to keep from bumping his head in the passageway of the ship.

Fortunately, the ceiling in his cabin was more adequate for his height. "I do believe I met the two of you at the Townsend ball, did I not?"

"Yes," agreed Ty sweeping off his tricorn and tucking it under one arm, "and my mother as well."

"Ah, yes." The captain smiled and nodded. "A lovely lady. She has invited us for lunch tomorrow, which pleased my wife considerably."

Ty smiled. Irish had been right. Being accepted into Charles Town society was important to Mrs. Woodford especially since the *Lady Margaret* would be making regular calls here.

Once in his cabin, the good captain offered seats and a choice of drinks from tea to rum to a good port.

Ty glanced at Douglass then shook his head and waved away the refreshments. "We are not here on a social call, I'm afraid, Captain," Ty said.

"No?" The captain's dark brows came together over his hawk nose and he sat warily on the edge of his worktable.

Clasping his hands behind his back Ty looked at the captain from beneath sternly lowered brows. "My brother Nathanial Fortune was...shall we say convinced to come aboard your ship last night. I do not believe that he would have joined his majesty's navy by choice."

The captain's brows arched and he stiffened for just a moment but then he shrugged. "Some of my men were on shore leave last night. I did send men out to round them up. If your brother happened to be among them, perhaps he did indeed sign the articles."

"I doubt very much that Nathanial would have joined your crew, Captain. He was out last night on a most important errand. He would not have abandoned his task."

The captain leaned back, clasping his hands on his knee. He had obviously played this scene many times before, wives, mothers, brothers coming to claim someone wrongfully signed on to his crew. He well knew the role he must play. He smiled. "Perhaps you do not know your brother as well as you thought. Perhaps he has secretly longed to sail away from Charles Town and saw this as his chance."

"Our family owns numerous ships, Captain Woodford. Nathanial owns two in his own right. He has no lack of opportunities if he wanted to sail anywhere in the world."

Woodford shrugged. "Then perhaps it was the hope of action in this war that prompted your brother to join my crew."

Douglass's hand shot out to restrain Ty when his fist clenched and he started to step toward the captain. "May we see the signature, Captain?"

Shrugging, the captain went around his worktable, putting it between him and his visitors. The paper Nate had supposedly signed was quickly found among the neatly placed papers on the table. Douglass took it from the captain and he and Ty looked at the signature.

"This is nothing like my brother's handwriting, Captain." Ty tossed the paper back onto the desk like so much worthless trash.

The captain picked it up and placed it back onto one pile, carefully squaring the corners. "That often happens when these young men come to us after a few rounds with some of my men. Their hands are often a bit unsteady. But they are good lads, nonetheless, and welcome aboard the *Lady Margaret*."

"And you will not release Nate?" Ty asked.

The captain dropped all pretense. "Mr. Fortune, I sympathize with you, but you must understand that we are at war and our need for men is desperate. If we must sometimes resort to…unusual means to get them…" he shook his head and sighed. "We do what we must for England."

"Would you consider a trade, Captain Woodford?" Douglass asked.

Woodford's brows raised questioningly and Douglass continued. "We have a young man who is willing to join your crew in exchange for Nathanial Fortune."

The captain was nonplused and waved a negligent hand. "If you know someone willing to sign on we would be more than happy to have an additional man, but I see no sense in trading a good, well-trained sailor for an unknown."

Ty took his tricorn from beneath his arm and slapped his thigh with it. It was clear the captain would not agree to an outright trade. But perhaps Irish's suggestion might work. "How is your wife enjoying Charles Town?"

Captain Woodford looked surprised at the apparent change of subject. "She seems to be enjoying the social whirl," he answered.

I'm sure she is, Ty thought. In London, as a merchant's daughter married to a second son, she would not have quite the entré that she did in Charles Town. "My mother also seems to enjoy balls and soireés. Indeed, many of the leading families look to my mother's example when deciding whether or not to open their doors to newcomers."

"I see," the captain said slowly.

Ty was not entirely certain the captain understood the full import of what he had just been told, so he continued. "My mother is so worried about her son that she is thinking of canceling some of her social engagements. I do hope that doesn't become necessary. It might mean that your wife would suddenly find herself with very few social engagements, herself."

The captain looked hard at Ty then sighed and opened a ledger. "On second thought, Mr. Fortune, Mr. Townsend, it does seem that the *Lady Margaret* now has a full complement of men. I believe we could exchange this man for your brother. So long as he is hale and hearty, that is."

Ty bowed to the captain. "Your new crewman is waiting in our boat alongside. If you would be so kind as to have my brother brought up on deck and released from service, Mr. Ian O'Conner will willingly sign on."

Woodford pulled out the paper Nate had supposedly signed and quickly wrote, "Released from service," on it, dated it, signed his name, and handed it to Ty. "Give my regards to your mother. My wife and I look forward to lunch tomorrow, Mr. Fortune."

When Ty and Douglass came back on deck a crewman brought Nate up. He was rumpled, his clothing torn and bloodstained, and from the look of him, some of that blood was his. One eye was swollen and his lip had a cut on one corner, but otherwise he seemed sound, and he grinned when Ty clapped him on the back.

Ian, on the other hand, was looking rather sullen, glaring at Ty. Matt stood at his back prodding him forward. He swallowed hard and looked around as if relishing his last moment of freedom. Then he signed the paper the captain presented and Nate was free to go.

Irish tried to keep from clasping and unclasping her hands in her lap as she sat in Douglass's office the next morning. She felt a little queasy. But there had been so much happening with Ian threatening her and with the heat—it was no wonder Daphne had had to bring her tea and toast to quiet her stomach before she could get up the last few mornings. She wished she had some now.

She hadn't been able to eat anything before she'd left.

Douglass's office was on the second story of a building on Queen Street, with two large airy windows. Sunlight streamed across his large paper-laden desk. Ty sat beside her, and he smiled at her reassuringly and patted her arm while Douglass pulled out some papers. But for once Ty's touch did not reassure her. All she could think about was the possibility of being publicly whipped and sold on the block.

Douglass finally found the paper he wanted and looked up at them. "I've talked to Judge Webb about you, Irish. He has agreed to settle your case privately."

She let out a breath she hadn't realized she was holding.

"But he still wants to see you and talk to you before passing judgment." Douglass glanced at the tall clock in the corner. "We have an appointment with him in just a few minutes."

"What will happen, do you think, Douglass?" Ty asked.

Douglass hunched forward and clasped his hands together on his desk. He looked at Irish. "You were sentenced to be sold as an indentured servant for life. The state is due the amount of that sale. I tried to convince him to let us simply put up the typical amount that a life indenture would sell for, but he was adamant that justice be served. You are to be sold."

Irish could not help but gasp even though it was what she had expected. Ty squeezed her hand, but not even the warmth of his touch could thaw the cold she felt in her heart at this pronouncement. It was her worst fear come true.

Douglass held up a hand. "It isn't as bad as it seems, Irish. He has agreed to let the sale be private and to Ty."

Irish looked at Ty with wide eyes. Ty would own her indenture? She would belong to him for life? Being tied to him by marriage was one thing, but she didn't think she liked the idea of belonging to anyone as a slave, not even Ty. She had a sudden thought and looked at Douglass. "Why can't I purchase my own indenture? I have more than enough money."

Douglass shook his head. "I didn't even bring that up to the judge and I suggest you don't either. You have basically been a runaway. In the normal course of things indentured servants often earn money of their own and pay off their indenture—with permission from their master. But you didn't have that permission. Everything you have earned belongs to your master, which is presently the state. Technically, the court could confiscate everything you have."

"So letting Ty purchase my indenture is my only choice," she concluded.

Douglass spread his hands. "It seems the best solution." He smiled at Ty.

Ty, in turn, smiled at her, but did not say anything.

Irish took a deep shuddering breath and looked from one man to the other, feeling trapped. She knew this was the best solution. The only solution. That didn't mean she relished the thought of being owned. But the men didn't seem to understand that. After all, wasn't a wife practically owned by her husband? They just didn't seem to understand the difference. Ty was assuming she was going to marry him anyway so why should he give her her freedom? And she did want to marry him--but as a free woman with a choice in the matter.

For now, there was naught else she could do but submit to having Ty buy her indenture. But perhaps she could convince him to sell her the indenture, giving her her freedom before they were married.

"It's time," Douglass said, glancing at the clock. He shuffled together the papers he had prepared and they left to walk the short distance to the judge's private office.

Judge Webb was large and florid and everything about him spoke of prosperity, from the huge size of his office and the family portraits that hung on the walls to the thick, soft carpet underfoot. His large mahogany desk would have dwarfed a lesser man, but the judge was a perfect fit for it and both seemed terribly intimidating to Irish.

He looked up as they entered and did not smile. This man could easily crush all her hopes and she felt small in this office with him looking at her so sternly. But she was not about to let him intimidate her. She lifted her chin and took comfort from Ty who had his hand at the small of her back.

"This is the woman?" the judge snapped.

"Yes, your honor," Douglass replied, laying the papers he had brought before the judge.

Judge Webb merely glanced at the papers then it seemed to Irish that he glowered at her from beneath thick, bushy eyebrows.

Irish had worn one of her better dresses, but one that still had a bit of wear to it. She hadn't wanted to look too prosperous, but she hadn't wanted to appear destitute either. For once, she seemed to have discovered Betsy's uncanny ability to match Ty's clothing with her own for they both wore indigo blue and cream, making them look of one mind.

"You have been living in this colony for two years?" the judge asked her.

"Yes, sir," she answered.

"Living with the Fortune family as a free woman?"

"Yes sir," she answered, again wondering why he was asking her questions he already knew the answer to.

"In what capacity?"

"I…as a friend," she said.

"As a friend." He made it sound like a crime.

"Sit on your backside and take advantage of it, do you?"

"She works hard, your honor. She does more than her share and—"

The judge held up a restraining hand to stop Ty's defense of her. "I'm speaking to the defendant, Mr. Fortune. I'll get to you later."

Ty clamped his jaws shut but she could almost hear him seething and it made her feel good to know that he had jumped to her defense.

"Well, young woman? What do you do for the Fortunes? Do you work like Mr. Fortune suggests?"

Irish's anger began to surface over the judge's insinuation that she was living in luxury and taking advantage of her situation. Her fists seemed to automatically place themselves on her hips. "The Fortunes have been very kind to me, and what kind of a friend would I be not to help out as much as I can? Of course I work. Do you think I'd want to spend my days in idleness when there's washing and milking and cooking to be done? Not to mention acres and acres of rice to tend. With Mrs. Fortune's husband gone privateering and her sons mostly gone, too, who else did she have to look after the dikes and see to their repair and see that the paddies get weeded properly?"

Irish would have continued her rant but Douglass laid a hand on her shoulder making her realize that she had almost been shouting at the man who held her future in his hands. She swallowed hard, hoping that her temper had not ruined what Douglass had worked so hard to accomplish for her.

"Your honor, I'm sorry–" Douglass began but the judge stopped him with an uplifted hand.

"Come here, girl."

Irish stepped closer to the judge's desk.

"Hold out your hands."

Puzzled, Irish wiped already clean hands on her skirt then held out her hands. She was a bit embarrassed to let anyone see them with their broken nails and work roughened surface.

The judge reached across the desk and grasped her hands, turning them palm up and running his thumb across them. He looked up at her and for the first time gave a small smile. "Ain't the hands of an idler." He released her, sat back and addressed Douglass. "Lots of people come into my court claiming one thing or t'other but they don't always tell the truth. The hands don't lie, though. Can tell a lot about a person by their hands. This'un here seems to tally up to what you've said of her."

He drew the papers Douglass had laid on his desk toward him, and picking up a pen, signed his name in letters as big and bold as the rest of him.

Handing the papers to Douglass he glanced from man to man then looked sharply at Irish and said, "With friends like these and the backbone you've shown me today you'll be a fine asset to this colony, Miss O'Conner."

Irish was so surprised at his compliment that she didn't know what to say, but she didn't have to speak. The judge had already pulled a pile of papers toward him and gone back to work, effectively dismissing them.

But still she said, "Thank you, sir," before turning and following Douglass from the room.

Ty met with the judge's clerk and paid her bond, then they headed back to Douglass's office.

Irish could not help but skip a step or two and kick up her heels right there on the walk. Her hands were not a lady's hands and neither was she. No lady would have been caught dancing on the streets. But she couldn't help herself. For the last two years she had lived in fear. Now, although she was not free, she no longer had to worry about discovery. She could walk down any street in Charles Town with her head up, and tell anyone her name.

She twirled around with her arms out and shouted, "My name is Kathleen O'Conner!" Then she stopped, suddenly aware of her prim and proper Ty. But he was not scowling at her. He was grinning as broadly as she was.

"Not for long, Irish!" He shook his head. "I've been trying for weeks to find out what you name is and now that I know it, I can scarcely wait to change it." He took her hand, and pulled her close with both arms around her waist right there in the middle of the street with who knew how many people looking on.

"Marry me, Irish."

She lifted her chin. "My name is Kathleen."

"Marry me, Kathleen. Marry me as Kathleen or Irish or Miss O'Conner. Marry me as whatever name you like, so long as you let me change it to Fortune."

She shook her head. "I can't."

Ty dropped his arms from around her and stepped back in stunned surprise. "What?"

"I'm not a free woman, Master."

He laughed and pulled her to him again. "I'm serious, Irish. Kathleen. Marry me. Marry me tomorrow. Marry me today."

It was hard not to put her own arms around him and hold him as close as he was trying to hold her but she pulled away from him. She had to have her freedom. She wanted to marry Ty more than anything else in the world, but she had to do it as a free woman.

"Perhaps we could finish up a few things in my office first?" Douglass suggested.

In his office Douglass gave Irish's indenture papers to Ty, wrote for a few minutes, then handed Ty another paper.

"A waistcoat of white linen, a blue apron, two caps of white linen, and a new pair of shoes and stockings," Ty read as Irish looked over his shoulder to see. "What's this?"

Douglass smiled at Irish. "That's what you, as her master, legally owe Irish when you give her her freedom."

Ty frowned and tossed the paper down on Douglass's desk. "I

don't need that. Irish is going to be my wife. As my wife she'll have a lot more than those few paltry items. She'll have whatever she wants." He took her arm. "Let's go, Irish. I promised my mother I'd be home in time for lunch with the Woodfords."

Douglass looked at Irish and shrugged.

"Thank you, Douglass," Irish said.

"I'm glad it all worked out well, Irish," Douglass said. "Or should I call you Kathleen now?"

Some of the joy had gone out of the day for her when Ty had tossed that paper down. She shrugged. "It doesn't matter, Douglass. Call me Irish. That's how everyone knows me."

She turned to follow Ty out of the office, but at the last moment she turned back and snatched up the list, folded it, and tucked it into her bodice. Some day she would legally have her freedom, she promised herself, whether she married Ty or not. And just maybe, if she turned him down long enough, he would realize how important this was to her.

As soon as they arrived home they found Mrs. Fortune and told her the whole story. She listened quietly and intently then simply held out her arms to Irish and embraced her.

"My dear, to think you've carried this for so long all alone!" she said. "You should have come to us sooner." She smiled at her son. "Thank goodness it's all settled now! And thank goodness you were willing to exchange your brother for Nate!"

Irish squeezed Mrs. Fortune's hand. "Nate is worth a hundred of Ian. But maybe the navy can make something of him."

"There's one more thing, Mother," Ty said grinning broadly.

Mrs. Fortune looked at her son expectantly. "Irish and I are going to be married."

Irish frowned at Ty. That had not been completely settled. But she bit her lip waiting for his mother's reaction. It was one thing to have someone you thought of as a heroine living in your home. It was quite another to have your son announce that he was going to marry a transported felon.

She didn't have long to wait for that reaction. Mrs. Fortune whooped, actually whooped with joy, and flung her arms around Irish. "Wonderful! I could not think of a better choice for Ty." She started babbling about when and where and dresses, then finally stopped and kissed Irish on the cheek. "But that's all for you to plan. But I do hope you'll let me help!"

Irish could only give her a wan smile. How could she tell her that she would never marry Ty unless she did it as a free woman, but that Ty didn't seem to think that was of any importance at all.

Daphne poked her head in the door then hurried over to her. "Miss Irish! The cook has been frettin' somethin' awful waitin' for you. That duck she's makin' for lunch is 'bout done and you said you'd make the sauce for it."

The luncheon with the Woodfords! She had forgotten. "I'll be right down, Daphne." She turned to Mrs. Fortune. "Under the circumstances, it might be best if I don't join the family for lunch."

Mrs. Fortune snorted. "You are going to be part of this family, Irish. And if that woman who did this to you is too high and mighty to sit down at the table with you she can leave. I know who I would prefer to eat with!"

"I agree," said Ty. He glanced at his mother. "We've agreed to sponsor the Woodfords into Charles Town society for releasing Nate"–he gave a wicked grin–"but if they don't choose to accept our hospitality, that is their own concern."

Mrs. Fortune looked thoughtful a moment. "My friends should be here well ahead of the Woodfords. Irish, dear, I think it best if I tell them your story. If Mrs. Woodford is half as spiteful as you say, and I have no doubt she is from meeting her that once, then your tale will be all over Charles Town by nightfall anyway. But if we tell it first, at least it will be our version that will be believed and spread."

Irish thought about it for a moment. She really didn't want anyone to know. But she was not at fault. She had not stolen anything. She lifted her chin. "Aye. That's the thing to do." Then she went down to the kitchen to help the cook.

Chapter Twenty-one

WITH ONE FINAL TASTE IRISH PRONOUNCED THE SAUCE finished, and she helped the cook pour it over the platter of roast duck. Everything was ready. The Woodfords had arrived and although Irish really didn't want to sit down to a meal with Amanda, at least she no longer feared that her former employee would expose her secret.

But Amanda might object to having a meal with an indentured servant. In fact, Irish thought, she was sure Amanda would object. There was sure to be some kind of scene. She grinned to herself. She was ready for it. In fact, she was spoiling for a fight.

Irish took just a moment to freshen up, washing face and hands, removing her apron, and tucking her hair in as best she could. Then she straightened her shoulders to march into the lion's den. She would have just enough time to be introduced before lunch was served. At least she had the advantage of surprise.

Mrs. Fortune, Matt, and Ty were entertaining the Woodfords and two other prominent Charles Town couples when Irish entered the parlor. Mrs. Fortune smiled and Irish went to her side to tell her that lunch was ready.

That's when Amanda saw her.

At first Amanda's jaw dropped and her eyes widened, but then she pursed her lips and lifted her chin and deliberately turned away from Irish as if she were the lowliest of servants.

When Irish sat down next to Mrs. Fortune on the sofa, Amanda returned to wide-eyed and slack jawed.

"I believe you are already acquainted with my friend, Kathleen O'Conner, Captain and Mrs. Woodford," Mrs. Fortune said calmly. "But we call her Irish."

Irish could tell that Mrs. Fortune was suppressing a grin.

Amanda Woodford jumped to her feet, her face red, her hands balled tightly. "Friend? She was transported. For life! She's no better than one of your black slaves! You dare to let her sit in the same room with visitors?"

"Amanda," Captain Woodford said, tugging on his wife's arm, "sit down. This is America. Things are different here."

Captain Woodford gave Irish a smile and a nod which she returned. She had always liked the captain even if her feelings had not run deep enough for another kind of relationship.

"Not that different," she shot back at her husband. She pulled herself up straight and looked down her nose at Mrs. Fortune.

"I have no idea how this hussy transformed herself from felon to friend, but perhaps you do not know what she was transported for."

"But I do know, Mrs. Woodford. Irish has told us the whole story. And her brother recently confessed to the crime she was accused of. It is unfortunate that you made such a mistake when you accused her, but I'm sure that Irish will forgive you."

Amanda's mouth opened and closed several times like a fish, but then she looked around at the other couples in the room and seemed to decide that if she wanted to be welcomed into their homes, she should make sure she remained welcome in this one. She sat down, clasped her hands tightly in her lap, and with pursed lips said, "Forgive me? I believe I was the one affronted."

"But not by Irish," Mrs. Fortune said softly. "You are the one who unjustly accused her."

"And you expect me to apologize to a servant?"

"We have never considered Irish a servant here," Mrs. Fortune said. Then she looked at Ty who had come up behind Irish and put a supporting hand on her shoulder. "Besides," she said turning back to Amanda and smiling proudly, "my son has told me that Irish will soon be part of this family which makes me extremely happy."

"Part of your family?" Amanda looked from Ty to Irish in amazement. Then her eyes narrowed and she glared at Irish. "You little hussy! You would have stolen my beau back in Ireland. Had it not been for your brother's theft... But now it seems you've landed on your feet." She jerked her head toward Ty. "What did you have to do to trap him? I'll bet it was more than stolen kisses in the parlor!"

Captain Woodford leapt to his feet and grabbed his wife's arm. "Are you saying...? You knew she was innocent?"

Amanda blanched. "No, I..."

Woodford looked down at his wife like she was spoiled meat.

"Harry, I...I couldn't lose you. I loved you!"

The captain's lip curled. "You loved the fact that my father was a landed baron." His grip on his wife's arm tightened. "I think it is time that you apologized to Miss O'Conner for what you did. You should probably do it on your knees, but"–he glanced at Irish–"I think Miss O'Conner is more of a lady than you'll ever be and wouldn't ask it of you."

The two other ladies turned to Amanda with expectant looks on their faces. Irish could see that Amanda was struggling. There was a venomous look on her face and her hands were clenched. She had a choice to make. Humble herself enough to apologize to Irish and congratulate her on her engagement, or walk out and never be accepted into Charles Town society.

Irish lifted her chin and waited. She had dreamed of this moment, the moment when she was acquitted by her accuser of any wrongdoing. It could never take away those humiliating days in an Irish jail or the weeks at sea in horrifying conditions, nor the rape she had suffered at the hands of the Spanish privateers, nor the months of slavery she had endured.

If Amanda apologized Irish knew she would be tempted to fling it back into her face. But Amanda's action had also brought her to Ty. She could only hope the captain was right. She hoped she was a better person than Amanda. She was hoping she could be gracious about what Amanda had done to her.

Amanda drew herself up and faced Irish squarely. "I'm sorry."

Irish waited for more but Amanda clamped her lips shut. Irish assumed that was all she would get. After all the woman had done, a simple, "I'm sorry," just didn't seem like enough. But she was just about to accept the apology when the captain nudged his wife and glared at her.

She looked up at him with a proud tilt of her head.

"If you can't find your own words, Amanda, perhaps I can help. It was wrong of me to so maliciously use you for my own personal gain," he suggested the words then glared at her again.

Amanda's gaze flicked from her husband to Irish. She swallowed then repeated what he had said. "It was wrong of me to so maliciously use you for my own personal gain."

"I apologize for all you have suffered because of me," the captain prodded.

Amanda's voice got smaller and smaller as she repeated the words. "I hope you can find it in your heart to forgive me," the captain suggested.

When Amanda had repeated those words, the captain and his wife both looked at Irish, waiting for her response.

It was harder than Irish had thought possible to accept that apology. But it helped knowing that, for the rest of her life, Amanda would have to deal with an irate husband who now knew the depths of his wife's perfidy.

She stood and stepped toward Amanda, and the woman actually flinched when Irish held out her hand. "I accept. I hope that there will be no hard feelings between us."

Reluctantly, as if her hand were filthy, Amanda took it and shook it briefly.

"You have always wanted to be a lady, Amanda. A lady would now offer her best wishes on the engagement," the captain said.

"May I offer you my felicitations," Amanda said and Irish thanked her.

The other two couples in the room began offering their congratulations to Ty and to Irish. The women came over to kiss her on the cheek and ask when the wedding would be.

Irish was beginning to feel trapped. She had not accepted Ty's offer, yet everyone, including Ty, was acting as if there were no doubt that they would marry. But this was not the time to say that nothing had been decided yet. So she only murmured to the women that a date had not been set.

When Daphne came in to announce that lunch was served, Captain Woodford took his wife's arm and bowed to Mrs. Fortune. "Perhaps, under the circumstances, it would be best if Mrs. Woodford and I left," he said.

Mrs. Fortune glanced at Irish and at her nod, Mrs. Fortune drew Amanda's arm through hers and said, "I think we all agree that the past be put behind us. I hear that the cook has prepared a wonderful meal. Let's not let it go to waste."

Graciously the captain again bowed to Mrs. Fortune and offered his arm to Irish. As they walked into the dining room together the captain leaned down to say, "Let me offer my apologies also, Miss O'Conner. Although I had just left on a voyage when those unfortunate events unfolded in Ireland, I feel that some of the blame must be mine."

Irish smiled up at the captain. "Thank you, Captain Woodford, but I have never blamed you in the least. Please absolve yourself of any guilt you feel."

The meal was delicious, but try as she might, it was still difficult for Irish to sit down in harmony with Amanda Collins. Added to that was the queasiness that had plagued her for the last week. She barely tasted her food.

Two days later, as Irish walked with the family to the Townsend wedding, Ty walked beside her with her arm drawn through his. "Would you like a big church wedding, Irish?" he asked.

"It's not the wedding that matters to me, Ty. It's the kind of man I marry."

He looked down at her with a grin. "Does that mean you'd wed me even in one of those heathenish Indian ceremonies Matt tells me about?"

She tossed her head. "And when did I ever tell you I'd wed you a'tall, Tyrus Winthrop Fortune?"

"Hah! On more than one occasion," he leaned close so that only she could hear, "and in more than one way."

She knew exactly what several of those ways were and, unbidden, they came to mind, causing her face to flush.

"When shall we wed, Irish?"

She lifted her chin and shrugged. "I'm not a free woman. I'll have to ask my master for permission to wed. And you know that masters usually don't like their female indentured servants to marry. Childbearing robs them of their services."

Ty leaned so close she could feel his breath touching her hair. "Your master gives you permission to wed, Irish. In fact, he is damn near insisting on it."

Fortunately, Irish didn't have to answer because they had reached the church and they took seats, listening to the music, and waiting for the ceremony to begin. Soon the music grew louder, and Ruth Townsend came down the aisle with her father. She was radiant and beautiful and looked at her groom with longing and love.

Irish didn't think she had ever seen a lovelier ceremony and wondered if this was the kind of wedding Ty had in mind for them. But she had meant what she said about a wedding. The ceremony didn't matter to her, only the man. She glanced at Ty. Yes, she wanted him. She wanted to marry him and have his children and grow old with him. But she wanted to do it as a free woman. Until Ty realized that her freedom was that important to her, she would continue to put him off.

At the reception and ball that evening, Irish enjoyed dancing time after time with Ty, with no worries that tongues would wag. The news was being spread even as they danced that they were soon to be wed.

Douglass and Betsy also danced more than their share of dances together. The Woodfords were there, having been invited before Irish's story came out. Now that it had, Amanda was finding her reception cool at best.

Irish, on the other hand, was the center of attention.

"Was your father really an earl?" one gushing young lady asked.

Douglass caught Irish's eye and winked, and she smiled back. She had given him permission to tell her story. She had just never thought he would include the part about her father being an earl and her mother the great-granddaughter of a duke. Apparently, Irish's earl and duke trumped Amanda's marriage to the second son of a baron, and Amanda was not looking very pleased.

Irish was not unhappy when she saw Amanda and her husband leave early.

For the rest of the evening she felt light and free, even though Ty still owned her. Even knowing all her secrets, Charles Town society accepted her. Everyone wanted to talk to her, congratulate her on her upcoming nuptials, and find out all the details of her unjust trial. For Irish, who had lived in fear for so long, the evening–most of it spent dancing with Ty–could not have been better.

The next morning Irish was gingerly sitting up in bed holding her hand over her queasy stomach and eyeing the chamber pot, when there was a tap on the door. Daphne had been bringing her some tea and toast every morning and it had helped. But when the door opened this morning it wasn't Daphne. It was Mariette bringing her tea and toast.

"Daphne told me you've been having a little sickness in the mornings," she said setting the tray across Irish's knees, then sitting on the edge of her bed.

Mariette had never been formally trained but she was the best doctor Irish knew. "I'm sure it's nothing. I didn't want to bother you with something so silly. You have enough to worry about with those twins of yours."

"Nonsense," Mariette said. "I'm right here in the same house, for goodness sake!" She clasped her hands over a belly that was still rounded from her recent childbirth. "Now tell me your symptoms."

Irish shrugged. "It's just a little stomach upset."

"Which happens every morning?"

"For the last week or so."

Mariette's eyebrows rose. "Are your breasts tender?"

Irish could not help placing one hand over her breasts, but she had to nod yes.

"And how are your skirts fitting you? A little tighter in the waist?"

Irish's brows came together. "How did you know?"

Mariette sat back. "One more question, Irish. How long has it been since your last menses?"

That was when Irish realized what was wrong with her. Her eyes widened, her mouth dropped open, and she clamped both hands over her mouth in dismay.

Mariette patted her knee. "I think you had better think about setting a date for your wedding, Irish. And the sooner, the better."

Irish's hands dropped to her lap. "But I can't be pregnant, Mariette."

Mariette leaned forward. "Well you have all the classic symptoms."

"But you and Alejandro...I mean...you were married over a year. Ty and I just..." she trailed off, embarrassed at what she had almost said.

Mariette squeezed her hand. "Sometimes it takes a year. Some women never get pregnant. For others, one time is all it takes. No one knows why."

Irish made a wry face. "I certainly never expected to be one of those lucky few, especially with no husband."

Mariette urged a piece of toast on her. "From what I hear, Ty has been asking you to marry him every day for the last month. Maybe it's time you took him up on his offer. I don't think it would be too great a hardship. I've seen how you look at him."

Irish dunked one corner of the toast into the tea and nibbled at the soaked bite. "I do love your brother," she admitted.

"Then why don't you marry him?"

Putting down the toast she took a small sip of the tea. Her stomach was already beginning to settle and she drew a deep breath. "Ty holds my indenture papers. I've offered to buy them from him. I have the money. I don't want to be owned by anyone, certainly not my husband. But Ty doesn't seem to think I'm serious. I thought if I kept refusing him he'd finally understand that I want to come to him freely, as a free woman."

"Ty the Tyrant," Mariette muttered. "That's what the rest of us called him when we were children. He was always so perfect and thought we should be the same." Then she smiled. "But he was so perfect he was always perfectly fair to us. He really wasn't a tyrant. Just such a good example that we all found him hard to live up to."

"You're very fond of your brother, aren't you?"

Mariette nodded. "I couldn't have asked for a better one. He might be a little hardheaded, but the idea of your freedom will sink in sooner or later."

"The problem is," Irish said patting her stomach, "I can't wait much longer."

"Then go ahead and marry him. He can sign your papers even after you are married. I don't think you should wait much longer."

Irish sighed and bit her lip.

"He'll make you a wonderful husband, Irish." Mariette stood up and went to the door then turned with her hand on the door latch. "Would you like me to give him a hint or two about your freedom?"

Irish shook her head no. "And Mariette, please don't tell anyone about the baby yet, either. I need some time to think."

Mariette nodded. "All right. But you'd better do your thinking quickly."

After Mariette left, Irish slowly finished her tea and toast, pondering what to do. She placed her hand on her belly. She had always loved children and had hoped for a dozen herself. For a while it seemed that her life would be spent alone and on the run, but Ty had solved that problem for her. And he wanted to marry her. How would he feel about the baby?

She smiled remembering what he had said about raising red-headed hellions. Maybe they wouldn't be so bad. Not with perfectly proper Ty as their father. Although he hadn't been behaving very properly when they made the little tyke. And hadn't he kissed her right out in the middle of the street? No, when you got right down deep underneath, Ty was just as improper as the next man. And she couldn't help loving him either way.

Taking a deep breath she set the tray aside and got up to dress. She wanted her freedom but now she had less choice than ever. For the sake of her baby she would have to accept Ty's offer and try not to worry about not being a free woman. Maybe Ty was right. Maybe it didn't matter after all. As his wife what difference would it really make? To her, a big one. But only to her.

The family moved back to the plantation the next day and Irish went with them. All the way up the river aboard the *Fortune* she thought of how she had planned to get her own place, be on her own, but always have to be looking over her shoulder, worried that the law would someday find her. That worry was gone but she was no longer free. She was bound to Ty by her indenture, by her love, and by the baby she was carrying.

She looked over to where Ty stood with Nate. Nate was a sailor born and bred. There was never such joy on his face as when he stood on the deck of a ship. But Ty was looking at the land as they passed. He loved the soil and growing things just as she did. They would do well together building a life on the land, raising rice and horses and children. If only she were free.

She would tell Ty tomorrow that she would marry him. Perhaps in a few years it really wouldn't matter to her any more that Ty held her indenture, that he seemed so indifferent about whether or not she was free. She gripped the rail as the ship rocked

on the waves and promised herself that she really would try to put
it behind her.

The next morning Irish pounded down the road aboard
Renegade. She had missed the great horse more than she realized
and was glad to be riding him again. When she had thought she
was leaving she had talked Abby's new husband, Joe, into learning
to handle him. Joe already rode well and although he was not an
accomplished horseman, he could at least control Renegade well
enough to exercise him.

Upon her return to the stable, Ty was waiting. He was dressed
for riding in buff breeches and a bottle green coat, but smiled as he
helped her down and let Mangus lead Renegade away.

"I suppose I'm going to have to get up pretty early if I'm ever
going to be able to ride my own horse," he said.

"Your horse?" she asked. "I thought maybe you'd give him to
me for a wedding present."

Ty stopped dead still for a shocked moment. Then he whooped
and scooped her up and whirled her around until she was giddy.
When he at last set her back on her feet, his face was radiant. "You
really will marry me, Irish? Soon?"

She nodded, feeling her heart torn between wanting her freedom first and wanting to marry Ty as soon as she could. "As soon
as you want."

"Tomorrow," he said firmly. "I want to marry you tomorrow.
I'll go into Charles Town this morning and get a license and a
minister and—" He stopped and looked at her with a thoughtful
frown. "But that's what I want. I know you said that the kind of
wedding you had wasn't important to you, but if you'd rather have
a big church wedding with all the trimmings, then that's what we'll
have. I saw how wistfully you looked at Ruth Townsend at her

wedding."

Irish shook her head. "No, I'd rather have a small, simple wedding, here, with just your family. Tomorrow might be a little soon, but I think day after tomorrow would be fine."

Cocking his head he looked at her a moment through narrowed eyes. "We've just been making wedding plans, Irish, which pleases me to no end, but I'm wondering why you don't seem quite so pleased."

Irish lifted her head proudly. "It's just that I was wondering what I should call you after we are wed, husband or master?"

He just smiled and pulled her close and held her tight, leaning his head against her hair. She could not help but respond to him, slipping her hand inside his coat and around his waist, even though he had once again avoided offering her her freedom. But Mangus was watching, so after a moment Ty pulled back from her and they turned to walk back to the house together.

Ty laughed and chucked her beneath the chin. "Oh, and since you'll be living in the house I'm building, you might want to look over the plans and ask Charlie to make any changes you might want."

That surprised her so much her jaw dropped, and she looked up at him with wide eyes.

He pointed toward the sun room on the side of the house. "You obviously know something about design."

"Thank you, Ty. I'll look over the plans tonight."

"And about Renegade," he said. "We're going to have to find a good mare to breed him with, and I'll be counting on you to help find one, and then maybe we can ride together every morning."

She smiled thinking of riding with him every morning, at least until she got too big and unwieldy to climb aboard a horse. Propping a fist on one hip she looked up at him and asked, "And which of us gets to ride Renegade?"

He grinned affably. "We'll take turns, my love."

My love. The words sounded good to her. They gave her great comfort. She might be Ty's indentured servant for life, but she knew as certainly and as deep down as anyone could know anything that Ty would never abuse her or force her to do anything she did not want to do. So why was she still so uncomfortable with the idea that he owned her?

Irish noticed that Ty didn't wait to go into Charles Town for a minister. As soon as they got back to the house, he nabbed Matt and Nate and they left.

She spent the time getting ready for her wedding. Ruby and Dee-Dee insisted on making every delicacy they knew how to make and Mrs. Fortune helped her add trim to the dress she had chosen to wear, a deep green one with a Wateau train.

Knowing Irish's condition and expecting the wedding, Mariette had not gone home yet. Alejandro helped her gather flowers and place arrangements all over the house. Even Charlie was called into service. He supervised the building of a bower in the side garden.

It was late the next afternoon when they sighted the *Fortune*. The small two pounder canon aboard announced something special so the whole family was gathered on the dock when the ship arrived. Nate waved jauntily from the bow next to a pale-faced minister who was gripping the rail as if his life depended on it, and gazing longingly at the dock.

Irish was only looking for Ty so she was surprised when Mrs. Fortune gripped her shoulder and gasped, "Sean!"

Mrs. Fortune's husband was standing on the deck, one hand grasping the tiller, his other waving. Mr. Fortune looked as much at home on a ship as his son, Nate. But where Nate was always as neat and trim as a navy captain, his father looked like a pirate working the tiller in a full-sleeved shirt open at the throat. He was slightly taller than his son and still lean-waisted. His black hair, tied into a queue at his nape, gleamed in the sun. The gangplank was not even out before Mr. Fortune was handing over the tiller to Nate and leaping over the side to the dock. Mrs. Fortune rushed toward her husband and they crushed together in an embrace so tight it looked as if nothing could ever part them.

Irish heard him say only, "Jessica!" as he buried his face in her hair and breathed deeply, kissing her tenderly. The two of them seemed oblivious to everyone else, oblivious to their surroundings, holding each other almost with desperation.

At last their embrace loosened and Mr. Fortune looked around with a wide grin. Without letting go of his wife he greeted Mariette, giving her a one armed hug, shook hands with Alejandro, and oo-hed and aahed over the twins.

Then his gaze came to rest on Irish. "Ty tells me I got home just in time for his wedding." He held out his arm and pulled Irish into a quick embrace. "Welcome to the family, Irish."

Irish barely had time to say thank you when she was being pulled from Mr. Fortune's arms and hugged again, this time by Ty.

Mrs. Fortune had her arm around her husband's waist and squeezed him. When he winced, she looked at him in alarm. "Sean! You're wounded!"

"'Tis but a scratch, Jessie. I'll mend. But it came close enough that I decided that this time, I'm home to stay. I've brought home enough rich prizes. These bloody wars never seem to end. I've had enough of roving for a lifetime."

"Come inside, Papa," Mariette said, "and I'll take a look at that wound."

He looked down fondly at his wife with a gleam in his eye. "Your mother can take care of it. Maybe she should have a look at it now."

Mrs. Fortune reddened but her lips turned up in a smile. She had to clear her throat before she could speak. "Yes, now would be a good idea."

Without a backward look, entranced only with each other, the two of them headed toward the house. They were almost to the door when Mr. Fortune swept his wife into his arms and carried her the rest of the way. No one saw either of them the remainder of the day.

For the rest of them, the wedding preparations went on. That night when Irish went up to bed, Ty went with her, kissing her soundly at her door and sending her alone to bed knowing that tomorrow night they would at last share a bed without having to fear discovery.

The next afternoon Mrs. Fortune helped her don the dress she was to wear for her wedding. Ruby and Dee-Dee were putting the finishing touches on the feast that would follow.

Irish had asked Mr. Fortune to give her away and he had agreed. Matt was going to stand up with Ty.

Mrs. Fortune was about to fasten a circlet of flowers that Abby had made in Irish's hair when there was a tap at the door.

"Miss Irish, could you come down to the kitchen?" Dee-Dee asked when Irish opened the door. "Ruby be havin' a time with that sauce she be makin'."

"Maybe Mariette can help, Dee-Dee," said Mrs. Fortune. "Irish is dressed for her wedding."

Dee-Dee looked askance at Mrs. Fortune. "You know what a disaster that daughter of yours be in a kitchen. Ruby said it's got to be Miss Irish who comes."

"It's all right, Mrs. Fortune. I'll be right back," Irish said and hurried down to the kitchen.

"I'm sorry, Miss Irish," Ruby said. "I guess I'm just plumb flustered over you gettin' married to Master Ty. I just can't seem to remember how much brandy to put in."

Irish shook her head in bewilderment. Ruby could make that sauce blindfolded. But she measured out the right amount and watched as Ruby stirred it into the sauce. Ruby had several other questions that made Irish wonder what was wrong with Ruby's mind, but finally, the cook smiled and dismissed her with, "I guess that be enough help, Miss Irish. You go on back to your room now."

Shaking her head, Irish climbed the stairs and opened the door to her room, then stopped in surprise at what she found there. Mrs. Fortune was gone but spread over her bed were papers and clothes.

Irish picked up the papers and looked at them. One set was the papers assigning her indenture to Ty. The next set was her freedom papers. With them was an inventory just like the one Douglass had written out for Ty listing all the things a master was required by law to give to a woman when she was freed. Across the bed were the items, not in the coarse, simple, cloth normally given, but in the finest of fabrics.

The two shifts were of the softest, finest linen Irish had ever touched, and embroidered with delicate blue flowers. The waist-coat and petticoat were not of half tick or coarse plain cloth but of softest cotton trimmed with lace. The shoes were soft black gleaming leather and the stockings were silk.

She heard a noise at the door and turned to find Ty leaning in the doorway, his arms crossed over his chest, a soft smile on his face. She had never seen him looking so splendid from his creamy white stock and embroidered waistcoat to his blue satin coat and buff breeches and black silver-buckled shoes.

"Is it all there?" he asked.

Irish could feel tears starting to form in her eyes and she bit her lip to keep from blubbering. She could only nod.

"Good, because I want to marry a free woman, Irish. I don't

want you to feel constrained in any way to marry me. I don't want you to come to me for any other reason except that you want to, that you want to be with me and live with me, and raise our children together."

"I do want to marry you, Ty," she said softly.

He walked toward her, his gaze never leaving her face. "It took you long enough to decide that."

Her chin came up. "It took you long enough to realize that I wanted my freedom."

He took her by the shoulders and leaned his head against hers. "Sometimes I can be a bit dim-witted, Irish. But when you kept insisting I began to think how I would feel if our positions were reversed. I thought I would give this to you for our wedding."

"I have something for you, too." She pulled his head down and whispered her last secret into his ear, that they would be raising a child sooner than he thought.

He started to whoop for joy but she stopped him by turning his face to hers, and giving him the kiss of a woman free to give her love wherever she chooses.

About the Author

Michele Stegman has loved history all her life. She lives in an 1840's log cabin with her husband, Ron, and enjoys spinning wool into yarn then using it for her weaving or knitting projects. She has learned to make her own soap and bakes her own bread.

From the time she was a child and realized that books were written by people, she wanted to be one of those people. In graduate school one professor told her she put too much romance into her history papers. Instead of taking it out, she put more in and began writing historical romance novels.

Fortune's Pride, a sequel to ***Fortune's Foe***, is available at all major online book retailers.

Visit www.michelestegman.com for information on her other books and to read excerpts. Or connect with her on Twitter at twitter.com/michelestegman, or on Facebook at facebook.com/MicheleStegmanAuthor.